Also by Fern Michaels . . .

FERN MICHAELS

Dear Emily

ZEBRA BOOKS
Kensington Publishing Corp.
http://www.zebrabooks.com

ZEBRA BOOKS are published by

Kensington Publishing Corp.
119 West 40th Street
New York, NY 10018

All Kensington titles, imprints and distributed lines are available at special quantity discounts for bulk purchases for sales promotion, premiums, fund-raising, educational or institutional use.

Special book excerpts or customized printings can also be created to fit specific needs. For details, write or phone the office of the Kensington Special Sales Manager: Attn. Special Sales Department. Kensington Publishing Corp., 119 West 40th Street, New York, NY 10018. Phone: 1-800-221-2647.

Zebra Books and the Z logo Reg. U.S. Pat. & TM Off.

ISBN-13: 978-1-4201-1172-9
ISBN-10: 1-4201-1172-8

First Trade Paperback Printing: August 2009
10 9 8 7 6 5

Printed in the United States of America

For my good friends,
Carol and Bob Ventimiglia

Part One

Chapter 1

Emily Thorn jerked to wakefulness, certain the sound grating on her ears was her husband Ian's alarm clock. Then she remembered Ian was off on a business trip. So, what was the sound? She scrunched her head into the feather pillow to blot out the persistent noise, aware of the birds chirping on her windowsill. They were waiting for the seeds and crumbs she set out on the deck every morning. Damn, she must have overslept again. She squinted at the clock: 10:15. "Damn," she muttered, "it's the doorbell."

A moment later she was out of bed, wrapping her robe about her as she stuffed her feet into felt slippers. By the time she got to the front door, struggled with the security alarm, the dead bolt, and the regular lock and opened the door, the Federal Express truck was halfway down the road. She leaned over, picked up the flat envelope, and carried it into the house. She didn't bother to look at the address; obviously it was for Ian.

In the kitchen she fixed the coffeepot, turned on the oven, and slid in a tray of sticky buns, the butter and frosting oozing down the sides. She poked around the refrigerator until she found the butter dish. The microwave would melt it to perfection. She poured a quarter inch of light cream into her oversize coffee mug.

While she waited for her breakfast, Emily ripped the blue rubber band from the morning paper. She yanked at her hair until she got it into an unruly bunch; the rubber band snapped into place. She really needed to get a haircut. She was too old for the long mane she carried around. "Crowning glory, my ass," she muttered. Today she would get it cut and styled. It would be something to do, a way to pass an hour or so.

She poured coffee, checked the sticky buns, decided she couldn't wait for them to brown. They were warm and would soak in the melted butter. She used a dinner plate, lining the buns up side by side as she drizzled the butter over them. She ate all six in under ten minutes, finishing her first cup of coffee. She poured again, adding cream as she did so. Now, with her sweet tooth sated, she could glance at the day's horror in the paper. As if she cared what went on in the world. Her own personal world was in such chaos she had neither the time nor the inclination to read about society's problems.

Emily rummaged in the drawer for a cigarette. A filthy habit. Ian smoked and he was a doctor so why shouldn't she smoke? She fired up, blew an artful smoke ring, propped her aching legs on the kitchen chair, and drew the paper toward her, bringing the Federal Express envelope she'd tossed on the kitchen table closer to her plate. Mrs. Emily Thorn. The sender was Dr. Ian Thorn. Emily blinked. Why would Ian be sending her a Federal Express letter? She pushed it away. He probably wanted her to do something. Ian always wanted her to do something. Someday, just for the pure hell of it, she was going to tally up a list of things Ian had asked her to do over the years. If she didn't open the letter, she wouldn't have to do anything. But then Ian would call for a progress report. Better to open it and get it over with. Whatever it was Ian wanted her to do could be done after she got her hair cut. Ian used to love her long, curly hair, said it made her look wanton when she tossed it from side to side. Emily snorted in disgust. Still, she made no move to open the Express envelope.

Emily was on her fifth cigarette and fourth cup of coffee when she snatched the cardboard envelope, opened it, and took out the letter.

The trembling started at the corners of her mouth, then spread throughout her entire body. She wanted to lean back in the swivel chair, but her body was too rigid. She wondered how she could tremble and be rigid at the same time. "Damn you, Ian, damn you to hell." Emily clutched the arms of the chair, twin lifelines, and stamped her feet. She remembered another day, long ago, when a letter had arrived from Ian. On the eve of her wedding. So very long ago . . .

"I can't believe I'm getting married. Do you believe it, Aggie?"

"I see the white dress and veil so it must be true," Emily's best friend said.

"I wish I wasn't so tired. I still can't comprehend that I worked last night. I must be out of my mind, but Friday night tips are so good I didn't want to give them up. Two banquets and I made a hundred and fifty bucks. Not too shabby."

"You look worn out. And yes, you were out of your mind to work until three in the morning. Emily, you are killing yourself."

"Maybe so, but look what I have in the bank. It's all paid off for Ian and me. We're finally getting married, seven years late, I grant you, but in a few hours I will be Mrs. Ian Thorn, wife of Dr. Ian Thorn."

Aggie's eyes narrowed. "It's that white shirt and tie thing, right?"

"That's part of it, but I love Ian. I've loved him since we

were in the ninth grade. He's a part of me just the way I'm a part of him."

"Right now, off the top of your head, don't think, just blurt the answer . . . how many times have you seen Ian in the past seven years?"

Emily's jaw dropped. "Seventy-five? That's a guess . . . it's probably more . . . that's a stupid thing to ask me, Aggie. You have no idea how hard it is for Ian to get fifteen minutes to himself. Most of the time he's half dead. We spoke a lot on the phone, sent cards. A day didn't go by when we weren't in touch. We agreed early on that sacrifices would have to be made. We knew what we were doing. We made it. Today is the big day. I've never been this happy in my life. Ian . . . he's . . . he's so happy he can't talk straight."

Aggie's lips compressed. "I'm glad you're happy, Emily. I could never do what you did." She shook her head.

"That's because you and Rob didn't have a dream, a plan. Ian and I did. I'm not saying that's wrong for you two. It was right for Ian and me."

"You always said you weren't going to have a backyard wedding with the potato salad in plastic bowls," Aggie groused.

"I did say that. It was silly of me. This wedding is only costing four hundred and fifty dollars. I'd rather have this and money in the bank. Ian agreed. I'm wearing my aunt's wedding gown and Ian is wearing his best dark suit. You have a lovely dress. It's simple, but it's what we can afford.

"Ian's friend is going to take some pictures. You made the wedding cake as your gift to us. So, what's missing?"

"Nothing, I guess. I just want you to be happy, Emily."

"You keep saying that. Right now I am the happiest almost-bride in Scotch Plains, New Jersey."

"Sit still so I can cover the dark patches under your eyes. Don't blink," Aggie said, sponging makeup under

Emily's eyes. "I'm going to use some extra rouge, your skin is too pale. A little sun wouldn't hurt you, Emily."

"No time for sunbathing. Do you know what I'm giving Ian as a wedding gift?"

"What?"

"The bank book. He has absolutely no idea how much money I've saved these past seven years. Do you believe he never asked? Not once."

"How much did you save?"

"I've got twenty-three thousand dollars. It's not all in the passbook savings account. I invested some of it. Ian's eyes are going to pop right out of his head."

"What's he giving you?" Aggie asked.

"I have no idea. I don't even know if he knows the groom is supposed to give the bride a present. Giving me his name is enough for me."

"Don't forget all those white shirts he's giving you to iron," Aggie said tightly.

"Am I wrong or don't you like Ian?" Emily asked.

"I like Ian. He's very charming. When he wants to be. But I do think he's taking advantage of you. Emily, you have worked like a dog since the day you graduated. You've been working seven days a week forever it seems. You're always tired and you don't remember what it's like to feel good. You're only twenty-five and already you have some bad varicose veins. You should have a doctor look at them."

Emily burst out laughing. "I think I'm going to have a doctor looking at them for a whole week. I'll respect his opinion."

"It's not funny, Emily. Jeez, I'm going to miss you."

"We'll write. Not a lot, but I promise to stay in touch. Ian still has another year and then his residency and more schooling if he wants to specialize, which I think he's going to want to do, and then, Aggie, it's clear sailing for both of us. I can start school, get pregnant, and have the best of everything. A few more years aren't going to matter. At least we'll be together. Be happy for me, Aggie."

"I am happy for you, Emily. All I can say is Ian better make you happy or he'll have to take me on. Rob and I will straighten him right out."

Emily's voice dropped to a whisper. "Aggie, I want to show you something. I want to share it with you so you won't worry about me. Last night when I got home, so dead tired I thought my legs and feet were numb, I was just going to fall in bed with my clothes on, but I turned on the light and taped to the outside of the window was a letter from Ian. He must have stopped by late and left it. It was so like Ian I cried and cried. I know it by heart, but I'm going to read it to you. Listen to this," Emily said, pulling the folded piece of paper from inside her bra. "I want to keep it close to my heart. This will set your mind at ease where Ian is concerned."

"Let's hear it," Aggie said, perching on the side of the bed.

Dear Emily,

I say "Dear Emily" because there is no dearer, sweeter person in the whole, wide world, than you, dear Emily. I love you so much I want to say all the right words, words poets write and talk about, but I don't know them. Please, know in your heart that I love you more than life itself. I never dreamed anyone could love me the way you do. Know that love is returned in the same way.

You are my life, my reason for being. Without you I would not be where I am today and where we will both be tomorrow and all the tomorrows yet to come. I am going to dedicate my life to healing the sick and to making you happy. The day will come when I can give you everything your heart desires for the rest of my days.

These last years have been hard, especially on you, Emily. We're going to see daylight soon. I promise to spend the rest of my life making it up to you for all your sacrifices.

I had to write this letter on this last night before we become one in every sense of the word. Thank you, Emily, for being you, for loving me. I will love you forever and ever. My heart is yours, dear Emily.

"That's beautiful," Aggie said.

"I'm going to read this every day of my life even though I know the words by heart. When I'm old and gray and sitting in a rocking chair with my grandchildren at my feet, I'm going to show them this and tell them that true love is worth waiting for, worth all the sacrifices that need to be made."

Ian and Emily settled into their new life with gusto. Atlanta, Georgia, was far enough away from New Jersey that neither Emily nor Ian worried about family visits. Ian settled into the Emory School of Medicine while Emily got a job working at a tacky lounge called Sassy Sallie's.

Ian studied. Emily worked. The only thing breaking the monotony was Ian's days off, which were few and far between. Emily found herself working double shifts just so she wouldn't have to be alone in the tiny apartment they called home. They were making it, though, unlike some of Ian's married friends who couldn't tolerate the long separations, the constant workload, and lack of companionship. Three couples had separated, the wives filing for divorce. At each new announcement by Ian, Emily hunkered down and worked more because of the worry in Ian's eyes. "It won't happen to us, Ian, I swear it won't."

Constantly she reassured her husband that they were different and they both understood what was involved when they got married. "I want you to succeed, to fulfill your dream, and then I'll get my turn." Ian always smiled when she said that. The smile, the warmth in his eyes, was what kept her going. Until the day she started to feel ill.

"Listen, Emily, you look dead on your feet," Carrie, the night hostess, said gently. "I've been watching you since yesterday. Go home and get in bed. You're the only one who hasn't come down with the flu, so it's your turn. Sallie isn't going to say anything. You're the best waitress she's ever had and she doesn't want to lose you. You look flushed to me. Bet you have a fever. Get your stuff together and go home. We aren't that busy. Look, the most you could make by staying till the end of your shift is maybe another ten bucks. Those guys drinking at the table in the corner are not big spenders. Go on, I don't want to hear another word. Call in tomorrow and let me know how it's going. If you can't make it, don't worry about it. Sallie has some reserves for the breakfast trade."

Emily sighed. "I guess you're right. Explain to Sallie, okay."

By the time Emily arrived at the small apartment, chills racked her body. She made tea but could barely drink it, so she swallowed four more aspirin and crawled into bed, but not before she slipped into a warm flannel nightgown and piled all four blankets on the bed. It wasn't until she was dozing off that she remembered that Carrie had slipped a bottle of brandy from the bar into her purse. She should have taken a few swigs.

Exhausted, she slipped into sleep.

The alarm shrieked at four-forty. Emily struggled to reach the button to turn it off so Ian could have an extra hour's sleep. She always woke him when she was ready to go out the door. Not only did she wake him, she handed him his first cup of coffee for the day.

She knew when her arm refused to move that she was sick—really sick. Whatever it was she had, she'd felt it coming on the past two days. Her ears ached, her throat hurt, and her eyes were watering so badly she could barely see the numerals on the clock. She tried to move, but she was so cold her teeth chattered. The flu? Who got the flu in May? Nobody but her.

"Ian, wake up. I'm sick." Ian mumbled something and then moved away from her. Without his body warmth she felt colder. Her teeth continued to chatter. "Ian, wake up. You have to call and tell my boss I won't be in." Ian bolted upright in the bed.

"What time is it? My God, it's quarter to five. You're going to be late, Emily."

"I'm sick, Ian," Emily croaked. "God, I can't get warm and I have a fever. Will you get me some aspirin?"

"Jeez, Emily, you're burning up."

"I felt it coming on. I've been taking aspirin for the past two days."

"That's just like you, Emily, trying to doctor yourself. This damn flu is going to lay you up for two weeks. We're going to lose ten days' pay. That was dumb of you, Emily."

Emily buried her face in the pillow. Was it her fault she was sick? Probably. Everything was her fault. Ian was right, it was stupid of her to try and medicate herself just to save ten dollars. "I'm sorry," she said. "It was stupid. Don't be cross with me, Ian."

"I'm not cross with you. Look, put this heavy sweatshirt on and these wool socks. I'll ask the super if he can give us a portable heater. They turned the heat off last week. The A/C is on now. We don't have any more blankets, do we?" Emily shook her head. "I'll fix you a toddy. Maybe you can sweat it out. What else can I do?"

"Call Sallie's."

"Right. I'm going to call in too. I'm staying here with

you," he said, his face a mask of worry. "You never get sick, Emily. In all the years I've known you only had one cold." He took her temperature then looked at her, startled. "God, Emily, it's a hundred and three. I'm going to call a doctor."

"No. You're almost a doctor. Just take care of me. There's nothing they can do for the flu and you know it. Fluids, rest, and aspirin for the fever. Trust me, Ian. Don't call a doctor." All she could think of was the ten days' pay they were going to lose.

"For now, but if your fever doesn't come down, I'm calling a doctor," Ian fretted. "Soup, do we have canned soup? I'll get some when I go out. I was going to make you a hot toddy. We have brandy, don't we? Coffee for me, maybe some toast. Do you want some?"

"Ian, go to class. Call me during the day."

"Absolutely not. I'm staying right here with you."

By midmorning Emily's fever was down a degree. Ian had used the last of the alcohol to rub her down three different times. She was on her second toddy when he announced that he had to go to the drugstore for more alcohol and aspirin.

Emily could barely keep her eyes open. "Swear to me you won't call a doctor. I'm feeling better, really I am. By this evening my fever will be down. I mean it, Ian."

"What the hell kind of doctor am I going to make if I listen to you, Emily? You need a qualified physician. This is home care at its worst."

"You're the best medicine for me. I want your promise," Emily croaked. "Besides, you're going to be spending money at the drugstore. I feel better. It has to run its course."

It took three days before Emily was able to shake the chills, the fever, and the sweats. The soreness in her throat eased some and her ears, with drops from the drugstore, ceased to ache. The toddies and the aspirin had finally worked. Or else, as Emily had said, the flu was running its course. She drank constantly, urged on by Ian, who sat at her side the whole time. "You look worse than I feel," Emily whispered when she woke from a nap on the fourth day.

"I feel like shit," Ian said quietly. "Sleeping in this chair has given me a permanent crick in my neck. Guess what, I ironed today."

"Good, the job is yours," Emily quipped. "It looks so nice outside today, Ian, open the windows and let's air out this room. I don't want you to catch whatever I have."

"I think it's a little late for that," Ian said, banging at the window. He finally raised it. "If you think you can handle being alone, I'm going back to class tomorrow. You have to promise to stay in bed, though."

Emily nodded. "I'll be fine. How far behind are you going to be?"

"I'll catch up."

"I'm so sorry, Ian. I appreciate all you've done."

"You were pretty sick. This is the last time I'm listening to you, Emily. This has been eating at me, your stupidity and my stupidity for going along with it. *I know better.*"

Which meant she was really the stupid one. She didn't *know* better. "I'm sorry," she said again.

"Emily, I was so worried about you. I felt so . . . helpless. You just lay there. I love you," he said gruffly. "But no, I am not taking over the ironing. How about some scrambled eggs?"

"Sounds good. No toast, though. My throat is still a little sore."

"Another toddy, okay?"

"Hey, I'm hooked." She smiled. "I love you, Ian, with all my heart."

"My heart returns the feeling."

Emily scrunched herself into the mound of pillows. Everything happened for a reason. She'd gotten sick and Ian had realized how much he loved her. He'd taken care of her, putting his own life on hold for a few days. "Thank you, God," she whispered, "for giving me such a kind, wonderful husband." Another part of her mind shrieked, fool, fool, fool.

Only time would tell if she was a fool or not.

Ian was right, Emily thought as she stepped from the shower. The last three years had gone by in a giant, tired blur. How was it possible that they were approaching their third anniversary? What she wanted, the only thing she wanted was a long, hot bath and one of Ian's soothing massages. A good dinner, a little wine, and then some lusty lovemaking. Instead she was going to celebrate her anniversary at a restaurant. She'd taken a shower instead of the long, soothing bath, and the dinner would be Chinese with carry-in beer. She did have a new dress, one that Ian said made her look like his own glorious rainbow. It was beautiful, she couldn't quibble with the colors, but the style didn't, in her opinion, suit her. Plus, she didn't have a single pair of shoes that matched the dress.

This was it, the end of the long years of studying, of sacrificing. Life was going to move forward now. Now she would be able to quit her job, get pregnant, and perhaps start school. It was her turn now. Tomorrow was going to be the first *real* day of her life with Ian. Tomorrow afternoon she was going to register for the fall semester.

Emily found herself smiling. Thirty-one wasn't too late to start her education. Tomorrow morning she was going to sleep in, then go by Sassy Sallie's and give her notice. "Thank you, God, for finally giving me this day," she murmured.

In the bedroom, Emily slipped on a robe before she settled down to paint her toenails. She was on her pinkie when Ian arrived. He picked her up, whirled her around, and then kissed her until she thought her chest would explode from lack of air. "Tell me we aren't still newlyweds!" he chortled.

"We're newlyweds, we're newlyweds," Emily laughed. "You're a half hour early."

"That's because I finally said to that old bear, today is my anniversary and my wife needs me. I wish I had done it more often. You aren't upset with me, are you, Emily?"

"Of course not. Do you really think I counted all the missed holidays, birthdays, and the last two anniversaries? And all those weekends when you had to cover for someone. Not on your life. That's all behind us now. We really need to talk, Ian, about the future."

"I know. Tonight at dinner. We're going to . . . guess, Emily?"

"The Chinese Garden."

"Wrong. We are going to, wait till you hear this, Adolpho's. I made the reservation last week. I don't care what it costs. Hovering waiters. Champagne. For you. You deserve the best and I'm finally going to give it to you. Listen, I know it's money you earned, but right now I don't have a pot to piss in. That's going to change starting tomorrow. Tell me it's okay, honey."

Emily stared at her husband. He hadn't changed a bit since their wedding day. His summer blue eyes could still beguile her. She fought the urge to brush back his wheat-colored hair. He didn't like it when she did that. He looked so incredibly handsome in his white Arrow shirt and Fabil tie. There wasn't a trace of a line or wrinkle in his face, whereas hers had several. Her early years in the sun, she supposed. The only thing was, Ian didn't look right to her unless he smiled. Right now, this very instant he looked chagrined, like a small boy who'd done something wrong. She and she alone could wipe the look away and replace it with a smile. So what if tonight's dinner would be two student loan payments? Once in a while you had to do something wild and crazy, and today was her anniversary. "Why don't we say we both deserve this night out and who cares what it costs? Promise me candlelight or I'm not going." Emily giggled. She could get into this; she'd had many years of practice making Ian smile. He did.

Ian smacked his hands gleefully. "I'm going to shower and then we're both going to get into our new duds and split this place. When we get back, I'm going to love you all night long. What do you think of that, Mrs. Thorn?"

"I think that's a *splendiferous* idea, Dr. Thorn." Please, God, don't let me fall asleep, she prayed silently. Let me get through this evening in one mental piece.

"I have a better idea, let's get a head start. C'mon, Mrs. Thorn, we haven't done it in the shower yet." He kissed her then until she thought her teeth would rattle. Her adrenaline kicked in. It had been over a month since they'd made love. "Do *that* again," she moaned. He did, all the way into the shower and while the shower was pelting them both. The exquisite release left her buoyant. They were both giggling like children when they left the apartment.

Twenty minutes later, they arrived at the restaurant.

"They give you a rose when you leave," Ian whispered.

Emily smiled. A rose would be nice, something to remember the evening by. She'd press it into her photo album when it wilted.

Ian frowned. "Promise me you aren't going to pick the service apart. Promise me you won't roll your eyes if the waiter makes a mistake."

"Only if you promise to leave a generous tip," Emily muttered.

"Okay, it's a deal. Forget that you're a waitress tonight, and for God's sake, don't tell anyone, okay?"

The edge was off her happiness now. "Why, are you ashamed of what I do? What *do* you tell your friends I do, Ian?"

"I don't tell them anything. It's none of their business. And no, I am not ashamed. Nobody appreciates what you do more than me."

"Appreciating it and being ashamed are two different things, Ian."

"We're getting off to a bad start here. Let's back up two steps and start over. I for one still feel like a newlywed so let's act like it. That's an order, Emily."

"Yes, sir," Emily said, snapping off a smart salute.

Ian's hand was on the doorknob when the door swung open. Ian stepped back, ushering Emily through the door as he nodded curtly to the doorman. Inside he maneuvered Emily to the secluded area where the head waiter stood discreetly with an immaculate white towel folded over his arm.

"Dr. and Mrs. Thorn," Ian said imperiously. Emily flinched.

It was a small restaurant with only twelve tables and as many waiters hovering against the wall. One-on-one service, she thought. She knew immediately that this was the kind of restaurant where the tables did not turn over. One seating, and the dinner would take three hours, possibly longer if they dawdled over coffee and liqueurs.

Emily gave her husband a gentle nudge and whispered quietly, "Ask for the table by the wall. You don't want to sit by the kitchen." Ian bristled as the waiter led them to a draped table one table away from the kitchen door. Emily nudged him again. She could see Ian's shoulders stiffen.

"This is unacceptable," he said quietly.

That was good, Emily thought. When you said something was unacceptable, it left no room for discussion. The waiter veered to the right. Emily felt herself nod approvingly. Ian's lips were compressed into a tight, white line when the waiter held her chair. If Ian wanted to pout, let him, she thought. If they were going to spend the kind of money she knew they were going to spend, then they deserved a good table. And if there was one thing she knew about, it was good tables.

"That really wasn't necessary, Emily," Ian said, smiling for the benefit of the other diners and the waiter as well.

"Yes, Ian, it was. We're celebrating so we should get the best for our money. Or is it that it was my suggestion that's bothering you?" She smiled sweetly to take the sting out of her words. "I guess this is the rose they give you," she said, motioning to a single yellow rose in a bud vase.

"No, they hand it to you when you leave. I saw them in a box by the front door." He always had to one-up her. There was no box by the front door on the little counter. She'd taken in the decor, everything, the moment they walked through the door. She let it go and nodded. "This is a lovely restaurant. I understand the food is wonderful, but incredibly rich. We're going to gain weight, Ian."

"I haven't gained an ounce in seven years, Emily. You, on the other hand, are getting . . . love handles."

It was true, she thought in dismay. She'd gone from a perfect size ten to an uneven size twelve. It was all the fast, greasy food she ate on the run, not to mention the sweets she was addicted to. Tomorrow she was going to go on a diet. "I know," she said miserably. "Starting tomorrow I'm going to switch up and go on a vegetable and fruit diet."

"Emily, Emily, you're kidding yourself. They don't serve fruits and vegetables in that dive you work in."

Emily's heart thundered in her chest, but she was determined not to spoil this evening. She leaned across the table to take her husband's hands in hers. "I'll give it a try," she said. "Tomorrow is a new day and I'm looking forward to starting college and being a practicing doctor's wife. How many committees do you think I'll have to work on? Ooohhh, this wine is wonderful."

"Have some more," Ian said, refilling her glass just as the waiter arrived at their table to pour it for him. Ian waved him away. "I hate hovering waiters," he whispered.

"Me, too," Emily whispered in return.

"Bet nobody hovers at that place you work at."

"You're right. Ian, what's the name of *that place* I work at?"

"What?"

"You know, the name of the lounge I work at? What's the name of it?"

Ian shrugged. "It escapes me at the moment. It'll come to me."

"No, it won't. You never asked me. I bank the checks so how would you know?"

"You told me, I guess. I've called you there."

"So how do they answer the phone?" Emily persisted.

"Jesus, Emily, what is this, twenty questions? Just because I can't remember the name of that joint doesn't mean I don't know it. I know the phone number by heart so why do I need to know the name of it?"

"What if something happened to me and you had to get there right away?"

"I'd call first. I have it written down somewhere. None of this is important, Emily."

"Yes, Ian, it is. The *dive* I work at is called Sassy Sallie's. That *dive* put you through medical school, paid our rent, bought our food, paid our utilities, helps to pay your student loans, paid for that suit, shirt, and tie, not to mention your underwear and shoes and socks as well as my new outfit. And this dinner. So, you see, it is important. To me. And it should be important to you too."

"Emily, that isn't what I meant. I meant the discussion.

Dive is just a word. You're the one who used it first when you first started to work there. I picked it up from you. I *am* appreciative. What is it you want?"

"Respect. Why did you tell me not to tell anyone what I do? You admitted you don't tell people because it's none of their business."

"It isn't. Do you tell people what I do?" Ian asked huffily.

"To anyone who will listen. I'm proud of you, Ian. Waitressing is honest work. Hard work. Look, let's drop it. I guess I'm just tired."

"You're always tired, Emily. Are you taking those vitamins I got you?"

"I take two a day and I'm still tired. I can't wait to sleep in and do nothing."

Ian shrugged. Their salads arrived. Ian refilled their wineglasses a third time.

A long time later, their soup and salad plates gone, Ian said carefully, "Listen, I don't have the foggiest idea of what I ordered for us. The menu was in French. I just pointed. I think it's some kind of fish. Let's not make a fuss if it's something we don't like. I'd hate to be embarrassed."

Emily felt her hackles rise as she thought about the hours she'd worked, the hours she'd stood on her feet to pay for a dinner she might not even like just so her husband wouldn't be embarrassed. She sighed and shook her head to show she would do as he wanted. She always did what he wanted. Always.

Ian ordered a second bottle of wine. It arrived when the dinner of salmon mousse was set in front of them. Ian beamed. Emily stared at her plate. She hated salmon. She'd rather have a greasy hamburger.

"You're a good sport, Emily," Ian said happily. "I love it when you look like you do right now."

"How's that?"

"Determined."

Emily burst out laughing. "This tastes like . . . like my father's muddy galoshes with a topping of Parmesan cheese." Ian choked on his food and then burst out laughing. He finished the wine in his glass at a gulp, his face red. "Is everyone looking at us?" he whispered.

"Uh-huh. I think we need a little more practice before we eat in restaurants like this or else we need a crash course in French." Emily giggled.

"I think you're right, Emily. We'll stop and get a banana split when we leave here."

"Are you kidding? We'll be too drunk to make it to the ice cream parlor. Besides, I thought you had other things in mind," Emily said, leering at him across the table. "Oh, Ian, I can't wait to give my notice."

"You look so beautiful in candlelight, honey. When we finally settle in somewhere, let's have candlelight every night."

"Okay. You're the handsomest man in this restaurant, Ian."

"How blitzed are you?"

"I can still see straight. You *are* the handsomest. Look around at the men in here. Pot bellies, bald heads, I'd wager half the women in here are mistresses. You know how you can tell?"

"How?"

"They're talking. Husbands and wives drink, eat, and leave. Lovers dally, smile, talk, and look into each other's eyes."

Ian looked around. "Jeez, you're right. That's disgusting."

"Will you always be faithful to me, Ian?"

"Of course. What about you?"

"Always," Emily said, her eyes shining with love. "I would never muck up what we have. Men . . . I'm not sure men feel the same way women do when it comes to affairs."

"I feel just the way you do, Emily. We are going to have the perfect life to make up for all our sacrifices. We deserve the best and I'm going to make sure we get it. That's my job."

Our sacrifices, Emily's head buzzed with the wine she'd consumed. She should be paying attention to what Ian was saying. She'd think about it tomorrow while she lay in bed. Maybe Ian would bring her breakfast. She didn't realize she'd said the words aloud until Ian said, "It will be my pleasure. How about French toast with melted butter, warm syrup, and sprinkled with powdered sugar or maybe that spice you use?"

"That sounds wonderful, Ian. Let's stay in bed till noon and have brunch."

"Sounds good to me. Here comes our coffee and we finished the wine. I need to talk to you about something, Emily."

"Okay, talk."

"Emily, honey, I want us to go back to New Jersey. This is . . . I don't know how to say it except to blurt it right out. I want to work for myself. I want us to open a clinic. I've talked, long distance, to a few bankers back home and the guy at First Fidelity said he didn't think there would be a problem loaning us money for a clinic. I thought Front Street in Plainfield would be good. A walk-in-off-the-street clinic, open to everyone. I didn't commit, said I had to talk it over with you. Two years Emily, if my predictions are right. Clinics are moneymakers. If you keep working, plus help out in the clinic, we can pay off my loans and the loan for the clinic. Two years. What's two years, Emily? Twenty-four months. Seven hundred and thirty days. We can do it, Emily, if you pitch in. It will be ours. You won't have to bust your ass anymore. I mean after two years. This is how I see it: You work mornings, seven to one, and then you can work the night shift at your old place, you know, what was it called, Heckling Pete's? What do you think, Emily?"

What she thought was she wanted to die, right here at this very table where she'd consumed almost a whole bottle of wine and eaten salmon mousse.

She chose her words carefully. "That means I have to put school off again. How's that going to look when I finally go back and everyone is years younger? I won't fit in. I was so looking forward to starting school. Ian, I don't know if I'm strong enough to put in two more years."

"The first thing we're going to do is some blood work on you. Build you up. That's a must. You're going to take a vacation and sit on your tail for ten whole days. I'm doing this for you as much as myself. If we don't take hold of this opportunity, we might not get another one. I swear to you, dear Emily, I'll make this up to you. I can't do it alone. I need you at my side."

"Oh, Ian, that means I'll see even less of you and I'll be working more hours. Before you said we were like newlyweds. That was wrong, we're like strangers. You didn't even know where I worked."

"I remembered Heckling Pete's and that was a long time ago."

"You really want to do this, don't you?"

"More than anything. We'll be on our own, making money, and we'll be our own bosses. I can treat people at affordable prices. It's a moneymaker, Emily. Two years. Can you see it in your heart to give me two more years? I know what I'm asking. It has to be your decision, though." His eyes pleaded with her.

Emily nodded because she was too numb to do anything else. Ian smiled, raised his hand for the check. "I'm going to make this up to you, dear Emily. The day is going to come when I will give you anything your heart desires. Anything. I promise, Emily."

She managed to say, "I'm going to hold you to it." She even managed a sickly smile for her husband's benefit.

They tottered home, holding on to one another, their futures settled for the next two years.

Chapter 2

Emily stared in awe at the Christmas tree she'd decorated to surprise Ian. The small apartment positively reeked of Christmas. She was going to bake the way her mother always baked for the holidays. She was going to wrap presents and maybe drink some wine while she was doing it. The day was hers to do with as she pleased. Heckling Pete's was closed for serious plumbing repairs and she'd pretended she had a cold and told Ian she couldn't work in the clinic. And here she was. Full of Christmas spirit.

She glanced at the pile of papers and ledgers on the kitchen table. She had to do the payroll, fill out insurance papers, make a bank deposit, pay the clinic bills as well as the household bills. She didn't want to do them, wasn't going to do them. She opened the cabinet under the sink, pushed aside her cleaning supplies. Then she swept the pile of papers into the far back corner.

This was supposed to be a real Christmas. Ian had promised. Last year the clinic had been opened and they had both worked and had a cup of eggnog in front of the plastic tree in the waiting room. They'd agreed not to exchange presents, but at the last minute she'd gone out and bought Ian a cashmere jacket she couldn't afford. He'd stuck to their agreement. She'd cried in the bathroom afterward. She would have been satisfied with a gift-wrapped Bic pen.

Emily looked at the pile of presents she was going to wrap in silver paper. Big, red, velvet bows would go on all the packages. She tried to imagine Ian's reaction to her shopping and decorating spree. Would he look at her with disappointment in his eyes or would he smile and say something kind and wonderful? Now, the clinic was in the black. Everything he'd predicted had come to pass. Six more months and his student loans would be paid off. For now, every extra cent went toward the loans and the cheap apartment they lived in.

Ian had worked even harder than she had in this past year and a half. He was as bone weary as she was, but it had been his decision to keep the clinic open twenty-four hours a day. When he came home at 11 P.M., he was on call during the night. She could count on one hand the nights he got to sleep through until morning. When Ian fell into bed, they cuddled and told each other it was just a few more months, then it was all going to be worth it. Every night he kissed her and thanked her for working at his side. Sex was just a sweet memory. Both of them were too tired to put forth any real effort, always promising one another the weekend would be for lazing about and making wild, crazy love. It never happened, though. The weekends were devoted to emergencies, grocery shopping, laundry, and her stint at Heckling Pete's.

They had a covering doctor now and a covering office manager. It had been Ian's idea so they could start the first of the new year fresh and with energy to spare. As if she would ever have energy again. All her git up and go had departed a long time ago. She wasn't sure about Ian's stamina. He looked weary beyond words. Was success worth all of this sacrificing? Their youth was gone, if they'd ever really had a youth. The early years of their marriage were gone, never to be recaptured.

The years between thirty and forty were supposed to be prime years. Would hers and Ian's be prime?, She wished for a crystal ball. She was still daydreaming when Ian walked through the door.

"It smells like Christmas in here," he shouted.

Emily threw herself into his arms. "You're early. Why? Is everything okay?"

"Of course. I came home to check on you. I called Garret to come in and cover. Allison is going to stop by and pick up the work I know you didn't do. She'll do it this evening."

"Are you really home for the night?" Emily asked in awe.

"Jesus, Emily, I try, I really do. Let's not get off track here. I'm here and we're going to glue ourselves to each other. I say we light the fireplace, pop some corn, and look at that gorgeous Christmas tree. Did you do all that yourself? It smells great. I'm sorry about all the past Christmases, Emily."

"Shhhh, me too. This is now and we're going to enjoy it. I can hardly believe Christmas is just three days away. Shall I bake a turkey?"

"You bet. With all the trimmings. Let's go to midnight mass too."

"Oh, Ian, really. Do you mean it?"

"I certainly do. We have to try going to church more often. We're going to start doing a lot of things we never had time for. It's time for us, Emily."

"Like what?" she said, snuggling into the crook of his arm.

"Like we should go ice skating when the ponds freeze. We should go to the mall and browse around, maybe take a ride to the shore and walk along the boardwalk and huddle into our winter coats. Remember how we used to do that? We'd walk for hours, freeze our tushees off, and then go for hot chocolate. I want to do that again."

"Oh, me too, Ian. I'd love it. What else?"

"Let's go to New York to see all the Christmas decorations. We can ice skate at Rockefeller Center." Emily clapped her hands in delight. "We can browse down Fifth Avenue and look at all the wonderful window displays. We'll buy ourselves new outfits while we're there."

"Pinch me," Emily gurgled. Ian obliged. "Ouch! Anything else?"

"How about five days in the Cayman Islands? Just you and me. I think we can take five days off around the middle of January if you want to go."

"Do I want to go? Do I want to take another breath? Of course I want to go. Pinch me again." Ian pinched her a second time. "Okay, okay, this isn't a dream."

"It means more now, doesn't it. I think we're both really going to appreciate it after all our hard work. We can't stay anywhere that's really expensive and we'll pretty much have to eat on the cheap because the air fare is expensive. Do you care about that?"

"Not a bit. Is this our Christmas present?"

"No way. I bought you a present. Did you buy me one?" he asked slyly.

"Yep. Oh, Ian, you are absolutely right, it means more now. I'm going to mark it off on the calendar and count the days, but not right now. Right now I want to stay here with you."

"Where you belong. God, I love you, Emily. You are one of a kind. You are the kindest, the warmest, the gentlest, the most generous human being I've ever met."

"Oh, tell me more. More," Emily begged.

"Not until I change my clothes, make a fire. Hey, does

that fireplace really work? What's for dinner? Let's eat in front of the fire."

"I think it works. The box of firewood the last tenant left is still in the corner. It should burn well. We're having pepper steak. Go ahead and get changed. I want to plug in the tree lights."

"My God, Emily, it's beautiful," Ian said, backing up a step to view the magnificent fir. "Where'd you get all the stuff? How long did it take you? I thought you didn't feel good."

"Doing it made me feel better. I just have a scratchy throat. Really, I'm fine."

"You're the best, honey."

Emily smiled and smiled. She smiled all evening long. She continued to smile when they made love far into the night. The smile stayed with her when she slept and was still with her when Ian nudged her in the morning and invited her to take a shower with him.

"I'm making breakfast for us this morning," he said.

"In that case, I'll have eggs, French toast, and bacon," Emily called over her shoulder as she scooted for the bathroom. "Make the coffee dark and sweet and don't forget the orange juice."

"You got it. Last night was great, wasn't it?"

"Oh, yes. I'm greedy, though. I want more."

"Okay, same thing tonight. I'm going in for four hours. I have a kid I have to check. He's worrying me. I might have to put him in the hospital."

"Over Christmas?"

"I've been pumping him full of antibiotics but he isn't responding the way he should be. He's running a fever too. He's a great little kid. Keeps asking me if I'm going to make him better. I tell him I'm going to try my best. He wants a pair of ice skates for Christmas. The family is too poor for gifts. I bought a pair for him, Emily, and a pair for his sister. Do you think it's okay? I mean will his mother think I'm—you know."

"Ian, that's wonderful. His mother is going to be very grateful. Thank you for doing that."

"Yeah, well, I did it for a few other kids too. Actually, twenty to be exact. You don't mind, do you?"

"Of course not. Christmas is for giving. I'm just grateful we can afford to do it."

"Actually, the corporation did it. It's a write-off, but that isn't why I did it."

"I know that, Ian. I knew I loved you for a reason."

"Will you still love me if you have to wrap them?"

"Now, why did I know you were going to say that? Of course I'll wrap them. Do you want them this afternoon?"

"Do I have a clean shirt for today; an ironed one?"

"Of course. They're hanging on the back of the door."

"Good girl," Ian said, squeezing her arm.

"I have to go now. I'll be back early." The phone shrilled to life in the living room. "I'll get it," Ian said. "It's for you, honey, it's Heckling Pete's."

Emily's stomach started to churn. He was ready to leave so why was he standing by the door? He'd kissed her cheek as she picked up the phone. He was deliberately stalling so he could hear her end of the conversation. "Hello," she said cautiously.

"Emily, this is Pete. Listen, the workers managed to get the back room ready ahead of schedule. We scheduled three Christmas parties for this evening. I know I gave you a few days off, but I'm short of help. I'll throw in an extra fifty bucks if you help me out."

"I can't, Pete. I have plans." She wouldn't look at Ian, she just wouldn't.

"What about tomorrow?"

"Can't, Pete, that's Christmas Eve. Sorry."

"Okay, no hard feelings. Have a nice holiday and I'll see you after Christmas. Stop by and pick up your schedule and your year-end bonuses."

"I will. Have a wonderful holiday."

"Can you believe that!" Emily said, turning to face her husband. "He had the nerve to ask me to work on Christmas Eve. You have to set Pete straight in the beginning or he takes advantage of you. Is there anything special you'd like for dinner?"

"How about stew. I like to eat stew when it's cold out. Put lots of carrots in it, okay?" He paused. "You're going to be losing a whole week's pay, right?"

"I really won't be out that much. Pete is generous; he gives everyone a Christmas bonus."

"Yes, but if you were working, we'd be that much farther ahead. What will he give you?"

"Probably a hundred dollars. That's what he gave us last year. It's generous. Most places don't give waitresses anything." She hated it when her voice turned pleading. Now she felt guilty for lying, guilty for not working the Christmas parties. She was letting Ian down. Her head pounded. "You better hurry, Ian, or you're going to be late."

All day, Emily was a whirling dervish, wrapping presents for Ian's patients, and then her own presents, cutting vegetables, making sure she added carrots, cutting the meat into cubes, flouring it and then browning it. When it was simmering, the apartment tidy, she showered, did her best to tame her wild mane of hair, and had a cup of coffee. Ian would be in shortly. Maybe she should walk out back and bring in some of the firewood the landlord said they could use. Three trips would about do it if they wanted the fire to last all night. Ian did love a fire, but then so did she. Yes, she'd do a fire, turn on the tree lights, and everything would look toasty and cozy. Ian would be so happy, and when Ian was happy, she was happy.

Wasn't that the way it was supposed to be?

Christmas Eve and Christmas Day were everything Emily dreamed of. Ian's gift of expensive perfume was a treasure to her. Secretly she liked the cut-glass crystal better than she liked the scent, but she doused herself to please her husband, who all but swooned when she put it on. The sweet, cloying scent gave her a headache.

When the Christmas dinner dishes were done and the apartment tidy, Ian drew Emily into the living room. They sat on the couch for a long time staring at the fragrant balsam. "I've never been happier, Ian. I wish this day could last forever. I just love Christmas, don't you?"

"*Hmmnnn.* It was nice. We're going to do this every year no matter what. We're going to stop and smell the roses. We have our vacation to look forward to. Let's go shopping tomorrow and get a few new clothes. You'll need a few sundresses for the islands and maybe some shorts and sandals. We can afford to splurge a little. Make sure you bring that perfume. It drives me nuts. I'm going to make sure you never run out. I told the girl in the department store to call me at the clinic if it ever goes on sale. She said she would."

Oh, God, Emily thought. He was tense and she wondered why. He was going to tell her something she wasn't going to like. She could feel it coming because she knew him so well.

"It's hard to believe a new year is just days away. Time is getting away from us, Emily. Opportunities have a way of knocking and people have a way of ignoring the knock on the door. I was never one of those people; how about you, Emily?"

She pretended not to know what he was talking about.

"Oh, you mean like me enrolling in school? My opportunity, that kind of thing? I agree. And me getting pregnant? I think I'll make a good mother, don't you, Ian? I'm going to make a great teacher, too, because I just love kids. I can't think of anything more rewarding than teaching little kids to read and write. I want to teach first grade. I'm really excited, Ian, that my turn is coming up."

It wasn't coming up, she could tell. Ian was going to spoil it. Still, she babbled on. "Remember our promise to each other, Ian. You promised me a baby and you promised I could go to school. That's not going to change, is it?" She was tense now, nervous. She could feel a scream building up inside her. "I want to take courses all summer. June will be my cutoff date for work. Then in September I can start full time and maybe work a little, a few nights a week, maybe three hours a night twice a week."

"You sound like you've really thought this all through, Emily," Ian said quietly.

"I've thought about nothing but this for months now. Ian, I am bone tired. I can't keep working like I've been working. I'm so frazzled at times I can't see straight. Is there something wrong?"

"It depends on your definition of wrong, Emily. I don't think there's anything wrong, and everything right about what I'm going to say, but I know you're going to think it's wrong. I want to say now, before I tell you what I'd like *us* to do, that it will only benefit us and that's what we set out to do. We're here for the long haul, Emily, we can't ever lose sight of that. Well?"

Emily could feel her heart start to flutter in her chest. "Well what? You've told me the *why,* you haven't told me the *what,* although I can guess."

"There you go again, Emily. What am I going to say?" Already Ian had inched away from her as he waited for her to say what was on her mind.

"I think you want to open a second clinic. I'm not as stupid as you think, Ian. I answered the phone when the bank called, not once, not twice, but at least a dozen times. Our accounts are in order so what else could it mean? I think you should have spoken to me about it before you went ahead and held discussions. We're doing fine, we're about to go into the black, in fact I think we're already in the black. You want to saddle us with more debt. What am I going to get out of this, more years of hard work, agonizing work? Ian, I want a baby, a life. I want to go to school. You promised me. We didn't agree to open clinics. One, yes. It will generate enough income for us to live quite well. I know how to manage money. We can have a wonderful life with time for ourselves. We can hire people and still have plenty of money. How much is enough? Tell me, how much? I see two hundred thousand dollars a year as a lot of money. That's ours after all the bills and salaries have been paid. And you want to know something else, Ian, this perfume gives me a headache. I can't wear it anymore. Well?"

"I can't believe this is you talking, Emily. When did you become so closeminded? I'm sorry about the perfume. I assumed because I liked it that you would like it. I'll take it back and get you something else. You're right about the banker. This is an opportunity not to be missed. It fell in my lap, Emily. We'll be fools to turn it down. We'll literally be sitting on easy street if we go for it. I swear to you the second clinic will net us three quarters of a million a year. Put that together with our income from the Front Street clinic and we'll be taking in a million a year. We'll be millionaires, Emily. You and me, millionaires. It boggles my mind. A year, Emily, just one more year. The bank wouldn't go for it if it wasn't a sure thing. How can you even *think* about turning this down? I can't believe that perfume gives you a headache. You're busting my chops, aren't you, Emily? Because you're being selfish. You don't want us to get ahead. You're one of those people with no visions, no insights. I thought we were alike."

"No, Ian, I'm not one of those people. The dream we had was limited. Family, schooling, success. I personally do not have any of the things *I* signed up for. I want a life, Ian. Can't you understand that?"

"What's a few years?" Ian huffed. "I'm not complaining, I'm the doctor here. I put in as much time as you do and I'm not whining about it. I'm prepared to put in another year to achieve what I thought was *our* dream. You're letting me down, Emily."

"Get off it, Ian. Arrogance should be included at the end of your name along with M.D. A few years, my butt! Try the word *eternity.* I've been working *forever.*"

"Emily!" Ian shouted in outrage.

"Ian," Emily shouted in return. She wasn't going to give in. Not this time. She tried to block out the tears in Ian's eyes, the quiver in his lips. She would have succeeded if Ian hadn't taken that moment to speak.

"I'm sorry, Emily. You're right, I am selfish and greedy. Of course you can go to school. We'll start trying for a baby, but I have to warn you, babies are expensive. There's college and then medical school. Our kid is going to be a doctor and I don't want him to have to struggle like I did. I know you, Emily, you'll want to shower him or her with everything, the best preschool, the best private school, the best prep school. We'll need a house with a yard, some household help for you, a station wagon, bikes, toys, that all costs money. Your schooling is going to cost a bundle, but I'm up for it if it's really what you want. But that two hundred thousand is going to whittle down to say, maybe thirty thousand. And we can't forget the insurance, more help at the clinic. Before you know it, we could be left with minimum wage as take-home pay. Let's go for a walk, Emily. The wood you brought in was wet and the room's kind of smoky. We need to clear our heads. We need to work off that grand dinner you made for us. A brisk walk will do us both some good. Later maybe we can have some turkey sandwiches with hot chocolate. I'll even fix them. Can you forgive me, Emily?"

Emily dropped to her knees and laid her head in Ian's lap. She cried. Ian cried too. "How long, Ian?"

"Fourteen months tops."

"What do I have to do?"

"Work in the Front Street clinic from seven till eleven. Then you'd go to Terrill Road and work till one. You can still work your job at Heckling Pete's because we'll need that money for our personal living expenses. I don't want to borrow more than I have to. It will be like now, you'll be on the books, but your money stays in the corporation. I need to know in my heart that you can handle this, Emily, otherwise there's no point in going ahead."

"What I did sign on for was till death do us part, for better or worse. I'm being honest, Ian, I don't think it can get worse so I guess you can count on me. I can't work seven days a week anymore, Ian. I need some time for myself. Fourteen months. Swear to me on our unborn child."

"Whatever it takes, Emily. I swear. You won't regret this, honey, I am going to give you everything in the world. You wait. That's a promise I mean to keep."

"All I want is an education and a baby."

"That too. Well, are you up for that walk?"

Emily tried to smile, tried to put some bounce in her step, tried to feel something for her husband at that moment, but it all fell flat.

Ian didn't notice.

Chapter 3

Things moved quickly after the first of the year. There were days when Emily barely spoke to Ian and days when she didn't speak to him at all. Only the thought of their trip to the Cayman Islands kept her sane. She was packed, had been packed since the second of January. All she had to do was stick her comb and brush and toothbrush into her bag.

Grudgingly, she had to admit Terrill Road was the perfect location for the second clinic. It was amazing, she thought from her position in the open doorway, how fast renovations could go in just two weeks. Ian must have promised the workers overtime and paid extra to have the equipment shipped out right away. When Ian wanted something, he left no stone unturned. For him it worked. For her it didn't.

She watched, huddled inside her heavy coat, as the examining tables were unloaded from a huge tractor trailer. Who was going to set them up? Her question was answered a moment later when four husky young men, probably Rutgers students on Christmas break, bounded out of a van. Two of them carried paint cans, another a tool kit, and a fourth was lugging boxes of tile. By nightfall, she was certain, everything would be in its place. When she stepped into what was going to be the waiting room, the shutters were up and painted on all the front windows. She shook her head in wonderment. Ian's philosophy was, hire somebody, pay them well, they'll do the job and get out and on to the next one. Not one minute wasted. Still, for all this to have happened in two short weeks meant the people he hired had worked round the clock.

Emily felt a chill wash over her. If everything was done by the end of the weekend, they could be open for business on Monday. It wasn't like Ian to open and then go off and leave the clinic to someone else to operate. The sign was already in the window.

Emily stepped outside. A light swirling snow was starting to fall. All thoughts of the island vacation was whisked away with the gusty wind. She might as well go home and unpack her bags. Now that she thought about it, she'd never seen the tickets. Her eyes narrowed. Ian wouldn't do that to her, would he? He never broke a promise. Intentionally. To Ian a promise was a promise. Maybe she wouldn't unpack.

Emily switched on the windshield wipers before she steered the six-year-old Chevy onto Route 22. She took the first turnoff, waited for the light before she headed back in the opposite direction. She almost missed the Somerset Street turnoff that would lead her to Park Avenue and the third-floor apartment they lived in. She was home in twenty minutes. She was stunned to see Ian sitting in the kitchen eating a cheese sandwich. "Want a sandwich, Emily? I opened some tomato soup and saved some for you—it's on the stove. I fixed an extra sandwich."

"How did you know I was coming home, Ian?"

"I heard you tell Esther. Your car was gone. I called over to Terrill Road and they said you'd just left. See, I'm a sleuth. I knew you'd be cold so I made the soup. Besides, I wanted to change my shirt. I have clean ones, don't I?"

"Of course. I ironed late last night, they're hanging on

the pantry door. Ian, do you know how long it takes to iron twenty-one shirts every week? I think we should start sending them out. I don't have the time anymore and do you *really* have to change your shirt three times a day? And when you get called out at night, you put on a fourth one. It's a bit too much, Ian."

"You're the one who got me into that. You specifically told me I should always look crisp and professional and you were right. I can't tell you how many compliments I get on my shirts. You know just the right amount of starch to put in them. The laundries either use too much or too little. I hate it when they do my shirts. You do it perfectly, Emily. Are you ticked off about something and taking it out on me?"

"Of course not." Damn, she should have reheated the soup. The sandwich on the plate looked dry; Ian didn't use mayo or butter the way she did.

"It's snowing out," she said, to have something to say. "Did you pack yet, Ian?"

"Not yet. I thought you were going to do it. I can do it if you don't have the time. You're too busy, right?"

Emily shrugged. "Where are the tickets, Ian?"

"In my desk at the office. I had them sent there because I had to sign for them and I'm never really here. Did the agent make a mistake or something?"

"No. I was just curious. Esther asked me if we had any stops and I said I didn't know. Do we?"

"Beats me, I didn't even look at the tickets. I just shoved them in the drawer. Emily, Emily, I can see right through you. You should know you can't pull off deviousness. You think I just made up the trip, that we aren't going because the new clinic is opening in a few days." He shook his head in disappointment. Emily looked away and said nothing. She bit into the cheese sandwich.

"Well, isn't that what you thought?"

Emily turned around and eyeballed her husband. "More or less."

"Dear Emily, we're going and we're going to have a wonderful time. I'm telling you now I'm not taking a lot of clothes. I plan to live like a beach bum the whole time. How about you?"

"While you're being a beach bum, I'm going to sleep on the beach. I plan to live in a pair of shorts and halter."

"I wouldn't do that, Emily. You don't have a midriff anymore. You need to be rail thin to dress like that. I thought women were self-conscious about things like that. If it doesn't bother you, though, it won't bother me. A tan will help your legs, cover those bulging veins a bit. I thought you were going to see Dr. Metcalf."

"When have I had the time, Ian? I plan to make an appointment in the spring. The support hose help quite a bit."

"You can't wear support hose on the beach."

"Then how about if I wear long underwear? That way I'll be covered from my neck to my ankles. Sometimes, Ian, you are very cruel and thoughtless. You don't seem to have any regard for my feelings."

Tears flooded Emily's eyes as she started to wash the soup mugs and sandwich plates. She didn't say anything—what was the point?

"See you, honey," Ian said, kissing her on the cheek. "I love that new shampoo you're using, smells like a summer breeze." He ruffled her hair. "Don't ever cut this wild mane; it's you, Emily. I think your hair is part of the reason I fell in love with you."

She was suddenly shy, confused, unused to compliments like this. "If it wasn't *soooo* curly . . ." She should be saying something witty, something with a double meaning, but the words stuck in her throat. "Guess I'll see you tonight."

She didn't want to think. Instead she moved by rote the way she did every day. First she shed her skirt and blouse, pulled on the thick support hose that were more elastic bandages than hose, and pulled them up. She was exhausted with the effort. If only she could take an hour-long bubble bath and then lie down. The long shift she had to work at Heckling Pete's loomed ahead of her. "Don't think, Emily, just move your butt and do what you have to do," she muttered to her made-up reflection. She did her best to calculate the minutes and the seconds until she could return to this tiny bathroom, shed the elastic stockings, and take a long, hot bubble bath. Of course Ian might have something to say about running the water at two o'clock in the morning. Once he'd said the light shining under the bathroom door bothered him so she'd resorted to taking her bath by candlelight and running the water through a bunched-up towel. "I'm crazy. Nobody in their right mind does the kind of things I do for Ian. They're going to come and lock me up."

"Do you believe this weather?" Ian asked, seven days later, as he snapped the lid of his suitcase. "God, we're going to be lucky if we make it to the airport. When was the last time it snowed like this?"

"About five years ago. I think we had fourteen inches. I'm going to the airport if I have to walk."

"We're going, so wipe that look off your face."

"Okay, Ian."

They were doing a last-minute check of the apartment when the phone rang. They stared at one another. "Don't answer it, Ian." The phone continued to ring, six, seven, eight rings. It stopped suddenly in midring and then rang again a few seconds later. Emily shook her head.

"I have to answer it, Emily. I'm a doctor."

Emily sat down on the arm of the couch and watched

her husband's face. When she heard him say, "I'll meet the ambulance at Muhlenberg. Not half as sorry as I am," she took off her coat.

"I have a patient in crisis, Emily. Mrs. Waller had a heart attack. At the clinic. They're transporting her as we speak to Muhlenberg. I have to go. Damn, she was doing so well too. I don't want to lose her, Emily." He was ripping at his heavy jacket, at his cable knit sweater. Emily automatically picked them up and folded them.

"What should I do?"

"Take the Honda and drive to the airport. Leave my ticket at the counter, and when I'm satisfied Mrs. Waller is in stable condition, I'll take the next flight. Check my bags with yours. It's the best I can do," Ian said, slipping into his coat. "Don't say anything, Emily. This is an emergency and I am a goddamn doctor. Go, get in the car and go. I'm the one missing out. I'm using your car."

He was gone. She could hear the Chevy sputter once, twice, three times before it caught and rolled over. Even if it didn't, Ian could walk the three blocks to Muhlenberg. Now what was she to do?

Well, she wasn't going to the Cayman Islands, that was for sure. In her heart she knew Ian wouldn't join her.

She leaned back on the sofa. The old lady had touched some deep chord in Ian just the way the children at the clinic did. Everyone appeared to love Ian. He had a wonderful bedside manner and he always seemed to know just the right words to soothe anxious patients. And it paid off in referrals. Everyone who came in wanted to be treated by Dr. Thorn.

Emily picked up her purse and threw it across the room. The airline tickets and colorful brochures of the Caymans spilled onto the floor.

Then she howled like a banshee.

Chapter 4

It had been a disappointing day in more ways than she wanted to think about. She'd slept for eleven straight hours. It was almost midnight, and the Cayman Islands vacation was dead in the water.

Groggily, Emily tottered into the bedroom to see if Ian had returned while she was asleep. He hadn't, the bed was neatly made, just the way she'd left it. It occurred to her then to look out the window. Her eyebrows shot upward. There was so much snow she couldn't see across the street and it was still snowing, which meant Ian would stay at the hospital. The Chevy wouldn't make it in this kind of weather and Ian hadn't taken his boots. Ian would never trudge through snow, no matter what. He hadn't called. Then again, maybe she hadn't heard the phone ring. Anything was possible. Possible, but unlikely. Ian thought she was in the Cayman Islands. She wished now she'd had the guts to brave the turnpike. Now what was she going to do? She was on a week's vacation with nowhere to go and no one to spend time with.

Emily marched into the kitchen and did what she always did when she was frustrated and angry. She ate. When she was finished, she said what she always said: "I wish I hadn't eaten all that food."

Emily stomped her way to the bathroom to fill the tub.

A bubble bath eased some of the tension that was settling between her shoulder blades. A big glass of wine would probably help even more. Then some more sleep. She felt sluggish with all the food and candy she'd eaten.

An hour later she was in bed, dressed in her long flannel, granny nightgown. She slept till three the following day, when she got up, showered, and ate a monster lunch of fried potatoes, Spam, and a whole can of creamed corn. She finished it off with a half a tin of butter cookies and two glasses of chocolate milk. She watched soap operas for the rest of the afternoon. When the commercials came on, she switched to the local weather station.

At noon of the third day, Ian arrived home in the middle of the day. Emily was sitting at the kitchen table with the newspaper spread in front of her, a cup of coffee in her hand.

"Emily!"

"Ian!"

"Emily, what the hell are you doing here? I thought you were in the Caymans. I called you all night long and there was no answer."

"I fell asleep, Ian. I guess I didn't hear the phone," she said. "I was afraid to go. Besides, I didn't want to go without you."

"Jesus Christ, Emily! You just blew two vacations. I better not hear you bitch about how tired you are and we never go anywhere. I had no choice; you did. Sometimes you are so goddamn stupid you boggle my mind."

Emily gulped at her coffee, which was mostly cream and sugar. "How's your patient?" she whispered.

"She died. A lot of people have died in the past few days. I worked around the clock and slept leaning up against walls, for ten minutes at a time. I just came home to get cleaned up. Mrs. Waller's funeral is this afternoon. I had to leave your car at the hospital and walk. My feet are wet and cold. Couldn't you at least have cleaned off the car?"

"I'll do it now."

"Don't bother, Emily. The snow is frozen on it. I hired some kids to do it."

"I'm sorry, Ian. Sorry about Mrs. Waller and sorry about the car. I should have done it. I don't know why I didn't. It's so cold outside."

"Tell me about it, Emily," Ian railed. "If it's not too goddamn much trouble, do you think you could make me an egg sandwich and some fresh coffee? I'll take it with me. In case you're thinking I'll be here for dinner, I won't. I have to go back to the hospital after the funeral."

"Is there anything I can do?"

Ian marched back to the kitchen. "Yes, Emily, there is. Make a chart showing how much money we lost. Tack it up on the refrigerator with a note saying, 'I am never going to waste money again.' I mean it, Emily, if I ever hear you bitch about not taking vacations or anything else for that matter, I'm leaving you. You had your chance and you muffed it."

He was tired, saying things he didn't mean. He wouldn't leave her. She was his wife, in sickness and health, for better or worse. Tears dripped into the mixing bowl as she beat the eggs into a swirling yellow fluff. Her life, as she knew it, literally flashed before her. Her hand froze on the wire whisk. What would she do if Ian left her? Die. She would simply curl up and die. Ian was her reason for living. But was this living? She choked back a sob. She felt guilty, ashamed, and wasn't able to look her husband in the eye when he reached for his sandwich and his Dunkin Donuts mug full of coffee, complete with sipping lid.

Emily ran to the living room window. She watched as Ian paid two boys and then climbed in the car. Even from the second floor she could hear the engine catch. Damn, why hadn't she cleaned off the car?

When the kitchen was cleaned up, Emily sat down and made two neat columns of figures. Well, there was only one way to make this right. She called Heckling Pete's and asked for Pete.

"Pete, I didn't make it to the airport. If you need me, I can come in for the next four days. Okay, I have to get the car from the hospital parking lot. It might take a while to dig it out. The main roads are clear, aren't they? I don't have four-wheel drive on the Chevy. I'll be careful. It's hard to believe business is brisk after a storm. Everybody unwinding, huh? Guess that makes sense. You'll see me when you see me. Thanks, Pete."

If she worked till closing and then went in for the break-fast trade, she could even up the money they'd lost on the vacation. Ian wouldn't be able to quibble with that or would he? She just didn't know anymore. She prayed the tips would be good.

After working her shift, Emily drove home and crept into the apartment like a thief in the night. Ian's car was in the driveway; he was finally home. She undressed in the dark, shivering in the cold apartment. She hugged the covers to her as she tried to still her quaking body. She didn't dare wake Ian.

Emily and Ian both moved the moment the alarm sounded two hours later. Emily went straight to the kitchen, allowing Ian the bathroom. She made one cup of coffee for herself. When the door to the bathroom opened, she carried her mug of coffee and her clothes into the tiny cubicle. She locked the door, something she'd never done before in her married life. She turned on the shower and sat on the edge of the tub drinking her coffee.

Emily peeled off her nightgown and was about to step

into the shower when Ian banged on the door and tried to open it. "Where's the coffee, Emily?"

"I drank it," she shouted as she lathered up under the warm spray.

"A whole pot?" Ian said in outrage.

"I only made one cup. If you want coffee, make it yourself. And on your way out, drop off your shirts at the laundry. And your other laundry too. I'm on strike. You can start eating out for all I care. Make sure my car is back here by noon or I'll tell the police you stole it."

"When are you coming out of there?"

"When I feel like it. Probably after you leave. I don't want to look at your face, Ian."

"You screw up your own vacation and you don't want to look at my face. God, Emily, that's just like you. How long are you going to pout this time?"

"Forever," Emily shot back.

She stayed in the shower until the water ran cold. Then she stepped out, but let the water continue to run. She applied light makeup, struggled with her curly hair, brushing it till it was smooth enough to twine into a neat bun. She was dressed five minutes later, at which point she turned off the water. Her ear pressed to the door, she listened for some sound in the apartment. Her watch said she'd been in the bathroom for ninety minutes. Ian wouldn't dilly-dally that long. Usually he gulped a cup of coffee and ran.

Coffee cup in hand, Emily wandered around the small apartment. First she checked the laundry basket. Ian hadn't taken his shirts with him. She counted them, looked in the closet. Two clean ones. He'd probably go out and buy more. His suit was thrown over the back of a chair, ready to go to the cleaners. Ian probably didn't even know where the cleaners was. She set her coffee cup down and made her side of the bed.

Petty, childish behavior. She didn't care.

"Enough, Ian, I've had enough." Two and a half more days until her "vacation" was over and she had to go back to the clinic every morning. Maybe she wouldn't go back. Ever.

It was a full three days before Emily found out Ian's reaction to her behavior to be no reaction at all. She sighed heavily; it was business as usual. He didn't even comment on the money she'd left on the kitchen table with the list he'd ordered her to prepare. On Monday morning the list was crumpled and in the trash, the money gone. But things weren't right between them even though they were both trying to act as though nothing had happened. Ian spoke in quiet tones, left early, and was asleep when she got home. At the clinics when he met her in the hallway or stopped by her desk, he smiled at her, but that was because there were patients milling about. It was clear to Emily that Ian was avoiding her and she did her best to avoid him, staying at Heckling Pete's as long as possible.

On the fifth day of what Emily considered their armed truce, Ian approached her and said, "Enough of this crap, Emily. We're like two tired warriors and I for one have had enough."

"I've had enough too," Emily said as she packed up her oversize pocketbook. It was one o'clock, time to get ready to head home to change her clothes and go on to Heckling Pete's.

"Then give me a big kiss and let's get back on track here." Emily dutifully held up her face and Ian kissed her on the cheek. "What is it you want, Ian?"

"Well, now that you ask, I think the fridge needs to be replenished. I couldn't find a grain of sugar or anything sweet in the whole apartment. I really hate to mention this, but the laundry is piling up."

"I know," Emily said.

"What does that mean, *I know*? Does it mean you

know and are going to correct the situation or does it mean who gives a good rat's ass? Or are you unaware? I prefer to think you're unaware because we've both been uptight."

"All of the above," Emily said, walking toward the door.

Ian followed her to the door and walked outside with her. "Well?" he said, a smile on his face for the benefit of a patient who walked around both of them to enter the clinic.

"Well what, Ian?"

"You really have a pissy attitude lately, Emily. I don't like it. At all."

"I know," Emily said, marching toward the parking lot. What was it her mother always said, don't cut off your nose to spite your face? Something like that. And that's exactly what she was doing. It was time she asserted herself where Ian was concerned. Right now the laundry was the biggest bone of contention. Grocery shopping the second. Their attitude toward one another. Slave-master relationships, Pete said, went out with the dark ages.

Maybe she had things out of order. She didn't know anything anymore. She was a robot doing things automatically. She didn't think anymore, didn't exercise her brain at all. All she did was work, eat, sleep, and cry.

Things were going to change, Emily thought as she jammed the key in the lock of her apartment door. And they were going to have to change soon.

Someday I'm going to live in a real house and this rinky-dink apartment and all my problems will be over. If you believe that, Emily Thorn, you're a fool. She sat down on the hard, wooden chair and stared into space. Someday . . .

Chapter 5

Emily stared at the laundry basket. in her eyes it represented an insurmountable mountain. Each day it got higher and higher. She stuck her foot into the basket and crunched down Ian's white shirts. She didn't feel any kind of satisfaction. Suddenly she wanted to count the shirts, needed desperately to know the numbers so she could calculate the days she and Ian had been at war. She upended the basket, kicking each shirt into the basket as she counted. When she was done, she jumped into the plastic basket and stomped with both feet. Forty shirts at three shirts a day meant thirteen and a half days. But then that wasn't right either because Ian hadn't come home for a few days during the snowstorm. She was stomping on two weeks' worth of white shirts, maybe more.

The refrigerator was still empty, and there were no goodies or munchies in the cupboards. She still made only her side of the bed.

The Thorns were at war.

Emily's nerves were in such a fragile state she no longer knew if what she was doing was right or not. If Ian would just say something, do something, make some kind gesture, she would react accordingly. Positively. She couldn't go on like this much longer. Emily looked at the clock.

Five minutes to midnight. She was home early tonight because Pete had decided to close early.

Emily raced for the bathroom and turned on the shower. When Ian wasn't home, she could make all the noise she wanted. She could stand under the shower for hours or until the water ran cold. Tonight she'd be able to wash her hair twice with the new coconut shampoo and hopefully get the stench of Pete's deep fryer out of her hair. The cigarette smoke she reeked of would disappear if she carried her clothes out to the kitchen and dumped them in *her* laundry basket.

"You are one screwed-up, mixed-up puppy, Emily Thorn," she muttered as she lathered up her hair. In some cockamamie way she justified the feeling by telling herself if she recognized that she was half nuts she wouldn't cross over the invisible line into insanity.

An hour later, Emily's hair was dry, she was powdered and dressed in a high-necked, flannel nightgown and in between the covers. She was almost asleep when she heard Ian come in. She felt a tremor in her body and then another. God, how she wanted him. More than she'd ever wanted him. But more than anything, she wanted to rear up in bed and scream at the top of her lungs, *I'm sorry! Love me, Ian, please love me. I'll do whatever you want. Say you love me, say this is just something married couples go through. Say it, say it even if it's a lie and you don't mean it.* She fought with herself, refused to give in. Instead she clutched the pillow and clenched her teeth.

Tomorrow was another day. Tomorrow there would be forty-three shirts in the basket.

"Emily." It was a whisper.

It was the dearest, the sweetest sound. A sound she'd hungered for so long. Her name. Ian was ready to make peace. Thank you, God, thank you.

"Yes, Ian."

"I don't want to live like this anymore, Emily. I feel like I'm living in a war zone."

"I don't want to live like this either." She didn't move, waited for his arm to reach out to her the way he used to do. When she finally felt his touch, she rolled over and snuggled close, her breath exploding in a long, happy sigh.

"This was the worst two weeks of my life," Ian said.

"Me too. Let's not ever do this again, okay?"

"Okay. You smell good. New shampoo?"

"Hmmmnn." He didn't smell good. He'd smoked a cigar and he hadn't brushed his teeth. "I haven't been sleeping well. I tried to wake you last night, but you were in a deep sleep."

"Really, Ian!"

"Really, Emily. Let's go out to dinner tonight. Just you and me. Call in sick or switch your hours with someone, okay?"

"Are we celebrating something or are you just being nice?"

"Both. I'll know more tomorrow. I'll dude up and you gussy up and we'll go out on the town. Your choice, Emily, where would you like to go?"

"Can I think about it?"

"Sure, honey. Listen, let's make a deal, okay. If you make out a grocery list, I'll get up early and go to that A&P that's open twenty-four hours a day. You wash and iron my shirts."

"Okay, Ian." She knew at that moment if he'd asked her to climb to the heavens she would have searched out a hardware store to see if they made ladders that reached that high.

Moments later, Ian's lusty snores permeated the bedroom. Emily waited ten minutes before she crept from the bed and out to the kitchen. She pulled on her down coat, gathered up the laundry basket as well as her soap. She let herself out of the apartment quietly and down the steps to the basement where the washer and dryer were located. While the shirts washed, she set up the ironing board and plugged in the iron. She'd gone without sleep before. She'd iron all night and surprise Ian when he woke to go to the A&P.

While she waited for the clothes to dry, she ran upstairs to make a pot of coffee, which she carried down to the basement. She switched on the landlord's portable radio on a shelf above the galvanized sinks. Golden Oldies wafted softly throughout the basement. It was warm, and she was doing something she did well, something Ian appreciated. If she was going to call in sick, she could nap in the afternoon. This was more important than sleep.

As she finished each shirt, she hung it on the clothesline that ran the length of the basement. The heat from the furnace would dry the dampness around the double thickness of the collar and cuffs.

At five-ten in the morning, Emily made four trips back and forth to hang the shirts in Ian's closet. Satisfied with her long night's work, she made a fresh pot of coffee and was sitting at the table trying to imagine Ian's reaction when he saw all his shirts hanging in the closet and on the back of every door in the apartment. She was about to take a sip of the freshly brewed coffee when she panicked and ran to the bathroom to check on the shirts, the last ones she'd ironed, the ones she hadn't hung by the furnace to dry. She was too late.

"Jesus fucking Christ, Emily, these shirts are still wet. I could get icicles on my neck. It's nineteen degrees outside."

Stunned, Emily backed up a step and sucked in her breath. "I made a mistake, Ian, the ones in the closet are the dry ones. I thought you'd take one from the closet.

You steam up the bathroom and it seeps out. I'm sorry. Here, let me get you another one," she said as Ian ripped off the damp shirt and tossed it in the corner. Emily cringed as though she'd been slapped.

The phone rang as Ian was tying his tie. Emily picked it up and listened before she handed it to her husband. "I'm on my way," she heard him say.

"Emily, I won't be able to do the A&P bit. Joshua Oliver is having another series of seizures. Damn, I thought we had those under control."

"I'll do it, Ian. Hurry," she said, holding out his winter jacket for him to slip his arms into.

"You're a sweetheart, Emily. I'm sorry about the grocery shopping and I'm sorry for going off on you for the wet shirt. It's gonna be one of those days. I'll see you around five, okay?"

"Sure, Ian," Emily said, tilting her head for his kiss on the cheek.

If you were keeping score, which Emily was, it was Ian Thorn 1, Emily Thorn zip.

Chapter 6

Emily sat at her desk in the Watchung Clinic—their third—her chin in her hands, her eyes staring straight ahead at the calendar propped up against the outgoing mail basket. There was finally light at the end of the tunnel. She x'd out the date. So many years, she thought wearily.

For the first time in hours, it was quiet. Somewhere in the background one of the nurses had a radio that was playing Christmas carols. Emily loved the carols and wished she were a youngster again, just getting ready to start her adult life, a life much different from the one she'd opted for.

Her heart missed a beat when she heard her husband say, "A penny for your thoughts, Mrs. Thorn."

"Right now that's about what they're worth. I was thinking I finally see light at the end of the tunnel and enjoying the sound of the Christmas carols. It's such a wonderful time of year, don't you think?"

"Get your coat on, Emily, you and I are leaving this place. We're going to Rickels and get one of those hot dogs from the guy with the umbrella and we're saying the hell with our cholesterol. Maybe we'll get two hot dogs with the works. Root beer. God, Emily, when was the last time we did that?"

"About twelve years ago."

"No!"

"Yes, Ian."

"God! In that case let's see if we can eat three. Are you game?"

"You bet," Emily said, slipping into her coat.

"I have a surprise for you, Emily, and this is my way of leading up to it. We're gonna sit in the car and eat with the heater running and the windows steaming up, right?"

They were kids again. After the hot dogs they'd make out in the back seat. She giggled.

"Right."

"But," he whispered, "we'll go home and make love in bed. Is that okay with you? I think we're both too old to scramble around in the back seat."

"Give me a clue, Ian. About the surprise."

"Nope. It's something you have to see. No clues, no hints."

"Will I like it?"

"You are going to love it. It's taken me almost two years to get . . . that's all I'm going to say. You're just going to have to wait and see it."

Later, when Ian carried six hot dogs with the works, plus two giant root beers, back to the car he said, "I'm going to be awfully disappointed in us if our eyes and memories are bigger than our stomachs. Five bucks says you burp first."

"Ha!" was all Emily said. Oh, God, this was so wonderful, she thought as she chewed her way through her three hot dogs. Ian finished his and gulped down his soda. She deliberately waited, knowing the fizzy soda would indeed make her burp. She cackled with glee when Ian, red-faced, finally couldn't hold it in a moment longer. She held out her hand for the five dollars. He paid up. Emily leaned across and tapped the horn for the Salvation Army volunteer to come over to the car for the money.

"That was a damn nice thing you just did, Emily Thorn."

"It was damn nice of you to pay up, Dr. Thorn."

"That's because we're just two damn nice people. Sometimes I lose track of that, Emily."

"I know, Ian, I do too." Either she was dead and in heaven or this was all a dream. Whatever it was, she didn't want it to end. Days like this, times like this, over the past years were so few and far apart she could count them on both hands. At that moment she knew she'd sell her soul to the devil if she could have wonderful moments like this every day for the rest of her life. Well, it wasn't going to happen, so she didn't need to concern herself with it. Instead she would enjoy today and pray that sometime soon another day such as this one would come along. She hoped it would be during the Christmas holidays.

"Well, if you're ready, we're off to my surprise. Actually, Emily, it's sort of a surprise and a Christmas present all rolled into one. It's for both of us. I know how women are about such things so I said it was for you, but I meant it was for us to share. I think you'll understand when we get there."

All Emily heard were the words *share* and *together*. A unit like cream and sugar, salt and pepper. Ian and Emily. A couple. Don't let this end, don't let it come crashing down around me, Emily prayed silently.

Twenty minutes later, Ian swung the car onto Watchung Avenue. They were driving past the clinic, but Ian didn't bother to even look out the window. They went through the traffic lights and up the hill. She couldn't make out the street signs at all.

"This is Sleepy Hollow Road. It's nice back in here, isn't it?"

"Maybe we should think about looking here for a house when we're ready to buy. I could see us living here, Ian."

"I can too," Ian said cheerfully. "We're here."

"Who lives here?" Emily asked in awe as she stared at

the brightly lighted English Tudor with the huge Christmas wreath on the front door. "Ian, if this is a party, I'm not dressed. We reek of onions and sauerkraut."

Ian literally dragged her from the car and hand in hand they ran to the front door. Ian continued to play the game by knocking on the door and then ringing the doorbell. "C'mon, open up," he bellowed.

"Ian, *shhhh,*" Emily said.

"Guess I'll have to open it myself." Emily watched, her eyes round, as her husband fitted a shiny new key into the lock. The door swung open.

Before she knew what was happening, Ian scooped her up and carried her over the threshold. "Welcome to your new home, Mrs. Thorn."

"What?" Emily squealed as Ian set her down. "*Ohhhhh,* Ian, this is too much. I know I'm dreaming." Ian pinched her rump and she squealed again. "Is this really ours?"

"In a manner of speaking. It belongs to the corporation, but technically, yes, it belongs to us."

"How? Where? I don't understand. It's wonderful. It's beautiful. Did you do all this yourself?"

Ian held up his hands. "Remember Mrs. Waller? The house belonged to her estate. The time was right, I guess, and no, I did not do this myself. I hired a decorator, and before you can think it much less say it, decorating isn't your forte nor is it mine. I told the woman what you liked and what I liked and this is what we got. Of course, if you don't like it, you can change it. She even put up the Christmas tree. The front door wreath was a gift from her. We have to decorate the tree. I know how you like to do that. I had some boys bring all the stuff from the basement over this afternoon. It's in the garage. I thought we'd do it later after the hot dogs digest. Do you like it, Emily?"

"Oh, Ian, I love it. However did you keep this from me?"

"It wasn't easy," Ian said jovially. "Why don't you look around while I pop the cork on a bottle of champagne. Emily, I'm trying to keep my promise to you to give you everything in the world. This is a start. Would you like a fire?"

Emily threw her arms around her husband. "Oh, Ian, I love you so much. Thank you for this, thank you so much. Yes to the fire and yes to the champagne."

When Emily returned from her inspection of the house, Ian said, "Did you go down to the basement. No! Half of the basement is for you so you can plant in the winter. I had them install grow lights. There must be at least a thousand flats down there and every seed known to Burpee. I expect some wonderful salads this summer with flowers in every room of the house. I'd appreciate it if you'd plant a lot of tulips, every color they come in. Will you do that?"

"Of course. Ian," she said, dropping to the floor next to him in front of the fire. "Why are we sitting on the floor?"

"I like sitting on the floor in front of a fire. I thought we could make love here. It's toasty and we need to christen our new house."

"Sounds good. Hit me," she said, holding out her wineglass. "Do we have any more of this. I *like* it."

"Two more bottles. One's for Christmas Eve, though. I want you to do something for me, Emily. Don't look like that, I'm not going to say I changed my mind about something. This concerns you," he said, handing her a pen and a paper napkin. "Write down every single thing you could ever possibly want. Everything, no matter how big or small. There's no limit. If you need two napkins, that's okay, too."

"Everything, Ian?"

"I promised you whatever your heart desires. Start writing, honey."

"My very own wish list. I don't know where to start. I

guess I don't have to put down a house since we already have it. I'll start big, okay?"

"Whatever you want, Emily?"

Emily wrote steadily for what seemed like a long time. When she had finished, she handed the list to Ian. It was a shy gesture, her eyes looking everywhere but at her husband.

Ian read the list aloud, to Emily's embarrassment. "Beach house, Sunfish, three vacations a year, Mercedes convertible for weekends, a Porsche for weekdays, pearls, every length, diamond earrings, diamond bracelet, lots and lots of diamonds. Mink coat, a sable coat, a fox coat. Three Chanel handbags, a live-in housekeeper to take care of us and wait on us, my very own checking account that I do not have to account for, money for my college tuition, a baby that looks just like you, and you, for all the rest of my days."

"That's an impressive list, Emily. Now here, sign it."

"This is fun," Emily said, scrawling her name. "Is there anything on the list you object to?" she asked, fear in her eyes.

"Not a thing. Those three vacations a year might be a problem if you want me to go with you. Both of us can't be away, but if you're speaking for yourself, then I can definitely guarantee them."

"Vacations are no fun alone," Emily said, sticking her tongue out at him.

"I'm serious, Emily. Will you settle for going alone if I can't go?"

"You're serious, aren't you?" Emily said, puzzled by his tone.

"Of course I'm serious. I made a promise to you and I intend to honor it. What's it going to be? If I can't get away, will you go alone?"

"Yes."

"Good. That's settled." He leered at her as he stuffed the napkin in his shirt pocket. "C'mere."

"This is nice, isn't it?"

"It's wonderful," Ian said. "What are you going to do with all your free time, Emily?"

"Well, now that you don't need me anymore . . ."

"Wait just a minute, Emily. Where did you get the idea I don't need you anymore? No, no, that's not what this is all about. You hung in there with me and now it's your turn. All you have to do is put in an hour each day at each clinic. That doesn't mean I don't need you. I don't ever want you to think that. You said you wanted to go to school. Just out of curiosity, what were you going to do?"

"I'll read, sleep late for a little while, watch some television, garden a lot, study if I go to school, wait for you to come home. Ian, are we making a lot of money now?"

"I think it's safe to say we're making a kingly amount."

"Can we start a baby, you know, can we start trying?"

"Don't see why not."

Everything suddenly felt flat. Ian didn't need her anymore. He was agreeing to everything; he was being so nice it was now suspect. She felt like a tired, old workhorse being put out to pasture. She didn't mean to say the words, but they tumbled out of her mouth.

Ian stared at her for a full minute, his jaw dropping. He cupped her face in his hands. "Emily, what do you want? What do you really want? I don't know you anymore. No matter what I do or when I do it doesn't make you happy. I thought you would be overjoyed, that all this was what you wanted for so very long. It's my turn now to pay you back and suddenly you make me feel like I'm doing something dark and ugly. You're spoiling things again. You, Emily, not me."

"I'm too old to start college now. Look at me and tell me I'll fit in. Go ahead, say it."

"You might not be as young as the freshmen, but there are a lot of people older than you who go to college. You don't want that degree very much, Emily. Either you want that degree or you don't. It's clear sailing for you, Emily. No loans to pay, you can buy your lunch or dinner, you can drive to class, come home and someone will be here to cook for you, to do all the chores. I never had it that good and neither did anyone else I know. I said three hours because I thought you wanted to keep your hand in the business. If you want to work all day, feel free. It's your choice."

"I don't know how to choose. There I was working sixteen and sometimes seventeen hours a day, trying to do my best. Then instead of being weaned away from that killer load I'm suddenly out in the cold. At least that's how I feel. I guess I just don't know how to react. I didn't expect this, wasn't prepared. I appreciate it. All I've ever known is work and more work."

"And now you don't have to work anymore. Now you can have your legs taken care of. All the things you couldn't do before, all the things you *said* you wanted to do. I think you need to finish this wine by yourself and think about things. I'm going to bed. By the way, I'm taking the green room at the top of the steps. Yours is the yellow one. This way I won't wake you up with my middle-of-the-night departures and the phone ringing."

"But Ian, I thought we . . ." *Don't beg, Emily, please don't beg,* she pleaded with herself. "Good night, Ian," she said quietly.

Separate bedrooms. My God, she thought. So it's come to this. She couldn't help but wonder if the try for the baby would be a one-shot deal or if he'd back off from her all together. She looked around at her new house. There was no way in hell she was climbing those stairs and sleeping in a yellow bedroom someone else had decorated.

God, what was wrong with her? Maybe she needed a shrink. Well, she could certainly find the time now to visit one. In secret, of course. Ian would explode if he thought a colleague was hearing her troubles. Maybe she could go into New York and give a false name and pay in cash. Maybe she'd get pregnant right away and she wouldn't have to do anything but take care of the baby. That would be blissful heaven.

She finished the wine before she curled into a tight ball and slept on the hard, new sofa that smelled of packing materials.

Emily woke to silence that was so total she shook her head to clear it. At first she felt disoriented, sluggish and then fearful. A faint amber glow from the streetlight outside gilded the middle of the room. Then she remembered where she was and why she'd fallen asleep on the scratchy new sofa. From somewhere in the house a clock chimed the hour. She counted one, two, three, four, five. Five o'clock in the morning.

The smelly pillows she'd been sleeping on caught her as she flopped backward. How could something beautiful and wonderful end so disastrously? Unless that was the way Ian had intended the evening to end. *Separate bedrooms.* Hers was yellow. She started to shake, was unable to stop, and there was no quilt, no afghan to cover herself with. She didn't even know where the thermostat was. She wanted to feel anger, to go upstairs and demand Ian tell her *exactly* what was going on in their lives.

Well, she was going to find out and she was going to find out right now. Her trembling ceased and was replaced with ramrod stiffness as she mounted the steps to the second floor. She thrust open the door and peered into the darkness. The bed had been slept in, but was empty now. Ian must have gotten called out to one of the clinics during the night. She turned on the light, gathering one of Ian's pillows to her chest. It smelled faintly of his after-shave, a potent concoction from a grateful patient. Tears dripped on the pillow. She brushed them away. Crying never helped. Crying gave her headaches. "Damn you, Ian." She wanted a friend then more than she'd ever wanted anything. Someone to call up and talk to. Where was her old friend Aggie? For years they'd sent Christmas cards and then one year there was no card and she didn't know where to send hers to so she'd scratched Aggie's name off her list. Well, she was going to have a lot of spare time now. Maybe she could track Aggie down.

Ian had his own bathroom. She looked around carefully. If she remembered correctly, this was the largest of five bedrooms—the master bedroom. The yellow room, hers, wasn't quite as large. Ian had huge double closets. The yellow room had an oversize closet with a mirror on the door. And why the hell not, Ian needed more room than three women with all his shirts and suits. Her own wardrobe was meager compared to his.

Who was going to clean this monstrous house? When was a housekeeper going to materialize? If that didn't happen, she and she alone was going to have to do it. It would take her all day to dust and polish, to keep things the way Ian liked them. She'd need two vacuum cleaners, one for upstairs and one for downstairs. A set of cleaning supplies would have to go into the upstairs linen closet. Or would Ian expect her to lug things up and then down?

From long habit, Emily made the bed, but she did it with anger in her eyes and murder in her heart. The linen closet in the hall was full of towels and sheets. There was no vacuum cleaner, no cleaning supplies.

Emily opened the door to the yellow room. It was pretty enough in a frilly kind of way. She almost choked when she opened the closet door to see her clothes hanging

neatly. She yanked at the dresser drawers to see her underwear, her stockings, her nightgowns neatly folded. She
pawed through them. How dare Ian do this to her! Her
personal things were no one else's business. She did cry
then when she saw her panties, the ones where the elastic
was coming away from the material, all neatly folded on
the bottom of the pile. Some stranger Ian hired had seen
and touched her underwear. She felt ashamed, embarrassed that she didn't have sexy, beribboned undies, the
kind you bought from Victoria's Secret. She didn't have time
to shop for such things, and goddamn it, she liked cotton
underwear. Size eight. She shuddered as she slammed the
drawers shut.

The yellow room had its own bathroom. It wasn't as
large as Ian's and didn't have a bidet and only one vanity.
She fingered the apple-green towels that were larger than
beach towels and twice as thick. They were called bath
sheets in the Sears Roebuck catalog.

There was a hollow feeling in her stomach when Emily
made her way downstairs to the kitchen. She passed the
thermostat on the way and turned it up to 80.

It was a beautiful, modern kitchen complete with dish-
washer, trash compactor, and garbage disposal. There was
a center island with cabinets underneath, lots and lots of
gorgeous oak cabinets, all of them full of new dishes and
copper-bottomed pots and pans. A string of garlic hung
from one of the beams, which had a little note attached to
the bottom that said, "Good luck in your new house."
"Up yours," Emily muttered.

Everything was where it should be, just the way she would
have positioned things if she'd decorated the kitchen herself. She made coffee, and while it perked, her mind raced.
Down the hall and around the corner of the steps was a
home office for Ian, completely outfitted. Suddenly it was
important for her to see that office, to see what was in it.

It was manly, professional-looking. An Ian office if there was such a thing. Wainscoting, deep leather chairs, chocolate-colored carpeting, a mahogany desk that was so shiny she could see her reflection in the top. Everything shrieked newness. It even had a fireplace, a neatly laid stack of wood waiting for a match to ignite it. Medical books lined the walls in what Emily knew were custom-made bookshelves.

In their entire married life she'd never, ever gone through Ian's things. Even at the clinics she'd never opened any of his drawers, never touched anything. She yanked at first one drawer and then another. Files, folders. Records. In the middle drawer where people had a tendency to toss bits and pieces because of convenience she saw a lone folder labeled Park Avenue Clinic. She read through it, stunned at what she was reading. When she was finished, she replaced it exactly the way she'd found it, closed the drawer, got up, gave the seat of the leather chair a hard smack to erase the indentation, pushed it back, and left the room.

Emily's eyes were wild when she poured coffee into a gaily colored mug. There seemed to be a set of cups, each with a flower painted on the side. The one she was holding was a pansy pattern with beautiful shades of purple. At first she thought it was a decal. On closer examination she saw it was hand-painted. It took both hands to hold the mug, to bring it to her lips. Until she tasted the scalding coffee she wasn't aware that she'd forgotten to add sugar and cream.

The Park Avenue Clinic was going to be an abortion clinic. Over her dead body. She had something to say about that. Ian knew she was going to object and that's why everything was so secret. Which just went to prove this new house, last night, was nothing more than window dressing until he got down to what he was setting her up for.

Was she supposed to go to the clinics today? She couldn't remember. Obviously it didn't make a difference or someone would have called by now to find out where she was or at least to ask if maybe she was coming in late.

Are you thinking of a confrontation, Emily? her other self asked quietly. At Ian's place of business? Think again, Emily. You really don't have any say in how the businesses are run. You refused to become an officer of the corporation. You gave up those rights and Ian will throw that at you with the speed of lightning. His attorney will back it up. You are a paid employee whose salary remains in the business. You are given an allowance by your husband; he takes care of everything. He's currently working on the list you provided, to give you everything you ever wanted in life.

The pansy cup fell from her hands and shattered on the terra-cotta floor. One down, five to go, she thought as her gaze raked the colorful cups hanging on a coffee cup tree that was too cute for words. Her arm swept out, sending the metal stand and the five cups crashing to the floor. Now she was going to have to clean it up and even from here she could see the nicks in the new floor. It was a stupid floor. Terra-cotta belonged outside, on a patio or a deck.

Maybe this was what wasn't sitting well with her. Ian's blind rush to start giving her things without asking her dislikes and likes. Why couldn't she be allowed to decorate her own home? Was her taste so terrible? The house was attractively furnished, but it wasn't her taste, and as far as she could tell, it wasn't Ian's taste either. It was probably some damn. twenty-five-year-old decorator Ian had flirted with.

Cry, Emily. That's what you always do when things don't go right. Instead of taking a stand, making your views known, you cry and give in. Like that time you ironed those forty shirts. Ian smiles at you, and you all but kiss his feet.

Emily walked into the living room. She needed to take a shower and get dressed. Then she'd go into the clinic and talk to Ian.

Her shower completed, she tried to dry herself with one of the large towels. The terry cloth refused to absorb the water because the towels were new and hadn't been washed. She picked up her sweatshirt, turned it inside out, and dried herself.

Naked, she charged into the yellow bedroom, where she rummaged for her clothes. How should she dress to visit the Park Avenue Clinic?

The Park Avenue Clinic, two blocks down from Maple Avenue, ran the entire length and breadth of the four-story building. It was going to be huge, bigger than the other three clinics. It was a perfect location. Rent was going to be very high. She walked down the nine steps to the basement, whose windows were above ground level. The workmen didn't pay any attention to her. She thought she recognized two of the men who worked on the Watchung Clinic. They nodded to her.

At least six thousand square feet. Really high rent. She was checking on the patient bathroom when she heard two men conversing on the other side of the wall. They were amused about something, she could hear it in their voices, but the words weren't distinguishable. She backed out of the bathroom and meandered closer to the wall. Now she could hear perfectly.

"I wouldn't lie about something like that, Walt. Doc Thorn told me himself just last week. This whole side of the building is for a sperm bank. It's gonna be a whole separate operation. Ten bucks if you don't believe me. Ask Dwight, he's the architect."

Emily's eyes rolled back in her head, but she didn't move. "Big money in sperm banks, the Doc said. They charge for the *donation* then they charge rent for keeping the *donation*. This isn't just going to be an abortion clinic. Some other doctor is going to be doing vasectomies. Now that's something I'd never even think of doing. What about you, Walt?"

"When I don't want any more kids, I might think about it. You can get it reversed later on if it turns out to be something you can't live with. My wife cut out an article for me to read. I'd consider it. One of the guys up front said the doc was thinking of converting the other clinics he has to this kind. Must be a lot of money in this. Doc Thorn wouldn't be considering revamping his clinics if he wasn't going to be making some mega bucks. My wife is pro-choice, what's yours?"

"Pro-life. Guess we're a wash if it comes to a vote."

"Yeah, guess so. Guess the Thorns are pro-choice."

Emily swayed dizzily before she felt well enough to leave the work area.

Sperm banks, abortion clinics. The family clinics she'd believed in, had worked in, were going to be done away with. And she'd made it possible with all her hard work.

She needed to talk to Ian and she needed to talk to him now. She was off the hook as far as invading Ian's privacy via his desk drawers. She could now honestly say she'd overheard the men at the clinic talking.

At home she called the three clinics to see where Ian was. "Pencil me in for lunch," she told the receptionist. "Tell Dr. Thorn it's very important I see him. I'm making a reservation at Jacques' for one o'clock. I'll meet him there."

Emily's stomach churned as she changed her everyday attire to an outfit more conducive to a Christmassy lunch at Jacques'. She pulled on a raspberry-colored sack outfit and dressed it up with a multicolored belt that matched the costume jewelry left over from her younger days. She felt elegant in her high heels which she hadn't worn in over a year. For the tiniest of moments she dallied with the thought of spritzing herself with the perfume Ian had given her years ago. He'd take it as a sign that she was ready to give in, as usual, to whatever he wanted. She put the bottle back on the dresser. She was never going to use this room. Never, ever. When this luncheon was all over, she might very well end up packing her bags and moving out. Sheer bravado as far as her thoughts went. In her heart and gut she knew only an act of God could separate her from Ian. He was her reason for living, her reason for *being*.

Emily's spirits lifted when she walked into Jacques' shortly before one o'clock. She took a moment to drink in the colorful poinsettias lining the foyer. The blooms were banked at the desk and up the steps and into the bar. Inside the main part of the restaurant they were featured in the boxed windows with porcelain dolls dressed in red velvet. Cheerful, colorful, a reminder that the holiday was just days away. She ordered a glass of white wine and settled down to wait for her husband. He was fifteen minutes late, a huge smile on his face when he was ushered to her booth.

"Scotch on the rocks," he said to the waiter at his elbow.

"Emily, you never cease to amaze me. To what do I owe the pleasure? This is *verrry* nice," he said, lighting a cigarette. "I don't think you ever really invited me to lunch before. Great idea. You're paying, of course."

How handsome he looked in his beige cashmere jacket. His white shirt was so perfectly ironed by herself she felt a ring of heat start to form around her neck. "Of course," she said carefully.

"Are you telling me you saved your *allowance?* Or are you holding out on me again?"

Emily's heart thumped in her chest. "Pete gave me a generous Christmas going-away present. I planned to use it for Christmas."

"And well he should. You worked your buns off for that man. He owes you. How much did he give you?"

"Five hundred dollars."

"In that case I think I'll order lobster." Ian flipped open the huge brown menu and pretended to scan the day's offerings. "Did you sleep well? I slept like a baby. When the phone rang at three forty-five I just got up and showered and out I went. I felt so rested. I really like the idea of my own room, don't you? Mine looks the way a man's room should look and yours looks the way a woman's room should look. I think it's one of the best decisions I've ever made. You have no idea, Emily, how many couples have separate rooms. I personally think it makes for a better marriage. I hope this lobster tastes as good as those hot dogs tasted last night. That was great, wasn't it?"

"I enjoyed the hot dogs. Ian, about the separate bedrooms, I don't like sleeping by myself. What kind of marriage is it when we sleep apart? We're supposed to be a couple. If I'm not going to work anymore and you're going to be gone all day and most of the evening, when will I see you? I don't like that yellow room. I slept on the couch." She put her hands in her lap and then between her knees to keep them from shaking. She wondered if he could tell she was trembling. Ian could sense everything.

"Emily, it's just for sleep. We both need a restful night. Did you look at yourself in the mirror before you left the house? You look positively frazzled. That's what sleeping on the couch will do to you. Now, look at me. I feel like the king of the mountain because for the first time in years

I've gotten a good night's sleep. Don't you care, even a little bit, about my well-being? I need my wits to take care of my patients. You're being selfish again. If you're worried we won't have sex, you can forget that. I'll knock on your door or you knock on mine. Or we can plan ahead and make appointments. Now, you have to admit, that's devilish."

Devilish. Did he think she was stupid? Obviously. "Why didn't you talk to me about it before you did it, Ian? You always consult me. At least you used to. I don't know us anymore, Ian." There was a quiver in her voice Ian was going to notice. Damn.

"And spoil the surprise? I thought I was doing something nice, keeping my promise to you. Consulting you would have ruined the surprise. And, dear Emily, I am aware, even if you pretend that you aren't, that you are a good thirty pounds overweight. That makes a difference in a bed when you flop around like you do. We need rest, Emily. Why are you being so damn hard to get along with? I thought we were here to have a nice lunch. This is just more of the same."

"We're drifting apart, Ian. I can see it, feel it."

"Now you're a seer. Come off it, Emily. It's your own insecurities. Suddenly you have all this free time and you're running scared. I suppose in a way that's understandable, but for God's sake, what more do you want from me? Women would kill for that house. Women would kill to have free days. Women would kill to have some man pay for everything so they can sit on a velvet cushion. Not you, all you want to do is bitch, whine, and then bitch some more. I think you need to grow up, Emily, and see how things are done in the real world. If you don't like the yellow bedroom, redo it. That's part of it too, right? You don't like the idea that a professional decorator made over the house. If I had let you do it, we'd be living in cutesy, snuggly Early American. I hate that stuff."

Two down, one to go. Emily took a deep breath, signaled for a second glass of wine. "I know about the Park Avenue Clinic. You should have talked to me about that, Ian, before you went ahead and set things up. I feel like you betrayed me. I don't know if I can forgive you for that. I went there this morning to see how things were going and I heard the workmen talking. Why didn't you talk to me, Ian?"

Ian's eyes narrowed as he leaned across the table. "Let me see if I understand this right, Emily. You're unhappy because I went ahead and made a decision without consulting you. You told me when it was time for you to quit working you didn't want any part of those clinics. You goddamn signed away your rights, on advice of your own personal attorney that I and the corporate attorney insisted you hire and paid for by me. You waived your rights. I retired you quite handsomely. So, what the hell is the big bitch here?"

Emily unclenched her jaw. "The bitch is you're turning family clinics into abortion clinics. Sperm banks! My God, Ian, here I am pleading with you for a baby and what are you going to do, you're going to terminate pregnancies. I want a baby so bad I can . . . You said we would have a family. I need to get pregnant before I'm too old. You yourself said it's not good to have a baby late in life."

"Correct me if I'm wrong, Emily, but didn't you on more than one occasion tell me and anyone else who would listen that you were in favor of a woman's right to choose? True, you always said it wouldn't be your own choice, for yourself, but you committed. You can't have it both ways."

"Why not? Isn't that what choice is all about? I would

never choose that for myself, but I don't have the right to make that decision for someone else. Don't put me on the defensive, Ian. You did something we agreed not to do early on. We said we would discuss everything, that we were a team and a team worked together. I guess what you're saying is we aren't a team anymore in more ways than the business. Now that you have your own bedroom, you've put me out. You've actually pensioned me off. How much do I get a month, Ian?"

"Is that what this is all about? You want a check?"

"Among other things. I've never taken a salary, but I'm on the books. I should get something. I want to see it in writing, Ian."

"How much do you want, Emily?"

"Two thousand dollars a month."

"Fine. I'll set it up. All you had to do was say that's what you wanted. You realize the money is going to come from the clinics, don't you?"

"What?" Suddenly she felt stupid and wished she could hide under the table. She'd never seen such a pitying look on Ian's face. Hold her ground now or make another stupid mistake like she'd made when she waived her rights to the family clinics. Tears of frustration burned her eyes. Three down. Suddenly all her expectations evaporated and she could feel her shoulders slump. "Why don't we just get a divorce and be done with it?"

"Is that what you want, Emily? On what grounds?"

God, no, it wasn't what she wanted. "Grounds?"

"Yes, grounds. Yes, if you file for a divorce, what grounds will you sue for? Are you going to say I've been good to you? That I'm trying to make life easier for you? Are you going to say I'm being generous and kind, I just gave you a magnificent house for a Christmas present? What are you going to charge me with? Oh, I get it, the separate bedroom thing. Well, when a judge hears that I'm on call twenty-four hours a day and need my sleep, what do you think he's going to say? You never think, Emily. I'll tell you what I think right now. I don't think we need to get a divorce. Yet. I think we should live under the same roof. You lead your life and I'll lead mine. In a year, if you want a divorce, I'll agree."

Emily's head reeled. She gulped at the wine. "That means we won't have a baby."

"Exactly. If you think I'm going to bring a baby into this world with your attitude, you have another thought coming. You expect me to have passion for you? Forget it, Emily. You know, I have here in my pocket two airline tickets to the Cayman Islands. See," he said, placing the tickets in the middle of the table. Another folder was added. "This is a first-class hotel, ocean view. It was another surprise. I thought we'd leave Christmas morning. I know how much you like Christmas Eve so I thought we'd celebrate then, and leave in the morning. I even hired a limo to pick us up. It was my way of making up for that other botched up trip we couldn't make. See this," Ian said, lifting the flap of the ticket that had her name on it, "now watch me carefully, Emily." He ripped the ticket in two and placed it on her bread plate. "Merry Christmas, Emily." A moment later he was gone.

The waiter appeared at her elbow. "Will Dr. Thorn be returning or did he have an emergency? Will you want to take his lunch home or shall I cancel it?"

"Cancel it, and yes, he had an emergency." She would have left herself, but she knew her legs wouldn't hold her up. She opted to stay and eat the lunch she knew would stick in her throat. She'd stay till most of the patrons were gone so she wouldn't look like the fool she knew she was.

Emily didn't cry until she got home. When she'd finished, she walked up the long staircase to Ian's room. His suitcase was gone and so were a lot of his clothes and toilet articles. Obviously he wasn't coming back home till after his vacation. She pulled back the spread on the bed and buried her face in her husband's pillow. She wished she could fall asleep and not wake up until she was old and gray, when things like this would no longer bother her.

Downstairs in the kitchen, Emily took stock of the refrigerator and pantry. She needed groceries if she was to get through the next week or until Ian returned from his vacation. She made out a list, ordering the best of everything. She called the Plainfield Market and told them to deliver everything by six o'clock and to charge it to the Terrill Road Clinic.

Emily stared for hours at the bare Christmas tree. Decorate it or not decorate it? At eight o'clock, after all the groceries were put away and she'd eaten a sandwich and showered, she dragged the tree through the living room and out to the foyer. She opened the door and gave the fir a mighty shove. It slid down the brick steps, the heavy, metal stand clunking and probably chipping the bricks. As if she cared. There were pine needles everywhere. She didn't care about that either.

She made a fire, turned on the television set, uncorked a bottle of wine, rummaged for a pack of Ian's cigarettes, and settled herself for the night. She drank herself into a stupor and repeated the process every day until January 2. A new year.

Emily woke with a hangover that was so bad she went back to sleep and didn't get up till noon, at which time she made out a schedule for herself that did not include Ian. She still hadn't slept in the yellow room and still had no intention of doing so. Something perverse in her made her carry her things down to the basement. It was all a finished room, carpeted and paneled with a bathroom and small summer kitchen that was outdated, but still worked. At the far side of the basement was what she referred to as her planting room. She could live quite nicely down here until she got some backbone and some guts to do something about her marriage. She knew she was being stupid, but she couldn't seem to help herself. She also knew she required some kind of professional help. She needed to get out her health insurance policy to see if it covered psychiatric care.

On the twenty-fifth of January, Emily signed up for classes at Middlesex County College. She scheduled a series of twelve appointments with a psychiatrist named Oliver Mendenares. She rebooked her appointment with the attorney on Park Avenue, kept it, and came away angry. With herself. Because of her blind stupidity, she'd signed away all of her rights to the family clinics. Either she could get herself a job or stay dependent on Ian.

She'd already made up her mind that she wouldn't take the two thousand dollars a month if Ian offered it. "Once a fool, always a fool," she muttered over and over to herself.

Ian's return was nothing short of anticlimactic. He went about his business as usual, spoke to her the way he'd speak to someone he'd just met. He didn't ask how she was, where she was sleeping, what she did with her days. He wasn't home at any one time to do more than sleep, shower, and change his clothes. The white shirts were still piling up.

Spring heralded bright, sunny days. A new housekeeper named Edna arrived as did a bright red Mercedes-Benz convertible. A week later a Porsche was delivered. Both vehicles had giant silver bows sitting on top. Cards stuck under the windshield said, "To Emily, as promised. Love, Ian."

The first thing Emily did when Edna arrived was to

show her how to iron Ian's shirts. She quit four hours later. A second, third, and fourth housekeeper arrived, but each one quit when the laundry basket was pulled out.

When the last housekeeper left after two days—the longest any of them had stayed—Ian came home with a wide smile and three jeweler's boxes. He magnanimously cooked dinner outside on the grill and presented her with the boxes, gaily wrapped. He smiled benignly as he offered them to her.

"These are lovely, Ian," Emily said carefully. "Is it safe to keep them in the house?"

"They're insured. Do you like them? I think I got everything on the list. The ring is two full carats, the band has two carats in smaller stones. The two bracelets are worth twenty thousand, at least that's what the appraiser said. Each set of earrings is two full carats each. You have five different strands of pearls. Are they what you like?" he asked anxiously.

"They're lovely," Emily repeated.

"I put thirty thousand dollars in your account for your three vacations. I think you can take a pretty decent vacation for ten thousand dollars each, don't you? The travel agent said it was more than enough. I'm working on the shore house and boat. Did I forget anything, Emily?"

"I don't think so," Emily said, her mouth a grim, tight line.

"You're trying to fool me, Emily," Ian said jovially. "In the living room are your furs. You should keep them in a vault. There's a place in Metuchen named Oscar Lowrey. You can store them there, but if you'd rather go someplace else, it's okay. What do you think?"

What did she think? Dr. Mendenares pretty much said Ian had a screw loose, but then he'd pretty much said she had one loose, too. "I'll think about it."

"Aren't you going to say thank you? I know you, Emily,

you thought I wasn't going to keep my end of the bargain we made. See, you should have trusted me. I always come through. You need to trust me more. What do you see as our problem in keeping a housekeeper?"

"Those white shirts, Ian. No one wants to iron them. Including me."

"Are you going to sit there and tell me, after all I've given you, you aren't going to iron my shirts?"

"I'm not going to do it. If you want to take back all these lovely things, go ahead. Dinner was . . . okay. I have to get back to my books now." She walked away, into the kitchen and down the basement stairs. Only here, in this underground cavern, did she feel safe, reasonably content and free of anxiety. She left the jewelry on the wrought iron table and didn't bother to check out the furs. She also left Ian with the dishes. The rule had always been: You cook, you clean.

Mendenares, if she was still going to him, would probably applaud her actions. But then, maybe he wouldn't. He'd told her she had to stand up for herself, take charge of her life and not be a doormat. That's when she stopped going to the sessions. At the beginning she'd made a pact with herself to take twelve sessions, and if she couldn't see the light after three months, she would need more than one forty-five-minute session once a week. How disgusted Mendenares looked when she told him she wouldn't be returning. "I have to work this out myself. I still love Ian. I will probably always love him. If that's my weakness, then that's what I have to work at. I want to try and save my marriage."

She hadn't done anything, though. She returned home and burrowed into the basement with her seedlings, her books, and her memories.

And now this strange dinner and gift-giving session. What did it mean? Everything Ian did was suspect. He was giving her everything he promised, everything she said she wanted. She hadn't been able to work up any excitement when the cars arrived. The furs would probably stay in their boxes until Ian hung them up. Mendenares said she had to force herself to look at things squarely and to be honest with herself. And she was trying to do that. Ian was not a kind, generous person. In her heart she believed Ian was paying her off, and as soon as his *debt* was paid, he was going to leave her.

She smelled his shaving lotion before she saw him. It was the first time, to her knowledge, that Ian knew she was living in the basement, the first time he'd actually come down the stairs. She looked up from the pile of books on the card table she was sitting at. He was angry but trying to control it.

"Emily, I think we need to talk." He looked around uncertainly. "Let's go upstairs where we'll be more comfortable."

She'd learned a thing or two from Mendenares. She couldn't give Ian any kind of an edge, because as soon as she did, she was lost to her emotions. "I'm comfortable right here. In case you haven't noticed, I live down here."

"I'm not blind, Emily. If you want to do something stupid like live in a cellar, that's your business. It's the same stupid principle that made you sign away your rights to the clinics. This is a magnificent house, a comfortable house. If you want to live like a mole, feel free."

"I am and I will. What do you want to talk about? If you want to *really* talk, then let's discuss that scene where you left me at Jacques' Restaurant and then let's talk about the clinics. In my opinion we do not have a marriage. If we did, you would never have left me and gone to the Cayman Islands by yourself. That was one of the cruelest things you've ever done to me and you've done quite a few. The list is long. I let you do it to me, though, so I'm as much to blame. You know it too. Giving me all those things is your way of trying to make yourself feel good. I thought it was a joke, a game we were playing when I made out that ridiculous list. I don't want *things,* Ian. I want a husband and a family. That's what I signed up for and you said you did too. I know you're a doctor, I know you have weird hours, but if I was important to you, you'd find a way to at least call me once a day, have dinner with me, bring me a flower once in a while, something to show me you care. You don't do any of those things."

"Are you saying this house is to make *me* feel good?"

Emily stared at her husband, pleased that her heart was beating normally, pleased that she saw his eye twitch, a sign that he was upset.

"Oh, you bet. You have the biggest, the best bedroom. You don't want me in it, but you were gracious enough to assign me one across the hall. When was the last time we slept together, made love? I remember the day, the hour, and what went on before and afterward. Women remember things like that. I don't like the yellow room and I resent that you would think I would. Take away the surprise element, Ian, and what do you have? I would rather have known about the house, done the decorating myself. And how do you know I couldn't do a good job? You don't know a goddamn thing about me and that's really sad. You broke my heart. You really did and I cannot forgive you for that. I'm still angry about those clinics."

"Those clinics netted a hundred and forty thousand dollars last month," Ian said coldly.

"How many babies did you kill for that, Ian? How many men jerked off in a bottle to store in your freezers? Give me a number, Ian."

"Don't go noble on me, Emily. Women have a right to

choose. I've always believed that. Jesus Christ, you don't even go to church, so don't start that morality crap. You believe they have a right to choose, too."

"If you truly believed that, Ian, I would know it in my heart and then I could live with the clinics, but you don't believe it. I know you better than you know yourself. You're in this for the money, and nothing you can say will ever convince me otherwise. You kill babies for money and then you buy me presents to try and ease your conscience."

"That's not true," Ian bellowed.

It was true, she could see it in his face, read it in his eyes. She felt no satisfaction, only a deep sadness. Suddenly she wanted to wipe the look off his face, kiss away the look in his eyes. He still had a hold over her. "Take back all those presents and go outside in the garden and bring me one of the tulips, pick me a dandelion, a green weed. I don't care what it is as long as you pick it because you want to give me something from your heart. Did you know dandelions are herbs?"

"No, I'm not taking back the gifts. I promised them to you and I never knowingly break a promise. The tulips are too pretty to pick and I think you know that. I didn't see any dandelions in the lawn when I came home. And why in the hell would I give you a weed. And no, I didn't know dandelions are herbs. I guess I wasn't in class the day they discussed dandelions."

"What else do you want to talk about?" Emily asked as she tapped her pencil on the table.

"Us." He walked over to the table and reached down for her hand. "I want you to move into my room. I'll order a king-size bed since we're both restless sleepers. We need to start working on that baby. If I broke your heart, I'm sorry. I didn't mean to do that. I'm a doctor, do you think

I can fix it for you? Will you let me try? Do you still love me?"

Emily thought her heart would burst right out of her chest. It was the first time Ian had ever said he was sorry about anything. Maybe this time he meant it. She wanted to believe it, needed to believe it. "I'm willing to try, Ian. I love you. I will probably always love you. Do you love me?"

"Of course. How can you think otherwise?"

"Because I need to hear the words, Ian. If you loved me, how could you go off and leave me sitting at Jacques'? And go away without me?"

"I don't know how I did that, Emily. It was a knee-jerk reaction and I was miserable. All I did was think of you and the business. I couldn't wait to get home to apologize, and when I did, you didn't want any part of me. I didn't know what to do so I didn't do anything. I was wrong and I admit it. What did you do while I was gone?"

"I drank myself into a stupor every night."

"We really messed up, didn't we?"

Mendenares's face flashed in front of her. "You did, Ian, I didn't."

"Guilty!" Ian said cheerfully. "God, I'm glad we settled all this. Come on, let's move your stuff upstairs. I'll help you. Then, if you are agreeable, we'll take a long, hot shower together and do our best to make a baby."

Emily smiled. It was a start. You always had to start somewhere. "Did you do the dishes? You cook, you clean, I'll watch you."

"That's fair," Ian said, bolting up the stairs to the kitchen. Emily watched as he dumped the dishes, the condiments, the silverware into the trash barrel on the deck. "Done!"

In spite of herself, Emily giggled.

It took four trips before they were ready to strip down in the shower.

Emily thought she could feel her heart start to mend when Ian said, "Let's get started on that kid who is going to look like you or me or both of us put together."

Her heart was mending, she was sure of it as she stepped into his arms under the pelting water.

Chapter 7

The house on Sleepy Hollow Road took on a new life, albeit Emily's life, over the following years. The days were busy days, the nights busier still with homework and the few hours Ian allotted to their "togetherness" program.

On the eve of her thirty-ninth birthday, Emily decided there was no such thing as pure happiness in a marriage. There was, she told herself, fulfillment and even contentment. Either you accepted or you rejected it, which was just another way of saying you went with the flow or you fought it. Emily opted to go with the flow, an expression she'd heard on television.

She'd finally given up on the idea of getting pregnant. It wasn't even something she could fault Ian for. They'd worked at it arduously, playfully, angrily, determinedly, to no avail.

Today was going to be a bad day. Emily could feel it in her bones.

"What's wrong, Emily?"

"I'm thirty-nine today. So tell me what are we going to do this weekend to celebrate this momentous day in my life?"

"We're going down to the shore house and take the

boat out. I bought you a Sunfish for your birthday. They delivered it yesterday."

Two whole days with Ian. They were going to celebrate her birthday. Maybe it wasn't going to be a bad day after all.

"We should have done something special to celebrate your birthday, Ian. Why didn't we?"

"Because I hate growing older. I don't even want to talk about it. Jesus, next year we'll be forty. Half our life will be over. The chances of us living to eighty are pretty slim, if you want my opinion."

"I plan on living to be a hundred. So there, Dr. Thorn."

"Plan on being a widow then, Mrs. Thorn. So there."

"Swear to me, Ian, that we aren't going to go through that midlife crisis syndrome you read about in all the slick magazines. Swear to me if either one of us feels something is awry, we'll talk about it. I'm really serious, Ian. I've read some real horror stories. Okay?"

"Sure," Ian said, snapping the lid of his suitcase. "Listen, Emily. I have a confession to make. I don't know if I'm ready to take that Sunfish out in open water. My stomach goes into knots the minute I start to think about it. I don't honestly know if I'll *ever* be ready to take it out."

Emily burst out laughing. "Why did you buy it, Ian?"

"Because it was on your goddamn list, that's why," Ian said, his eyes wild.

"I think you should sell it. Maybe someday we'll take a cruise. That will be boat enough for me." How endearing, Ian admitting to a mistake, letting her see his vulnerability. This was the best birthday present. To think it took living thirty-nine years for Ian to show this side of him.

"I guess we can go then. God, I feel like a hundred pounds has been lifted from my shoulders."

"Ian, can I say something here, something that's important to me?"

"Sure, fire away."

"The feeling you're experiencing right now, I never had that. The relief, the weight taken off my shoulders. So many times I wanted to blurt things out, to tell you how I felt, but I was afraid of your reaction. I'm not talking about the dumb mistakes I made over the years. It's okay now, we can't go backward, I just wanted you to know. Life is too short to dwell on the bad things, and, Ian, there were a lot of bad things."

"God, Emily. I don't know what to say."

"You don't have to say anything. It's history. C'mon, let's start to celebrate my birthday. I want it to be a great one."

"I'll make sure of that, Emily," Ian said, smiling.

But before they were halfway there . . .

Emily opened her eyes and returned to the present . . . and the Federal Express letter that lay before her. "I've had enough of Memory Lane. I've had enough of you, Dr. Ian Thorn. Enough!"

She lumbered up from the sofa and made her way into the kitchen. She wished for more sticky buns, anything to stuff in her mouth to make the pain go away. On her way to the refrigerator she passed the open doorway to the downstairs bathroom. She must have left the light on earlier. Surely the hag staring at her from the mirrored wall wasn't herself. She was so uncertain, so disbelieving, she walked into the bathroom and looked at herself. No, this wasn't Emily Thorn. The only thing reminiscent of Emily Thorn was the bush of wild hair. Frantically she rummaged in the vanity drawer for a pair of scissors. She couldn't find any. She ran to the kitchen, yanked open a drawer, and ran back to the bathroom with a pair of kitchen shears. She started to chomp and slice at her hair. Ian had always said he loved her hair. "Fuck you,

Dr. Ian Thorn," she blubbered. When she couldn't hold her arm up any longer, Emily quit cutting. She looked like something out of a horror movie. She still didn't look like Emily Thorn, wife of prominent physician, Dr. Ian Thorn.

If it wasn't Emily Thorn in the mirror, then who was it? Emily leaned closer. Once it had been Emily Thorn, but years of abuse had turned her into this creature who was forty pounds overweight, had bags under her eyes and three chins. When and how had her complexion gotten so bad? Grease and sweets was the answer. She stretched her lips so she could look at her teeth. Good teeth. Pedigree teeth. Didn't breeders check dogs' teeth to see if they were fit? Well, hell, she was no pedigree. She was nothing but an ugly stray whose husband didn't want her anymore.

The person in the mirror started to cry. That was Emily Thorn. Emily Thorn always cried when things went wrong. Emily Thorn was speaking so she had to listen. "I wasted my life. Wasted it. I have nothing to show for it, but this . . . this . . . whatever I've become. I gave away my life, the best of my years for a smile, a pat on the head, and 120 white shirts. I just up and gave it away. And there's no way for me to get it back. I'm forty years old. Where do I go now, what do I do?"

Emily turned out the light and sat down on the toilet seat. The Emily Thorn in the mirror went away immediately. Emily clenched her fists and beat at her fat knees until she howled for mercy. If she kept up this abuse on her person, she was going to cripple herself.

She didn't like the dark, had never liked the dark, but hadn't she been living in the dark for a long time? There were no mirrors in the kitchen, she could go back there and be as miserable as she was here in this windowless bathroom.

In the kitchen again, with the bright sunlight shining through the windows, she fired up a cigarette and chain-smoked for almost an hour before she reached for Ian's letter. The last thing she was ever going to get from Ian. She brought it close to her face. A tear splashed downward. This letter was written to the Emily Thorn in the bathroom mirror, the one who had wasted her life. She stared at the letter. How many times would she read it? She knew the contents by heart, mouthed the words aloud as she read the letter yet again. Even now, in this, the last thing she would ever get from Ian, he was placing all the blame on her. He was blaming her for his leaving, saying she pointed out to him certain things he never would have thought of himself. "Liar!" she screamed. "Dirty, low-life liar! Lying sack of shit!"

Dear Emily. "You bastard, the only time you ever called me dear Emily was when you wanted me to do something for you."

I wish there was another way to do this, but there isn't. Trust me when I tell you I am deeply sorry. I won't be back, Emily. Our marriage hasn't been working for a long time and we both know it. Knowing you as I do, I know you would never be the one to take the first step. You can file for a divorce anytime you want. I sold the clinics, or maybe I should say the assets of the corporation have been sold. I'm moving on. I'm tired of working, tired of the clinics. I'm forty, as are you, and I want to experience life a little.

No, Emily, I don't feel any guilt at all. You made out your wish list and I gave you everything on it except the child. I would have given you that, but I couldn't. I didn't find out until a short while ago that I'm sterile. I guess it was from the mumps as a child. So you see, I did what you asked. I'm not leaving you destitute, Emily. I would never do that to you. The cars, the jewelry are yours as is the shore house, the

Sunfish, and the house on Sleepy Hollow Road. The houses have large mortgages so you might want to think of selling them. You will get a small amount of equity out of them. The vacation money piled up nicely and quickly, and it's yours, as is the personal account with ten thousand dollars in it. I did my best to calculate the amount of money you earned over the years and I think I've been more than generous. We're even now.

Take care of yourself. You'll always have a special place in my heart, dear Emily.

Affectionately, Ian.

"Eat shit, Ian," Emily sobbed.

Emily ripped at her clothes as she stumbled her way into the dark bathroom. She flipped on the light to stare at the Emily Thorn in the mirror. "You are fat. No, you are obese. Look at those rolls of fat. There's absolutely no sign of a waist line. Your boobs are almost to your belly button. Ponderous. Look at your upper arms, at your neck, all the skin is loose and flabby. You can't even look down and see your pubic hair because of the rolls of fat. Gross."

The Emily Thorn in the mirror said, "This is the person Ian saw every day. This is the person he didn't want to live with anymore. Can you blame him?"

"No, no, I can't blame him for that," Emily whispered. "If he'd said something, if he'd talked to me, really talked to me, treated me like a real person, I would have made the effort."

Forty years old, fat and ugly. Unloved. Dumped. She was now an official *dumpee*. A fat ugly woman who had wasted the best years of her life in the name of love. "Oh, God!" she moaned.

Emily ran upstairs, so winded she had to sit down on the stool in the bathroom until she could breathe normally. She looked awful, felt worse than awful. The thick support bra she struggled into made her wince. Once, long ago, she'd worn lacy bras with an underwire for support. Now, with all the weight she'd gained, it was necessary to wear ugly, cotton bras with wide straps that cut into her shoulders and covered her entire back. Once she'd been able to wear size five bikini panties. Now she was wearing size nine cotton briefs. Two rolls of fat bulged between the top of her panties and the bottom of her bra. In frustration she brought her hands down on the vanity with so much force a bar of soap sailed across the room.

From the hook on the back of the bathroom door, Emily pulled a sack dress with no detail, no belt, and nothing to distinguish it from any of the other sack dresses she'd been wearing the past year. She stuffed her feet into sneakers, bent over to work the Velcro bands into place. She was breathing hard with the exertion.

Emily trundled down the steps, taking them one at a time because of the tears in her eyes. She didn't need a fall now. At the bottom of the steps she opened the hall closet and pulled out an old raincoat of Ian's that she couldn't button. A minute later she was outside, squeezing herself behind the wheel of the Mercedes coupe. This was a joke too. She was so uncomfortable she wasn't sure she was going to be able to drive.

Well, by God, she was going to drive. She wanted to see for herself, needed to see if the clinics had really been sold off. She needed proof positive the letter from Ian wasn't some kind of cruel joke or a nightmare that she would wake from momentarily.

The clinic on Terrill Road had a sign on the window that said UNDER NEW MANAGEMENT. The one on Mountain Avenue said the same thing. Watchung's sign said CLOSED TEN DAYS, UNDER NEW MANAGEMENT. Her face was grim when she drove down Watchung Avenue, where she made a right onto Park Avenue. She refused to even look at the building where she'd lived with Ian for so long. When she came to the clinic, she pulled into the parking lot and cut the engine. She struggled from the car, her purse hindering her as she inched past the steering wheel.

"We'll make it easier for you, just hand it over," a voice said from the other side of the car. Emily looked around to see who was talking to whom. In stupefied amazement she watched as four unsavory-looking youths came around the back of her car. "Give us your purse and we won't hurt you." Emily clutched the purse tighter.

"Get away from me or I'll scream," Emily threatened.

"Nobody's going to hear you. Hand it over," one of the youths said brazenly. "C'mon, or we'll take the car too."

Emily saw the knife, the wicked-looking, gleaming piece of steel. The moment when she should have screamed was past. She didn't know what was in her purse—very little money, that much she did know. A few credit cards Ian had probably canceled. She was about to hand it over to one of the youths when it was snatched from her hand.

"Don't think about running after us either. You stay planted right here for ten minutes or we'll come after you. Your address is right inside your wallet, lady. You hear me?" Emily nodded.

A second youth laughed cruelly. "Fat-ass tub of lard ain't going to be doing any running. Don't go reporting this to the police or we'll get you when you ain't expecting it. We got lots of friends. You understand, lard-ass?" Emily nodded. "Git in that car and sit there for ten minutes. Now!"

Emily did as instructed, her face burning with anger and humiliation, not because she was being robbed and threatened but because of the names they'd called her and the fact that they were laughing at her as she struggled to get into the sports car. She sat in the car for ten minutes before she drove back to her house on Sleepy Hollow Road.

The moment she was inside, she bolted all the doors and put on the alarm system. Would they come back? Maybe, when they saw how little cash was in her purse. She hung up Ian's coat, saw the camcorder on the top shelf. She'd bought it to take videos of her garden to submit to the Garden Club. She could feel her eye start to twitch when she reached for it. She carried it into the living room, where she placed it on top of the wide-screen television. She turned it on before she backed up to sit down on a brocade love seat that clashed with the green dress she was wearing. She stared straight ahead, her eyes on the camcorder as she recounted the past forty-five minutes. Her voice broke when she described the dialogue between the youths and herself. She stood up, fumbled with the buttons of her dress, pulled it over her head. She closed her eyes and took a deep, searing breath. She turned slowly for the camera's benefit. Tears rolled down her cheeks. "I am Emily Thorn. This is what I've become. I did . . . it doesn't matter how I got like this. What matters is I did it myself. I am Emily Wyatt Thorn and I am fat and ugly. I am a poor excuse for the woman I once was. My husband has just left me. This is the Emily Thorn he saw every day when he woke up and when he went to bed." She advanced on the camcorder in her underwear and turned it off. Then she carried it back to the closet and placed it on the shelf. Someday she would look at the video.

Someday.

Part Two

Chapter 8

The day after. There was always a *day after* when a disaster occurred. Emily peered through the miniblinds in the kitchen to her outside world. It was morning, the young sun was already a glorious ball in the sky. The dark night was over. Had she slept through it? How did she get to this hour of a new day? She looked around to see if there was a wine bottle on the table, but there wasn't. There were a lot of cigarette stubs in three overflowing ashtrays, lots of coffee grounds spilled on the counter and floor, lots and lots of bread crumbs all over the kitchen. She was wearing the same clothes she'd worn yesterday; at least she thought they were the same clothes. The Federal Express envelope and Ian's letter were still on the table, staring up at her like two square, hateful eyes.

She was numb, her eyes puffy and red, her ribs hurting from all the crying and sobbing. Her feet and hands hurt. She must have hit or kicked something. All in the name of sick, obsessive love and a pile of white shirts.

Yesterday she'd thought there were no more tears to shed. How wrong that was. Tears dripped down her cheeks. She was never going to see Ian again. She'd never been truly alone in her life before. She'd gone from her parents' home to life with Ian. How was she going to live? The world stopped for a second when you hit forty, time enough to get your bearings, then time picked up its feet and raced toward that goal no one wanted to reach. "You're born to die," she muttered.

Mendenares. She would call him today for an appointment. She'd go in, get on the couch, wail and moan for three sessions before anything constructive came out. "So, who needs him?" The attorney she'd gone to see might be able to make sense out of this. Emily snorted. One had to be deaf and dumb as well as blind not to see what had happened. "So, who needs him?" Ian really thought she was going to file for a divorce. "Well, think again, you son of a bitch. If you want a divorce, *you* get it!"

In some foggy recess, way in the back of her mind, she knew she and she alone had to deal with this. By herself. She'd dragged herself down to this point in time, with Ian's help. Now, because Ian was gone, she was alone and she had to crawl up and out of her pit.

Why hadn't she seen this coming the past year? Maybe if she'd moved into the yellow room, maybe if she'd stayed in the basement, this wouldn't have happened.

Emily ran to the windowless bathroom and turned on the light. She had to see the other Emily Thorn, the real Emily Thorn. She jabbed a finger at the mirror. Her eyes narrowed as she backed out of the bathroom. She was in the kitchen again, her back to the gas range. She reached behind her for the tea kettle, grasped it firmly, and headed back to the bathroom. "I hate you, you bitch!" she shouted. "I never want to see you again." The tea kettle sailed through the air. The mirror shattered into thousands of sparkling shards of glass. She stepped back just in time. When the glittering pieces littered the floor, Emily thumbed her nose at the blank wall with its globs of dried cement and bellowed, "You don't exist anymore, Emily Thorn!" She slammed the door shut.

* * *

"And what did that little tantrum get you, Mrs. Thorn?" She had to stop talking to herself. Or were you allowed to talk to yourself and it was only bad when you answered yourself? Whatever it was, she didn't care. So, the old Emily Thorn was dead, she'd smashed her to nothing. Now she had to come up with a new, improved version. Was she losing it? Was she going off the deep end? Only time would tell. The spatula was suddenly in her hand. "You're born right now, Emily Thorn." She tapped herself on the head three times. "Happy birthday! You're alive. You are reasonably healthy. You are overweight. You are alone, which makes you a free spirit, and free spirits are not accountable to anyone. You can do whatever you want, whenever you want."

She was exhausted. What was on her schedule for today? Gardening in the morning, two classes in the afternoon, grocery shopping, cooking dinner, studying. "Yeah, well, that was yesterday's schedule. No more schedules, no more busy time, no more anything that had to do directly or indirectly with Dr. Ian Thorn."

Emily marched upstairs into the bedroom she had not shared with her husband. It was dark and somber. She ripped at the hunter green comforter, at the matching drapes. She carried them out to the top of the steps and pushed them over the railing. She made four more trips with sheets, Ian's leftovers. The laundry basket on the floor in the linen closet was stuffed full of white shirts. They went over the railing too. She couldn't help but wonder how long it had taken Ian to fold the shirts that had hung in the closet. He must have packed his things when she was at class.

Don't think about Ian. Fix this room so you can sleep here. You have to sleep here. This room is part of what happened; you have to come to terms with it. Clean the bathroom, make the bed, make it *your* room now.

Emily followed her own orders. She put on a baggy jogging suit, brushed at her cropped hair, and went downstairs to make fresh coffee. No breakfast today. Today was Day One of Ms. Emily Thorn's new life.

As she drank her black coffee, Emily made a list of things she wanted to do for the day. Go to the library, the bookstore, the vegetable market, the grocery store. Clean out the refrigerator, get rid of all the fattening foods, go to Herman's sporting goods store. The bank had to be her first stop. Set aside some time to go through records, providing Ian left records to go through. Think about framing Ian's letter. Better yet, maybe she should tack it to the wall and throw darts at it.

It was four o'clock when Emily returned to the house on Sleepy Hollow Road, her car full of purchases that took a half hour to carry into the house. She felt pleased with herself until she entered the kitchen and reality slapped at her. Always before, she knew Ian would be home *some*time during the day. Now she had to deal with the fact that he was never going to walk through the door again. Think positive, Emily, think about all those damn white shirts you are never going to have to iron again.

She made coffee, cleaned up the grounds because she was not a sloppy person. She marked the calendar, the first day of her new diet, one she would stick to or die trying. She was going to exercise too. One of the Herman's employees was going to drop off the treadmill and the exercycle she'd purchased.

A brand new day. The *first* day of Emily Thorn's new life. "I'm going to do it. I'm going to do it," she said aloud.

Emily stared down at the bags and bags of groceries she'd purchased. She had at least fifty cans of tuna fish, seven boxes of tissues, bags of apples, oranges, celery, and carrots. Two whole bags full of diet drinks and two bags of Evian water. Ten pounds of coffee and five boxes of herbal tea. Four boxes of artificial sweetener. A new scale whose huge, digital numbers glared up at her like red eyes. Two bottles of super-duper vitamins guaranteed to fill her body full of energy. She felt a wild burst of confidence, then scotch-taped Ian's letter on the bulletin board next to the phone. She tripped over the bags in her frenzied search for the darts she'd picked up at the hardware store. Eight darts. She stood back, took aim, and missed every single time. Well, she'd do better next time. Besides, it was good exercise to bend down to pick them up. She felt pleased with herself.

The refrigerator was a definite challenge. She tossed everything into huge, green lawn bags and then dragged them outside. Who in her right mind kept seven gallons of ice cream in the freezer? Who in her right mind kept dozens of frozen pies and cakes next to the ice cream? Who in her right mind kept bags and bags of chips, candies, and cookies in the cabinet? Obviously, she was the guilty one. So, I wasn't in my right mind for a long time. I'm going to get through this, I really am. She felt dizzy with the declaration.

She washed out the bare refrigerator and stocked it. It looked good. All the vegetables and fruits were washed, the vegetables pared into snack-size bites and placed in Ziploc bags. The fruit went into a huge bowl on the kitchen table.

Done.

Now, where was the exercise equipment going to go? In Ian's office, of course. Because, she told herself, there's a television set and VCR that I can watch while I'm doing my exercises. She pulled and tugged, shoved and grunted as she put her ample rump up against Ian's desk to shove it through the deep pile of the carpet to the far side of the room.

Done.

Back in the kitchen she poured a third cup of coffee and fired up a cigarette. She was going to quit smoking too, but not just yet. If she tried too much, she'd probably kill herself. But, she would quit, she promised herself. She threw all eight darts and nicked the letter once, but the darts fell to the floor. She bent down, picked them all up, and placed them in the corner.

She was so hungry her stomach was growling. This then was her first major challenge. She devoured a whole bag of the cut vegetables and ate two cans of tuna. She munched down two apples and still wasn't satisfied. She made a cup of herbal tea and tossed in the contents of three Equal packets. God, it was so sweet, so delicious, so satisfying, she made a second cup. Any other time she would have eaten her way through a box of Twinkies or half a frozen pie. She still wanted to do that, but she wasn't going to. Willpower was half the battle.

"I hate you, Ian Thorn, for doing this to me. I hate you." He didn't do this to you, you did it to yourself. Yes, he left you. He saw that Emily Thorn you saw in the bathroom mirror. But he didn't make you what you are, grossly fat, a martyr. You did that to yourself because you have no guts. Get it together, Ms. Thorn, or you ain't goin' anywhere.

"All right already," Emily said, slapping the palms of her hands on the table. I did it, but I did it because he . . . because he . . . didn't love me. He had a part in this. He's to blame too. He sucked my life's blood is what he did.

"He took the best years of my life and trampled them, then put me out to pasture like some old cow who can't give milk anymore."

Rage, unlike anything she'd ever experienced in her life, rivered through her. Somewhere in this house, unless Ian took it with him, was a copy of his medical license. Where did she put it when she moved here? She gouged her way through all the downstairs closets. When she finally found it, she smashed the glass on the doorknob and ripped the diploma from the frame, a triumphant look on her face. She stormed her way to the kitchen and scotch-taped it next to Ian's letter. Over and over, until her arm was tired, she threw the darts, picked them up, and threw them again.

Emily heard the doorbell ring at nine-thirty. She supervised the placement of her treadmill and exercycle, tipped the boy, and locked up for the night.

Emily stared at the machines for a long time. Today was the beginning of a new regime in her life. It was late; should she exercise or not? Better to wait till tomorrow. Somewhere she'd read that a person shouldn't exercise before bedtime. It made sense. She was too tired, could barely keep her eyes open. She opted for a warm bath and bed. Tomorrow was a new day too.

Emily's sleep was invaded by demons, all of whom wore Ian's smiling face. When she staggered downstairs, she felt more tired than she had before she'd turned in for the night.

She made coffee, lit a cigarette, put a check next to the list she'd made for cigarette consumption. She wasn't ready to quit, but she was going to cut down. When she scoffed down a melon that was hard as a rock, she daydreamed about mainlining double chocolate Oreo cookies. In times past she'd eaten a whole bag at one sitting. Oreo cookies, like Twinkies, were things that belonged in the past with the old Emily Thorn.

Emily poured a second cup of coffee, lit a second cigarette, and dutifully checked her list. Finances. She had to deal with whatever it was Ian had left her. She hoped he'd left the files, prayed he wasn't bastard enough to make her flounder through the bureaucracy of mortgage companies and banks.

In Ian's office that still smelled like Ian, Emily went through the desk drawers systematically until she found everything she needed. A vision of Ian sitting at the desk writing out checks flashed in front of her. She made her way back to the kitchen, lit a third cigarette, forgot to mark it down as she opened first one folder and then the other.

Two cups of coffee and three cigarettes later she knew she had a financial problem. The house on Sleepy Hollow Road carried a twenty-five-hundred-dollar-a-month mortgage payment. The shore house had a hundred-and-fifty-thousand-dollar mortgage. Household daily expenses, including food, ran to well over a thousand a month. To keep the electricity, water, and phone turned on at the shore house cost another two hundred and fifty dollars. The car insurance was so outrageous she squeezed her eyes shut. Life insurance and health insurance premiums caused her heart to palpitate. So much money. How in the world was she to live? Even if she worked around the clock cocktail waitressing, she wouldn't make a dent in the bills. She would have to sell everything just to keep up her life and health insurance. Maybe she could sell the cars and get a good secondhand one and not carry collision insurance. She could get a part-time job to pay for her food and rent if she moved into an apartment. The cars would net some serious money if she was able to sell them. It didn't make sense—Ian had paid cash for cars but wouldn't pay cash for the house. Obviously it had had something to do with write-offs. Then there was her jewelry and the furs she'd never worn. She looked at the appraisal forms and knew she'd never get what they were worth. Then again, maybe she'd get lucky and she would sell them to the first person who showed up at the door.

Emily rummaged until she found the passbook savings account. There was one hundred and twenty thousand dollars in it. She blinked in stunned surprise. For some reason she'd thought there would be a lot less. She took a deep breath and let it out in a long sigh of relief. According to Ian's letter, her personal account held ten thousand dollars. Thank God she wasn't going to be out on the street in the next week. She had breathing room now. Time to make decisions she could live with, time she could take to get her life into some kind of sane order. Time to try and make over the Emily Thorn in the bathroom mirror, the Emily Thorn Ian had rejected.

It would take months to sell the house, possibly a year, and during that time she would still have to pay the large mortgage. The shore house might sell quickly since summer was only months away. Unless . . . unless she rented it. She could rent out rooms here in the house too. She'd lived in the basement, and if she could do it, someone else might want to. The house had six bedrooms; she used one. Five rooms to let with kitchen privileges. The small apartment over the three-car garage could be made livable, the junk thrown out. If she had to, she could invest in some new appliances and furniture and rent it out furnished. Utilities would be the tenant's responsibility.

Intruders would invade her quiet life. They would tramp through the house and leave their mark. She had to decide if she cared. She decided she didn't. It had never felt like her house. Ian and a decorator had done everything. No, she didn't care. Renting out rooms would keep her money safe. She was, after all, forty years old with no retirement fund. It wasn't going to be easy to get a job at her age.

Emily's stomach rumbled. She drank two glasses of water, scrambled an egg, and ate a whole melon. Already she was looking forward to the cottage cheese and fruit she'd have for lunch.

She drank more coffee. In his letter Ian said she should think about selling the house and the shore house. "Well, guess what, Ian, I think I can make it on my own. The last thing I'm going to do is something you tell me to do. Never again." She was off the kitchen chair in the blink of an eye. The darts sailed through the air, one after the other. Twice she hit Ian's name on his medical diploma. Once she nicked the letter toward the bottom where he had signed his name. As entertainment it left a lot to be desired, but it was the best she had at the moment. "I need to do this. I really need to do this," she said.

For the first time since she'd awakened, she became aware of the rain outside the kitchen window. The kitchen was suddenly as dark as her mood. She switched on the overhead lights. Her mood started to lighten almost immediately.

A physical fitness book in hand, Emily tromped down the hall to Ian's study. Midway, she turned back and scribbled a sign she pasted on the door that read EMILY'S WORK-OUT ROOM. "Whatever it takes," she mumbled as she scanned the digital panel on the treadmill. She flipped the On switch. She lasted exactly seven minutes before she literally fell off onto the floor. Grossly out of shape. When she had her wind back, she drank two glasses of water. She lasted eleven minutes on the exercycle. It was a start. To-morrow maybe she could last a few more minutes. And, she could go on later and again in the evening. The day had twenty-four hours. In the meantime she would sit at the table, drink coffee, and take care of business.

Business consisted of placing an ad in the *Plainfield Courier*'s classified section under furnished rooms to let. The second order of business was to call the *Star Ledger,* whose circulation was larger than the *Courier*'s to place an ad to sell her cars. The third order of business was to call a real estate agent to list the shore house for rent. She copied the ads neatly onto lined paper and took them with her to the A&P, where she placed them on the bulletin board. When she returned to the house, she climbed the stairs to the apartment over the garage. It held junk, cartons, and boxes from the last tenant that had never been taken away. She maneuvered her way around the cartons and old furniture to check out the minikitchen and bathroom. Years of dust, grime, and grease could be cleaned. A paint job and some curtains would give the small apartment eye appeal. The furniture would need to be shampooed. The biggest hurdle would be carrying the junk out to the curb for disposal. A challenge.

She ate her lunch—cottage cheese, a lettuce salad with lemon and spices, melon, and two diet drinks. She was starving, wanted a Big Mac so badly she had to stop herself forcefully by throwing the darts again and again. "I didn't give in, Ian. You aren't going to lick me again. I'll beat this, you'll see, you son of a bitch!"

Emily climbed in the car again and headed for Bradlees, where she bought curtains, paint, a gallon of window cleaner, a degreaser, floor wax, and three gallons of white paint. On her way home she stopped at Public Service and ordered the power turned on. From home she called the water company. Service would be restored by noon tomorrow.

With grim determination, Emily attacked the treadmill and cycle again. Her time was identical to the morning's time. This time, however, when she fell to the floor after her strenuous pedaling, she stayed on the floor and slept for an hour.

In the kitchen with fresh coffee and a cigarette, she

wondered why she'd never had the guts before to do what she was doing now. What did it matter? She was doing it now and that was all that mattered. No, it wasn't all that mattered. Even if she'd dieted and looked like a million dollars, Ian still would have dumped her. She didn't know how she knew, but she knew and subconsciously she'd always known it. None of it was worth the effort. So, why is it important now? "Because," she insisted, "that Emily Thorn in the bathroom mirror isn't me." She blew her nose in a paper napkin and tossed it in the general direction of the waste basket. It was still raining. She'd always loved rain. Once she'd asked Ian if they could go for a walk and get soaked to the skin. "And ruin my clothes and shoes. Are you out of your mind? Only romantic fools in movies do things like that." She'd never asked him again and she hadn't done it on her own. Well, by God she was going to do it now. Before she could change her mind, she was out the back door. She stood on the flagstone walkway until she was drenched, at which point she picked up her feet and walked around the house three times. When she squished her way back into the kitchen, she decided Ian might have been right, there wasn't anything romantic about being this wet, this chilled. Obviously one needed a partner to shiver and cuddle with. She turned up the heat, drank more hot coffee, and longed for a double cheese pizza.

The next few weeks were busy weeks for Emily. She rose at five and was in bed by nine-thirty, exhausted. She stuck to her diet, did her best to exercise three times a day. She drank water constantly. The apartment over the garage was ready for an occupant. She had a list of twenty or so names of people she'd interviewed along with extensive notes. She needed to make up her mind, as both mortgages were due to be paid by next week. The most difficult decision had to do with renting the shore house. Did she want to rent it for $850 on a twelve-month lease or rent it for three months at $3000 a month and worry about a new tenant in the fall? If she took the summer rental, she would be able to use it in the off months if she didn't find a winter rental. She finally opted for the twelve-month rental with a substantial security deposit as well as first and last months' rent. Emily checked off the shore property on her list. One less worry.

The offers she had on her cars were below what she'd hoped to get, but the insurance premiums were due, so she sold both of them and received cashier checks in the amount of $65,000, which she banked immediately. A three-year-old Ford Mustang with 30,000 miles on it now sat in her driveway. "That's what I think about you, Ian, and your foreign imports," Emily grumbled.

There were now charts all over the kitchen—one for cigarettes, one for weight loss, one for the treadmill, one for the exercycle, one for her dart game, one for the payment of bills. There were also yellow sticky reminder notes on the refrigerator—do this, do that, with the dates and times.

Emily looked at the charts and notes now to plan her day. Aside from her daily routine she had no errands, no grocery shopping. Just her midafternoon walk around the house and choosing who her new tenants were going to be.

Suddenly it overwhelmed her and she almost burst into tears. Things weren't moving fast enough. She still looked the same. Fat, ugly Emily. Yes, she was taking charge, but where was her life? How long was she going to live like this and what was she going to do for the next thirty years, provided she even lived to seventy? One step at a time. You didn't get into this mess overnight and you aren't going to get out of it overnight, she counseled herself.

By nightfall, when she stepped on the treadmill for the

third time, she had her new list of tenants in hand. All five bedrooms had been rented for $250 a month each. The basement area for $350 a month. The apartment over the garage for $600. The three-car garage was rented for $400 a month to a local vendor who needed space to house his pinball and bubble gum machines. In her head, for the hundredth time, she calculated the amount of money. She would make the mortgage and have a hundred dollars left over, which she would apply to the water bill. On the phone she'd told all her new tenants if the electric bill and the water exceeded a certain amount she would have to increase the rent. All of them had agreed. She included these facts into the homemade lease agreement she drew up. It was going to be interesting to see how these people interacted with each other. The best part was everybody worked, and her days would be free of people and chatter. For the first time since she received Ian's letter, Emily smiled. She had close to $200,000 in the bank and would have more once she sold her jewelry and furs. All she needed now was a part-time job to pay for her food and the rest of the household bills. The ten thousand dollars in her personal checking account could be dipped into if need be. She was safe for at least a year. A whole year where she didn't have to worry about a roof over her head or food in her stomach, and if she was lucky, her nest egg would be secure for her future when she couldn't work any longer. She smiled again and realized she felt good about things, about herself. She offered up a small prayer that nothing would go wrong.

It took Emily four months before she felt confident enough to make an appointment with a divorce lawyer. She needed to know where she stood legally and had no intention of filing for a divorce. That was Ian's job.

She dressed casually, pleased that over the four months she'd lost twelve pounds, a slow weight loss, but a safe one.

It was a warm August day with a hint of a summer shower in the air. She could smell the delicious scent of newly mown grass as she walked along Park Avenue toward the lawyer's office. It was shady on the street, the trees giant umbrellas shading the cobbled walkways. Overhead a lazy bird chirped from time to time to let passersby know he was still in residence in the lush greenery overhead. Cars whizzed by, radios blaring through the open windows. To her right was a Dunkin Donuts shop. Emily stopped in her tracks. More than anything in the world she wanted one of the juicy, sugary donuts. Nothing in the world would taste as good as their special blend of coffee with sugar and real, honest-to-God cream. Two donuts, one jelly, one Bavarian cream. If she went across the street now, she'd have to gulp them down and not be able to savor the sweet she adored. Better to do it after her appointment. She deserved to reward herself for the strict discipline she'd imposed on herself these past four months. It would be something to look forward to after the meeting.

The appointment lasted exactly forty-five minutes. It was Emily who called a halt to it.

David Ostermeyer was a tall, imposing attorney with graying hair, a pristine white shirt, and a perfectly tailored dark suit. His eyes were as gray as his temple hairs. He was briskly professional. Emily felt he never smiled, probably didn't know how. A legal Ian. "Who does your shirts, Mr. Ostermeyer?" she blurted out. She knew her face was red with embarrassment, but she didn't care.

"I beg your pardon?"

"I like your shirt. I was wondering who did them for you."

He blinked. "My wife. Sometimes the housekeeper. Now, what can I do for you?" Emily held out her folder and told him her side of the story. He stared at her with disgust and pity.

"Let me be sure I understand this," he said, tapping his pen on the yellow legal pad in front of him. "You put your husband through college and medical school. You worked seventeen hours a day for many years. You worked in the clinics and then went on to a second job. How am I doing so far?" Emily nodded. "You then signed away your rights to the clinics over your husband and his attorney's protests. They told you to get an attorney to represent you, who then argued with you telling you what you were giving up and asking if you understood clearly what you were doing. Is that right?" Emily nodded again.

"My God, Mrs. Thorn, why would you do something like that?"

"I'm not sure I know why. Now, I think I understand my actions a little better. Back then I didn't. I think I was trying to make some kind of statement. To myself. I wanted to think Ian would take care of me forever, that all I had done was a kind of hold over him. If I signed, that meant . . . it was business. I don't know. I do know now that it was stupid of me and I regret it. However, I can live with it because I have to live with it. The house and shore house are in both our names. I am currently making the mortgage payments. Does Ian . . . is he entitled to half if I'm forced to sell?"

"Of course. It's called equitable distribution. If you file for divorce, you can sue for alimony. Is that what you want to do?"

"No. Ian will have to file. I just wanted to be sure I understood things. The clinics . . . that's a closed issue."

"I'm sorry I haven't been of more help to you. This isn't

going to make you feel any better but the sale of those clinics came up at one of the Chamber of Commerce meetings. The sale figures they were bandying about took my breath away. I'm sorry you lost out. You would have been quite comfortable for the rest of your days. Do you know where your husband is living now?"

"No. All I have to do is call the AMA and they'll tell me, providing I want to know, which I don't. At this point in time it doesn't matter where he is. Actually, Mr. Ostermeyer, I'm quite comfortable now. Thank you for your time. I really like that shirt; I couldn't have done it better."

"I see," the attorney said.

Emily laughed. "No you don't. My husband used to say that all the time and he was clueless. Shall I pay the receptionist or do you send bills?"

He looks at a loss, Emily thought as the attorney rose to see her to the door. "Good luck, Mrs. Thorn."

"That's about what it comes down to, Mr. Ostermeyer," Emily said, her mind on the donuts and coffee that were moments away.

In the parking lot of the donut shop Emily made up her mind that she would go inside and *smell* the baked goods. She wouldn't buy anything. Or maybe if she absolutely couldn't resist the temptation, she would buy some of the holes that were sprinkled with powdered sugar. Munchkins, that's what the holes were called.

Inside she was a kid in a candy shop. She wanted one of everything. "I'll take a dozen. Four jelly, four Bavarian cream, three Boston cream, and one glazed. A dozen Munchkins. One large coffee, heavy on the cream with three sugars." Emily wondered if her eyes were as glazed as the donuts in the case. As soon as she got into the car, she was going to rip into the donuts and slurp at the coffee. She slapped the exact amount of money onto the counter, grabbed her bags, and with her rear end backed out through the plate glass door.

Emily was almost into the car, one foot was straddling the seat when she turned around and dumped her purchases into the trash container to the left of her car. "Oh, well," she sighed. The anticipation of buying the donuts and coffee, and paying for them, was almost as good as tasting them. "So there, Ian, so there."

It was a milestone. A kind of insurmountable hurdle. She'd come through, her willpower intact. It wasn't even a setback because she hadn't weakened. "Atta girl, Emily," she chortled to herself on the way home.

"Paulena, you're home. Is everything all right?" Emily asked her new tenant, a widow whose husband hadn't provided for her.

"Fine. Today is my early day. Tomorrow is my late day."

"What's all this?" Emily asked, pointing to an array of bottles.

"When I got off work at the Acme, I went to my part-time job at the health food store and my boss loaded me up with all these vitamins and herbs. He's good to me that way. I'll share some with you. There's a vitamin and herb for everything. If you like, I'll bring you some books tomorrow. Good nutrition is the key to weight loss. You can make teas from the herbs for sleeping, all kinds of good stuff. I was working at the health food store before my husband died and I learned about all this."

There was an easy, comfortable familiarity between the two women. Lena, as she preferred to be called, usually arrived home just as Emily was finishing her afternoon stint on her exercise equipment. While she had coffee, Lena had herbal tea and they talked. Emily hoped a friendship would blossom and they would become confidants, best friends.

"I'd like that. I read while I exercise. I suppose I should pay attention to what I'm doing, but it's easy to walk and read. I'm not losing as much weight as I'd like to lose. I'm sticking to my diet. God, today I bought donuts and then threw them away. Do you believe that?"

Lena hooted. "Sure. We all do dumb things from time to time. Like me trying to bleach my liver spots with Clorox. Now that's dumb, but I do it anyway."

"Call them freckles and you'll feel better about them. They go with your red hair and hazel eyes. Listen, Lena, if you want, you can use my exercise equipment. I ordered a NordicTrack. It should be here this week sometime."

"That's kind of you, Emily, thank you. It's all working out for you, isn't it? I mean with all the tenants and all. I know it's a zoo around here at dinnertime, but this past week I saw that most of the kinks are being worked out. I find something very comforting about all of us living under the same roof and doing our best to be considerate of each other."

"That's a lovely compliment, Lena. Listen, bring your tea and come into my workout room and talk with me. It will make the time go faster, and when I'm done, you can give it a try." Emily held her breath, waiting for Lena's response. Was she moving too fast in her desire to make a friend?

"Sure."

Emily was up to twenty minutes on the treadmill. Today she stayed on for forty-five minutes without realizing the time. To date, thirty minutes on the exercycle was all she could handle. She lasted an hour. "I should hire you," she gasped when she dropped to the floor to swig from her water bottle. "Your turn, Lena."

"I'm tired just watching you. I'll think about it. Actually, I'm comfortable with my fifteen extra pounds. As long as I'm in reasonable good health and eat right, I'm happy. I hope I'm not stepping over the line here, but you seem to be . . . obsessed with this program and your diet. I can't help but see the way you . . . you know what I mean."

"I guess I'm an obsessive person. Do you want to know why?"

"Not if it's going to bother you to talk about it."

"I won't know that unless I try. If it bothers me, I'll stop and continue some other day."

A long time later, when Lena filched stove time from the tenants to boil water for fresh tea, she said, "Emily, I'm so sorry. It must have been terrible for you."

"I don't want to waste the rest of my life. I need to do something. I need to do something to help myself, to prove to myself that I am a worthwhile person. That shrink I went to for a while said I had low self-esteem and he was right. I existed only for Ian. Do you think I'll ever get over Ian, Lena?"

"I don't know, Emily. They say time heals all wounds. I still love my husband and I know I'll never get married again. It's something I know and feel. I think you're different, though. Is there anything you want to do with your life? I mean something special?"

"I've been taking classes for years now. I only need twelve more credits to get my degree. I thought for a long time that, if I had a degree, I'd be worthy of Ian. Is that sick or what? I can see these things now. Why couldn't I see them then?"

"You didn't want to see them, Emily. It was easier to shift into neutral and coast. You trusted Ian and he didn't come through for you. That doesn't mean you can't trust people, another man, in case you meet one. Those white shirts now, that's something else. You literally created a monster, you know that, don't you?" Lena giggled.

"Oh, yes, I do know that. Nobody, according to Ian, could iron a white shirt like me. You know, when he left, when I got the letter, I really gave serious thought to taking in ironing. I panicked. I'm still in a state of panic each time I have to pay a bill. I gave myself a year to get it all together."

"And then?"

"And then I don't know. I have to think about my future and how I'm going to get by. I want the second half of my life to count for something. I don't want to look back and say to myself, I should have done this or I shouldn't have done that. I can't change the past. At night, when I can't sleep, I do that and then I really can't sleep. Everything reminds me of Ian. This room reminds me of him, but it's the only available space for these machines."

"Then I say we get rid of everything in this room that reminds you of your husband. I know how to wallpaper. Let's rip off this oh so manly plaid paper and put something up with some zip to it. I have a portable sewing machine I can let you use if you want to make some new curtains. I'd do valances. You'll get more light. If this wainscoting is important to you, leave it. If it isn't, paint it. Make it your room. I'm off this weekend and I can help you." This last was said so shyly, Emily wrapped Lena in her arms. "I'd love some help if you're sure you don't mind."

"Weekends are hard for me. My husband and I used to spend all our time together. I'd probably just read. Besides, the physical exercise will be good for both of us. Do you like this dark carpet?"

"I hate it."

"We'll work it in to our project. I can't wait. I love transformations. Let's go for a walk if you don't have anything else to do. I never really walked around Sleepy Hollow. It's beautiful out here with all the big, old trees. I bet you're going to get a lot of exercise when the leaves start to fall. I'll help," she said magnanimously.

"I accept. A walk would be nice."

A friendship began, a bond formed that would last both women the rest of their lives.

Chapter 9

There was a party going on at 47 Sleepy Hollow Road. Balloons and colorful streamers were everywhere. Music blared from Ian's stereo system throughout the house while a magnificent repast was being prepared in the kitchen.

"I love celebrations," Lena chortled as she cut the greens for the salad. "Tell me again exactly what we're celebrating."

"The list is endless," Emily said, and laughed, a sound of pure mirth. "First, and most important, we're celebrating your two years here with me, you and the others. I thought most of the women would be transients, but they're happy here. I'm just overwhelmed that you all feel this is a nice place to live. We're celebrating my fifty-pound weight loss even though I reached my goal six weeks ago. We're celebrating my degree. We're celebrating the fact that I obliterated Ian's name from his framed medical diploma and we're celebrating my Dear Emily letter that hangs in shreds in the workout room."

"Impressive indeed." Lena smiled.

"I don't know if I could have made it without you, Lena. Do you believe the saying that when God closes one door, he opens another?"

"One hundred percent. Moving here was the best thing

I ever did. I have more money in the bank than my husband and I ever had at one time in our lives. I'm not saying money is the end-all, but it is security. We have such a wonderful friendship. I guess this was meant to be. When are you going into that bathroom, Emily?" she asked quietly.

Emily's hands started to shake. "Maybe tonight. Maybe tomorrow. I don't know."

"You don't ever have to do it. If you aren't up to it, Emily, don't do it. You've built this up so in your mind it's become another obsession for you. Don't torture yourself. You've come a long way to get to this point in time. If it's something you can't handle . . ."

"I can do it, Lena. It's the timing. I have to work that out in my head. Let's change the subject. I, for one, cannot wait to sit down to this dinner and stuff myself. When the dishes are cleared away, I'm going to go for that five-mile walk, and when I get home, I'll do an hour on the Nordic-Track to work off more calories. If my eyes aren't bigger than my stomach, I'm going to have two pieces of apple pie with two scoops of ice cream."

"You've earned it, Emily. Indulgences are fine if you keep them within bounds. You've done everything right, your weight loss was slow, your exercise program was just what your body could handle, and you did it on your own. You're down to six cigarettes a day. Now, that's something to be proud of. I say we have another party when you finally kick the habit. I'll cook that dinner."

"Make that a promise and you have a deal," Emily said happily.

"It's a deal, Emily. What time is dinner?"

"Seven. Everyone will be home by then and cleaned up. Listen, Lena, I did something . . . now I'm not sure if . . . it was one of those spur-of-the-moment things people usually regret later, but I wanted this to be a bang-up affair. Balloons, streamers, dinner, and a rich dessert didn't seem like quite enough so I . . . what I did was . . . Maybe I can cancel," she dithered.

"Cancel what? What did you do? Emily, look at me, what did you do?"

Emily took a deep breath. "I hired a male dancer. He's coming at nine o'clock. He dances on the dining room table. He takes off his clothes. Well, not all of them. I think he wears something skimpy. Oh, God, I thought it would be fun."

Lena doubled over laughing. Tears rolled down her cheeks as she removed the granny glasses she wore perched on her nose. "Emily, you have come a long, long way. I think it's great. Does he gyrate and do we put five-dollar bills in his . . . whatever . . ."

"I guess we could," Emily said weakly. "I have to tip him. Yes, yes, let's do that. I have some five-dollar bills. I went to the bank yesterday. I think we should hoot and holler like they do on television."

"Absolutely," Lena gasped. "They gyrate right up against your face. I saw that on television."

"Don't tell me that!"

"You hired him so you're the one he'll do that to. Oh, I can't wait to see this. Nice going, Emily! I thought you said we were going for a walk after the kitchen was cleaned up."

"I lied."

"Does he have a name?"

"Uh-huh."

"What is it?" Lena giggled.

"The Liberated Stud."

"I like that," Lena said with a straight face.

"You do!"

"I guess that means he's uninhibited, loose as a goose, that kind of thing."

"I have a picture. He sent one in the mail when I called him. He said it was a professional shot. He has . . . he said he has a portfolio."

"Well, let's see it!"

Emily reached into the cabinet where she kept the trash bags and withdrew a manila envelope. She licked at her lips as Lena cackled gleefully, smacking her hands in anticipation.

"What do you think?"

"*Oh, myyyy Goddddd,*" Lena said, holding the glossy photograph this way and that way. "On his best day, my husband never looked like this. How about you, Emily?"

"Ian couldn't measure up anywhere near this guy. Even when he was twenty. Does this make us two dirty old women?"

"Yeahhh, but who cares? If you have an old frame lying around, I think you should stick this in it and put it on the dining room table so we can all look at it when we're eating."

"Are you serious?"

"Oh, yeah, I'm serious. I wouldn't know what to do with someone like that, would you, Emily?"

"I'd make it up as I went along. Listen, we're in our forties. That doesn't mean we're dead. I bet we could teach him a few things. These young hunks think women are going to be so mesmerized with their perfect bodies they aren't going to want anything but . . . you know. Guys like him probably don't know how to please a woman. Did your husband please you, Lena?"

"He tried. He wasn't . . . ah . . . adventuresome. How about Ian?"

"Sometimes it was good. Most times it was for him. A

lot of times he was too tired and I got to the point where I refused to ask because I didn't want to be told he was tired. Hey, I was born tired, but I did . . . do like sex. You?"

"How can you like something you never really had? My husband thought foreplay was something only hookers and johns practiced. He was very straightlaced, but I loved him."

Emily stared at her friend. "But? There's always a but."

"No buts. Now, where's that frame?"

"Upstairs on the hall table. Lordy, it's almost time for everyone to come home."

Dinner was a festive affair with many toasts to the photograph of the oiled body flexing his muscles in the center of the table. When the dishes were done and the dining room chairs were placed in a semicircle far enough back into the room to afford a good view of the dancer, Emily poured fresh wine into long-stemmed flutes. "We're ready!" Lena bobbed her head. "He brings his own music."

"How long is he going to dance?" a library assistant from the Plainfield Library asked.

"An hour," Emily said happily. "When you want more, just ask."

"Does he wear a cape?" a nurse's aide said.

"He starts *out* with a cape."

"I hope he wears feathers around his ankles. I think that's sexy," Kelly said. "Do you know, Emily?"

"If you want feathers, I can go upstairs and take some out of a pillow. Lena knows how to sew so she can string them together."

"That's okay. I'll pretend he's wearing feathers."

"I hope he throws his pelvis out a lot. Lots of bump-and-grind stuff. Do you realize, ladies, that women have finally come to a place in time where we can do something like this? Before it was men with hookers at stag parties. I say we exploit this guy, heckle the hell out of him. Just the way they do to women."

Martha Nesbit laughed uproariously. "I want to borrow that picture so I can put it on my desk tomorrow morning. I want all the salesmen to see it when they come in. I'm gonna say he was my date for this evening."

Emily poured more wine.

The Liberated Stud arrived promptly at nine. The women gave a collective gasp of approval before he banished them to the kitchen so he could "get ready."

In the kitchen the women, half drunk and still drinking, let go of their inhibitions and cackled in delight. "Did you see those loins?" "You read too many romance novels." "Rippling thighs." "Ohhh, I like that." "Sleek." "Did you see that wry grin? He's gonna get off on us, you wait and see."

"Emily, this is the best idea, the very *best*. We are all going to dream about this tonight. I love living here, Emily. We're like sisters. I can't wait to go to work tomorrow. You're taking pictures, right?"

"Oh, my God, I don't have a camera. I should have thought about that," Emily wailed. "Of course we want to take pictures. How could I have forgotten something so important?"

"I have a Polaroid camera," the assistant librarian said. "I'll just scoot up the back staircase and get it."

"Hurry," they called in unison.

Emily uncorked another bottle of wine. They liked living here. The women liked her as a person. They thought of themselves as sisters. They liked what she planned. Everyone was happy. For once she'd done something right. There was no Ian to criticize her. And when the night was over, there would be no one to say, dear Emily, don't forget to iron my white shirts. She was giddy when she saw Zoë Meyers trot into the kitchen waving the camera. Emily immediately filled her wineglass.

"Oh my God!" they cried in unison when a trumpet beckoned them into the dining room.

"He has clothes on," the assistant librarian complained as she tried to focus the camera.

"It's one of those Velcro suits that come apart at the seams," Emily hissed, never taking her eyes off the dancer in the middle of her dining room table.

A cane with a sparkling knob at the end snaked downward to press the button of his tape deck. Loud music, runway music, stripping music, blasted into the room. The women sat back.

He danced. He pranced. He gyrated. The sleeves came off his jacket. The rest of the jacket followed in slow, tantalizing motions, the dancer never losing a beat. Emily felt her forehead bead with sweat. She wondered if she was going to slide off her chair.

"Take it off," Nancy Beckenridge shouted hoarsely.

"Everyyyyything!" Lena tittered.

"Let's see what you got," Kelly Anderson leered.

He showed them. His pants sailed over his shoulder in one swift, fluid motion. His red satin jock strap pulsated. The women clapped enthusiastically. Zoë whistled between her teeth. Lena hooted, and so did Emily. They all stamped their feet.

He was off the table in the blink of an eye and then he was in front of them.

"He's going to throw his back out," Martina, the nurse's aide, whispered.

"Who cares?" Kelly said, reaching out to touch his oiled thigh. She squealed her pleasure. She recoiled at once when he thrust out his pelvis. Emily tweaked the elastic on the jock strap. "Is this a jock strap?" she asked hoarsely.

"It's whatever you want it to be," he leaned over to whisper. He did a wild series of bumps and grinds ending with a thrust of his pelvis in Emily's face.

Emily did something then she never thought she would ever do. She cupped both her hands and brought them up like a cradle to cup the quivering red satin. The girls stamped their feet and hooted their approval. Her eyes wild, Emily smashed her face against the mass in her hands.

"*Ooohhh,* that feels *goooddd,*" the Stud said, a wicked grin on his face.

"My turn, my turn," the others called. Emily dropped her hands and pushed her chair back. Suddenly the camera was being thrust at her. She snapped and snapped and kept right on snapping until the dancer was back on her dining room table whereupon she thrust the camera back into Zoë's hands.

My God, did she just . . . yes you did, Emily Thorn, you grabbed that guy's balls and mashed your face in them. And you liked it, didn't you? Damn right I did, she said, swallowing hard.

And then it was over and the Stud was wearing a red satin cape that matched his outfit. The raucous music ended and was replaced with Paul McCartney singing "My Love." The Stud jumped from the table, landing in front of Emily. "Mrs. Thorn, would you do me the honor of sharing this dance with me?"

She fit perfectly in his arms. "Did you get your money's worth, Mrs. Thorn?" he whispered.

"Yes, yes, I did. You gave an excellent performance. My friends enjoyed it immensely. Perhaps someday when we're celebrating something, we'll call you again. With a different routine, of course."

"Of course," he said, cradling her against him. "I have a

wicked yellow Speedo that will drive those women to the brink."

Emily smiled up at him. "It was a fun evening. You're going to dance with all of them, aren't you."

"Yes. I try my best to leave everyone happy."

"You succeeded. Your turn, Lena," she said, stepping aside.

Emily watched as he danced with each woman to the strains of "I've Been Waiting for a Girl Like You."

When the tape deck was packed in his huge duffle bag, Emily asked if he would like a glass of wine.

"Sorry, I have another gig at ten-thirty. Listen, I don't know if you're interested or not, but I sell a set of my pictures. Twenty bucks for twenty pictures."

They each bought a set.

Before he left, he kissed each of them on the cheek.

When the door closed behind him, Emily said, "He's some mother's son. I thought he was rather gallant, all things considered. What *are* we going to do with these pictures? Ohhh, I *like* this one."

"I have an idea," Lena said. "Let's make a border of them in the kitchen. We can use wallpaper paste. Eye level, of course, and we can stare at them as much as we want. We have six sets. They should cover every wall in the kitchen."

"Sterling idea," Emily said. "Let's do it now. Tomorrow we won't have the nerve. The paste is in the workroom closet."

"It's crooked," Nancy said two hours later, "but I like it. I think we should get that one with Emily blown up to poster size and put it on the back of the kitchen door. Let's vote."

"I'll take it to that one-hour photo place," Lena volunteered. "I think posters take about a week."

"Hear! Hear!" Emily said.

"Let's finish the pie and coffee. I'll get it ready," Kelly offered.

"It was a fun night, Emily. It really was," Zoë said.

"Who says you're dead after forty?" Lena chortled.

When their coffee cups were full, Zoë made the toast. "To Emily, to calories, to caffeine, to wet dreams, and to our newly decorated kitchen."

The Demster twins, Rose and Helen, who rented the apartment over the garage, slid off the kitchen chairs at the same time. "They do everything together," Nancy said. "They were snakeroot after the first glass of wine. I think we should just cover them up."

"Okay," Emily said agreeably.

Martha Nesbit, a friend of the Demster twins, and who never said two words if one would do, looked down at the twins, reached for a cushion from the kitchen stairs, and lay down beside them.

"Great evening," she said before she fell asleep.

"I have the early shift at the hospital tomorrow," Martina said. "Leave everything. I'll clean it up before I leave. I had a great evening, Emily. It's real nice living here. Night."

"Want to go for a walk, Lena?"

"Sure."

"Just up and down the street. It's a nice evening." They walked a block in silence, then Emily began to speak. "You know, Lena, it's been a long time since I really noticed anything but my own misery. I know I've had too much wine but that has nothing to do with it. Take right now, for example. The stars are out. I can see the Big Dipper. It looks like someone shook out a blanket full of bright sprinkles. The air around us is like crushed velvet, all soft and silky feeling. That's because there's no humidity tonight. The moon is gorgeous. Tomorrow it will be full and we'll all get cranky and out of sorts. Way back when I used to work at the clinics, you'd be surprised at the things that happened when there was a full moon. I can smell honeysuckle. It's late this year, probably because we haven't had much rain.

"I need to do something, Lena. I realized that tonight more than ever. Two years out of the mainstream of life wasn't in my game plan—not that I have a game plan, but I need to get one. I need a life, a goal, something to work for, or toward, however you want to say it. I want to think and feel again. Tonight I did for a few minutes. I don't mean that silly thing I did with . . . that silly thing I did. I'll chalk that up to the wine. How about you, Lena?"

"I'm content, Emily. It doesn't take much to make me happy. I feel like I found a family in my middle years. We all tried to tell you tonight, each in our own way, how grateful we are to you. Me especially."

"Is that another way of saying you're content to stay in the supermarket and be on your feet for eight hours and then go on to a part-time job?"

"I need the benefits, Emily, you know that. My husband, as well meaning as he was, thought any kind of insurance was a waste of money. I have no other choice so I accept it."

"If I found something, a business, something that would earn us both a living, would you be interested?"

"If you provide benefits, I'd be delighted to join you."

"I'm going to work on it. Maybe I can come up with something."

"It would be great."

"I wish every day could end as nice as this one did," Emily said, turning around to head back for the house.

"I'm glad we took the time to become friends. My husband used to want all my time when he was home. I didn't begrudge it, but I see now that I missed a lot. You're a nice person, Emily."

"I know that. Now. For so long . . . Forget it, that's all in the past. I don't live there anymore."

Lena waved her arms about. "Welcome to the world, Emily Thorn."

Chapter 10

Emily groaned when she sat down at the table for her first cup of coffee. This was her first hangover. The ones with Ian didn't count. But it was worth it. The evening had been everything she'd expected it to be. If she hadn't known before, she knew now that the diverse group of women who were her boarders, and now her friends, were true friends. They all had problems, though some were quicker to talk about them than others. Actually, what they were was a support group, something she'd only read about until now.

A gurgle of laughter bubbled in her throat when she stared up at the latest decorating endeavor. The laughter exploded when she tried to imagine the meter reader's expression when he came to calculate her electric bill. He had to knock on the door and go through the kitchen to the laundry room. "Life goes on," she muttered.

She had plans for today. She was going to hire a personal trainer to help her tone up her body. Weight loss was one thing; loose, flabby skin was something else. She didn't even know if she could tone up, but she was going to find out if women over forty still had elasticity.

She eyed the bathroom door, looked away. Not yet. Soon. Maybe. Maybe never. Her gaze rose upward. Ian never looked that good. He'd been thin, stringy actually. For a fair-haired, fair-skinned man, he'd had little body hair, and what he did have was golden so it was hardly noticeable. Chest hair on a man was so . . . so . . . sexy.

"You are horny, Emily Thorn. You need to get laid, Emily Thorn." She stared at the Polaroid shots on the wall and at the series of photos they'd all paid for. *"Yesssss,"* Emily said, breathing hard.

The realization that she wanted sex, needed it, was another milestone she'd conquered. Not too long ago she thought all her emotions were dead. The young, glistening body last night had proved how wrong that kind of thinking was.

Emily poured a second cup of coffee, lit her first cigarette of the day. She savored it. Okay, number one on her list of things to do was to get laid. Number two was to find a business she could go into and earn some money. Number three was to provide jobs and security for the women who now lived with her.

All of her boarders had been done in, one way or another, by men. Some willingly, some unwillingly.

Lena's husband hadn't provided for her in the event of his death because he didn't want to pay premiums. Now she was forty-four, cashiering in a supermarket because she needed health benefits. She had nothing of her own, no nest egg in case something happened to her. Twenty years from now, if she was lucky, at sixty-four, she'd be ready for Social Security and still living in a furnished room, here or somewhere else.

Nancy, with no college education, was working as a clerk in the lumber mill for $6 an hour. Her husband had left her for life on the open road. She was forty-five and had nothing to her name but her personal possessions because she'd been forced to sell off the furniture in her one-bedroom apartment. She had limited health benefits and a bleak future to look forward to.

Martina, a nurse's aide, had walked out on a husband

who was a drinker and who refused to get help. She was in the process of getting a divorce, but the drunkard had a better attorney than she had. With almost no equity in the four-room house, she didn't stand much of a chance of providing for her old age when and if the house was finally sold.

Kelly Anderson, age forty-four, held down two part-time jobs and had no benefits at all. She'd never been married, but had been in a fifteen-year relationship with a traveling salesman who said he would marry her, but died instead. Her future looked as bleak as the others.

Zoë Meyers, the assistant librarian, was poorly paid, and according to her, an old maid. She was forty-eight, the oldest of them all, but she was the one who might eke by with her small pension and Social Security.

Rose and Helen Demster, the forty-five-year-old twins, ran a tree-cutting service and lawn maintenance company. They had a small nest egg, but that could be wiped out in one bad year. They'd given up their garden apartment to move into the apartment over Emily's garage. Neither had ever been married. Helen said it was because they wore bib overalls all the time and Rose said it was because they had big butts and no boobs.

Martha Nesbit, age forty-two, had been dumped by her husband of twenty years after she put him through law school. His parting remark had been, "Martha, living with you is like watching paint dry." She'd gotten a $25,000 settlement and lifetime health benefits, but she'd blown the $25,000 in the hopes of snaring a husband. It hadn't worked so she got a job as a mail carrier. She had bunions and bursitis from walking and carrying the mail bag. She hated men, lawyers in particular, and her car carried a bumper sticker that said FIRST WE KILL ALL THE LAWYERS!

All of them, including herself, were emotional cripples. Emily knew in her gut that none of them, including Lena, had the courage or the motivation to do anything about it except to go on as they had. If things were going to change, it would be up to her to change them.

Of all of them, she was the best off, if there was such an expression. She had a nest egg, the jewelry, and the furs. While she hadn't actually received a salary while working for the clinics, Ian had paid into Social Security for her so she could count on that when she reached sixty-five. Few people could survive on Social Security alone. She didn't plan on being one of those few people. She couldn't, ever, lose this house. If she did, she would feel personally responsible for all her boarders' lives. They were her friends now and she had to help them, the way she'd helped Ian. Only this time her reward would be different. There would be nothing sick and obsessive about her help, and there would be no white shirts. In her heart she knew that if she came up with a business that could earn them all a living and give them back their self-esteem, they'd work like Trojans. None of them would be an Ian Thorn. They would all give back, a hundred percent. Women helping women. She liked the way it sounded.

Emily let her gaze go to the closed bathroom door. It was amazing, it really was, how none of the women had ever asked questions about that particular bathroom.

Before Emily left the kitchen to get ready for the day, she gave a jaunty thumbs-up salute to the dancer cavorting around the walls. "Nice buns." She laughed. "Real nice. I mean *really* nice."

Outside, Emily took time to admire the garden she'd planted years ago and still tended. Some of the flowers were going to seed, and the grass between the flagstone walkway needed to be sprayed. The lawn needed water, but she hadn't been using the sprinkler system these past two years because she didn't want high water bills. She didn't care too much about the lawn because it would come back, but the shrubbery, which added eye appeal to the house, needed water desperately. She added it to the list of things she had to do at the end of the day. And if she didn't get around to it, one of the other women would do it. Nancy liked to work outside and, from time to time, gave each bush and shrub a five-gallon bucket of water if it didn't rain. If you watered by the bucket, you didn't waste water, she said.

Emily reached down to check the dirt in the clay pots that lined the walk. Someone had watered the New Guinea impatiens and her glorious pots of bicolored dahlias. In another month the summer flowers would be replaced with mums and pumpkins. Her flowers and the garden had gotten through some bad times.

Emily gave herself a mental shake. The bad times, as far as she was concerned, were over. There might be a setback from time to time that she would have to endure, but she could handle it.

Her first stop on her list of things to do for the day was the ATA Fitness Center. She walked away with the names of three personal trainers who would come to the house. From ATA she went to the Inman Racquet Club and was told all their trainers were booked solid. She tried the YMCA in Metuchen, where she was given two more names. She then stopped at the First Fidelity Bank, where she asked to see a loan officer—the same loan officer who had given Ian the loan for the first clinic.

Five minutes into their discussion, Emily knew she would be fighting a losing battle to try and convince the officer that she was entrepreneurial material.

"Mrs. Thorn, you aren't actively employed and you haven't worked in some time. You have no collateral. I'm sorry, but I—"

"You should be sorry, Mr. Squire, because I'm going to get a loan somewhere. You couldn't wait to lend my hus-

band money when he hadn't even started to practice medicine. Who do you think set those clinics up? Me, that's
who. I know everything there is to know about operating
a clinic. All my husband did was treat patients. I'm not
trying to make light of his abilities, but I'm the one who
paid off those loans by working nights and half days at the
clinics. That should count for something."

"It should, but it doesn't, Mrs. Thorn. This is a bank
and without collateral we can't help you. You could try
the SBA, but in the end you have to go through a bank.
There's tons of paperwork involved."

"Are you trying to discourage me, Mr. Squire?"

"No."

"All your loans were repaid, by me, in a timely manner
and still you won't help me. Is it because I'm a woman?"

"Absolutely not. Are you planning on opening a clinic
on your own?"

Was she? Why not? "Yes," she said.

"A family clinic?"

"No. What difference does it make if you aren't willing
to lend me money?"

"Mrs. Thorn, do you have any personal credit? I don't
mean credit cards with Dr. Thorn's name where you sign
your name on purchases."

"No. I don't use credit cards. I pay cash for everything."

"What about your utility bills?"

"They're . . . in Ian's name. I never changed them over
when he . . . when he left."

"You need to do that right away. You say you've been
paying them for over two years?"

"Yes, I have. Am I going to need a credit card?"

"Bankers like to see a credit history. I truly am sorry,
Mrs. Thorn. I don't think you'll have much luck at any of
the banks in the area unless you have collateral to put up.

Sometimes collateral isn't the answer either. Banks don't gamble."

"You gambled on my husband."

"He was a doctor, Mrs. Thorn. Doctors are usually very successful. He had a profession that was unequaled in the eyes of most bankers."

"You know what, Mr. Squire? That stinks, and if my words offend you, I'm sorry. Thank you for your time."

Purse in hand, Emily walked to the low gate on the platform that led to the main part of the bank. She was about to unlatch the gate when she changed her mind and walked back to the banker's desk. He looked up, a frown on his face. "When I'm as successful as Ian was, I'm going to come back here and show you my bank balances in other banks. That's a promise, Mr. Squire. Now I'm leaving."

Emily didn't start to shake until she got to the car. She fired up an unauthorized cigarette and smoked it down to the filter. She lit a second one, then made a mental note that she had to forgo the two cigarettes she allowed herself in the evening.

So she was stupid. She should have thought about the utilities, should have thought about a credit card. She had collateral at the First Jersey Bank. She should have told him that. As long as she wasn't borrowing more than the collateral there shouldn't be a problem. Unless she failed. And then her old-age nest egg would be gone and she'd be in the same position as the women at the house. She might not even have a house if that happened. "And there go all my wonderful plans," Emily muttered as she slipped the car into gear.

Fear. That terrible, awful feeling that made you sick to your stomach. She'd read, somewhere, that there was nothing to fear but fear itself. Whoever said that must be a man, she thought.

Ian had had no fear when he'd started out. And why should he—he had me to do all the worrying, all the work. He just sailed in in the morning and sailed out at the end of the day and everything was taken care of, right down to those awful white shirts and his underwear. Ian didn't know the meaning of the word *fear*. Maybe there was a lesson to be learned here. If it wasn't for her, he wouldn't have succeeded. She corrected the thought—he would have succeeded, but not as quickly. If I could make it work for him, then why can't I make it work for me? The question is, Emily Thorn, do you have enough faith in yourself, in your ability, to make things right, to give up your financial security? Think about that.

Emily pulled into the parking lot of the United Jersey Bank. She pep-talked herself for five minutes. If I'm going to give up my nest egg for a loan I'll be paying interest on, what's the point? If I'm going to do this, I can use my own money and not worry about a payment to some bank which will end up owning my very soul. Ian always said never use your own money, use the bank's money. Well, that was fine for Ian to say because he had an Emily in the background. She didn't.

Emily backed out of the parking lot. She needed to go home and sit down at the kitchen table with coffee and another unauthorized cigarette. If she kept this up, she'd be into tomorrow's allotment. Whatever it takes, Emily.

Damn, she was mad now. She stayed mad all the way home. By the time her coffee was ready, she was seething with fury. Instead of drinking it and smoking a cigarette she wasn't supposed to have, she opted for her workout room, where she put in three hours on the treadmill, the NordicTrack, and her exercycle. Dripping sweat, she stretched out on the floor to think.

"Are you dead?" Lena asked from the doorway.

"I know first aid," Martina said, peering over Lena's shoulders.

"Listen to this," Emily said, rolling over on her belly. She told them about her day. "I have a germ of an idea. If I can make it work and all of you are willing to work for very little. Actually, you have to work for nothing. For a while. Listen carefully. Mr. Squire asked me if I was going to open a clinic and I said yes. I said that just to have a response, but I've been thinking about it. That's how Ian started out. A storefront clinic. Walk-in-off-the-street kind of thing. I can start an exercise clinic. Not a health club, but a clinic. The biggest expense would be the rent and the machines. We might be able to lease those. I already have three. I have tons of books on nutrition. Lena knows all about herbs and stuff. We can buy wholesale and package the stuff ourselves. If we all commit and work at it, I think it might work. Those house payments ... that's the only thing that worries me because I need your rent to pay the mortgage payments. Any ideas?"

"We can't give up our benefits, Emily," the ever-practical Lena said.

"I know, but we can take out a group policy. It will be cheaper than what we're all paying now. Yours are still high, Lena, and your employer pays most of it. We'll all be partners. I can put up the money. How much is twenty-five hundred dollars times twenty-four?"

"Sixty thousand dollars," Martina said.

"Okay, I'm going to pay two years ahead. I don't care if it's stupid or not. We'll all feel better knowing we aren't going to lose the roof over our heads. The shore house pretty much pays for itself, and if I sell, Ian gets half and I don't even know where he is to have him sign the papers. Do you think the others will go for this?" Emily asked anxiously.

"If somebody offered this to you, what would you do, Emily?" Lena asked.

"I'm all for taking chances. We aren't kids anymore. I think all of us have learned a lot these past few years. Since there isn't anyone around to take care of us, not that we want that, but since there isn't, we have to do it ourselves. I'd love to know I"m going to have a stress-free, luxurious old age. I don't want to struggle and just get by. I had that for too many years. I want better now and I'm willing to work my tail off if you girls will agree."

"No more bedpans," Martina chirped.

"No more coupons, no more paper cuts from the grocery bags," Lena said. "Exercise clinics. Sounds promising."

"For women our age," Emily added. "Nutritional, exercise clinics."

"What makes that different from health clubs?" Martina asked. "In case you haven't noticed, there's a health center on every corner."

"And who do you see going in there? Certainly not women our age. Two years ago when I first started my exercise routine, I would have died before I walked into one of those places. My fat rolls had rolls of their own. Furthermore, I didn't think they made those cute little workout suits in my size. I'm still not sure they make them, and even if they do, can you see one of us in one? If we can get this off the ground, it's something we should look into. If we're going to sweat, we should look as good and be as comfortable as we can. The way I see it, shame and embarrassment are going to be our two biggest hurdles. This is all off the top of my head now. I was so angry with Mr. Squire's negative comments that I blurted out I was going to open a clinic. Then I ran with it and I'm still running."

"We're going to need a plan, for home and for your

clinic. Businessmen are always talking about a well-oiled machine. We need that," Lena said.

"Yes, we do. We have to assign out our house chores. Someone has to cook, no more of this each person making her own food. Someone has to help with the yard work. Someone has to pay the bills. I guess that's me. We're going to have laundry and grocery shopping to do. None of that is going to change, but we can work out something. I want us to have pension plans," Emily added. "It's a must."

"Are we going to incorporate? I think you need to do that or you pay a lot of taxes. We'll have to hire an attorney."

Emily turned white. "I . . . I have to think about that. Tonight, after we talk to the others, I'll make out a list. Do you think the others will go for this?"

"I think so. When it comes right down to it, what do any of us really have to lose? It won't be a hard sell if that's what's worrying you," Martina said.

Four hours later she said, "See, I told you it wouldn't be a hard sell."

"Details to be worked out. I say we all give our notice tomorrow," Nancy said. "Let's vote."

"Guess that means the die is cast. In two weeks we'll all be unemployed. Fresh coffee is called for," Zoë said, hopping off her chair. "I don't know the first thing about running an exercise clinic," she called over her shoulder.

"I don't either," Emily said cheerfully. "We're going to learn real fast, though. Now listen to this. When Ian and I opened our first clinic, we more or less fell into it. At least that's the way Ian explained it to me. We did them one at a time, I think, and this is just my opinion, that we should open a bunch all at one time. Storefronts, so rent is low. We can fix them inside. So what if they aren't fancy from the street. It's what's inside and the people working there that are important. Word of mouth is going to help." Her voice was confident sounding.

"What's a bunch?" Kelly asked anxiously.

"Well, there's eight of us, so I say we go for eight."

"Oh, no," Rose and Helen said together. "We have to be with each other. What's wrong with seven?"

"Eight is better. There are two of you and two pensions and two sets of health plans. It has to be this way or it won't work," Emily said gently.

"Cut the umbilical cord already," Martha said, passing coffee cups around the table. "Sure it will be different in the beginning, but like anything else, you'll get the hang of it. Think of it as the ultimate in adventures. Or this is where they separate the women from the girls. You aren't girls anymore. You need to think about the future. How much longer can you go on with your tree-cutting business? You said business isn't that good."

"We've never been apart," Helen said miserably.

"You can talk on the phone. You can meet for lunch. You can ride to work together, one drops the other off. You can do it," Lena said positively. "Think of it as a monster tree that needs to be topped and no one wants to do it but you and Rose. You know it can be done. So can this.

"It's going to be as new to us as it is to you. The good part is we'll help one another," Lena said. "I can't wait to see our screwups."

"Will you give it a try?" Emily asked.

In unison the twins bobbed their heads.

"Good. Tomorrow I'll call an agent and scout around for storefronts. I think strip malls might be a good idea or someplace that's in close proximity to a supermarket. Lena, can you post a notice on the bulletin board once we get started?"

"Sure. I can get a list of all the customers at the health food store. The bulk of them are our age or older. This might surprise you, but most of the people who work in the supermarkets, especially during the day, are women my age. I can get a list from the shop steward. I might even be able to get a list of *all* the employees from other supermarkets too."

"I can put a notice up at the hospital," Martina said.

"I can do the library. We have a lot of chubbies who love to read. I'll take on all the libraries in a five-mile radius. We're staying local, right?"

"For now I think so," Emily said.

"I'm off tomorrow. Do you want me to call around about the equipment?" Nancy asked.

"That would be great. Find out about leasing versus buying outright. We'll need eight of everything so you might be able to cut a deal. All those places have 800 numbers, so you can spend as much time on the phone as you want. Find out about service contracts and what their time record is for repairs. We need professional machines, not the kind I have," Emily said.

"One of my customers is a lawyer. Would you like me to call her after work and set up an appointment to work out details?" Lena asked.

"Okay, that's your job, Lena."

Emily looked at the twins. "How busy are you for the next few days?"

"Slow," they said in unison.

"Okay, then it's your job to call insurance companies for quotes on health insurance. Can you handle brokerage houses to find out about how you go about setting up a pension fund?" Both heads bobbed up and down at the same time.

"Lena, while you're getting the lists from the health food store, can you find out where we can get herbs and vitamins wholesale?"

"Can do," Lena agreed.

"Zoë, you're the librarian. Find out about health codes, licenses, and all that stuff. Especially bathrooms. We'll need showers. Most storefronts don't have anything like that. It could be costly. It's possible the owners might make some concessions.

"Martha, you check out printers for mailers and business cards and advertising. We want anything that's free or has a discount attached. Push eight clinics and don't be afraid to mention the word *competitor.*"

"What are we going to call ourselves?" Zoë asked. Seven pairs of eyes stared at her blankly. "We need a name."

"Yes, we do. Okay, everybody, let's see what we can come up with," Emily said.

"It should have something to do with Emily. It's her idea and she's the one putting up the money," Martina said. "God, I just love the idea of us being our own bosses. I never, ever thought this would happen. More coffee, Zoë."

Suddenly, Emily felt like the proud mother of eight grown children. It was a wonderful feeling, sitting here with her friends, all of whom were bending over backward to be fair to her, complimenting her and doing it sincerely, from their hearts. This is going to work. It has to work. I'm going to make it work.

They brainstormed far into the night with no results. What one person liked, three persons disliked. "I say we call it Emily's Blast-off Clinic and be done with it," Martina said wearily. She was booed lustily.

"I like the Figure Perfect Clinic," the twins said at the same time.

"I like the Fresh Start Clinic," Zoë grunted.

"Tell me one thing that's wrong with The Second Chance Clinic. I happen to love it because that's exactly what it is," Lena grumbled.

"Yeah, well, I happen to like Starting Over Clinic," Nancy said.

"Listen, all of you. None of the names you came up with have Emily's name in them. I say we vote right now to call it Emily's Fitness Clinic," Kelly said.

The women stared at her, their mouths open. "No one came up with that name all evening," Zoë said. "I like it." The others agreed.

"What do you think, Emily?" Lena asked.

"If you all agree, then it's okay with me. A show of hands. Okay, we are now, officially, Emily's Fitness Clinic. Good night everybody."

Emily slept deeply and peacefully. Tonight there were no demons invading her rest.

Chapter 11

It took a full thirty days before Emily's Fitness Clinics were ready to open. All the legalities, all the permits, all the licenses were finally posted on the walls of the eight locations. The last bathroom, then the last inspection, was completed.

Emily had been stunned when the attorney told her the others wanted her to have a full half of the business, the other half to be divided seven ways. Emily agreed, but only if a sizable bonus was given to each woman at the end of the year. She herself would forgo the bonus. It was so agreed among all eight women.

"I feel like a fidgety cat who's about to get neutered," Emily said on the morning the keys to the eight locations were handed over by the rental agency.

"This is the best part, prettying up the places," Lena said. "When things look pretty, women feel pretty. Pretty makes you smile. Pretty makes you happy doing what you're doing. I'm glad we all agreed on our decor."

"Listen up, everyone," Lena said. "Do not forget today is the day the *Courier* is coming to take our pictures. Do you all have your sweatshirts that I very lovingly stitched the words *Emily's Fitness Clinic* on? We're wearing them. It's free publicity. The *Star Ledger* is tomorrow and the *News Tribune* is Friday."

Emily felt like an indulgent mother as she watched her friends leave, their cars loaded down with supplies and what Lena called "decor." She was going to her location as soon as she finished working out with her personal trainer, Ben Jackson. She looked at her watch; he was five minutes late. Usually he was on time or early. She drank a cup of coffee standing by the window. She wanted one of her cigarettes, but she tried never to smoke until an hour after her workout with Ben. She was down to five cigarettes a day.

She smiled when she saw Ben's car, grinned when she saw him pick a flower, which he would hand to her when he came through the kitchen door. He was a handsome man, physically fit, divorced. More important, he was a kind man with a gentle smile.

"I picked this just for you. I have to treat my clients right." He smiled. His smile was contagious. It set the mood for the workout session. "Catch!"

"Ben, these are ten pound weights. I have trouble with five. C'mon."

"Let's go, Emily. You want to tone up, this is the only way to go."

"How come you were late this morning?"

"Business to take care of," he said curtly.

"In other words, none of my business. Sorry I asked. You don't look happy, Ben."

"Don't talk, work. I'm counting, let's go."

When the hour session was over, Emily collapsed on the mat in the middle of the floor. Ben handed her a bottle of water. She gulped at it then wiped the sweat from her forehead. "Forget these weights. I'm going back to five next time."

"Then get yourself another trainer," Ben said.

"Testy, aren't we? This is too much for me, Ben. I'm breathing like a racehorse."

"I wouldn't have you use a ten-pound weight if I didn't

think you were ready. I'm the trainer, remember? Are you sure you aren't the one who's testy?"

"I am uptight. Today we start to get the clinics ready. The others have a head start on me. Ben, sometimes it helps to talk things out. You said that to me a few weeks ago. I have a good ear."

"My ex is getting married in two weeks. That means my son is going to have two fathers. They want to adopt him. I said no. They said I wouldn't have to pay child support anymore. I said no again."

"What does your son want?"

"To live with me. His mother won't allow it. He's only eleven so what he wants doesn't count," Ben said, flopping down on the mat next to Emily.

"I guess you aren't looking for advice, huh?"

"Not really. He's my son and I'm not giving him up. God, I love that kid. Just because his mother and I couldn't get along doesn't mean he and I can't have a relationship."

Emily wondered why he hadn't married again. A good catch, she thought. "Would it make things different if you were remarried? Would you have joint custody then instead of visitation rights?"

"I'd have to go back to court. Hey, you're looking at one burned fella here. I'm never getting married again."

"I feel like that, too," Emily said, hugging her knees. "We aren't being fair, you know that, don't you? There are a lot of nice men and women out there. Take my room-mates, they're the best. I offered to introduce you to them, but you said no. You've been divorced for seven years. Life is going to pass you by."

"What would you say if I said I wanted to kiss you?"

"For starters, I'd say what took you so long?"

"Brazen, aren't you?"

"It goes with the new me."

"You see, that's my problem, I'm still the old me."

"Do you get off on wallowing? It only works for a while. I'm the living proof, Ben. You haven't severed your ties yet; at least that's the way I see it."

"And I suppose you have?"

"I'm trying. I'm moving on, trying new things, doing new things. I want to learn how to laugh all over again. I still cry sometimes. It seems to me you're just going through the motions of filling up your days."

He kissed her then to shut her up. She responded hungrily, demanding he carry the kiss further. He pushed her away.

"I don't know about you, but I *liked* that. Let's do it again."

"I don't like to be used," Ben said flatly, his gray eyes full of pain.

"I don't either," Emily said. She crooked her finger under his nose. "C'mere."

They whispered and tussled, each afraid, yet unafraid, as they tried to shed their clothes without ungluing their lips.

"It's been a long time," someone whispered.

"Too long," someone else whispered.

The plastic mat was slick with sweat, but it had the effect of a dose of cold water. Emily jerked away, her arms crossing her breasts. "I . . . I can't do this . . . I'm sorry, Ben. I . . . I thought I could, but I'm not ready . . ."

"Hey, don't mind me, I'm just a guy sitting here with an erection even I can't believe. What the hell happened?" he groaned.

"It's me. The physical side of me wants . . . but my head . . . I'm not ready. Please don't be upset."

"Well, goddamn it, Emily, I am upset. You get me all lathered up, I'm buck-ass naked in front of a client. I'll turn around and you get dressed. Look, I'm not angry. I think I even understand."

Fully clothed, they sat on the mat and stared at one another. They burst out laughing at the same time.

"Friends," Emily said, holding out her hand.

"Friends," Ben said solemnly. "For whatever this is worth, Emily, you're the first woman I've gotten close to for a long time. You're special, Emily. For some reason I don't think you know that yet, but you are."

"That's the nicest compliment anyone's ever given me, Ben." Suddenly, she was shy, unable to look at the man whose naked body she'd just mashed herself into.

"Well, I gotta be on my way. I have to go all the way to Murray Hill for my next session. Good luck with your decorating. If you need someone to hang curtains or drive nails, I'm a phone call away. I'd like to help, I really would."

"If I need you, I'll call," Emily said in the kitchen doorway. "Drive carefully."

"You're the only person who ever says that to me." Ben grinned. "I will. Have a nice day and don't overdo it."

"Bye, Ben."

"Bye, Emily."

Her adrenaline was still pumping so Emily opted for her second shower of the day. An hour later she was carrying boxes and bags into her new fitness center that was off Highway 27 with easy access from the road. There was adequate parking, and if she ever needed an overflow, the side streets would be handy.

It's ironic, she thought, that I'm between a bakery and a pizza parlor. Think positive, Emily. The rent was just right and the management company had agreed to install two showers and add a second bathroom. They agreed to pay half for the mirrored wall, but refused to lay down new tile or buy blinds for the huge plate glass window. She'd taken a three-year lease. She didn't know if it was a mistake or not. If things worked out, the rent was secure with no raises. Time to get things off the ground.

Emily looked around. Two thousand square feet seemed like a lot when the room was empty. Now with the rows of machines it didn't seem so big. Everything looked new, fresh and unused. Women liked things like that. At least she did. She dusted her hands dramatically before she started to unpack the boxes and bags.

She blinked when she held up the valances that matched the lightning bolt wallpaper Zoë said was a must. "You look at it and you want to move." The jagged streaks were every color of the spectrum and Zoë was right—just looking at the paper gave you an itch to move. The chairs and desk were plastic, bright in color and bought from Ikea. The floor was white and would be washed and waxed each night before closing. Modular shelves, all colors, rose from the floor to the ceiling behind the bright blue desk and Stop sign red chair.

The small room off the main exercise room was decorated in a soothing pale shade of green. It was carpeted in a deeper shade of green, still soothing and comfortable-looking. Nine futons lined the walls. Soft music would play in the background. This was the cooling-down room where clients would go to when they finished working out.

A small refrigerator filled with water, juices, and diet soft drinks stood in the corner. A bank in the shape of a large green apple was on top. Customers were on the honor system to deposit seventy-five cents if they bought a drink. The only other thing in the room was a small fish tank with two tropical fish named Harry and Harriet. Supposedly, watching fish swim relaxed a person. Ian had installed them in all his clinics and patients had commented on it. Ian went so far as to say watching the fish would bring a person's blood pressure down.

The bathrooms, with two showers each, were tiled, one in blue, one in pink with matching floors. The towels were pink and blue, all of them sewed by Lena, who'd bought toweling by the yard. They'd saved a small fortune by hemming their own and the plan was to install four sets of washers and dryers between the eight locations. According to Zoë, the machines would pay for themselves within a few months, provided they had customers who would use the towels. Emily had gotten a cramp in her stomach the day she wrote out the check to Tops for thirty-four hundred dollars. If things were slow, they could do their personal laundry, which Zoë said was advisable because they weren't paying for water and electricity at the clinics. It still boggled Emily's mind that the management company had agreed to absorb the electric and water bills. Possibly it was her grim determination, her don't-haggle-with-me,-I-have-other-places-I-can-rent attitude. Whatever it was, she'd made a good deal and she knew it.

The bright yellow phone on the bright blue desk rang. Emily sat down in the bright red chair and grinned from ear to ear. "Emily's Fitness Center," she said cheerfully.

"*Ooohhh,* call me back so I can say the same thing." Lena laughed. "You sound so good. How's it going?"

"I got the valance up. It looks great. All the towels are folded. My appointment book is still empty and so is the registration book. I just love it. I feel like I should be jumping around, doing something."

"That's the object. Did you hang your bell over the door?"

"Nope, that's what I'm going to do next. Do you think we made a mistake by not putting in some green plants? What do you think?"

"They cost money. I'm finished here so I can pick some up at the greenhouse if you think we need them."

"We don't *need* them, but they would look nice. They'll

reflect off the mirrors and look like we have twice as many. Some greenery on the shelves behind the desk would look nice. Maybe some philodendrons in clay pots or bright-colored pots. Do you have any money on you?"

"Three bucks, just enough for lunch. We need to start bringing lunch. Buying out is going to cost all of us. Kelly said she'd be willing to pack lunches for a while then we can take turns. I'll stop by for a check and head over to the greenhouse."

When Lena returned at two o'clock, her car loaded down with greenery, they transferred half of it to Emily's car and delivered the plants to the other six clinics. The philodendron for the shelves were in red, blue, and bright yellow pots. "It cost a little more, but I thought it added something," Lena said. They all agreed.

At four o'clock they were lined up like kids for a camp picture, dressed in their new sweatshirts, smiling for the reporter and photographer from the *Courier*. When it was over, Emily said, "I think it went well. I bet women flock in here day after tomorrow when we open for business. Get out your quarters, everyone, we're going to toast something."

"What?" Lena demanded. "We can't just make toasts willy-nilly. We need a reason."

"Well, we just had our picture taken, the clinics are technically open for business, we bought green plants, Kelly is going to start making lunches for all of us. All of that should be worth a toast. And if you don't like that list, how about I *almost,* the key word here is *almost,* had sex with Ben this morning. I fizzled out."

She was sharing with her peers, her friends—something she'd never had the opportunity to do before. They weren't going to judge her nor would they heckle her. If anything, they'd offer advice which she might or might not take.

"What kind of body does he have? Did he look like the Liberated Stud?" Martina demanded.

"Who had time to look? All of a sudden, there I was, drenched in my own sweat on that slick mat and I couldn't do it. I pulled away and covered my breasts with my arms. I suppose I acted like a fool, but I . . . I wanted to, but part of me wouldn't follow through. He was real nice about it; he even looked away while I put my clothes back on. After a while we both laughed about it. Do you think it means I'm still wrapped up in Ian? God, what if I can't be with another man? I like sex. It's that physical *fix* everyone needs from time to time. I'm tired of channeling my sex drive in other directions. I want it!"

"Good for you!" Martha chortled.

"Have I embarrassed any of you?" Emily asked. "I never really had friends to share things with. Oh, I had a friend during high school, but we didn't share intimate things. It seems like I'm a late bloomer in more ways than one. I guess I trust all of you."

"Emily, there is nothing wrong with you. You're being cautious. There's nothing wrong with being cautious. You haven't known Ben that long. Liking sex is fine, so don't be defensive about it. When it feels right, you'll do whatever you feel at the moment. I think you're still a bit vulnerable. Time will take care of everything," Lena said in her best motherly voice.

They shared confidences for a long time. It was almost dusk when they locked up, saluted the front door smartly, and left to return to the house on Sleepy Hollow Road.

The clinics didn't take off like a rocket, even with all the publicity the local newspapers generated. The word of mouth Emily counted on didn't happen. Five weeks into her endeavor, she started to panic when she wrote out rent checks and lease payments on the exercise equipment. In the five weeks since their grand opening, they'd netted only $965 on all eight clinics. She dipped into her nest egg with fear in her heart.

"It takes time to get a business off the ground," Lena said at their weekly meeting over the kitchen table.

"I don't understand. Ian opened the clinic and the next day we were swamped with patients and he wasn't that cheap either. We're cheap. What are we doing wrong? We have a walk-in policy and we have a membership policy. We take credit cards. Maybe we need some kind of entice-ment, a gimmick. Something. Instead of opening the clin-ics, maybe we should have gone around to big businesses and offered to open a clinic on their premises. Lunch-hour physical fitness, that kind of thing. I'm not giving up, but our money or our lack of money is going to start hurting real soon."

"We're saving on our water; we're showering at the clinics and doing our laundry there too."

"I have a cookbook with a hundred and one recipes for tuna fish," Zoë said. "I filched it from the library. We can't eat any cheaper or more nutritionally than we are. Is there anyplace else we can cut back?"

"Heat. We'll turn down the thermostat when we leave in the morning. That's going to help some. Maybe we should open later and stay open until eight in the evening. I think we should vote on that. A lot of women commute to New York and don't get home till six or seven. If we stay open till eight, we might have a shot at them."

"Or we look for a gimmick, like you suggested," Lena said.

Emily, her eyes on the Polaroid of the Liberated Stud, shouted, "That's it! Let's use him! I paid him fifty bucks plus tip for an hour to entertain us. We have eight clinics. We can each hire him for an hour. He can get his tips from the customers. It'll be good publicity for him and for us.

What do you think?" Emily cried excitedly. "If he agrees, we'll get that frontal shot of him flexing his muscles and have it blown up to poster size and plaster them all over the place. It might work. Let's call him and ask him to come over."

"Emily, that's four hundred dollars a day. Two thousand a week. That's an awful lot of money," Lena said, panic in her voice.

"He'd be a fool to turn it down," Emily said. "We'll figure out how much we have to take in in order to pay him and tell him in the beginning he's pretty much going to be doing it for nothing. If it takes off, he's going to make a lot of money. I think he might see the possibilities. I'm going to call him right now. Let's vote. Okay, the ayes have it." Emily rummaged in the kitchen drawer for the Stud's business card. Her eyes were wild when she dialed the number. She listened intently. She mouthed the words, He's on a gig, but will check his messages on the hour. The girls nodded. "This is Emily Thorn. My roommates and I have a business proposition to offer you. It's ten o'clock now. We'll be up till midnight. Please call, or stop by on your way home. My number is 555-7026."

After she'd hung up, Emily asked, "How'd that sound?"

"If it was me, I'd stop by," Lena said. The others agreed.

"Gin rummy, anyone?" Nancy asked, getting the cards out of the kitchen drawer.

At ten minutes of twelve the doorbell rang. As one they scrambled to the front door.

"What's your real name?" Emily demanded.

"Charley Wyland. What's up, ladies?"

Emily told him. "We're investing in you. The question is, will you lend yourself to us and invest in us? If we get off the ground, you stand to make a lot of money. What do you normally do in the way of work during the day?"

"I wash cars. I can't do anything too physical, can't ruin

this body, you know. How long before the money starts rolling in?"

"In a way, that's going to depend on you. We're going to target the housewife. Each hour you'll do a different clinic. We're going to be staying open till eight. Will that cut into your nighttime job?"

"No, I usually don't start till nine. I'll give it a try. A month. If it doesn't work out, I'm gone. I will need gas money, though, and lunch money."

"No, no, no, you eat the lunches we prepare. We're on a tight budget," Zoë said.

"You ladies drive a hard bargain," Charley said.

"Who knows? Chippendales might offer you a job when we're done with you," Emily quipped. "We need you to sign something that says it's okay to make up posters. You pick the photo you want. We'll do the rest. Can you be ready to start a week from today?"

"I'll be ready. That one," he said, pointing to the picture Emily and the others favored. "I like your wallpaper." He grinned.

"We've had many lively discussions out here looking at those photos." Emily laughed. "We'll make up a schedule and I'll give you a call."

"See you around."

Whatever it takes. Whatever I have to do, I'll do, Emily thought as she made her way upstairs. It was going to work, she could feel it in her bones, feel the success, the satisfaction. Whatever it takes.

It was two weeks before the women were satisfied with what they called the Charley Wyland blitz promotional package. They literally worked around the clock and aired the video Emily insisted Charley make on all the cable channels in the area. The newspapers carried a regular rogue's gallery of shots showing Charley in every imaginable pose in their weekend Lifetime sections.

According to Charley, he was getting calls for gigs and was booked into the following year. It was Emily's suggestion that he hire a group of dancers and train them to put on an all-male revue every so often. "It'll be your own business on the side and you take a cut of the profits," she said to encourage him.

Charley countered with, "Emily, I'm not sure you're heading in the right direction. It all sounds great and I love the idea of performing for all your ladies, but I think you're losing sight of what it is you're hoping to accomplish. Your clientele is middle-aged women. I think you need older men, men like Ben who are fit and look good. I'm a fantasy and I say this with great modesty. I don't think that's fair. I can see the revue as a fun thing, but I think you need to rethink this strategy."

"How old did you say you are?"

"Twenty-four."

"You know what, Charley, I think you are absolutely right. I guess I'm so desperate to make this a success, I didn't think it through. The others followed my lead. It's kind of late to switch up now; all the publicity is in place."

"I can be a Grand Opening flash and you phase in the other way a little at a time. I'd hate to see you fail, Emily. You ladies have all worked so hard. Think about it."

"I think you're right, Charley. I'll call a meeting and see what the others have to say. Would you be amenable to hiring some older men and training them too? Stress physical fitness above dancing, though."

"Well, sure. Ben probably knows a lot of guys who might be interested. Women tend to think only women teach aerobics. With serious-minded men teaching classes, the women will try harder. That's my opinion."

"It's a good one, Charley. Thanks for the advice."

"You have a lot of money tied up in this venture, don't you?"

"My retirement money. When it's gone, if this doesn't work out, I'm back to waitressing. My degree can never earn me the kind of money I'll need for my twilight years. God, that sounds terrible—twilight years. I don't imagine you can even comprehend that."

"Are you kidding? My dad split fifteen years ago and my mom had to take over. She works in the office of a lawn maintenance company. She works weekends cashiering at a drugstore. She put me through junior college, but we both realized that wasn't for me. I help out; in fact, I give her most of my money. She doesn't have any kind of pension and my dad's insurance ran out a long time ago. If you ever get this off the ground, maybe you can hire her and put her in your fund. You did say this was about women helping women, right?"

"Yes, that's what it's all about. I'll do my best, Charley. Are you nervous?"

"Nah. Well, maybe a little bit. If this works out, I want to get into bodybuilding. That's *my* dream. My mom can take over the training class if we get this off the ground."

"We'll help in any way we can," Emily said. "That's a promise, Charley. And . . . Charley, I want to ask you something, and after you answer me, I want you to forget I asked. Agreed?" Charley nodded. "Am I, in your opinion, exploiting women? I'm sure with all the publicity you've gotten in the past few weeks you've heard a lot of . . . you know. I don't want to do anything that will degrade you or the ladies who come to the clinics to work out."

"I asked my mom that same question and she said no. The way I see it is you're trying to get a business off the ground. Your goals are what's important. I entertain. You're hiring me to give your ladies incentives to be the best they can be. Look, Emily," Charley said, placing his hands on her shoulders, "you do whatever you have to do to get this business off and running. If for some reason it doesn't work out, and I don't think that's going to happen, but if it does, you'll know you gave it your all. Keep your goals in mind and do whatever you gotta do."

"That's pretty much how I look at it, but I am so worried I won't be able to pull this off. On paper it looks good. In theory it looks even better. The reality is what I fear."

"Hey, Emily, you know what they say about fear. There's nothing to fear, but fear itself."

"I seem to recall hearing that once or twice in my lifetime," Emily said wryly.

"Third time's the charm." Charley laughed. "Chin up, Emily."

The Emily's Fitness Centers' second grand opening happened precisely at noon the following day. Women attired in business suits and high heels and carrying briefcases stood next to mothers with tots in strollers who mingled with students from the local college. Charley arrived in his yellow satin cape with matching Speedo suit. Emily didn't know what to expect, catcalls maybe, shrill whistles, but it didn't happen as the women lined up for the aerobics class while others took to the machines. Mentally she tried to calculate the money the hour was going to bring in as she settled herself behind the desk, registration cards in front of her.

Emily listened in awe as Charley gave a brief speech about nutrition, caring for one's body, self-satisfaction, and the rewards that would follow if all of the above were adhered to. Then he turned on his tape deck and proceeded with the first of his two thirty-minute aerobics classes. This time Emily did hear little sighs of pleasure from the women on the machines.

When the hour was over, the women again stood in line to sign up and pay for their membership. There were so many queries Emily found herself hard-pressed to answer them all. The main question seemed to concern the aerobics class. "Three times a week is what we're scheduled for at the moment. We're working on the schedules. The clinics are interchangeable. If you can't make it at this location, you can go to one of the others. The aerobic fees are separate, but they do entitle you to use the machines for thirty minutes after the class."

No one complained. Everyone left with tired smiles. One and all were invited back for a free orientation class at closing, which was scheduled for eight-thirty. Emily stressed the word *free*.

One by one the women straggled back to the house on Sleepy Hollow Road. Emily was the last to arrive at ten-thirty. Zoë poured hot chocolate for Emily and offered her a sugar cookie, which she devoured greedily. She immediately lit a cigarette. "I didn't smoke today. I didn't have time. I can hardly believe it," Emily said wearily. She tossed her cash bag on the table. "Someone else has to count it, I'm whipped."

"Let's do it in the morning," Lena said, gathering up the bags to put in the freezer; their in-house safe. She whirled around to set the security alarm.

"Turn it off, we have to go home," Rose said. The others waited for Helen to speak, and when she didn't, Emily burst out laughing.

"You did it, you broke that cord. How'd it go?"

Helen smiled. "I was so busy trying to explain how the digital gadgets work on the machines I didn't have time to worry. I didn't even call Rose until seven o'clock. I did everything myself. For the first time in my life."

"Rose?"

"It worked the same way for me," she said shyly.

"That's more important than anything else we did today," Emily said. The others agreed.

"You guys go ahead and talk. I'm going back to the apartment and soak in a hot bath. You coming, Rose?" Helen asked.

"No, I'm going to have another cup of hot chocolate. I'll be quiet when I open the door."

"Okay," Helen said cheerfully.

"I'm going to bed too. Listen, let's meet here in the kitchen and talk in the morning. Charley and I had a talk early today. We've got some kinks to work out and one of my machines isn't working properly. Whose towels am I doing tomorrow?"

"Mine," Lena said. "They're in my car. I'll load them in yours in the morning and pick up your clean ones. Next week I do the laundry, right?"

"Yes. See you in the morning."

In her room, Emily stripped down and fell into bed. She was almost asleep when she remembered she had to call Ben Jackson. He wasn't home so she left a groggy-sounding message asking him to stop by the clinic around noon. She was about to drift off when it occurred to her that it was after eleven. Where was Ben at this hour? Not that it was any of her business. Or was it?

Chapter 12

Shortly before noon the next day Ben Jackson entered the clinic and said, "Whoa, you need sunglasses when you come in here. Sorry I wasn't home when you called last night. How'd it go with Mr. Sex Appeal?"

"We had a *great* day financially. If it keeps up, we'll do okay, but I'm realist enough to know it can't keep up like that. Charley and I had a talk yesterday. Meet me in the cool-down room; I have to explain how these machines work to that lady in the green sweat suit."

"If you tell me where the cool-down room is, I'll be glad to meet you there."

"Around the corner. If you get bored, feed Harry and Harriet." Emily grinned.

When Emily joined Ben fifteen minutes later, she laughed at the way he was sprawled out on the futon, his eyes glued to the fish tank. "Before you ask whatever it is you're going to ask me, I want to ask you something. Will you have dinner with me on Saturday night?"

"You mean a date?" She felt flustered, remembering the time they'd been glued to the workout mat.

"*Date*'s a good word. Two people having dinner. I can pick you up and then it's a real date. If you meet me at the restaurant, we're two people having dinner."

Emily's face was as pink as the towel in her hand. "Okay. You can . . . you can pick me up."

"Okay, that sounds good. Chinese, Italian, French?"

"Chinese. I like Italian and French too," Emily said carefully.

"Well, I guess we could go Chinese for the wonton soup, hit the Italian for the ravioli, and then go French for some chocolate mousse," Ben said with a straight face. "Busy night, though."

"Chinese."

"Sounds good. I'm looking forward to my fortune cookie already. How about you?"

"Can't wait."

"Six-thirty okay?"

"Six-thirty's good. We close at six. Pick me up here, okay? I hate to admit this, but we're showering here at the clinics to save on our water bill at home," Emily said.

"Makes sense. Now, what do you want to talk to me about?"

Emily told him about the conversation she had with Charley. "I think he's right. These clinics are geared to middle-aged women. You're middle-aged and you look . . . good. They'll be comfortable with you."

"Comfortable!" Ben protested. "Comfortable!"

"You know what I mean," Emily said, remembering the feel of his body next to hers.

"I'm not into satin capes and Speedo tights or whatever that . . . that thing is the guy wears."

"It's a bathing suit. They sell them everywhere."

"To exhibitionists," Ben grated. "I'm not shaving the hair on my body. And I'm not oiling it either."

"Does that mean you'll do it?"

"It means I'll think about it," Ben said.

"You'll have to sign up for Charley's class. I'll pay for it."

"Emily, I'm forty-five years old. Do you really expect me to get up there with those young studs and do . . . well, whatever the hell it is they do? Oh, no, that's not for me."

"How about private lessons?"

"If you give them to me. You've seen the video a hundred times. But at your house. I still have to think about this. I'm not committing."

"A private lesson is good," Emily said weakly. "Do you think it will help, Ben? Your honest opinion."

"Sex sells. Everyone knows that. Alluding to sex sells. Sex is fun. I'm just not sure I'm up to peddling my body. At my age it seems a little decadent." There was a hint of a smile on his face, Emily noticed.

"Uh-huh. I guess that's a good answer. What you're saying is it will probably work. At least for the time being. Decadent is in," she said devilishly.

"On that thought, I'm going to leave you. I have to go to Princeton to do a workout with some executive who's seventy-eight pounds overweight. I'll see you Saturday."

"I'll look forward to it."

"See that you do," Ben said, rapping her butt with one of the pink towels.

He's flirting with me. A man is flirting with me. A man has asked me out on a date and I said yes. A man is really taking me out to dinner and he's going to pay for it. Oh, my. What to wear?

Seven phone calls later it was agreed that she was to wear a dress with a long, circular skirt with an Indian pattern, low-heeled shoes because she was just as tall as Ben, with a single strand of pearls and pearl earrings. When Emily hung up the phone, she decided her friends were more excited than she was.

She thought about Ian then because she always thought about Ian when things were going badly or particularly well. Where was he? Had he filed for a divorce? Bastard.

He'd never called once to see if she was alive or dead. You're renting space in your head to Ian and he isn't paying for it, Emily. Shelve it. Think about your date with a very nice man. Think about how well you get along. He likes you. He teases you, flirts with you. When did Ian ever do that? Only when he wanted something from you.

Business was brisk, but not overwhelming. Slow and steady. Emily had time to do some of the laundry, chat with her new customers, and still call the other clinics to see how they were doing. All of them gave positive reports.

How long was it going to last? Ben didn't seem overly optimistic. Sex sells, he'd said, but what happened when women got tired of looking at young muscular bodies? What happened when they decided they didn't want to look at Ben Jackson? Then I'm just another exercise clinic or health club. What made her clinic different from a health club? A club had members who gathered for a common purpose whereas a clinic was a facility for diagnosis and treatment for outpatients. She truly believed in her heart that, psychologically, women in midlife felt more comfortable knowing they were in a clinic as opposed to a club.

"Whatever will be, will be," Emily murmured. "If I fail, I'll go on to something else." She looked at her watch. Fifteen minutes until the ladies on the NordicTracks were due to move on to the treadmills. Time to read up on the herb book Lena had given her. She made notes as she read. It was all so interesting she had to be called twice when the buzzers on the machines went off.

Inside the workout room, Emily addressed the nine women on the machines. "I'd like to ask you a few questions. How do you all feel about herbs? What I mean is, if I told you there were herbs you could take to keep your bodies in good shape, would you take them, knowing what we all know about osteoporosis in women our age? Just raise your hand. How about teas made from the herbs— would you drink them?" All nine hands shot in the air. "Would you drink them here or would you make them at home?" Fifty fifty.

"Let me ask you something else. If I held a class over the weekend at one of the clinics on nutrition, herbs, and vitamins, would any of you take the time to come and listen? The class would be free, of course." Seven hands shot in the air.

"I work weekends," one woman said.

"I go to Pennsylvania to see my mother in a nursing home," the other woman said. "I'd take any literature you have, though. If you had a class during the week or at lunchtime, I might be able to make it. Is it a one-time class or is it ongoing?"

"I'm not sure. I just want to get a feel for how receptive you ladies are. It's preventative. However, there are herbs for ailments too."

"Give us an example of both," a woman on the exercycle called out.

"A tea made with mistletoe will help to bring down high blood pressure. You can mix it with angelica root, ground fine, mix two teaspoons of each in a pint of water and bring to a boiling point, cool it and drink two or three cups a day. You might be interested to know mistletoe is the only herb mentioned in the U.S. Dispensatory as a treatment for high blood pressure. That's if any of you are interested.

"Here's one for hair. It prevents you from going gray. I'm going to try it myself. You make a tea from the leaves of a grape vine and wash your hair in it once a month. Supposedly Indians used it. Some lady in Utah says it works. I guess you could use it as often as you wish."

"You got any more, Emily?"

"How about flushing out fat and cholesterol with garlic and vinegar."

"If it works, you could probably make a fortune."

"Better be prepared for the medical profession to come down on you real hard."

"I'm for whatever works," a woman doing leg lifts gasped.

"That's pretty much how I feel about it," Emily said. "I'm not saying people shouldn't take prescription drugs. I'm saying if there's a way to treat a condition or ailment without drugs, try it." The women concurred.

This from someone who used to be married to a doctor, Emily thought as she made her way to the front desk to answer the ringing phone.

Emily listened for a moment, her eye on two of the women on the machines. She rattled off her spiel automatically. "We have a pay-as-you-go program or we can do a full year's membership. I offer one-on-one counseling. We suggest before embarking on any physical fitness program that you check with your doctor. Yes, our machines have pulse and heart monitors. We'll teach you how to take your own pulse when you're doing aerobics. We have showers and a cool-down room. So far we haven't had any men sign up. We're a chain organized for middle-aged women. Most of our clients are over forty. Yes, we know when to call a halt if you start to sweat too much. Of course we have a television set for you to watch while you're exercising. I understand you want to watch your soap operas. Killing two birds with one stone is good if that's how you feel. Food? We'll give you a wide selection of diets to follow. Of course it's the honor system. Yes, it is your body. Freeze-dried food? We're working on it, but as of now, no, we don't have it."

Emily hung up the phone and rushed to turn off the

treadmill. "That's enough for you, Mrs. Sanchez. Tomorrow you'll increase it by two or three minutes. You didn't put that weight on overnight and it isn't going to go away with a few sessions. You want to do this right and lose your weight slowly. Inches are important. We're striving here to lose body fat. Twelve minutes on the exercycle and then you cool down. Can you read while you're cycling? Good, here's a book on herbal medicine I'd like you to peruse. You're doing well, I'm proud of you," Emily said, patting the chunky woman on the shoulder. The woman beamed with Emily's praise. *And I would have killed for a kind word while I was torturing myself.* One woman helping another, that's what it was all about.

Emily woke on Saturday with a feeling that something wonderful was going to happen. While she dressed, she played her date back and forth in her mind. Dinner meant dinner. Nothing was said about after dinner. Maybe they'd stop at Charlie Brown's for a drink since the Chinese restaurant didn't serve liquor. And then . . . and then . . . back to her house or back to Ben's apartment? Did she have the nerve to go? Would he ask her back to see his etchings? Did they use that term anymore or did they say something like, Let's go back to my apartment to see my new CD player or let's check out my big screen TV? Maybe they were even more risqué and suggested X-rated movies. She needed a plan. Asking her roommates would be futile since they'd been as dateless as she was. She could follow Ben in her car, since he was picking her up at the clinic.

She caught her reflection in the mirror. Emily Thorn stared back at her. She squinted, trying to see traces of the long-ago Emily, but age and the ravages of her life had definitely taken their toll. With her index finger she pulled skin toward her ears, from around her eyes. Makeup could only do so much. A facial even less. The loose skin around her neck bothered her, but at least she'd lost most of her triple chin. She was not pretty, didn't consider herself attractive at all. Why was Ben taking her to dinner? What did he expect? Better yet, Emily, what do *you* expect? What I expect is . . . is a nice dinner with someone I'm comfortable with, maybe a drink afterward and then . . . and then, perhaps a long, lingering kiss. Nothing more. I wish I could turn the clock backward, erase the calendar, become the old Emily with a twitch of the nose or an airy wave of a finger.

In the kitchen over a bagel and coffee, Emily listened to the good-natured teasing about her date. Her face was warm, but she loved every minute of it. A collective "Don't do anything we wouldn't do" rang in her ears as she scurried through the door, her dress and makeup bag under her arm. "I'll see you . . . whenever." She smiled as she listened to the hoots of laughter that followed her to the car.

The hours passed quickly. Saturdays, she'd found out, were her busiest days. She had a system now for the machines as well as the aerobic classes. "Smooth as silk," she'd told the other girls. Damn, she felt good. Really good. She was doing something she loved, something she was convinced in her heart would work, and while she was doing it, she was helping other women.

The hours passed, and before she knew it, the last group of women were packing up to leave. They called her Emily and asked her advice on their workout clothes, on any number of things. She was a mentor now and she thrived on it.

"C'mon, c'mon," she said, making shooing motions with her hands. "I have a date and you guys are going to make me late. You don't want that on your conscience, do you?"

"We want to hear all about it next week," the last woman through the door said, grinning. "Take notes."

"You bet," Emily promised. She locked the door, closed the blinds, and sprinted for the shower.

When her hair was dry, her large, gold hoop earrings in place, she stood back to admire her reflection. The Indian print skirt was perfect. The wide leather belt with its ornate clasp riding low on her hips with the top bloused over it was more than fashionable. Kelly's contribution. The suede boots, a rich copper color, were comfortable—contributed by Martina. The burlap carry bag with its leather handles and buckles were donated by Nancy.

Emily opened her makeup bag. She had one of everything. It really wasn't going to help her to make up. If anything, makeup, no matter how skillfully she applied it, would call attention to the fat deposits under her eyes, announce the deep creases around her mouth and nose. Better to smile a lot and pretend they were laugh lines. Her fingers found the loose skin under her chin. Too much, way too much. And she was getting liver spots. She wasn't sure if she could tolerate the ugly, brown blotches much longer. She had one in the middle of her nose that definitely had to go, but it was the ones on the backs of her hands that bothered her the most. If she wanted to pay out the money, she could go to a good dermatologist and have them singed off. She made a mental note to call the first of the week for an appointment. She made a second mental note to seriously look into cosmetic surgery. A nip, a tuck, or an entire overhaul. If she sold her furs, it would probably cover the cost. Something for herself. And she was going to look into the possibility of having the veins in her legs stripped. She wondered what it would be like to be free of the awful ache in her legs. She'd lived with the aches and pains for so long it was a way of life.

Emily made a face at her reflection before she applied her lipstick and a little mascara to the tips of her eyelashes. She dabbed a little perfume, perfume she'd bought herself, which she liked, behind her ears, in the bends of her elbows.

Emily turned off the light, then walked to the front of the clinic to unlock the front door so Ben could just walk in. She walked back to the cool-down room and sat down on one of the futons. She watched Harry and Harriet as they cavorted in their tank.

"Emily!"

"Back here," Emily called back. "I just have to get my coat and I'm ready. I can follow you, Ben; this way you won't have to take me home."

"Hey, when I pick up a date, I take her home. Or in this case, I'll bring you back here to get your car."

"Okay," Emily said.

"It's raining out. I parked at the far end of the lot. Do you have an umbrella? No, huh? Okay, I'll drive around and pick you up in front."

"No, it's okay. I like walking in the rain, do you?"

"Hell yes, it's one of my favorite pastimes. My son and I slosh around in the rain all summer long, to his mother's horror. I'm forever buying him new sneakers."

"Really! Then let's walk. Wait a minute, I want to close all the blinds."

Outside in the rain, Ben asked, "Don't you worry about your hair?"

Emily laughed. "It just gets curlier. Oooh, look at that big puddle." She let go of his arm and ran forward to stomp in the circle of water that covered her boots. She turned to see Ben stomp in it right alongside her. "Let's find another one," she suggested. "There's one over there and there's another one! *Ooohhh,* here comes a pickup."

No sooner were the words out of her mouth when the puddle splashed upward, drenching both of them.

The pickup stopped then backed up. "Hey, I'm sorry. Can I give you people a lift?"

"No way," Emily said.

Ben grinned. "I'm with the lady."

"Okay, I'm sorry."

They received a second drenching when the pickup's tires spewed water as it sped away.

"You know what, Emily Thorn, you look green and purple under these lights," Ben guffawed as he pointed to the arced lights in the parking lot. "Listen, we can't go to a restaurant looking like this. We can either go back into the clinic and dry our clothes or we can go to my place and I can whip us up some supper, or as a third choice, we can stop and take some Chinese home. Your call, Emily."

"Can you cook?"

"Of course I can cook. Not well, but I can throw things together. My specialty is bacon and eggs. I have both."

"I love bacon and eggs. I haven't had them in a very long time. I like to dip my toast in the yolk and then dip it in coffee."

"I do too. My mother used to tell me I couldn't do that in a restaurant, and then when I was old enough to eat out on my own, I saw everyone do it. I like the yolks best in fried eggs, but I like the whites best on hard boiled eggs. I throw away the yolks."

"I do too. Imagine that," Emily said, climbing into Ben's car. "Do you have a dryer at your place?"

"Sure do. My son gives it a workout every time he comes to visit. I tried to make my place an extension of his home with his mother. He has his own room, his own things, his own television. Divorce is hard on kids. Be glad you didn't have that problem. I don't mean . . ."

"I know what you mean," Emily said. "Was it hard on you?"

"Yeah, it was, but you go on because that's all that's left for you to do. You don't look back. I learned that the hard way. Things are better now. Now I look forward to getting up in the morning, I look forward to what the day will bring and talking with my son at night. It gets lonely sometimes, but those times are almost over. I have a life like you do now. The bottom line is you go on. Some people never learn that little fact. I have a friend who refuses to let go. His wife cleaned him out; she got everything. He spends so much time and energy on ways to harass her, he isn't living, he's existing. Just two weeks ago he slashed the tires on her car in the middle of the night. A month ago he hid in the bushes and threw rotten fruit and vegetables he'd been saving for weeks up against her front door. He gets caught and then she has to talk to him. She won't press charges so he keeps doing it. Now, I ask you, what's the point? She has a new boyfriend and is getting married in a few months. She's going to move out of state to get away from him and he's trying to fight it with the legal system."

"What will happen to him if his wife moves away?"

"First of all, they're divorced, so she isn't his wife anymore. He's going to get a dose of hard reality when she marries and moves away."

"Be there for him, Ben. I didn't have anyone for a long time. I know how he feels. Rejection is . . . it's so demeaning. You want to hide in a dark closet."

"Here we are," Ben said, steering his car into his assigned parking space. "When I bought this place, I had a choice of a garage or a fireplace. I opted for the fireplace. My son is a Boy Scout and he loves to make fires. In the winter we build a fire and tell scary stories at night and toast marshmallows. I make a lot of popcorn. I have one of those poppers they make just for fireplaces. It's great!"

She liked this man. She almost said, Have you ever made love in front of a fireplace, but she bit her tongue instead. "I'm freezing."

"That will teach you to walk in the rain and jump in puddles." Ben laughed as he opened the front door and turned on the light. "Upstairs to your left is my son's room. It has a bath. In the hall closet next to the bathroom you'll find a robe. Bring your clothes down and I'll dry them."

"What about you?"

"I have some clothes in the laundry room. I want you to look now, I got spiffed up for this date," he said, opening his jacket to reveal a pullover sweater over a neat white collar. His cords were sharply creased but drenched around the ankles. He dripped water on the beige carpet.

"Duly noted," Emily said as she made her way up the stairs.

She didn't take note of the boy's room until she was dressed and warm in one of Ben's robes. It smelled like him. It was a wonderful room filled with sports equipment and bright color. A parade of toy soldiers, worn and handled, marched along a white shelf next to a pile of teddy bears that were equally worn and handled. In the corner, a baseball bat, a glove, and a box of balls sat waiting. A lamp whose base was a real football stood next to the bed. It was an old football, probably one of Ben's from his youth. She touched the leather, noted the frayed strings that had been sprayed with some kind of lacquer. Next to the closet door was a sled, a Flexible Flyer with the Y in flyer almost obliterated. It must have been Ben's sled that he'd saved for his son. She knew he was a wonderful father. Three-shelf bookcases were under both windows, jammed with all kinds of boy's books: the Hardy Boys, the Bobbsey Twins, Huck Finn. All of them were old ones, well thumbed, the pages yellow. New books, most of them adventures, were squeezed in between the old books. Puzzle books, books about sports, trains, and airplanes were jammed every which way on the bottom shelf next to a string bag of Leggos. A desk with a swivel chair was opposite the bed. Cups of pencils, all the erasers gone, stood sentinel on each end of the desk. Tablets of school paper and spiral notebooks sat in the middle of a doodled pad. She turned, tested the mattress of the single bed. Firm, but comfortable. She liked the baseball figures at bat that speckled the cotton spread. The drapes matched the spread perfectly.

"Is everything all right, Emily?"

She hadn't heard him come up. "I bet your son loves this room," she said quietly. "It's wonderful. Did you do it yourself?"

"Ted and I did it together. When I first moved here, I was tapped out as far as money went. I pretty much lived out of cartons for a while, but the courts said I had to have a room for Ted with his own things so I got stuff out of storage, from my parents' house. Stuff my wife didn't want. I asked Ted and he loved the idea of having some of my old things so that's the route we went. He likes coming here, looks forward to it. I think it's a happy room, what do you think?"

"Oh, yes. I'm sorry I never . . . Ian had our house decorated . . . I didn't even . . . that's all in the past. So tell me, how's our supper coming?"

Ben laughed. "I've been waiting for you to do the toast. I softened up the butter for you. I have jam, not jelly. What's your feeling on that, Emily?"

"I adore jam, hate jelly sliding all over my toast."

"Me too," Ben said happily. "How about the bacon?"

"Extra crisp, snap in two. Four slices."

"A lady after my own heart. How about the eggs?"

"Over easy, I want the yolks really runny. I think I'd like three."

Ben threw his head back and laughed. "Emily Thorn, your taste in food is impeccable. As you can see, I have eight slices of bacon all laid out as well as six eggs. Three slices of toast each, right."

"Uh-huh. Are we having dessert? I like something sweet after a meal like this. Usually I eat mandarin orange slices."

"Jesus," Ben said, opening the cabinet over the sink to reveal nine cans of mandarin orange slices. "I want my own can," he said.

"I do too," Emily said.

They stared at each other, their eyes wide with wonder. Emily was the first to look away, her neck warm.

They ate like starving truck drivers, finishing at exactly the same time. They ate their orange slices out of the cans and drank the juice the same way.

"We are not going to do the dishes. I have to get up early tomorrow to pick up Ted so I'll do them then."

"That's the nicest thing you've ever said to me, Ben Jackson," Emily said, getting up and beelining for the living room. Ben followed her with a tray that held fresh coffee and a bottle of brandy. He set them down on the coffee table. "You pour and I'll light the artificial log. One log or two?"

Emily giggled. "Two. I like big fires. Don't you use wood?"

"I need to get some. Ted and I will probably pick some up tomorrow at the supermarket. Did you know you can buy bundles for three bucks each?"

"I didn't know that. Anytime you want *free* wood, go by my house. I have a ton of it stacked up behind the garage."

Ben sat down next to Emily and propped his feet on the circular table. Emily did the same. Outside, the rain pelted the windows. "Do you like rainstorms in the summer— you know, lots of thunder and lightning?" she asked.

"I do. There's nothing like a storm to clear the air. I like watching it through the window. My parents used to have a screened-in back porch and I'd sit on the swing and watch until it was over. It made my mother nervous. Ted likes storms too. He's a lot like me. How about you?"

"I watch through the window too. For some reason when a storm is over, I always feel better. These days I'm grateful for most anything that makes me feel good," Emily murmured.

"You mean things like this?" Ben said, leaning over to kiss her lightly on the mouth.

Emily smiled. "Yes, things like that."

"I can do it again if you like."

"I like." Her smile was wider this time.

"Maybe we should stop now before . . ."

"No. That was then, this is now. How about we agree now that it's going to be whatever it's going to be and nei- ther one of us is committing to the other. I think I need to keep that clear in my head."

"We could talk this to death if we keep it up, but okay." He reached over to gather her in his arms.

Suddenly she was all over him, her hands feverish, her mouth crushing his. Breathless, he pulled away and said, "Whoa, Emily, what's going on here?"

"*Shhhh,*" she said. "This is what you want and I'm going to give it to you."

"No!" It was a thunderbolt to her brain. She blinked, reared back, a look of stupefied amazement on her face. She shook her head to clear it. "No! Is that what you said?"

"That's what I said. Listen, I . . . I might be off base

here, but I have the feeling you think I'm somebody else . . . your husband maybe. I like rousing lovemaking as well as the next person and I like to give as good as I get, but you aren't giving me a chance. I'm not your husband, Emily. I'm me. I want to make love to you. I don't want to rape you and I don't want you to rape me. Lovemaking takes two people. There's one person too many in this room, and if he doesn't leave, we don't stand much of a chance."

Mortified, her body flushed with shame, Emily gathered the robe about her, refusing to meet Ben's gaze. "I . . . call me a taxi, please. I'm sure my clothes are dry." Her tongue felt like it was triple in size. In her life she'd never been so shamed.

"Emily . . ."

There was no moistness at all in her mouth. She had to defend herself. How? How did she do that?

"Emily . . ."

Emily sprinted for the stairs before she realized her clothes were downstairs in the laundry room. She ran back down, tears streaming down her cheeks. She would not look at the man who'd just humiliated her. What had she done to make Ben react the way he had? Taken the lead? Weren't women supposed to do that sometimes. All the slick magazines said a woman was supposed to tell her mate, her lover, what she wanted. Did they mean words instead of actions? Obviously, she'd missed the point in the article she'd read.

In the laundry room, with the door closed, Emily yanked at the robe and pulled on her clothes. Her breathing was ragged, her eyes full of misery as she pulled on her boots. God, where was her coat? Hanging over the back of a chair by the fireplace. Which meant she had to go back into the living room, pass Ben, look at him, talk to him. The stubborn streak in her surfaced as she noticed for the first time the door that led to a small outdoor patio. She knew she was being stupid when she opened the door. Rain splashed inside. Was she really prepared to walk five miles to the clinic, where she'd left her car? Deal with this, Emily, then you can move on. You're past that other garbage. Open the door, call the taxi yourself, and then you can wait outside on the little porch.

Emily opened the door. How did one cover shame? With one's head up in the air, eye contact, words? All of the above. Act like nothing happened, put on your coat, call the taxi. But something did happen. Something that was going to set her back emotionally. If she let it happen. Dignity. She needed it now. She marched over to the wall phone, dialed the number for the South Plainfield Taxi Company, gave the address, and was told a cab would be there in seven minutes.

"Thank you for dinner. I'm sorry you have to do the dishes. I called a cab; it will be here any minute now. I'll wait outside."

"Emily . . ."

"I think it best if I withdraw my offer to you to work in the clinics. I don't think I'll be needing a personal trainer any longer. If I owe you any money, send me a bill. Goodby, Ben."

"Emily . . ."

Emily closed the door before she realized the little porch didn't have a roof. It really wasn't a porch at all; it was a concrete slab with a rail around it but no roof overhead. She was drenched in seconds. Twice in one night. "Who gives a good rat's ass?" she muttered.

The taxi arrived just as Ben opened the door. "Goddamn it, Emily, get in here. We need to talk."

"You already did that," Emily shouted to be heard over the pouring rain as she sprinted to the cab. She was shivering violently when she settled herself in the backseat. Her teeth were chattering when she gave the driver the address of the clinic. She did her best to scrunch herself into the corner. Shame rivered through her. She wanted to cry, needed to cry. You always cry, Emily. Crying doesn't solve anything. You should have listened to what he had to say. You never listen; you act and then you're sorry. It's that same stubborn streak that made you sign away your share of the clinics. Stupid, stupid, stupid.

Emily thrust a five-dollar bill at the driver, keys in hand, as she jumped out of the cab. She had the door to the clinic opened in seconds, the blind pulled, the door locked. She ran through the room in the dark, skirting the machines, to the back and into the bathroom. She slammed the door shut, locked it before she turned on the light. She peeled off her clothes for the second time, turned on the shower and stepped in. Maybe she could wash away Ben's words, her shame, her rejection. She lathered and scrubbed, lathered again and again. The bathroom was so steamy she couldn't see her reflection in the mirror. That was good. She had no desire to see Emily Thorn. Seeing her and being her were two different things. "I liked him. I really liked him," she blubbered.

She was pulling on her sweat pants when she heard someone bang on the front door. Ben! She turned off the light in the bathroom, crept out into the little hallway. She could see his shadow outlined on the blinds by the front door, heard him call her name, heard him say he was going to stand there all night until she was ready to come out and talk to him. "So stand there, be a jerk, see if I care." She inched her way into the cool-down room and dialed the house on Sleepy Hollow Road. "Lena, it's me, just listen and do what I tell you. Come to the clinic, drive around by the back and pick me up. Please. Ben's banging on the front door and he says he won't leave. I'll tell you about it when we get home. I'm sorry to ask you to come out on a night like this. I'll be ready when you get here. Thank you, Lena," Emily said, her voice breaking.

Ben was still banging on the front door when Emily opened the back door a crack when she heard the sound of a car's engine. It was the Demster twins with their van, all of her roommates inside. She was so overwhelmed with relief she collapsed against Martina, who held her close, crooning soothing words of comfort. "Don't put your lights on; drive to the end and leave by the back entrance," Emily croaked.

"Here, take a slug of this," Lena said, holding up a pint bottle of brandy. Emily obediently took a healthy pull and sputtered, her eyes watering.

"Should I burn rubber, Emily?" Rose Demster asked, her shoulders squaring over the wheel, her grip firm.

"Go for it," her twin ordered.

They roared into the driveway sixteen minutes later. Nancy raced ahead to open the back door. She stood aside as the mad rush for warmth and light tracked her. Lena shot the bolt on the door and punched in the alarm's code. "Safe!"

"If we think Mr. Jackson is going to come here, I suggest we relocate to my rooms in the basement," Martha said. "We can make coffee and tea down there. Bring that brandy bottle and another one if we have it."

"All we need is a fire and we could pose as the Campfire Girls," Lena said solemnly as she took her place in the circle on the floor. "This is warm and cozy. It really is warm down here. I just love the sound of coffee dripping and perking, whatever it's doing. I like that tray in the middle of the circle. It kind of makes things official, that this is an important . . . pow-wow." Lena passed the brandy bottle around the circle. Each woman took a stinging gulp before she passed it on.

"Did he try to rape you?" Martina asked. Her eyes were murderous.

"No. No, nothing like that. I'm sorry if you all thought . . . let me tell you what happened. It's the end I can't . . . just listen, okay."

Emily looked around the circle. They were her friends. They would understand; she was sure of it. They would be objective, possibly see something she didn't see, help her to understand. She started to speak, haltingly at first, and then the words tumbled out, faster than she thought possible. "It's the shame. I've never been with a man other than Ian. I thought . . . how was I supposed to know . . . I'm middle-aged, I'm not up on all the . . . I ran. I panicked and ran. He wanted to talk to me, but I was so ashamed and I don't know why I'm ashamed. There we were, doing what I thought we were supposed to do, and suddenly, wham . . . You can be objective—what did I do? What should I have done?"

The faces staring back at her were nonplussed. One by one the women ventured an opinion, their talk graphic, supportive.

"How much foreplay was there?" Martina asked.

"Actually, there wasn't any. I said something earlier about not committing—whatever happened would be whatever it was, something like that."

"Are you saying you just . . . went at it?" Martha asked.

"Well, he kissed me. I liked it. He's a real good kisser. I said I liked it and he said he could do it again and he did. I liked it even better. I took that as a . . . that we were going to have sex so I did what I always . . . I did what Ian and I always did . . ."

"But you weren't with Ian, you were with Ben. Apples and oranges, Emily," Kelly said.

"Who was the aggressor?" Zoë asked.

"Me. My God, I was all over him. I attacked him; I honest to God attacked him. He . . . ah . . . he didn't seem to be responding so I got more . . . aggressive. Ian liked . . . oh shit!"

"What were his exact words?" The Demster twins asked in unison.

"He said no first. It wasn't just no, it was *no*! I said, 'This is what you want and I'm going to give it to you.' That's when he said *no*! Then he said he didn't want to rape me and he didn't want me to rape him, something like that. He said some other things too, but the last thing he said was there was one person too many in the room, and if that person didn't leave, we didn't stand a chance. All I felt was such shame, that this man I was prepared to make love with was telling me I was doing it all wrong. I took it as rejection. Shame and guilt are so awful. I had years of it. That's how I know exactly what I feel now. It's the same now as it was with Ian. A no from Ian was a cringing slap in the face. I'd run and hide. Sometimes for days I'd avoid looking at him, speaking to him. That's what the word *no* meant to me. To hear it from another man was all I needed . . ."

Lena put her arm around Emily's shoulders. "It's okay to cry, Emily. All of us understand. Look around. Do you see anyone judging you? Do you see anything but compassion in any of us? Well, do you?"

"No. No, I don't. Years ago I wouldn't have been able to open up to anyone. I kept it all inside. I don't mind any of you knowing I do stupid things. I'm not a perfect person. I have feelings and I hurt like everyone else. What should I do?"

"What do you want to do?" Lena asked.

"Hide in a corner and suck my thumb. It wasn't Ben, it was me. It was, wasn't it?" As one, they nodded.

"I don't think you've let go of Ian yet, Emily," Lena said.

"But I have. I hardly ever think of him anymore."

"He's still a part of your life. You aren't divorced; you're still married. File, Emily, get it over with."

"He left me; he should file. He's probably with some . . . some bimbo and he's using me as an excuse not to marry her."

"Men have been known to do that, but then so have women. You need to cut him out of your life. Until you do, he's going to haunt you. Like tonight, you slipped back into the old way. You've come a long way, Emily, and you can go further if you want. How am I doing so far, girls?"

"Great," they chorused.

"Emily?"

"Okay, I'll make an appointment and file for divorce. It will be quick, since Ian and I have been apart a few years. I think it's eighteen months. Should I charge him with desertion?"

"Whatever you can get away with. Ask for alimony. Do you want alimony, Emily?"

"Not if it comes from abortion clinics. Actually, no, I don't want it. I'd rather make it on my own. I can. I know I can. *We* can. All of us can as long as we stick together. Like now, I came home like a scalded cat and together we talked it over and things don't seem so bad."

The brandy bottle made its way around the circle again. Emily was just bringing it to her lips when she jerked around. "Did you hear something?"

"Someone's at the back door," Lena said. "Off the top of my head, I'd say it's probably Ben Jackson."

"Well, we aren't going to answer it," Emily said firmly.

"Why not, Emily?" the Demster twins asked at the same time.

"Because I don't want to deal with Ben Jackson right now, that's why."

"He must care about you to follow you to the clinic and then here," Zoë said.

"I bet he's cold and wet and he's going to get sick," Martina said quietly. "It's a cold rain out there."

"I got cold and wet too."

"Because you were stubborn and wanted to get cold and wet to punish yourself," Kelly said.

"You're going to have to talk to him sometime, Emily. Why not do it now, clear the air, and then if you want to sever your friendship with him, do so. Don't be a pisspot about this," one of the Demster twins said, but Emily wasn't sure which one had said it.

"It's easier to talk with your clothes on," Lena said. "Emily, you didn't do anything wrong. You simply reacted the only way you knew how. No one can fault you for that. I think the man likes you. A lot. You'll sleep better tonight if you talk this out. Remember what you told us when we opened the clinics. Get to the business at hand, deal with it, and move on. Business, financial, emotional, it's all the same. You can't keep on carrying baggage around. It gets in the way. We all found that out, thanks to you. Now it's your turn to practice what you've been saying for months and months."

"I say we all go to bed, think about the waffles I'm going to make us for breakfast, and let Emily handle her business," Zoë advised. "We're a shout away if you need us. He's still banging on the door."

They scattered. Emily was the last one up the stairs. She waited until she was sure Rose and Helen were on the front porch before she opened the back door.

"I should kill you, Emily Thorn. I should whip your butt for pulling this stunt on me. I already feel a cold coming on and I've been sneezing for the past twenty minutes. Do you care? Hell no, you don't, or you would have opened the door twenty minutes ago. You damn well sneaked out the back door of the clinic. It took me almost an hour to figure that one out."

"Come in, Ben. I'll make you some hot tea and brandy. Go into the laundry room and put your clothes in the dryer. I'll get you a robe. I was too ashamed, Ben. I'm sorry."

"Be sure you don't give me some damn old robe that belonged to your husband," Ben said, sneezing three times in a row.

"What's your feeling about flowered terry cloth?"

"I'll take it," Ben said, slamming the door of the laundry room.

In spite of herself, Emily smiled as she made her way to her room and the flowered terry-cloth robe. At the last minute she pulled out a pair of wool socks from her drawer. When she returned to the kitchen, the tea kettle was whistling. She turned it off, knocked on the door to the laundry room, and handed the flowered robe through the small crack in the door. "Don't be shy; I saw many naked men when I worked at the clinic. And if you care to remember, I've seen you naked too."

"Shut up, Emily. I'm pissed and I deserve to be pissed so don't try and be nice to me now."

"Then why are you here?"

"Because I know how you feel. At least I think I do. I needed to know you were all right. You're a nice person. I care about you." He sneezed again, four times.

Emily opened the Tylenol bottle sitting on the windowsill, shook out three, and placed them on the table. A heavy mug of tea was steeping on a colorful braided mat. She removed the tea bag and poured generously from the brandy bottle.

"Flowers become you. Is it warm enough?" Emily asked when Ben sat down at the table. He reached for a tissue from the box Emily set in front of him.

"I just want to know one thing, Emily. Do you read romance novels? I'm talking about ravage and plunder here, or was I right about there being a third person in the room?"

"No, I do not read romance novels, and yes, you were right." She looked away, at the clock on the wall and then at the array of cereal boxes on top of the refrigerator. "This is none of your business, but I'm going to tell you anyway. I've never been with a man other than my husband. I didn't know, and I am ashamed to admit this, but I didn't know there were new rules. I should have known that, maybe I did, but didn't want to act on it. When you said *no* the way you did, it triggered something in me and I reacted. I am sorry."

"Emily, when a couple decides to . . . to make love, the couple flounders a bit until they get comfortable with each other. Sometimes the first time is a real flop. If there's a second time, it usually goes a little better. Do you understand what I'm trying to say? I've been known to do some heavy-duty bellowing, so much so you can hear me in the next county. That's good. That's uninhibited. I'm not your husband and you aren't my ex-wife. I can sound like this because I did just about the same thing you did my first time out. I'm not judging you; I would never do that. Do you have slippers to match this robe?"

"No."

"I'll buy you a pair for Christmas. I like this robe."

"I'll buy you one for Christmas just like it."

"See, we're saying we're going to be around at Christmas time. As in together. Now, aren't you sorry you didn't open the door sooner?"

"No. I had to do what I did to get to this place in time. I have a long way to go, Ben. I made up my mind tonight to file for divorce. I'm also going to go and get a face-lift. I'm doing it for myself, not for you, just for me."

"What's wrong with your face?" Ben asked curiously. "I think it's kind of nice."

"I think I look . . . like three miles of used road. Too much excess skin. See, when I do this," Emily said, pulling the skin back from her cheekbones, "what a difference it makes."

"It does look better, but are you sure you want to go under the knife for something that isn't crucial?"

"I think so. All this loose skin, my look, it's the old Emily, the Emily that thought she belonged to Ian. I want *me* back and I'm not confusing aging with the way I look. I don't expect you to understand. I do and that's all that's important. Thanks, though, for saying I look okay."

"To me you do. Tell me now, am I fired?"

"Yes."

"Good," Ben said, smacking his hands together. He blew his nose lustily before he said, "Emily, I have an idea. See what you think of it. I think, and this is just my opinion, but I think it will take you right to the top if you go for it."

"Wait a minute. Are we done with that business at your house?"

"I never dwell on something when it's settled. We settled it. When and if we ever decide to make love, we'll do it the way Ben and Emily want to do it. Maybe it will happen, maybe it won't. We're friends again. That's important to me. Do you want to pick it apart?"

"No. What's your idea?" she asked, her eyes wide with curiosity. There would be a next time; she was sure of it.

"Do you remember telling me about that video you made of yourself a long time ago?"

"The one where I let it all hang out, where I'm in my underwear?"

"That's the one unless you made another one. Do you have the guts to show that to your customers? Instead of Charley with his satin cape and me doing your aerobics, which is going to get stale real quick. I think you can make that tape work for you. Look at you now. You are the living proof. Show them the tape. Give it to them so they can see that if you could do it, so can they. I want you to think about that, Emily."

"I never showed that tape to anyone. I made it to torture myself."

"How many times have you looked at it?"

"I've never looked at it. I would rather take a physical beating than look at that tape."

"That's the wrong attitude, Emily. You should be proud of all you've accomplished. You yourself said it was a long, hard road."

"I'm still traveling that road. You really don't think Charley is going to help me in the long run, do you?"

"No, Emily, I don't. Gimmicks are okay once in a while. They're fun, but your business isn't a fun business. You're trying to do something, build something that will give you and your friends a future, so you have to take it seriously. Yes, business dictates you do whatever you have to do to get customers in the door, but you have to be able to back that business up with a product or a service. I want you to think about it. And I want you to think about something else. Is it possible you went too fast, opened too many clinics all at once? In the back of your mind, were you trying to one-up your husband by opening eight where he opened four?"

"Oh, no, Ben, that had nothing to do with it. I did eight so each of my roommates and myself would have a clinic to operate. We're partners."

"As long as you're sure. By the way, I feel like hell."

"You look like hell too. Do you want to stay here tonight and leave early in the morning? I can make up the couch for you. It's still raining outside."

"No, I have to go back. I might be able to convince

Ted's mother to drop him off in the morning if I don't feel better."

"I'm sorry about this evening."

"And well you should be. Be sure to bring me chicken soup if you don't hear from me. I'll call you tomorrow night when Ted leaves. Thanks for the tea."

A smile tugged at the corners of Emily's mouth when she held out her hand for the flowered housecoat. "Promise me you'll go straight to bed. Drink some more tea and stay warm. Take a hot shower before you go to bed too."

"Yes, Mother," Ben said wearily.

"Good night, Ben."

"Good night, Emily."

Chapter 13

It was a cloudy, overcast day with a hint of snow in the air when Emily unlocked the kitchen door. She'd closed early because she thought she was coming down with a cold. As she set about making tea, however, she knew she wasn't catching a cold—it was just an excuse to come home and go over her books.

Two weeks until Christmas, two weeks and one day until her surgery in New York. Maybe she should cancel the face-lift and use the money for the clinics. It didn't matter that she and the others had taken a vote and all had agreed that she should go ahead as planned. Someway, somehow, they'd manage. The seventeen thousand dollars she'd gotten two weeks ago for the sale of her fur coats was to be used for the surgery, since her health insurance didn't pay for cosmetic surgery. It was decadent of her to do this, but she didn't care.

Her head pounded and her shoulders were so tight she felt like a wooden doll whose owner was about to snap off her arms. She lit a cigarette, her first in weeks, and gulped at the black currant tea before she opened the ledger she'd carried home. What *was* she to do? They were deep in the red. Charley had given his notice and would be leaving the first of the year. Bodybuilding, his obsession, beckoned, as did a girl named Winona who professed to love muscles.

Charley was going into training so he could do the circuit, whatever that meant.

Emily turned the pages of the ledger to the last page, where her personal finances were listed. She needed only one page. It was time to sell her jewelry, time to put the shore house on the market. Ian's share would be put into an escrow account should he ever come back. Maybe she could take out a small second mortgage on this house.

Did she have the guts to dip into the last ninety thousand dollars of her retirement money? Whatever it takes, Emily. You can do this. You have to do it. You committed. So did the others.

She finished the tea, made another cup. She was on her second cigarette when she started to think about the video she'd made the day she got mugged. Ben's words rang in her ears. Was he right? More than likely. How was she to show that video to the world? Ben was a man; he didn't understand shame, guilt, and rejection. He didn't understand rolls of fat, sagging breasts, thighs that rubbed together, a big ass whose excess fat formed rolls where the elastic on her panties met. He didn't understand slumped shoulders because of low self-esteem and a fat, ugly body. Ben saw his clients in drop-dead sweat suits with pretty little sweatbands. So what if there was fat underneath? He didn't *see* it, so he didn't know what he was asking her to do.

Once Ian had said she was as pretty as a butterfly. She burst into tears. Damn, she thought, she was past this sniveling. "I hate you, Ian Thorn. God, how I hate you. I hope your damn white shirts are full of messy wrinkles." She finished the last of the tea and crushed out her cigarette. The others wouldn't be home for another hour and a half so she had time to . . .

A moment later she was off the chair, pulling the camcorder and video off the shelf in the closet. It took another minute to turn on the VCR and the TV. She sat down on the chair, the remote in her hand. She shrank into herself as she stared at her reflection. Her eyes filled again when she stared at her underwear-clad body. She rewound the tape, played it three more times before she pressed the Stop button. She could continue the tape now if she wanted to. Part two, so to speak. The question was, Did she want to? My God, no, she didn't. Whatever it takes, Emily. The worst is over. The first part is the *before* part. This second part is the *after* part. Get your face right up there so everyone can see what the years did to you. Take off that sweatshirt and let everyone see what you look like in your pink leotard. Let them see the deformed butterfly. Whatever it takes, Emily, you can do. For yourself, for the others, and for everyone who is going to see this video. For free yet. God!

Emily pressed the Record button and backed up to the chair she'd been sitting on. "This is Emily Thorn," she began. "If you're watching this, it means you've seen the first part of the video I made when I was at the lowest point in my life. I didn't have the courage, the guts, if you will, to look at it until today. A long time ago my ex-husband said I was as pretty as a butterfly." She moved closer to the camcorder. "I don't look like a pretty butterfly and I don't feel like one either. However, I feel fit and healthy, and beauty, as we all know, is in the eye of the beholder. Easy to say, right?" She backed away again. "Take a good look at me, ladies." She turned around, did a few deep knee bends, did a few pirouettes, dropped to her stomach and did some pushups with rapid-fire motions. "I can do this now. I'm in shape now without one extra ounce of body fat that my body doesn't need. Today I can eat anything I want as long as I practice moderation."

Emily licked at her lips, her eyes filling again. "About thirty minutes ago I was sitting in my kitchen drinking tea and smoking a cigarette, which I know I shouldn't have done, but I have virtually kicked the habit. Anyway, I was sitting there thinking about my appointment to have a face-lift after Christmas. I thought of it as an investment in myself. But I was kidding myself. I was doing it for pure vanity. I wanted to be the Emily Thorn who was as pretty as a butterfly. I realize now I'm not a butterfly nor was I ever a butterfly. I'm me, Emily Thorn. There were never two Emily Thorns. That's where I went wrong, but I am now correcting that mistake. Please, bear with me for a few moments until I can get my thoughts together so I can go on to part three of this video."

Emily tried to marshal her thoughts. If Ben was right, then what she said was paramount and it couldn't be rehearsed. She had to say what she thought, what she believed. She stared into the single eye of the camcorder and said, "I want to believe I am a survivor. Now, many of you are going to ask yourselves, What does any of this have to do with physical fitness? For me, it had everything to do with getting my life on track. Now, as I look back, I know that I wasted half of my life. My husband left me after I put him through medical school. He didn't leave me destitute. He left me some money and a house with a huge mortgage and . . . and sixty-two pounds of fat; my fat. Fortunately for me I have a wonderful support system that came about because of all of this. All of us at Emily's Fitness Centers will be your support system. It doesn't matter what your reasons are, we'll be there for you. We'll teach you how and when to exercise, how to eat, how to treat your body kindly to attain the best results for you. You, as an individual. We are women helping women. I don't know who you are so you are going to have to come to us. Don't waste your life; don't give it away. Live it to the fullest. Dare to be you.

"And now I'm going to pause this camera one more

time and go to one of our clinics and show you what we're all about." Emily pressed the Stop button. Tomorrow she would take the camcorder in early and have Lena or one of the girls help her finish the video. She was totally exhausted. There really was such a thing as mental torture. Did mental torture burn off calories?

In the kitchen, Emily looked at the clock. She might as well make dinner since she was home. Broiled chicken, steamed vegetables mixed with lemon and dill, baked potato, a lettuce and carrot salad with a honey Dijon dressing, and sugar-free strawberry Jell-O. She'd baste the chicken with Sausy Susan and, *voilà*, a substantial dinner as well as dessert with very little sugar.

She enjoyed the dinner hour with her friends more than she enjoyed the food. Before, she'd lived to eat; like the others, now she ate to live. Tonight while they sat around the living room, they'd snack on popcorn and drink herbal tea.

Her eyes clouded with worry, Emily set the table. She was folding the napkins when Ben knocked on the back door and let himself in at the same time. "Just in time for dinner. Sometimes I do things just right," he teased.

"Shall I set another place?"

"If you're inviting me, yes."

"What brings you here at this hour?"

"I have a new client on Woodland. It was so close I just decided to stop and see you."

He looks wonderful, Emily thought. Even at the end of the day in his sweats, he looks like a man with a purpose. He was handsome in a homely, rugged kind of way. She felt a tingle of something she hadn't felt in a long time. "I'm glad you did," she said warmly. "I was wondering if you'd like to have dinner with me this weekend. My treat. Or is that one of those *no*, whoa, things?"

"If you want to pay, it's okay with me. I find it . . . titillating that a woman is asking me for a date, but I want you to know I'm modern enough to accept and be gracious in my acceptance. I'll look forward to it. And no, it's not a *no* or whoa thing." He grinned from ear to ear. "I thought you were going to bring me chicken soup when I was sick."

"I didn't have any chicken. That was a long time ago. I also remember you saying you were going to call me that Sunday and you didn't."

"I was too sick."

"Same principle as me not having any chicken, eh?"

"Or tit for tat," Ben said breezily.

"I thought about you a lot after that . . . that evening."

"I thought about you too, Emily. Actually, it's getting close to the holidays and I wanted to be around real people. My wife and her new husband are going to California for the holidays so I'm kind of bumming, if you know what I mean."

"I'm sorry, Ben. Don't you get holiday visitation rights or do you alternate?"

"We're supposed to alternate, but this is a delayed honeymoon for them. I get Ted for the next two Christmases. She was civil about the whole thing. Ted wanted to go, so what could I do?"

"Just what you did. You're welcome to spend Christmas with us if you want. We plan on doing it up big Christmas Eve and sleeping in Christmas Day then having a big dinner. Big dinner on Christmas Eve too. Hey, let's all go together to pick out a tree next weekend or even this weekend, if you want. Sunday would be good. I know where there's a wonderful tree farm down off Route 130. I love Christmas. I have boxes and boxes of ornaments and lights." Her voice was breathless as she waited for his reply.

"I accept. I'll bring the wine."

"You'll have to do better than wine. You need to show

up with *presents*. Shopping bags filled with presents. There's eight of us," Emily twinkled.

"Duly noted. Wine and presents. I hope it snows."

"I do too. They said it might snow over the weekend. Wouldn't it be great if we were out choosing a tree and it started to snow. Jeez, it would make me *soooo* happy. The girls are home," Emily said as she turned on the broiler. "If you want to help, you can pour that dressing on the salad and toss it. I'm doing the potatoes in the microwave so we'll be ready to eat in fifteen minutes."

Having a man in the house, in the kitchen, *did* make a difference, Emily thought as the group teased and laughed, poked and ribbed each other.

They didn't talk about business at all. Instead the conversation concerned Christmases of long ago, selecting the right tree, getting "dolled up" as Martina put it, for midnight services, opening presents afterward, toasting each other and then going to bed.

Emily sat back and watched the interaction between Ben and her roommates. In all the years of her marriage to Ian, they'd never had a dinner party, never had guests to their home. Once or twice they'd eaten out with one of Ian's colleagues and each time it had been a disaster afterward. She wasn't dressed quite right, she didn't sparkle enough, she didn't contribute to the conversation and then the ultimate punishment of silence on Ian's part; sometimes for days, sometimes for weeks. She knew she was smiling and it felt good. She was living; finally.

"Lordy, lordy, everything is gone," Kelly said, getting up to clear the table. "I love healthy appetites."

"Invite me again and I'll do the same every time. I can cook, but I find it easier to just grab something. This was a nutritious meal. I can see why you're all slimming down. I can help with the dishes or I can go home," Ben said.

"I'll wash; it's my turn," Emily said. "You can dry."

"I break a lot of dishes," Ben said.

"In that case, here's your coat," Lena said, ushering him to the back door. Hoots of displeasure followed him out the door. "Just like a man. Eat and run. Go on, see if we care. Next time you're washing and drying. Bring your own paper plates." The kitchen was suddenly a beehive as the women pitched in to help Emily.

"I want to call a meeting," Emily said, hanging up the dishtowel.

"We knew," Zoë said. "That's why we shooed Ben out."

"How'd you know?" Emily asked, her face full of amazement.

"We're women," Lena said as if that explained everything. "Are we right?"

"Let's go into the living room. I want to show you a video, but before I do, we need a short business meeting." The women trooped into the living room. Nancy was the last to take her place in the circle around the floor. She placed the tray with the Styrofoam cups and the coffeepot next to her. She poured and passed the cups to the others.

"We're at another low. Charley's moving on. We knew he would and he was a gimmick. We can't afford gimmicks any longer. We can stay in business for another six months, but then I'm tapped out. There won't be anyplace else to get money. The banks still won't lend us any; that much I'm sure of. That means we have to make it on our own."

"How bad off are we?" they asked together.

"Bad. There's no place else to turn. I don't have a magic wand. We have all tried so hard, given it everything we have. There's no place else to cut back. We have some goodwill, some word of mouth, but it isn't enough for now. I've made mistakes that have cost us money."

"We all have a little savings. If we give it, will it help?" Martina asked.

"Of course it will help, but I can't ask all of you to give up what little security you have," Emily said.

"You did," the Demster twins said smartly.

"Yes, but I still have some left. You'll be giving up everything."

"It's our decision. You said share and share alike. We'll put in the money we got for selling our business," the twins said quietly. "Let's see how much we can come up with between all of us."

When the count was final, Emily stared at her roommates. "It's a princely sum. In case any of you are *really* interested, I've decided not to get my face-lift. I sold the furs so that money, combined with yours, will go a long way toward what I propose. Okay, here's the plan."

"Wait, wait, I want to get the brandy bottle. I think this is a momentous announcement and I think we should be prepared to toast it." Zoë was up and out to the kitchen as the words tumbled from her mouth. She poured generously into their coffee cups. "Now, Emily, tell us."

"Wait a minute, I thought you wanted that face-lift. You said you *needed* it. If it's going to make you feel better about yourself, you shouldn't give it up. You said it would build your self-esteem, give you confidence," Lena said.

"So I lied. You guys make me feel good. Look at us. You're all willing to put your last dime into this venture. I don't *need* a face-lift. I might *want* one. Therein lies the difference. Maybe someday, and then again, maybe not. Look at this face, all of you. Do I have character or what? I earned every goddamn wrinkle and I'm not sure I want to part with them. Me. You aren't making this decision for me. Neither is Ben, who by the way said, 'What's wrong with your face?' He meant it—you should have seen the strange look on his face when he said that. So, let's put my face-lift behind us and move on to the matters at hand,"

Emily said. Seven pairs of hands stretched out. Emily grabbed Lena and Zoë's hand.

"To us, win or lose," Martina said happily.

"Okay, this is my plan so listen up. I have a video I think we should have copied and given away for free. It's going to cost a bundle of money to do that. Volume might get us a break. We'll saturate Plainfield and that covers South Plainfield, Edison Township, Metuchen, Woodbridge Township, and the Brunswicks, and that covers north, south, and east. I propose we hire people the way the phone company does when they give out the new telephone directories. We put the videos in little plastic bags and hang them on doorknobs. In the end, and I'm not sure about this, it will probably be cheaper than mailing them out, and we don't have mailing lists to cover all the areas. You have to pay for mailing lists. Christmas break is coming up so we should be able to hire college kids and seniors from the local high schools to help us."

She paused. "Now, I have all the information on the freeze-dried food. We're going to start selling it. *That's where the money is,* ladies. It will be perfectly proportioned, no fuss, no mess. Just take a minute to think about this. If you're serious about weight loss and an exercise program and you work or if you're a busy housewife and mother, wouldn't it be great to just pop something on the table for yourself and know it's been measured, is nutritious, and gives a guarantee that you will reach that goal you're striving for? I understand it's actually pretty tasty and looks good on the plate. That's important. There's a good selection. Variety is important too. No one wants to eat the same thing all the time. I have to be honest with you, I now hate tuna fish. We've all eaten a ton of that stuff these past few months, and if I have to eat one more piece of broiled chicken, I'm going to start clucking."

"When are we going to start?"

"Soon. Somehow or other we lost sight of the target we were after, which is middle-aged women like ourselves. I have no idea how that happened. I guess we were too busy with Charley and quick fixes. Anyway, women our age with midriffs like ours don't go to workout places and clubs, for a reason. We're ashamed of our bodies, at the extra pounds around our middles, our saddlebags, our drooping butts. Who do you see in those commercials? Eighteen- and twenty-year-old girls who say they need to lose a pound. One pound. They work out to lose one stinking pound. I believe in my heart they go there to meet men so men can see how cute they look in their spandex outfits. What forty-year-old woman who is fifteen to twenty pounds overweight is going to set herself up for something like that? It's easier to do nothing and hide your fat under the kinds of clothes we've all worn. That's why I think this new idea of mine might do it for us. If this doesn't work, then we're out of business. Understand one thing here: we're going to be paying for and giving away a lot of free videos that aren't going to our targeted audience, but we have to take the good with the bad. Do any of you disagree with anything I've just said?"

"When are we going to start this new project?" Lena asked. "We all agree, don't we ladies?" The others nodded.

"Okay, I'm going to show you the video," Emily said. "This, if we decide to go ahead with it, is going to take mega work. Ben will help, but he's just one person. By the way, we have a date on Saturday. I asked him out, and on Sunday he's going with us to pick out the Christmas tree. I invited him for Christmas Eve too. I hope you don't mind." Emily flushed at the looks of approval on the women's faces.

"Okay, here goes. It's not complete; I still have to do part three. I have a favor to ask all of you. Please don't say anything until you've seen it all."

Emily leaned back against the sofa and pressed the Play button. She closed her eyes for a second. She listened to her voice, watched herself, tried to imagine what the women on the floor were thinking, what they would say when she pressed the Rewind button.

Emily's thumb pressed downward. She wanted to look away, but she didn't. What were they going to say? She waited.

"Exactly what kind of underwear were you wearing?" Lena asked.

"Extra large, one hundred percent cotton. It wasn't big enough."

"You're telling me," Zoë quipped.

Emily burst out laughing.

"I like underwear that has the days of the week on it," Martina giggled.

"What's part three?"

"Like I said, I'll show one of the clinics, maybe have a few customers say something. I'll mention the food, maybe the herbs. I'd like your feedback on that. Aren't you going to say anything?"

"About what?" the Demster twins asked.

Emily squirmed. "You know, about the way I looked."

Martha laughed. "I understand you being squeamish about letting it all hang out like that, but Emily, do you have any idea how many women look like you did back then? I never used to look in the mirror when I got out of the shower. If you're comfortable with this, then we're behind you one hundred percent and I think I speak for everyone."

Emily looked at her friends. She didn't see pity or shame. She saw friendship mirrored in their eyes, support and a let's-go-for-it attitude. "I'm comfortable with it," Emily said quietly.

"Now we can make our toast," Martha said, holding

her coffee cup high in the air. "We need to say something meaningful." Her face puckered into a frown as she sought for just the right words.

"How about to Emily's coming of age," Lena said.

"How about to the greatest group of women in the state, women who are going to succeed because we're sharing and working together for a cause that will help other women and at the same time secure our futures?" Emily said, clinking her cup against the others.

"Perfect," the others said in union.

"Okay, now, down to work. Pads and pencils, phone books, our ledgers, our bank books, and more coffee," Emily said.

The women scattered to return with everything Emily had suggested. The coffeepot was filled and refilled throughout the long night. They were still at it at dawn when they called a halt, pleased with the progress they'd made over the past hours. They split up to shower and head off to their respective clinics with the promise they'd close up shop at five o'clock, order Chinese, and pick up where they left off.

Two days later they had a concrete plan of action that allowed for every screw-up known to man, a work schedule, a buying schedule, a plan to hire more people, mega expansion complete with maps garnered from the local Chamber of Commerce offices listing locations for additional clinics, distributors for the videos. A commitment to air commercials on the local cable channel was a day away from signing on the proverbial dotted line.

The possibility of failure was never mentioned, nor was it alluded to in any way.

Emily called an estate jeweler and made arrangements to sell her triple-strand pearl choker, her twenty-one-inch pearl necklace, her twelve-inch strand, two pairs of pearl earrings, and the diamond studs she'd worn three times.

The Rolex watch, the three diamond bracelets, the diamond pendant, and the three lapel pins would be held in reserve to be sold if needed.

The last piece of business they agreed on was Emily would, after the first of the year, travel around the local area to all the large corporations to try and offer management a program designed for employees to be conducted on the premises and called Lunch Hour Physical Fitness. Emily's Fitness Centers would take full responsibility for maintaining and renting all exercise equipment to be installed on the premises. The fee was outrageously high, but as Emily put it to the girls, "We need to hire the best and that means a high salary. It will be a write-off for the company and those guys will get their pictures in the paper. All we have to do is sign up a company like Johnson and Johnson and the others will follow. I feel it. I smell our success," Emily said, excitement ringing in her voice.

The women toasted the moment with cups of Celestial Seasonings Lemon Zinger tea.

The holidays passed in a blur, with a promise that next year they'd have a real, bang-up Christmas and a truly boisterous New Year.

Seventeen months later, Emily's Fitness Centers were a household word. They opened a corporate office in Raritan Center, hired people to manage the original eight clinics, plus nineteen now in total. They had nine corporations they serviced, advertised on cable as well as the Fox Network, and were working out a deal for the three major networks. The freeze-dried meals were netting them more money than they had ever dreamed possible.

By November, four months later, Emily was approached by a team of lawyers asking them if they'd consider franchising Emily's Fitness Centers. The women huddled, said no, took down names and phone numbers, and toasted that particular moment with a batch of Alabama Slammers in the middle of the day.

"We're on a roll, ladies," Emily said, throwing the empty pitcher against the wall. The women threw their empty glasses against the wall. "Call maintenance to clean up this mess, or better yet, let's not call. We'll put a note on the door. Our days of cleaning up are long gone," Emily said breezily as she shooed the women out to the hall. "We're going home, take our shoes off, and do absolutely nothing. Or we can start to plan for Christmas. We promised ourselves, remember?"

At home with a batch of Fuzzy Navels, the women settled themselves in the living room with their shoes off, their faces elated and happy. "Ben should be here," Lena said. "Let's call him."

"Can't. He's on the road. Our roving ambassador is busy from morning till night. I haven't really talked to him in almost two weeks. He's doing a wonderful job. If we lose him, we're in trouble. He's like a . . . cohesive that keeps it all together." Emily made a sour face.

"You guys are getting on pretty good, huh?" Zoë asked slyly.

"Pretty good," Emily said honestly. "I really like him, but I don't think I'm in love with him. I don't think he's in love with me either. We're kind of like a ham and cheese sandwich; we go together. For now.

"We need to talk, ladies. Today we were paid, as far as I'm concerned, the ultimate compliment—we were made an offer to franchise. I don't think it gets any better than that. By spring we're all going to be paid back the monies we advanced. It's my considered opinion that we are now set. I think we should look into the franchising bit, find out all we can. Those guys, I don't know, I didn't like them for some reason. I think they thought they were dealing with a dizzy, greedy bunch of women who would jump at their offer. If we're going to go that route, we need to be prepared, on our terms. Think of it like this: every single franchise has to buy their equipment, the videos, the freeze-dried food from us. That's all profit after we pay for it wholesale. Then we get the up-front buy-in money. Even if we franchised just eight clinics, that's our nest egg for the future. Invested right, it will grow to a healthy sum. Our yearly contributions will be the icing on the cake. We did damn well, ladies. I am so proud of us I could just . . . bust."

"Does that mean we have to move, get our own place?" Helen Demster asked.

Emily stared at the twin. "Why would you ask me something like that, Helen? Of course not. If you want to move to have more privacy or if . . . if you don't want to be a part of . . . our family, and to me you all are my family, I understand."

"Oh, no. I don't want to move, and neither does Rose. I just thought that now that we're successful and have money we . . . you . . . all of you . . . might want to change things."

"Families don't split up. I like things just the way they are. We need to take a vote here," Emily said, her voice as anxious sounding as she looked.

"See," she said moments later, relieved, "everyone voted to keep things just the way they are. God, Helen, you scared the hell out of me. I can't imagine life without all of you."

"How about some Singapore slings?" Lena asked.

"You make 'em, I'll drink 'em," Rose said sprightly.

"We're becoming regular lushes," Martha said happily.

"Yeah, right, twice-a-year drinkers," Lena snorted. "Toasts don't count. We only drink when we toast something."

"Yeah, like Christmas, Easter, the Fourth of July, Memorial Day, Labor Day, everyone's birthday, everyone's personal day, our anniversary, the day we moved in here, the day we officially became a success," Nancy said.

"None of that counts." Lena trotted out to the kitchen.

"Our workout suits are great, but we have to find a way to have them made cheaper. We're not going overseas to have it done either. We make and buy American. Who wants to check into the cottage industry and see if we can't come up with something better than we're paying now?"

"We'll do it," the Demster twins said.

"Great," Emily said. "You know, somewhere in this house is a book Ian had with names of people who gave him good prices on things. It seems to me there were two ladies in Perth Amboy who made white lab coats for almost nothing. The place where he got the material was in the book too. I'll look for it tomorrow. I bet we could cut some kind of deal with a sneaker company, too, if we really tried. Anyone want to give that a try?"

"I will," Martina said. "You know, we never really did make a decision about giving away those tote bags with our name on them. Maybe we can get the person who does the suits to make the bags. It really is good advertising. Rose, Helen, what do you think?"

"We'll check it out. I like giveaways," Helen said, "and it's a write-off."

"Here we are, ladies. What are we toasting this time?" Lena said, placing the tray in the middle of the circle on the floor.

"Who cares? Let's just drink this ambrosia and plan on what we're going to try next. We need to be more worldly. I used to order white wine when I was out because I didn't know anything about liquor," Zoë said.

"Harvey Wallbangers," Kelly said. "We'll just taste them so Zoë gets an idea of what they're like."

"A Mimosa."

"That's a sissy drink like a Shirley Temple. You drink those at brunch or for breakfast," Martha said.

"Well, this isn't brunch or breakfast so we aren't drinking them. The Harvey Wallbangers are next," Lena said.

Hours later, when they were finishing the pitcher of Bahama Mamas, Emily looked up to see a figure in the doorway. She pointed a finger and said, "Look!"

"You're drunk. All of you! Your back door was wide open. What if I was an ax murderer?" Ben said, his face registering disgust.

"Don't scare us," the Demster twins giggled.

"They're right," Emily chimed in, then hiccupped. "Why are you scaring us? We said such nice things about you tonight. We found a way for you to get a real big bunch of money so you can send Ted to a fancy Ivy League college."

"What?"

"What what?" Emily demanded.

"What did you come up with?"

"I can't remember," Emily said, doubling over with laughter.

"What are you celebrating?"

"Something. Something stupendous," Emily said, flopping about on the floor.

"Tell me."

"I can't remember. Tomorrow I'll remember. You look mad. Are you mad, Ben? Do we care if he's mad?" Emily asked the others.

"Only if he quits," Zoë muttered.

"Is this going to go on our resumés?" Martha asked in a squeaky voice.

"What resumés?" Ben demanded. "How long have you been drinking?"

Emily's arms flopped in the air. "Thirty minutes," she said defiantly.

"In your dreams. Come on, ladies, up and to bed. Tomorrow is another day, one you are probably all going to regret."

"We're going to sleep here tonight. We do that sometimes when we're discussing important things. Isn't that right, Emily?" Lena said.

"That is absolutely right. Lock the door when you leave, Mr. Jackson." She was slurring her words so she had to be drunk. It annoyed her that Ben was right. She narrowed her eyes in order to get a clearer vision of him. He's angry. Why, she wondered. "We're home. So what if we had a few drinks to celebrate. I never had a Bahama Mama before. It sure beats Lemon Zinger. Oh, God, I'm going to be sick." Emily made a beeline for the stairs, Ben on her heels.

"Leave me alone . . . I can throw up by myself . . . why do you want to watch?" Emily yelped between heaves. Her eyes watered, her stomach muscles pulled and protested the violent spasms. She was on her knees, her head in the bowl. "Go home, Ben. I don't want you to see me like this," Emily pleaded. "Don't you ever listen? I'd like to be alone with my misery."

"You'll never make a drunk, Emily," Ben said cheerfully.

"Thank God," Emily muttered. She heard water running, felt something cool on the back of her neck. "I've never been drunk before. Like this I mean," Emily gasped.

Ben was on his knees, his arm around her shoulders. "One more good one and it's over." His voice was soothing, calm, a balm to her quaking body.

"How do you know?"

"I've been where you are. When my wife left me, I did this almost every night. I wasn't celebrating, I was mourning. You should have stuck to the Lemon Zinger. What the hell were you all celebrating anyway? Come on, brush your teeth and use some mouthwash. I'll make you a cup of peppermint tea and that will help your stomach a little.

So, what were you celebrating?" He squeezed blue tooth-
paste onto a yellow toothbrush.

"Franchises," Emily said around the bubbles in her
mouth. "Some lawyers came by the offices today and more
or less offered us . . . told us to think about it and they'd
be willing to set it up. It sounded real good, but they were
a pair of sharks. I hate lawyers as much as I hate used car
salesmen and insurance agents." She spat in the sink, then
rinsed her mouth until Ben jerked her head backward.

"That's enough, you'll wear out your tongue."

"You're too damn bossy, Ben Jackson. I told you to go
home. Now, every time I look at you, I'm going to remember you watching me puke my guts out. We're thinking
about it because it will give you lots of money to send Ted
to an Ivy League school like you want. I look awful, don't I?"

"Yeah. Wait till tomorrow when you wake up. You're
going to feel like you look."

"Oh, shut up, Ben. Get some blankets so we can cover
everyone up."

"Mother Emily. Always thinking about other people."

"What's wrong with that?" Emily grumbled as she
pulled blankets from the linen closet.

"There's nothing wrong with it and everything right. It's
who you are, Emily. I think you were born to nurture."

She was walking like a puppet on a string as Ben guided
her down the steps and into the living room, where they
covered the sleeping women, then led her out to the kitchen,
where he put water on to boil. "I want a cigarette."

"You don't need a cigarette."

"Don't tell me what I need and don't need. I want one.
I'm going to get one. It's my last vice, and when I'm ready
to give that vice up completely, I will, but not one minute
before or when some damn man tells me I have to."

"Fine, burn your lungs out, see if I care."

"They're my lungs, so shut up, Ben Jackson."

"You are the damnedest, the stubbornest female I've *ever* met. I don't know why I love you, but I do."

"What's wrong with being stubborn? I have a right to my convictions. I . . . what did you say?" Her head reeled as she reached across the table to the pack of cigarettes she'd left there earlier.

"The part about you being stubborn or the part where I said I love you?"

"That part . . . about loving me. Are you *in* love with me or are you saying you love me. The way I love all the women."

"I love you and I am *in* love with you."

"That's not good, Ben. I don't want you to be in love with me. I don't think I'm capable of . . . what we have is wonderful, an easygoing, comfortable relationship with mutual respect on both sides. I'm not prepared . . . I probably will never . . . I wish you hadn't said that."

"Drink this," Ben said, setting the tea in front of her. He sat down, reached for her free hand. "Emily, every man in the world isn't like Ian Thorn. Some of us are rather nice. Take me, for example. I'm a loving guy. I treat old people with the respect they deserve. I'm kind to animals. I love children, especially my own kid. I have an honest job I work at because I love what I do. I'm considerate and I don't think I have a malicious bone in my body. I go to church on occasion, donate on occasion, do my share of volunteer work for the community, and I try to give back as much as I can. I'm pleading with you. Jesus, I'm pleading with you to love me." His face was full of dismay. "Good night, Emily. If I intruded, I'm sorry. I hope you feel better in the morning. Call me if you need me."

Emily burst into tears. Ben Jackson was indeed all those things he'd said. He was everything Ian wasn't. And he loved her. He didn't care about her wrinkles and the fat pads under her eyes. He'd seen her puke her guts out, held her hand, made her tea, and then announced his love. He'd seen her at her worst, seen her when she was at the bottom with nowhere to go but up. He'd made sweet, gentle love with her, held her in his arms when she cried. He'd kissed away the tears. He was that oh so rare person called friend. The friend who was there no matter what, just like the women. He was part of them, part of the family. He belonged to all of them.

Emily finished the tea because Ben had taken the time to make it for her because he cared about her. She set the cup in the sink. She was still crying when she climbed the stairs to her bedroom.

Emily flopped back onto the pillows. Maybe she didn't know what love was. This warm, gentle feeling she felt for Ben was like cuddling with a giant teddy bear. Love meant putting the other person first. She'd done that with Ian, but in a sick perverted way. Days and weeks could go by where she didn't see or talk to Ben, but that was okay because she knew all she had to do was pick up the phone and he'd be there for her. Was she using him until something better came along? Was there in fact something better than Ben Jackson? She doubted it. Where were the fireworks, the butterflies in her stomach, the wild anticipation? Were those just clichés slick magazines wrote about? And where in the hell were the multiple orgasms? Myths. Myths designed by men to make women miserable.

Emily rolled over, reached for the phone. She dialed Ben's number from memory. She smiled when she heard his voice. "I called to say good night and thank you. Everyone is sleeping peacefully and I'm ready to turn in myself."

"Did you turn the alarm on?"

"Yes, and all the doors and windows are locked. The television is off and so are the lights. Good night, Ben."

"Good night, Emily. Dream sweet dreams."

"I'll dream about us walking through a meadow filled with clover and daisies. You dream the same thing, okay, but put a lake in your dream. Tomorrow we'll compare notes. Thanks again, Ben."

Emily turned off the light and rolled over. Damn, she'd forgotten to turn the heat down. Oh, well, she wouldn't need any covers and the girls would wake up warm instead of shivering.

Emily was asleep almost immediately. She knew she was going to dream as soon as she closed her eyes and slipped into that dark place called sleep . . .

She thrashed about as she tried to free herself from the strings attached to her wrists and ankles.

"Do as I say," came the iron command.

"I can't unless you loosen these strings," she wailed. "How do you expect me to move the iron while you're jerking the strings. I can't put the shirt on the hanger and I can't hang it on the door. Take the string off, Ian. Besides, it's too tight, it's hurting me. Don't you care that you're hurting me?"

"What's so damn hard about ironing shirts? You said you loved to do it." The string jerked, almost pulling her arm out of its socket. She whimpered.

"It's too cold. I shouldn't be shoveling this snow. I shouldn't be doing half the things I do. Oh, sir, thank you for offering to help me." She was breathless from her exertion to do more than hand the shovel over to the good Samaritan, who in turn handed her a bunch of daisies wrapped in green tissue paper.

"Why were you shoveling the snow?" the man demanded.

"Because I did something terrible and I have to try and make it right." She held the daisies up to her cheek. How pretty they were, but they were going to die out there in the cold. She said so.

"I'll buy you some more."

"Why would you do that? You don't even know me."

"Yes, I know you. I've been waiting a long time to meet someone like you. I'm not like that person who tied the strings to your arms and legs and I know you didn't do something terrible. I wouldn't give you daisies if you weren't a nice person. I'm a good judge of character."

"Do you think I'm as beautiful as a butterfly?"

The good Samaritan stopped shoveling to stare at her. "No. Butterflies are free with no shackles; that's what makes them beautiful. Their coloring is just window dressing. You could be as pretty as the first star at night, as pretty as the first spring flower if you'd smile from your heart and let it reach your eyes. You seem to have lost your spirit."

"Can I get it back?"

"I don't know. You have too much laundry piled up. You're never going to see the bottom of the basket. Okay, get in and start the car and let's see if it moves. I might have to shovel some more."

Emily held out the daisies. "I can't get in that car," she cried.

"Why not?"

"Look! There's no room," she said, pointing to the mounds of white shirts stuffed into the car.

"Throw the shirts away. I'll help you."

"I can't. I can't do that."

"Then I'll do it for you," the good Samaritan said, opening the door of the car. White shirts sailed upward in the gusty wind, white kites flying in every direction. "See, they're like the butterflies. Now do you believe me?"

The good Samaritan held out his hand. "Come with me. I know a place where there are no white shirts, no strings, no butterflies. Come with me, Emily."

"I'm married," Emily said sadly.

"Will you always be married?"

"Forever and ever. Marriage means forever and ever." Emily dabbed at her eyes.

"*Forever and ever* are just words, wishes. Sometimes it doesn't work out like that."

"It has to work like that. Ian promised me. He promised me!" Emily screamed.

"Promises, promises, promises," the good Samaritan said as he backed away from the car.

Emily rolled the window down. "Tell me your name."

"You know my name, Emily."

"No, no, I don't. Tell me."

Emily woke, her eyes wild as she scrambled from her bed.

She must be out of her mind. Nobody with any sense left a warm bed at three in the morning to go and visit someone else who was sound asleep. And just what in the hell was she going to say when she got there? Listen, Ben, I had this bad dream and I didn't want to be alone. I have the Queen Mother of all headaches and I need . . . I need . . . comfort. Well, hell yes, Ben would absolutely understand that, especially the comfort part. After all, that's what he'd been doing now for almost two years. Comforting her, making love to her, making her life easier when he could. Ben was her port in a storm. Everyone needed someone like Ben in their life.

Emily parked her car next to Ben's. She wondered if her stomach was going to rebel. She sat with the window rolled down, drinking in the cold, night air.

The townhouse was dark. Inside she knew there would be a dim nightlight in the kitchen to aid Ben in his nocturnal wanderings looking for sweets. His Achilles' heel.

Emily let herself into the house, closed her eyes to get her bearings in the dark, and removed her jacket, dropping it by the front door. With the heels of her feet, she kicked off her sneakers.

Cold moonlight sliced into the room through the blinds, outlining the chrome and glass in Ben's living room. A beer bottle stood out starkly on the coffee table next to a pile of wrappers from a bag of Hershey Kisses. She skirted the table, walked around Ben's recliner, and made her way to the carpeted stairs. As always, she paused on every third step to stare at the pictures of Ben's son. One of Ted on his first pony ride, one holding a fish that was almost as big as he was, one of Ted in a pool with his water wings. Her favorite was a snapshot blown up to poster size of Ben and Ted with knapsacks on their backs and wide grins on their faces. Ben was a wonderful father, a wonderful friend, a wonderful lover, a wonderful human being.

Emily stood in the doorway, uncertain if she should call Ben's name, walk over to the bed, and shake him gently, or just crawl into bed next to him. She shivered, then opted to crawl into the queen-size bed with the brown and white sheets that Ben preferred. She squirmed and snuggled until her backside curved into his stomach.

"Emily?"

"Uh-huh. Sorry if I woke you."

"What's wrong. What the hell time is it?"

"Three o'clock, maybe later. I left around three."

"Are you sick? Is something wrong?" He was wide awake

now, propped up on one elbow. Somehow in his maneu-
verings, he'd turned her around so she was facing him.
"Talk to me, Emily."

"If you were going to give me flowers, Ben, what kind
would you give me?"

"You came over here at three in the morning to ask me
that? Why didn't you call? Wait now, don't take that
wrong, it's okay that you came here. Flowers . . . Jesus, I
don't know. Colored ones, maybe roses. Maybe those big
ones that look like pompoms. This is important to you,
isn't it?"

"I had a bad dream and you were in it. It's the same
dream I always have, but with a few variations."

"Maybe you should tell me about it," Ben said, drawing
her close.

She told him. There was silence in the bedroom for a
long time before Ben spoke. "You need to let go, Emily. I
thought when you got your divorce papers, it was all
over."

"I thought so too. I don't have the dreams as often, but
they still come. Especially when I'm tired or stressed out."

"Part of your dream was true, the part about me. I do
love you, Emily. I think I'll probably always love you. In
your heart, in your subconscious, you know that. I can
handle it if you don't love me. It is my . . . opinion, you
won't ever be able to love anyone until you put Ian behind
you. You say you have, but you haven't, not really. Look,
this is going to come at you from left field, but you can, if
you want, track Ian down through the AMA and go to
wherever he is. I think you need that confrontation. That
final ending where you get to say something. I don't know
what that something is. Ted has a saying when we're at
odds. He always says, 'Dad, I didn't get up to bat.' What
that means is it can't be just me talking to him, giving orders. He has a voice and he wants to be heard too. Then,

after he has his say, it's okay for me to exert my parental authority. It works, Emily."

"Go to see Ian?" Her voice was a harsh whisper.

"I think it's time to do that."

"My God, what would I say?"

"Whatever you want. I think it's safe to say you've earned the right to punch his lights out if that's what you want to do. Of course he might call the cops and you'll have to deal with spousal abuse or some damn thing. If you decide to do it, you'll know what to say when the time comes."

"Do you really think I should do that?"

Ben listened to the excitement creeping into her voice. He squeezed his eyes shut. "Yes, Emily."

"Let's make love, Ben."

"No."

"No? Why?"

"Because there's one person too many in this room. I suggest we go to sleep now and talk some more in the morning. Good night, Emily."

Emily dutifully closed her eyes, knowing she wasn't going to fall asleep. Suddenly she wanted to go home, back to her room, the one she'd shared with Ian. She needed to think about what Ben had said. She waited until she was certain Ben was sound asleep before she crept from the bed and let herself out of the townhouse. Before she got back into her car, she looked toward Ben's bedroom window. She thought she saw him outlined in the moonlight. She waved at the shadow.

It was a quarter to five when Emily carried a cup of tea and her cigarettes to her room. She closed the door, and for some unexplained reason, she locked it.

Aside from the pounding inside her skull, Emily felt buoyant. Ben had just given her permission to seek out Ian. He said she needed to do it, to confront her ex-husband.

As if she needed permission. Of course you do, Emily. You could have done it anytime these past years, but you didn't. You've been waiting for someone to tell you it's okay to do it, which doesn't say much for you, Emily Thorn. Admit it, you want to see Ian so badly you can taste the feeling. Admit it. Admit it and go on.

Emily started to plan.

Chapter 14

A year later, on the second day of the New Year, Emily Thorn checked into the Plaza Hotel in New York City. She unpacked her bag, then checked the contents of her purse before she locked it in her suitcase. In the pocket of her coat she had a wad of traveler's checks and forty dollars in cash. Enough to pay for a taxi ride to and from Columbia Presbyterian Medical Center.

Three days before Christmas she'd called the center to make an appointment to consult with a plastic surgeon and was fortunate enough to be given another woman's canceled appointment for January second to have a face-lift. According to the receptionist, the woman had the flu and had to be rescheduled. Emily had taken the train the day after Christmas, did all of her pretesting, and was home by six o'clock.

Now, here she was. Her heart skipped a beat as she slipped on her coat. She was getting a full face-lift and getting her breasts lifted. Hospital time was three full days, then she would return to the hotel and go back every other day for two weeks until all the sutures and staples were removed. Three more weeks for the bruising and swelling to go down, at which point she could return to New Jersey and try to explain all the lies she'd told everyone. She stared at the mountain of books on the dresser that she planned to read while she hid out. Her eyes burned unbearably as she made her way to the elevator. There are some things you don't share with anyone and this is one of those things, she told herself.

Emily wasn't a religious person, but she blessed herself when she entered the hospital. Her surgery was scheduled for noon. It was now 7:30 A.M.

Surprisingly, there was little pain. Emily slept, drank through a straw, and refused to look in a mirror. When she was discharged three days later, she left the hospital with a colorful Hermes scarf draped half over her face. The bandages had been removed and all she could smell was her own clotted blood. Her hair was matted, glued to her head. The staples felt huge, as if they should be in planks of wood instead of her head. She still didn't look in the mirror.

The stitches had been removed from her eyes before she left the hospital. Her eyes felt gritty and she felt incredibly dirty for some reason. She bathed, but wasn't able to wet her face or head.

On the seventh day, the staples were removed and Emily was permitted to wash her hair. She still avoided the mirror and hid in the room, telling room service to leave her food outside the door.

On the tenth day she left the hotel for a walk in Central Park. She sat on a bench and ate a hot dog, the most delicious meal she'd ever eaten. She shared part of the bun with the pigeons who flocked around her feet.

At the end of three weeks, Emily felt confident enough to leave the hotel and venture into the Manhattan stores, where she bought six frilly bras with an underwire, bikini panties, and two Donna Karan suits.

At the end of the fourth week, with most of the swelling and all of the bruising gone, Emily made an appointment at Elizabeth Arden for The Works, with the stipulation that her hair be cut in a room without a mirror.

On the forty-second day, the surgeon discharged her. Emily felt like singing. Five weeks and she was a new person.

Two more days before she was to return to the house on Sleepy Hollow Road.

Dressed in one of the Donna Karan suits, sporting a fashionable haircut, her feet shod in Louis Jourdan shoes, Emily closed her briefcase, which held a list of corporations she planned to visit that day.

Now it was time to look in the mirror. She inched her way into the bathroom, her eyes squeezed shut. Now was the moment. She opened her eyes, stared, then burst out laughing. The surgeon had somehow, miraculously, erased ten years. With a skillful application of makeup, she could erase another five. "Emily Thorn, you are a little devil!" she chortled. The makeup went on with sure, deft strokes. Not too much, less is more, she cautioned herself. Done. She smiled. The Emily Thorn in the mirror smiled back.

Earrings. The last and final touch. She'd brought them with her—wide, thick, solid gold hoops she'd bought herself one year for Christmas when she was still married to Ian. She'd never worn them because they never seemed to go with any outfit she wore and her hair was long then, shrouding the elegant earrings. "You are one classy-looking chick, Emily." She twirled for the benefit of the Emily in the mirror, then she laughed, a sound so rich in happiness she wanted to cry with the sheer delight she was feeling. "I'm me again. I really am me again."

Emily sat down on the edge of the bathtub. All the bad was suddenly washed away. Her shoulders were lighter, her smile radiant. I earned this moment.

Emily was aware of the coveted looks she received in

the elevator, more aware of the looks she received when she strode through the lobby. The limo she'd hired for the day to take her from place to place was waiting at the curb. She stepped into it, the smile never leaving her face.

If possible, her smile was even more radiant at four o'clock when she stepped from the limo and walked into a fiber-optic firm, whose headquarters were between Madison and Park Avenues.

Emily handed her business card to the receptionist and was ushered into Keith Mangrove's office immediately. "I can give you exactly ten minutes, Miss Thorn. That is all you said you needed. Is that right?"

"Yes, Mr. Mangrove, that's all the time I need. Come with me, please. I want a five-minute tour of your facility." She was moving out the door, down the hall past a large open room and then down a corridor with mini-offices staffed by women who appeared to be middle-aged. "I think it's commendable of you to hire middle-aged women. Their children are grown, and they've elected to go back into the work force to help with college and to buy that vacation home. Tell me what you see, Mr. Mangrove?"

"Women working."

"What else?"

"Nothing else. Am I missing something here?"

"Yes." Emily looked at her watch. "Work productivity at this hour of the day is slow. The women appear to be sluggish. How many candy bars and soft drinks do you see on the desks? Look at the women. How many of them can stand to drop ten or fifteen pounds? You have a wide range of porkers in here, Mr. Mangrove. I can use that word because I used to be one of those porkers. When I leave, I suggest you make this tour again, slowly, get a feel for it. And by the way, I have the perfect exercise that can take three inches off *your* waistline."

Emily looked at her watch again, turned on her heel,

and started back the way she'd come. "We have a program called Lunch Hour Physical Fitness. We install and maintain our exercise equipment. You pay for the lease. Our rates aren't competitive because we don't have any competition. We are however, reasonable. We guarantee a twenty-five percent productivity rise within the first six months. My staff can be here in seven days. You can be operational in ten days. If you go along with this, I'd suggest you make the program mandatory for your employees. Time's up." Emily handed a thin envelope to Mangrove and prepared to leave the office. "You can reach me at the Plaza until tomorrow morning. Or you can call the corporate office in New Jersey. Or if you want to, just call and find out how to take off those three inches." Emily was in the reception room. She tilted her head, knowing full well Mangrove was behind her. "Ask her how much overweight she is," she whispered.

"Wait, I have a few more minutes," Mangrove said. "Miss Devers, how overweight are you?" he blurted out.

"I beg your pardon, Mr. Mangrove. That's a bit personal, don't you think?"

"No, I don't think any such thing. Answer the question, please. I don't want you snacking on that caramel corn anymore either."

"You gave it to me, Mr. Mangrove," the woman sputtered. "Sixteen pounds," she whispered. Emily grinned.

"Wait a minute, Miss Thorn, I have a few more minutes."

"But I don't, Mr. Mangrove. I said ten minutes and I'm a woman of my word." When she walked through the doors, she heard him say, "That caramel corn was for clients to snack on."

In the limo, Emily kicked off her shoes and poured herself a glass of wine from the console. She was so certain she'd locked up all six corporations that she drank to her own success. Wait until she told the others and Ben. They were going to be as delirious as she was. If all six corporations signed on, they were going to be $400,000 richer in a year's time. If they sold their freeze-dried food, she could double it in a year. She poured a second glass of wine. When she finished it, she asked the driver how far they were from the hotel.

"Eight, ten minutes, depending on traffic," was the response.

"Good, let me out here. I'll walk the rest of the way."

Standing on the sidewalk, Emily squelched the urge to throw her arms in the air and shout. Instead she gave her skirt an imaginary twist, tugged at her jacket, and started off down the street. Strut, Emily. You earned this too.

When she reached the Plaza, she was grinning from ear to ear. She eyed the doorman for one split second before she made a wide, dizzying circle and then slapped her knees in glee, to the doorman's amusement. "I don't think it gets any better than this," she said, laughing in delight. People smiled at her, enjoying her happiness.

"It's my turn at bat," she called over her shoulder.

She laughed again when someone shouted, "Make sure it's a home run."

She was going home in just a few hours. The anticipation was almost more than she could stand as she tried to envision the looks on the girls' faces and then seeing Ben's reaction. Lord, she'd missed them all so very much. She wished now that she'd called at least once, but that would have ruined everything. These last six weeks were something she had to go through alone with no support from anyone. Even now as she packed her bags with all her new purchases, she wasn't sure she'd done the right thing, but it was a done deed.

She'd deliberately timed her arrival for the dinner hour so she could make her grand entrance. Originally, the plan was to leave early in the morning and arrive home as everyone was getting ready to leave, but she wanted to do some last-minute shopping for the women and Ben as well.

Emily looked at the list on the bed of things she still had to do. At the top of the list was a call to Mangrove at the fiber-optics firm to set up an appointment for Ben, get valuables and traveler's checks from the safe downstairs, check out, call to be sure the limo was on time, then have her bags and boxes carried downstairs. Allowing for traffic, she should arrive home at approximately 6:30. Dinner would be under way, the women buzzing about the kitchen. God, she was excited. She'd plop down, they'd all, as in one, demand details, every single one, and then they'd *ooohh* and *aaahhh* over her new face and hairdo. Maybe she wouldn't mention the breast lift. Over dessert she'd give them their presents—Chanel handbags—and again listen to the *ooohhs* and *aaahhs*. When the kitchen was cleaned up and they had their last cup of coffee and were all talked out, she'd go over to Ben's and get his reaction. He'd look at her, grin from ear to ear, scoop her up in his arms and say, This can't be the Emily Thorn I know and love. She'd squeal and say, Yes, yes, it's me. They'd rip off each other's clothes and head for the bedroom, where they would make slow, lazy love for hours. Everything was going to be so wonderful. Wonderful because it was Valentine's Day.

"Perfecto!" Emily chortled. "I might even accept Ben's proposal this time. She looked at the special box on the bed that held Ben's valentine gift and one for his son Ted.

The limo driver said, "Are you sure this is where you want me to drop you off?"

"I'm positive. I'll walk down the driveway. Just unload the bags and boxes by the mailbox. I'll take them in later. This is sort of a surprise visit. If I go clunking down the driveway or they see your headlights, it won't be a surprise." She handed over a generous tip even though she knew a tip was included in the chit she'd signed earlier. She didn't care.

She was home. Really home. For the first time in years she really felt like this house on Sleepy Hollow Road was hers; truly hers. Inside where it was warm, her family waited, and less than five miles away her lover waited. "All good things come to those who wait," she murmured.

Emily sucked in her breath and let it out slowly. Her breathing quickened, exploding in hard little puffs of vapor. Until now, she hadn't been aware of just how cold it was. Dark and cold. She was also aware for the first time of all the cars parked on the side of the road and in her driveway. She counted six strange cars. What did it mean? Her feet refused to move. She shivered inside her new cashmere coat. She began to feel a curl of fear in her stomach.

Overhead the stars sparkled, the moon a half slice, beaming down directly in the driveway. The sodium vapor lamps on the street cast everything, even the shrubs with their heavy coat of frost, into steely blue objects. Hard and cold. As hard and cold as she felt.

Emily started down the driveway, weaving her way in and out of the parked cars, strange cars she'd never seen before.

Scorching an anger rivered through her when she turned her heel over, knowing full well she'd broken it. She felt her gloved hands turn into clenched fists. This was her house. What the hell was going on here? She looked for her car, saw it three cars ahead, blocked in completely. How was she to get to Ben's? She couldn't even take one of her friends' cars because the strange cars were blocking them in too. "Shit!"

Something was wrong, either with her or inside the well-lit house. She hadn't felt anger like this since the day she'd received Ian's termination letter. Now, like then, she felt terminated, displaced.

Emily walked around to the back of the house and up to the kitchen door. She peered through the glass. The table wasn't set, but the kitchen was a mess. They must be eating in the dining room. They never ate in the dining room. Not even on holidays. Instead of opening the kitchen door, she walked around to the front of the house which would give her a clear view of the dining room. She took another deep breath before she advanced far enough on the walkway to afford her a clear view. Emily blinked at the strange faces seated at her dining room table. Men! Seven of them! Seated next to her friends. Boy, girl, boy, girl. They were laughing and joking as they ate. Turkey, the carcass almost picked clean. A valentine party. In her house. The women were dressed up, the strange men in suits. Nice-looking men, all of whom wore white shirts. Emily swayed dizzily. She gave herself a mental shake. When she opened her eyes again, the rotund gentleman seated next to Helen Demster leaned over and kissed her cheek. Emily gasped. Helen Demster, admitted virgin, smiled coyly. Her twin laughed aloud. The others smiled benignly. A twin of the rotund man blew in Rose's ear. "Oh my God," Emily gasped a second time.

Emily backed up against a gnarled sycamore tree, her eyes glued to the dining room window. Now she knew what it was that bothered her: The men appeared to be twins. They probably belonged to the twin organization Rose and Helen belonged to. They were couples, units, salt and pepper shakers, shoes and socks. True, the seventh man didn't appear to have a male mate, but he was paired off with Zoë, who wore the sappiest expression Emily had ever seen. If she went in now, she'd spoil things. Never mind that this little party had spoiled things for her. In her damn house, no less.

She was jealous. Infuriatingly so. And she was freezing. Inside it looked warm and cozy. The remains of the dinner looked wonderful too. She realized she was starving. They'd gone ahead and done something on their own, and from all appearances, it was working out. They looked so happy, so contented.

She felt betrayed. They didn't need her. Right now, this very second, she should storm into the house and boot their asses out into the cold. She was instantly ashamed of her thought.

Emily walked back to the top of the driveway, looked down at her suitcases, at the boxes of gifts. She pushed and shoved them under the spreading yews that lined the driveway. Damn, she didn't even have a car to sit in. The keys were inside.

The anger surfaced again as she made her way down the road to her neighbor's house. The Mastersons were elderly and never left the house after dark. Perhaps they'd lend her their car so she could drive over to Ben's house. For years she'd given them blooms from her flower garden as well as vegetables from the garden. Surely they'd oblige her and let her drive their car this evening.

Emily walked around to the back of the house and rapped softly on the kitchen door. They were having dinner. Harvey struggled up from his chair, walked over to the door, peered out, and said, "Who is it?"

"It's Emily Thorn, Harvey. Can I talk to you for a minute?"

"Emily. How nice to see you. Would you like some dinner?" the old gentleman asked.

"No, thank you. I need a favor, Harvey. My car won't start and I was wondering if I could borrow yours for a little while. I promise to be careful."

"If you put gas in it," Harvey said slyly.

"Is anything wrong, Emily?" Evelyn asked, speaking slowly. Evelyn did everything slowly, because as Harvey put it, she came from the South and they do everything slow down there.

"No, everything is fine, Evelyn. I guess my battery is low or something. I'll have it fixed tomorrow."

"Did that handsome husband of yours give you a valentine, Emily?" Evelyn smiled. "Harvey gave me one. Never missed a year in all the years we've been married."

Emily's vision blurred for a second. "A very pretty one," she lied. There was no point in telling the Mastersons that Ian had been gone for years. For the most part, both of them were forgetful and lived pretty much for the moment.

"Here are the keys, Emily. Be careful. Sometimes the clutch sticks. Bring the car back tomorrow. Evelyn and I are going to spoon for a while and then we're going to go to bed and talk about the good old days. If you bring the car back here, we'll hear it and it will break the spell." He made a grimace that was supposed to be a sly smile and then he winked. Emily winked back and let herself out the door.

Twenty minutes later she parked the car in a spot down the way from the two spots allotted each owner of Ben's complex. She locked the car and walked over to Ben's car. He must be home. She didn't recognize the car parked next to his. Possibly someone with company had used his extra spot the way she'd just used someone else's spot.

Ben's key was in her hand. Maybe this is a mistake, she thought uneasily. Maybe Ben had company. Better to ring the doorbell and not use the key. "Don't be shy, Emily, use the key anytime of the day or night." He'd said that so often she'd lost track. Still, she'd only really used the key three times.

Emily retraced her footsteps and stood looking down at the car in Ben's second parking slot. It was a bright red sports model. She bent lower, a Mazda something or other. A younger person's car. What to do? She'd forgotten the present for Ben and Ted and the valentine was inside her suitcase. "Shit!"

Emily walked back to the Mastersons' car and got in. She huddled into her coat, but didn't turn on the engine or the heater.

Maybe she should go to a hotel and not spoil anyone's evening. It was bad enough that her homecoming was spoiled; why spoil her friends' party? You don't know that you would spoil it, she argued with herself. Of course I know it. Those men don't know me so conversation would be difficult. The women will probably feel uncomfortable. Why would you go to a hotel when you own a house other people are partying in . . . without you, her other self argued in return. I thought . . . I expected . . . that things would be the same as when I left. Obviously things have changed a great deal. Everyone appears to have someone. In my house. Their house too; they pay rent. That entitles them to entertain. You yourself said they could do that. Yes, but I expected to be part of . . . If I go into the house, I'll be like a fifth wheel. "Shit!"

How long are you going to sit here and freeze? Aren't you going to go up and ring Ben's doorbell or open the door with the key? Better to go home and try to sneak upstairs from the kitchen.

Emily opened the car door and got out. Her face grim with purpose, she walked up to Ben's door. She shoved the key in her pocket and rang the bell.

Emily's first thought when the door opened was, I was this young once. I even had a ponytail. I don't ever remember my skin being that clear and blemish free. She had to do something, say something. She forced a smile and said, "I believe I have the wrong house. I'm looking for 2112."

"This is 2121. It's easy to mix up the buildings. The one you want is three streets over. Baddinger runs both ways and curves around. You think it's three streets but it's really all the same."

"That explains it," Emily said, backing down the steps. From inside she heard Ben call, "Who is it, Melanie?" And Melanie's reply. "Someone looking for 2112."

Melanie yet.

Emily ran to the Mastersons' car. She wanted to cry, but the tears wouldn't come. "And a happy Valentine's Day to you too," she said bitterly as she turned the key and then the headlights.

The Mastersons' house was dark when she returned home. She parked across the street from her own house, got out, and walked down the driveway to her own kitchen door. She opened it, walked across the kitchen to the back stairs and up to her room, her eyes smarting with unshed tears. She closed and locked the door to her room.

They don't need you, Emily. Not anymore. Your friends have come into their own. Her other self presented an argument. You, of course, are basing all this on what you saw through a window. And that sweet young person who opened Ben's door.

Men!

She hated them all.

Men were the reason for all her unhappiness. Before and now.

Go figure.

Emily took her time undressing, hanging up her new suit. Why in the world was she saving these shoes with a broken heel? She tossed them in the wastebasket in the bathroom. She washed her face, brushed her teeth and her hair, hung up her towel. Another minute was used up putting on her nightgown and crawling into bed.

The long night stretched ahead of her. She knew she

wouldn't be able to sleep. She could never sleep when things were bothering her.

Emily cringed, her nerves tingling, when a burst of laughter from the dining room wafted up through the heat register. If she wanted to, she could go over to the wall, sit on the floor, and listen to everything that was being said. If she wanted to.

She absolutely would not do that.

Emily tormented herself further by letting her mind, her memories, take over as she lay in bed, in the dark, listening to the sounds of her family. She wanted to be there, to share, to laugh with them. Instead she was lying in bed, in her own house, hiding out. By her own choice.

Ben. Don't think about Ben.

Emily moved from one side of the bed to the other. She fluffed the pillows, straightened the covers, blew her nose, dabbed at her eyes.

Hours passed. The clock on the night table said it was 12:30 when she heard footsteps in the hallway. From outside she could hear the sounds of car engines, one after the other. Valentine's Day was over.

And then the house was quiet, settled for the night.

Emily continued to think about the past, the present, and the future. When the clock said it was 4:30, she dressed in sweats and warm slippers. Why should she shiver? Who cared if her boarders sweated under their bed covers. She gave the thermostat a vicious twist and set the heat to 80 degrees.

Downstairs she stopped at the last step and looked around. The dining room table was still full of dishes. The turkey carcass loomed in the center of the table. The crystal winked at her with the aid of the moonlight filtering into the room in long silvery shafts.

In the kitchen, rage overtook her. There were pots and pans everywhere. They hadn't even been put to soak. The table was so cluttered with wine bottles, glasses, snacks, hors d'oeuvres, dirty ashtrays, and used silver she couldn't find a place to set her coffee cup. The pot was dirty, the grounds still in the stainless steel basket, the red light blinking. The smell of burnt coffee permeated the room. Fire hazard. How could they be so stupid? One, yes, maybe even two of them, but all seven? The oven was still on, too.

How dare they do this to her?

She didn't stop to think, didn't stop to weigh the consequences when her arm sent everything on the kitchen table flying and crashing. Then she pressed the panic button on the alarm system, stood back to listen to the wild, shrill whistles and screeches that ricocheted throughout the house. That should bring them on the run, even the Demster twins from the apartment over the garage. The phone rang a second later. ADT. "Sorry, this is Emily Thorn. I set it off by mistake. The code word is clinic. Sorry," she said, replacing the receiver.

It took three minutes before they were all standing in the kitchen, the Demster twins banging on the back door.

They stared at her with sleep-fogged expressions.

"Emily!" they chorused.

"Clean this kitchen. *Now!* You left the coffeepot on and the oven. Your *guests* blocked in my car last night. I wanted to use it. I had to borrow the Mastersons' car. Correct me if I'm wrong, but this is my house, isn't it?" She was so angry she started to tremble. She had to get out of here before she said something she was going to regret. She turned on her heel and stomped her way back upstairs to her room.

This time she did sit down on the floor next to the heat register and listened unashamedly. However, there was nothing to hear except the sound of dishes and silver being moved around. She gnawed at her thumbnail.

Was she being petulant, childish? Damn right and she didn't care. She wasn't going to open herself up to the same kind of hurt Ian had inflicted on her. That was never going to happen to her again. She'd get rid of them before they got rid of her. Betrayal had to be the worst sin in the world.

All because of a party you weren't invited to, Emily? How could they invite you, you didn't even tell them where you were going, when you would be back. They pay rent and they have rights. You said they could entertain. Would you really stand in the way of their happiness if it meant they were going to break away and find a life with a man? That's what this is all about, isn't it? Did you really think all of you were going to spend the rest of your days here in this house playing Campfire Girls?

Yes, yes, I did think that. I wanted that. I wanted to belong, to have a family. I wanted us to share, to confide, to be there for one another when . . . for the bad times. We were doing so well, everything was working out. The business is a success, our futures are going to be secure. And . . .

And what? Is that all there is—security and work? What about living a life? Sharing it with someone who cares for you. Love? What's wrong with that? You don't have the right to tell the others what they can or can't do in their personal lives. It was a party, Emily, a Valentine party. If you hadn't gone away, you would have been sitting at that table with Ben. You went away; it was your decision. Suck it up, Emily, don't make waves. Life is going to go on no matter what you do so make sure it's what you really want. Think about how much you enjoy the women; think about how well you all get along.

Ben.

The soft tap on the door forced Emily to her feet. Had she locked the door? She sighed with relief when she saw the lock button was straight up.

"Emily, it's Lena. I brought you some coffee. Emily?

Please open the door. I know you're upset. Can't we talk about this?"

Emily sat down on the bed and hugged her knees. She felt like a wounded bird whose wings had been clipped. Once she'd felt like a tired, old dog. She didn't know which was worse. All she knew was that her heart was sore and bruised.

Last night you stand outside like a thief and spy on your friends. Today you are hiding out in your room as if you've done something wrong. Oh, you've come a long way, Emily. Go downstairs, clear the air. Don't let this fester.

"I can't," Emily whimpered.

Yes you can. You can do whatever it takes. That's how you've gotten this far. You can do this, I know you can. They have the right to be heard.

Emily brushed her hair, then stared at the person in the mirror. She'd actually forgotten about her looks. Suddenly what she looked like didn't matter. What mattered was who this person in the mirror was.

They were in the kitchen, seated around the kitchen table, coffee in front of them. Her chair was empty; so was the coffee cup at her place.

"It must have been some party," she said quietly.

"It was. Actually we were celebrating more than Valentine's Day. Zoë signed up a huge insurance company in Raritan Center, and Martha signed up a chemical company in the Middlesex Industrial Park. Ben was supposed to clinch a deal with that new company that opened up behind the Foodtown. He called last night to say it's a done deal. He was supposed to come to dinner but his kid sister came in from Tampa, where she's going to college, and he was taking her and his son to the Poconos skiing today. It wasn't as frivolous as . . . as it must have looked when you got home." Lena's voice was weary-sounding, her eyes tired.

"Sit down, Emily, I'll pour you some coffee," Kelly said quietly.

"I guess you want to know who . . . whose cars were in the driveway. Well, they . . . Rose and I invited the girls to a belated New Year's party the twin organization had and . . . only twins can belong, but the party is open to guests . . . that kind of thing. The . . . others all seemed to hit it off pretty well and there were some new members and those members brought other sets of twins we'd never met before because they hadn't joined up . . . we thought . . . it was so nice to enjoy their company and I am babbling and don't know why," Rose said.

"You made us feel like we did something wrong," Lena said coolly. "I guess it was wrong to go to bed and leave the mess, but we agreed to get up early and clean it up. We drank too much wine. So, if that's a sin in your book, we're sorry."

"We didn't know you were coming home last night," Nancy said. "Why didn't you join us instead of going upstairs? I think your whole attitude stinks, Emily. Why are you making us . . . at least me, feel like we did something sneaky and underhanded? We live here too. You said we could entertain or did that mean only when you were here?"

Ben's kid sister. Relief washed over her. She should say something, give some indication that it was all right. But it wasn't all right. She knew before the words tumbled out of her mouth that she was, as Ian always said, cutting off her nose to spite her face. Her stupid, stubborn streak was going to do her in again. Maybe they'd just met the men a few weeks ago, maybe they weren't really involved, but they would be sooner or later. And then, one by one, they would leave. And she'd be alone.

Emily nodded. She felt uncomfortable, as if she didn't belong anymore. "Of course you have the right to have a party. Congratulations on getting the new business. I got some myself in New York. It's all in the envelope on the counter. This is very hard for me to say, but I think it's time you all moved on, found your own place. We can't be the Campfire Girls forever. I'm . . . ah, I'm going to sell the house and get a townhouse or a condo. Maybe in Park Gate. Take your time, there's no rush. Actually, take as long as you like." She set her coffee cup down on the counter and left the room.

In her room, secure within the confines of the four walls, Emily cried like a baby, hiccupping and sobbing into the pillow. Damn, it wasn't supposed to hurt like this. Being the initiator was supposed to ease the pain of the eventual parting.

And all because of a stupid party. Well, she couldn't backtrack now. Even if she wanted to. Which she didn't. Get on with it, Emily, do what you have to do. But what the hell is it that I have to do?

You have to stop depending on other people for your happiness. You need to get a life of your own. Put all your old ghosts to rest and that means Ian too. Then you go on. Again.

What do you want Emily?

"I want . . . to be happy, contented, to have someone to talk with, to share with, the good as well as the bad, someone who isn't judgmental. Ah, but isn't that what you just did? You not only judged, you tried and convicted all your friends. Even Ben. You are a mess, Emily."

A moment later she was out the door, taking the steps two at a time. She ran through the rooms, careening around the dining room table and out to the kitchen. She skidded to a stop. They were all crying. She was crying.

"It's okay if you leave. I just didn't want to have to go

through it seven times. I thought if I told you all to go I'd only hurt once. I can't stand . . . I didn't think I could take it again. I watched all of you through the dining room window and you all had someone and I just knew, just felt, that . . ." For a moment she thought she couldn't go on. "I'll work at it," she managed to say. "Don't be angry with me. It was stupid of me. In my mind I was coming home with presents, new business, new face, new boobs and I wanted us to . . . to . . . it doesn't really matter now. I was stupid and doing exactly the same things I did when I was with Ian. I had hoped I'd grown, gotten smarter, but emotionally, I guess I screwed up."

They were all over her, touching her face, peering at her, standing back to check out her bustline, as Nancy put it. Then they were all talking at once, about the different sets of twins, what each had to offer, about business, the weather, the house, everything under the sun. The bottom line was, "We missed you, Emily. It wasn't the same without you."

"I missed you too," Emily said, dabbing at her eyes. "I went over to Ben's last night when I saw you all through the dining room window and this young girl answered the door. I pretended I was looking for another address. I thought he'd given up on me. Everything kind of overwhelmed me after that. Can you forgive me?"

"Of course. Isn't that what family is all about?"

"Are we blessed or what?" Emily asked happily.

Blessed.

Chapter 15

"Emily, will you marry me?" Ben asked. "This is the fifteenth time I've asked you in the last two years. Is this going to be my lucky day?"

"I'm afraid not, Ben. I'm not marriage material. We both know that. Stop trying to make an honest woman of me. I like my independence. If I got married, I'd smother you. That's my nature. It's better this way. For me. If you . . ."

"Don't say it, Emily. I don't want anyone else. I love you, have always loved you. We're so good together."

"And I want to keep it that way. For some reason that piece of paper that says you're man and wife changes things. Can we talk about something else?"

"What would you like to talk about, Emily?"

"My upcoming trip to Los Angeles to see Ian."

"So, what else is there to talk about? You're going, you made up your mind, so what is there to discuss?"

"I guess I just want your opinion."

"I'm the one who suggested it, remember? Is there something else on your mind? If so, tell me. I'm not a mind reader, Emily."

Emily smiled. "I leave in the morning. Want to come along?"

"Nope. I'll be here when you get back."

"You are the sweetest man I know, Ben Jackson," Emily said, cuddling next to him.

"I'm not sure I like being called sweet. What's wrong with rugged, handsome? I like sinewy."

"All those things." Emily smiled. "I can't imagine my life without you and my housemates."

"Emily Thorn, I swear that is the nicest thing you ever said to me."

"Shut up and make love to me."

He shut up and did as instructed.

She didn't just look good, she looked smashing. A mover and a shaker. Or a woman on the prowl.

The Armani suit was perfection in itself, the shoes positively sinful, showing off her legs to their best advantage. Her makeup was flawless, her hair so fashionable she fit right in with those on the fast track.

She had an appointment at the Bayshore Clinic in the name of Ann Montgomery for three o'clock with Dr. Ian Thorn.

What she hadn't counted on, wasn't prepared for, was the crowd of protesters outside the clinic with their home-made signs and pamphlets that they tried to shove in her hand. She brushed them aside as she struggled past the knotted groups. She wondered if she'd come at a bad time or if this was a daily happening.

Inside, she took a deep breath, announced herself to the receptionist. When the nurse on duty handed her a form to fill out, Emily smiled and said, "I'm here for personal reasons." She handed the clipboard back to the nurse.

"Doctor will see you now," the nurse said five minutes later. "First door on the left."

The urge to cut and run was so strong, Emily clenched her fists and dug the heels of her shoes into the carpet. Deep breaths. Real deep breaths. Okay, walk slowly, open the door just as slowly. You're lookin' good, Emily. Act like it.

This wasn't Ian. Not this pudgy, balding man whose hand was trembling as he held it out to her. "Miss Montgomery, my nurse said you're here for personal reasons. A lot of patients say that at first. Sit down, relax."

"Ian, don't you recognize me? It's me, Emily."

"Emily!" Shock. Disbelief. Outrage. It was all there for her to see in his red face. He's drinking too much, Emily thought.

"That's my name," Emily said, sitting down. She crossed her legs, pleased at the way the Armani skirt hiked up. "I came all the way across the country just to see you."

"Why? What do you want? What did you do to yourself?"

"Actually I don't want anything. There's not a thing you have that I would ever want. I just wanted to see you. Well, maybe I wanted to tell you something. I burned all your white shirts." She paused a moment, for effect. "I guess it's my turn to ask you what you've done to yourself. You look like you've been rode hard and hung up wet. The good life, huh? If I was one of those women out there, I'd never let you take a knife to me. Your hands are shaking. You have the face of a drinker. You must be what, forty pounds overweight, and is that a smudge I see on that white shirt? *Tsk, tsk,*" Emily said, clucking her tongue.

"What do you want, Emily?"

"Nothing. Truly, Ian, I don't want anything. Now, how much do you charge for your initial visit?"

"A hundred dollars," Ian said automatically.

Emily wrote off a check and placed it precisely in the middle of Ian's desk. "See, I'm even paying for your time. I said I didn't want anything. I wanted to see if the years were as good to you as they were to me." She stood up, twirled around for his benefit, then sat down. "What you did to me was unconscionable, but I survived. Bet you don't know a thing about me. Or do you?" Ian shook his head. "I am Emily Thorn of the famous Emily's Fitness Centers. Of course we're mainly on the East Coast so it's possible you haven't heard about us. I make"—she leaned over the desk to whisper—"seven figures a year." Of course it was a lie, but he didn't need to know that.

"Come off it, Emily." At the same time he rang for his nurse. When she poked her head in the door, he barked, "Call Stan Margolis, my old attorney in New Jersey, and ask him to tell you everything he knows about an enterprise called Emily's Fitness Centers. Do it right now."

Emily shrugged. "How's business? Why didn't you have the guts to tell me to my face you were leaving instead of sending me a Federal Express letter?"

"I didn't want a scene. You loved scenes."

"How many clinics do you have out here?"

"Six, not that it's any of your business. I'm thinking of getting out. Every day I have to fight those people out there. We've been fire-bombed twice, robbed six or seven times, and now it's worse. I didn't bargain for this," he said, his words coming out in a tumbled rush.

The phone on his desk buzzed. Ian picked up the receiver and said, "Dr. Thorn. Stan, good to hear your voice. Fine, fine. Yeah, lots of smog. I have a patient sitting here."

Emily smiled at the expression on Ian's face. How was it possible that she'd been so besotted with this man?

Ian hung up the phone, an ugly look on his face. "I want half."

"Of what?"

"Whatever you have. I gave you your start. Turnabout is fair play."

"What about the start I gave you?"

"I gave you everything you wanted," Ian snapped. "Pay me off and I can stop slicing up women for a living."

"Go to hell, Ian. I divorced you. Long ago. You have no claim on anything I have."

"Do you still have the house?"

"Oh, yes with two mortgages. I took out an equity loan in case you decided you wanted your half. It's yours; name the time and date when you want to take possession. I've kind of let it go. Now I have a condo in Park Gate. The house is worth very little," Emily lied. "I'll give you five thousand for it or it can go into default. Darn, I meant to bring that up. Thanks for mentioning it, Ian. Well, I really should be going now."

"Why should I believe you?"

"You always did. When did I ever lie to you, Ian?"

"All right, I'll take it."

"Not until you sign this waiver. And this transfer for the deed."

"Write the check," he said, signing. "What about the tulips?"

"What about them?" she asked as she wrote out a second check and placed it on the first.

"Did you keep up with them?"

"For a while. There aren't any flowers now. I don't have time to tend a garden." Then Emily asked softly, "Are you happy, Ian?"

"Who the hell do you know who's happy, Emily? You always did ask stupid questions like that." He shoved the checks in his desk drawer.

"Aren't you going to ask me if I'm happy?"

"Well, are you?"

Emily smiled. "Very happy. You broke my heart, Ian. I mean that literally. But it mended. For a while I didn't think it was possible. Sometimes it's nice to be wrong.

Once I realized I'd wasted half my life on you, the comeback was relatively easy. What's happened to you, Ian?"

"Nothing. Don't go looking for things to say just to be nasty."

"You're wasting your life the way you wasted mine. It's too late for you, Ian, you've lost your edge. Look at the tremor in your hands. You need to give this up before something goes wrong. Go into dermatology." She began to walk toward the door.

"Come on, Emily, you must still have some feelings for me. We were together a long time. Let's have dinner for old times' sake. Don't you remember the good times, the good old days?" His voice was desperate-sounding.

"Ian, this is me, Emily. What good times, what good old days are you talking about? All my feelings for you are gone. You pretty much repulse me right now. All that education, all that medical knowledge, and look at you. You're pathetic. You're also a pisspot," she said over her shoulder.

Ian opened the drawer of his desk and stared at the checks Emily had given him.

Time to go home, to the big, lonely house in the hills that was full of treasures, all bought and paid for with abortion money. He removed his surgical coat and slipped into his sports jacket. He wished then, the way he wished every day, that there was a back door to the clinic so he wouldn't have to fight the protesters outside.

As he made his way across the parking lot, the noise and babble finally got to him. He raised his fist and shouted obscenities. He heard the shot, even thought he saw the sun spear off the barrel of the gun. He felt himself lose his balance, his arms grappling with the thin air. He felt his face mash into the dirty asphalt.

And then nothing.

*   *   *

Emily packed her small overnight bag as she waited for Room Service to bring the garden salad and vegetable soup she'd ordered for dinner. She snapped the small bag she would carry on the Redeye she was taking to return home in a few hours.

Today's visit with Ian had taken its toll on her. Her bravado and smart-aleck talk with her ex-husband had confused her. She still wasn't sure why she'd come here. The business with the house had merely been an excuse. With Ian she had always needed an excuse for everything. Old habits were hard to break. Until she'd seen him face to face, she'd felt connected to him even though they were divorced. Now, though, she was finally able to say there was nothing about Ian she ever wanted to see or hear of again. If there was a connection, her visit had severed it once and for all.

Maybe now she could give some serious thought to taking back her maiden name; legally. It was something she'd thought about many times, but had never acted on.

Emily carried her bag over to the door just as a knock sounded. She opened it to admit the waiter with her dinner. "I didn't order this," she said, "but it's okay, leave it. You might have a problem with the person who gets my salad and soup, though." She signed the slip, added a generous tip, and sat down to eat a thick ham and cheese sandwich with potato chips and pickles on the side. The frosty bottle of Budweiser looked wonderful. She loved beer, but rarely drank it. She turned on the TV and leaned back in the chair, propping her feet on the bed while she munched contentedly.

Until she saw Ian's face flash on the screen. She turned up the sound that she'd lowered when the waiter appeared. Her eyes were wide with shock as she tried to comprehend what she'd just heard. Ian was dead, shot in the parking lot by an abortion foe. She'd just spoken with him a few hours ago, she'd called him a pisspot, and now he was dead. She would never, ever, hear his voice again. He was out of her life. Forever.

Emily cried then, deep, bone-searing sobs that rocked her body.

Hours later, when there were no more tears, Emily washed her face, brushed her hair, put on fresh lipstick. Her eyes were red-rimmed now, slightly swollen. She opted to forgo eye makeup, knowing she was going to tear up again and again.

What was she to do now? Should she return home as planned? Should she go to the police station? And say what? Ian was her ex-husband. She wasn't involved in his life anymore. Who would handle his affairs? Did he have a live-in love, a wife somewhere? Who was his local attorney? Maybe she should call Stan Margolis back in New Jersey and ask his advice. Who was going to plan his funeral and where was he to be buried? Ian never wanted to talk about life insurance or discuss cemetery plots. In these past years did he do any estate planning? Was she obligated to stay and . . . and what? Emily threw her hands in the air.

Emily placed the call through the operator, telling her she didn't know the number. "Tell whoever answers the phone that this is an emergency, a life and death matter. Actually it's death. Yes, I'll hold," Emily dithered.

The attorney's voice when it came on the line was professional-sounding, much like Ian's. She took a deep breath and explained the situation. Finally she said, "I don't know what to do. What I mean is I want to do the right thing. Leaving sounds so . . . callous. I'm willing to do whatever you think is best."

She was frazzled now, pacing and wringing her hands. Margolis was going to call the police, explain, and call her back. Should she call home? It was nine o'clock back in

New Jersey, six here. Her friends would be home now. Usually the first thing they did was turn on the little television set on the kitchen counter for the evening news. Ian's death would have been on the news; she was certain of that. Violent deaths always made the news. Call now or wait till Margolis called her back? Cancel her airline flight or not?

Emily finished the beer in the bottle. She continued to pace.

It was six-thirty when the attorney in New Jersey called her back. "The police would like to talk with you. It's a formality, but I do think you should make an appearance. Delay your flight till tomorrow. If you need me, call." Emily copied down his home phone number and stuck it in her purse.

She used up another twenty minutes canceling her flight and calling the women, who had already heard the news. "No, no, there's nothing any of you can do. I'll call you when I get back from the police station. Do me a favor and call Ben."

At the police station Emily was taken into a small room, where she explained her visit to a man who said he was a homicide detective. He listened intently. "I knew he wouldn't . . . at least I thought he wouldn't want to talk to me if he knew it was me . . . I suppose this doesn't make sense to you . . . right now it doesn't make much sense to me either. I can't explain why I came here to California at this particular point in my life . . . perhaps because . . . because . . . I might be getting married. More likely than not I won't . . . that didn't make sense, did it? Something told me to come and . . . and I did . . . I don't even know if Ian ever got the divorce papers. What should I do now? Who's in charge of his affairs? I don't want to step on any toes, but if there is no one, out of decency I'll make the final arrangements. When will . . . when will . . . Ian be . . . do you know?"

"The coroner said he'll release the body late tomorrow. We've spoken to Dr. Thorn's head nurse and to his office manager. His attorney is down the hall. If you like, you can talk to him. We'll have your statement typed up and you can sign it. I don't see any problems here. You have my sympathies, Mrs. Thorn." Emily nodded.

"Aaron Jessup, Mrs. Thorn," a tall man with gray hair and eyes to match said when the homicide detective ushered her into a long, narrow room.

"Emily Thorn," Emily said, holding out her hand. "Do you know if Ian had any . . . any . . . did he want a burial or a cremation? When we were married, Ian would never discuss such things so I have no idea what I should do, if in fact I'm the person to do anything at all. I'm willing to make the arrangements, take him . . . home . . . but I don't know if he considered New Jersey his home anymore. He has three brothers, but as far as I know, he never spoke to any of them once he left home. His parents are deceased. I have no idea where the brothers are."

The attorney cleared his throat. "Dr. Thorn consulted with me shortly after he moved out here. His affairs are pretty much in order. He asked to be cremated and he wanted his ashes spread around the Mojave Desert." Emily's eyes widened.

"Ian wants . . . wanted cremation?"

"Yes. And he wanted tulips dropped from an airplane. Tons of tulips. Now, that may seem bizarre to you and me, but to Dr. Thorn it was something he didn't feel he had to explain. I can assure you he was quite sane when this will was written."

Emily wondered why the man sounded so defensive. "If that's what he wants, then it should be done. Are you the executor?"

"Yes."

"I was supposed to return home tonight on the Redeye, but I canceled my flight. I'm staying at the Beverly Hills Hotel if you want to call me. I can stay on for a few days."

"I would appreciate that."

Emily nodded. "I'm afraid I don't know much about cremation. I don't even know who to call. Do you call a mortician or . . . I . . . I'm not sure he'd want me to be doing *anything.* I've always believed a dying person's last wishes should be given serious consideration but I don't think I . . . I can do whatever you want," Emily said flatly.

"Dr. Thorn was a complex man. He was also a very wealthy man. He left everything he owns to you."

"*What?*" The single word sounded like a gunshot as it exploded from her mouth.

"Dr. Thorn left everything he owns, his entire estate to you. He made the will when he first moved here and consulted with me. When the divorce papers arrived, I made a point of asking him if he wanted to change his will and he said no. He said he owed it to you, that without you he wouldn't have been able to practice medicine."

"Ian said that?" Emily crumpled then, tears rivering down her cheeks. "I don't understand. I don't want his money," she sobbed.

"Dr. Thorn said you would say exactly what you've just said. He also said, and this is a direct quote: 'It will be interesting to see what she does with all my money. You tell her I'm going to be watching.' End of quote."

"Even in death he threatens me."

"He did say one thing I've never forgotten. It was in passing and neither of us dwelled on it. He said it after he signed the will."

Emily blew her nose lustily. "I don't think I want to hear it."

The attorney smiled. "Dr. Thorn said that, when he met

you, you were as pretty as a butterfly. I never found Dr. Thorn to be a complimentary man so the comment was significant. You are very pretty, Mrs. Thorn. The analogy, in my opinion, is on the money. That was another favorite expression of Dr. Thorn's. Well, I guess we can wind things down here. It's getting late. Can I drop you off at your hotel? It isn't out of my way. You did say you were staying at the Beverly Hills Hotel, didn't you?"

"That's very kind of you, Mr. Jessup. Thank you."

It was eleven o'clock when Emily called the house on Sleepy Hollow Road. The phone was picked up on the first ring. Emily sobbed out the night's encounter and all the information the attorney had given her. "What do you think of that threat?" she squealed.

"Emily, honey, don't take it as a threat. Think of it as what he said: he'll be watching, knowing you'll do the right thing," Lena said soothingly.

"It's a test. He was forever testing me. This . . . he dies and leaves me with a test. What if I do the wrong thing? What if it isn't what he wanted or intended?"

"He left that up to you. He could have left his money to anyone, to charity, to the homeless, to some medical fund, but he left it to you. I think he trusted you in his own way. Look at the positive side of things. Don't load your shoulders down. By the way, Ben is on his way. Zoë drove him to the airport. Don't sit around the hotel and think, Emily. Go to the airport, where it's busy and there are people. Wait for Ben."

"Is he really coming here, Lena? I wanted to call him to ask him to come, but it didn't seem fair. Yes, yes, I'll do that. I don't know if I can handle this, Lena. I have my limits."

"You can do it, Emily. When you come back here, you'll be free of all the old ghosts. It was a long time in coming, sweetie. Don't think about the past; it's gone. Deal with the here and now, and on a lighter note, Miz Thorn, Dudley Duhoefer popped the question to Miz Martha Nesbit. Miz Nesbit said yes. Do you believe that? Tonight, it happened tonight after dinner. He showed up at the back door and got down on one knee in front of all of us. It was *soooo* romantic."

"Damn, I missed that. Do you think he'll do a replay?" Emily said.

"I'm sure he will. I can tell you this—it was a struggle for him. He's kind of arthritic. It just makes it all the more endearing. Now, you're going to the airport, right?"

"Yes. Lena, talk to the girls. Ask them if they have any opinions as to what to do with Ian's money. What do you think I should do with it?"

"Emily, you are asking the wrong person. I can't think above a hundred dollars. I know we have monies in our funds, but I can't comprehend that either. Don't be in a rush. How much money are we talking about?"

"I have no idea. Everything was invested. Wisely. A lot, I guess. All I know is, I can't keep it. Thanks for listening. Give my regards to the women and tell Martha congratulations. I'll see you in a few days."

Emily was standing outside the jetway at LAX when Ben walked off the plane. Her eyes filled with relief at the sight of him. This man, this person she called friend and lover, could handle anything. The knowledge made her knees weak. She leaned into him as they walked down the concourse.

"We're heading for the bar. You look like you could use a good, stiff drink. I'm buying."

"In that case, I accept," Emily said wanly.

Emily was almost finished with her third beer when she said, her words slurred, "Ben, why did I come here now? Why did I choose this particular time? Was I meant to do this? I called Ian a pisspot; those were the last words he heard me say. Then he . . . then he died. I have to live with that. How am I going to do that, Ben?"

"You go on, Emily. You don't dwell on the past and you don't look back. Yesterday is gone and you can't get it back. You have no choice but to go on."

"Yes," Emily whispered.

"In your heart do you think he wasted his life and yours?"

"Yes," she whispered again.

"What constitutes a pisspot? Is he one?"

A smile worked around the corners of Emily's mouth. "It's another way of saying he was a jerk. A little more graphic, I suppose, and yes, he is . . . was one."

"I rest my case. Come on, you have a snootful. Time to put you to bed. Tomorrow's another day. Actually, it's tomorrow already."

"I'm glad you're here, Ben. Thanks for coming."

"My pleasure," Ben said, guiding her from the airport lounge.

In bed, the pillows propped behind her, Emily did her best not to cry. "Someone should cry for Ian, Ben. I'm crying, but I'm not crying for him. Who am I crying for? Do you know, Ben? I'm glad you're here. Did I say that already?"

Ben smiled. "Go to sleep, Emily. It's okay, to cry, and it doesn't matter if you're crying for Ian or for yourself. I slept on the plane so I'll be out in the sitting room watching television. I'm sorry, Emily. It's always hard when someone we know dies. Those of us left behind tend to say we weren't ready, that it wasn't time. There isn't a given time. It happens and you make the best of it. Everything will be all right, Emily. I promise."

"I just need to know why I came here now, at this particular time. God must have decided to let me see Ian one more time so I could finally see for myself that I was . . . I'm glad you came, Ben. Oh, I said that, didn't . . . ?"

She was asleep. Ben smiled as he leaned over to kiss her cheek. He closed the door softly. He settled himself in a chair, then turned the sound on the television set low. He was asleep within minutes.

Emily woke with a pounding headache. Today was . . . the day she was . . . to . . . God, what was today? A real funeral with a hearse would have been simple. That she could cope with. Cremation was . . . different. Scattering ashes, Ian's ashes, was going to be traumatic. You can do this, Emily. Swing your legs over the side of the bed, pick up the phone, and call Mr. Jessup. That's the first step. Don't think, just do it.

"Mr. Jessup," Emily said. "I need to know where to have the florist deliver the flowers. I guess I have to hire a helicopter to make the arrangements. This is something I myself have to do," Emily said, her voice brittle.

But in the end, it was Ben who helped her make the arrangements.

"You've come a long way, Emily," Ben said, in the cab on the way over. "I wish you'd think about going the rest of the way with me. Will you think about it?"

"Yes, Ben, I will. I have a lot of things to think about. It seems like I've come full circle."

"That you have, Mrs. Thorn."

"What do you think about me taking back my maiden name?"

"Do you feel like an Emily Wyatt, or do you feel like an Emily Thorn?" Ben asked. "Or is it possible you could feel like an Emily Wyatt Thorn Jackson?"

"You're pushing it, Ben. Here's the florist. Let's do our

thing and go for a drink," Emily said tightly. "This do-good stuff is making me thirsty."

"Now, let me make sure I understand this," the florist behind the counter said. "You want all the tulips I can get and you want me to take them out to the airport tomorrow morning. You're going to call me with the exact location. You're paying me a deposit now and will pay the balance in the morning on delivery. You want all colors."

"That's right," Emily said. "I don't mean just a few dozen, I mean hundreds and hundreds of tulips. If this is going to be a problem, I need to know now so I can make other arrangements. They're for a . . . funeral. Last wishes and all of that."

"Here's my card. I'm writing my home phone number on the back since we close at six. I'll have your tulips wherever you want them."

From a phone stall on the street Emily again gave her credit card number and made arrangements to hire a helicopter for three hours the following morning. She copied down directions carefully.

"Everything's been taken care of. Let's go for that drink and let's not talk about Ian Thorn or Emily Thorn. Let's talk about green meadows and blue skies and tell pet stories."

"Whatever you want, Emily."

There was only one bad moment as the pilot circled over the desert, but it was solved immediately by Ben. Emily fretted that the ashes in the urn would spiral upward into the rotor blades. The pilot did some fancy maneuvering as Ben let the box go. Emily upended the boxes of cut flowers, one after the other. It looks pretty, she thought, a rainbow of flowers over the desert. She shed a tear. Ben wiped it away.

"You can go back now," Emily said in a choked voice. Ian's at rest, finally. She raised her eyes upward. *He's all Yours now. If I might offer a suggestion, I'd put him in charge of complaints.*

Good-by, Ian.

Part Three

Chapter 16

Emily stared at the calendar in the kitchen. A year had gone by since Ian's death. Where had the time gone? Why wasn't she feeling something—happiness, sadness? Something. She looked around. She didn't even know why she was home today other than she didn't feel like going to the office. She could do that now, take time off when she felt like it. All of them could, for that matter.

Yesterday, for some unexplained reason, she'd gone through the employee files. She should give some kind of commendation to all the people she employed. But what?

Damn, she was so out of sorts today. Maybe she needed to pick a fight with Ben or one of the women. An exercise in futility—they wouldn't fight back and she had no reason to pick a fight. Then do something outrageous, something decadent. But what?

Maybe she needed to talk to someone. Someone. Who? Someone who wasn't involved in her personal life. A priest, maybe.

Emily didn't stop to think. She dialed 411 and asked the information operator for the number for Saint John's Catholic Church. She copied down the number and dialed again. She waited until she heard a voice on the other end of the line. "Father, this is Emily Thorn. I think I might be in need of a little spiritual guidance. Tell me, what does one do when one reaches one's goals? Do you set new ones? Do you mark time? What does one do with one's time? I'm not happy, nor am I unhappy. It just seems to me there should be more . . . of what I don't know. Am I being selfish in wanting . . . that's it, you see, I don't know what I want. I thought I wanted . . . needed to prove . . . I did all that . . . I came to terms with so many things, but it still isn't right for me."

"Perhaps you need to go back to the beginning. To do all the things you were never able to do. Peace and happiness come from within. You need to accept yourself for who you are. God didn't waste his time when he created you. If you had a wish, just one wish, what would you wish for?"

"Oh, Father, that's a serious thing to be asking me."

"Yes, it is. It's something that requires much careful thought. You must be careful not to waste that wish, for there is only one."

"Father, I wanted children. Unfortunately that didn't happen. I think I would have been a good mother. I wasted half my life because I was stupid. The best years of my life. Maybe that's what I should wish for; that half of my life that was lost to me."

"Perhaps you should make a list before you make your wish. Sometimes when you see it in black and white, it isn't what you want at all. It could be as simple as going away for a while, getting a fresh perspective. I don't know if this will be of interest to you or not, but I will mention it. There is a place called Black Mountain Retreat in the Great Smoky Mountains you might wish to visit sometime. I was there once. It was wonderful. You don't have to be religious to go. The mountains are breathtaking, the streams are crystal clear, the walking trails are scented from heaven. The food leaves a little to be desired, but the coffee is wonderful. It's a coming together of strangers, sharing, looking at your inner self. But only if you want to explore that avenue. If you want to spend all your time hiking, eating, and sleeping, that's okay too. It's a plain, simple life so don't take fancy clothes if you decide to go."

"Thank you, Father, for talking with me. Is it all right if I call you from time to time?"

"Anytime of the day or night, child. I'll be here as long as God wants me to be here. Bless you, child."

"Father, wait, don't hang up yet. Tell me, do you know . . . what I mean is, how will I know when I've reached that . . . that place of . . . contentment and inner peace?"

"If you're asking me from personal experience, I can try and give you an answer. When you wake in the morning and you feel like singing, when you hate going to bed because there's more to do. When you forget to eat because there's something more important for you to do. When watching a sunrise or a sunset gives you pleasure and you can't wait to see another. Simple things. Everyday things. A flower, a bird soaring in the sky, having your trash hauled away so you don't have to deal with it. Smiling for no reason. Laughing aloud. I find my heart is full to bursting at the sight of children playing. These are things that make me want to wake up in the morning and get on with the day. Today young people talk about priorities, look at their watches a hundred times a day. In my day we called it living life to its fullest because we don't know what tomorrow would bring. You simply cannot waste a minute of life. It's here to enjoy and live. Have I helped you, child?"

"I don't know, Father. I think I stepped off the path and took the wrong turn. I'll find my way back. I don't know if I should look for my starting point or just go on. What do you think, Father?"

"I don't have your answers, Emily. They're within you. If there's anything I can do, call me."

"I will. Thanks for listening, Father."

Emily hung up the phone. She didn't know if she felt better or worse.

Emily walked through the house, touching the back of a chair, a knickknack, staring at a picture on the wall. Maybe her mistake, if it was a mistake, was staying here in this house. It was hers now. Paid for with money she'd earned from her own sweat.

What do you wish for, Emily Thorn? That's just it, I don't know. What I do know is I have to get away before I really lose it. I have to get away from here. I'm going. I'm going to pack and go. Now, I'm going to go now, not tomorrow, not later today, now. I can get a map at the gas station. I'm going to call the women and Ben and then I'm going.

She'd come to love this house during these last years. The house was so lived in, so warm and cozy with each of the women adding her own personal touch—the green plants, the copper in the kitchen, the braided rugs, the knickknacks on the windowsills, the mayonnaise jars full of beach glass that winked and sparkled when the sun hit them through the kitchen window.

One of the women had made checkered curtains for the kitchen windows and back door, but she couldn't remember which one. That was good, she thought. They blended in, belonged; they were a team, each doing something to contribute to the everyday living.

Emily stared at the door to the bathroom off the kitchen. She'd locked it, told the girls it was off limits. It was years since she'd even thought about opening the door. The mirror was still in a million pieces on the floor. Why was that? She should open the door and clean it up, arrange to have the mirror replaced. Lord, where was the key? Probably in the junk drawer. The tip of a steak knife would open it too. And if that failed, all she had to do was take the door off the hinges. If she wanted to.

Her eyes still on the door, Emily thought about the priest's words. When was the last time she woke in the morning and felt like singing? The day I got married. When was the last time you hated going to bed because you had something more important to do? The night before my wedding. What about the sunrise and sunsets? Never. When was the last time a flower or a bird gave you joy? Never. Well, do butterflies count? Once, the day of my wedding when Ian gave me a butterfly I had to set free. I am grateful when they take my trash away but it doesn't make me happy. Laughing and smiling? Hardly ever. Children laughing and playing? Seeing children makes my heart ache. How can I laugh and smile and pretend when my heart is broken?

Emily rummaged her junk drawer for the key, found it, then clutched it in her hand. Her back stiff, she marched over to the door and inserted the key. She turned on the light, stared ahead at the bare wall where the mirror was. Black globs of glue stared back at her. On the far corner a shard of mirror still hung from the top border. If she stood on a chair, she could see into it. If she wanted to. She backed out of the bathroom to search the laundry room for a sturdy wastebasket, dustpan, and broom. She scooped up as much of the glass as she could, then she vacuumed the floor. Wearing rubber gloves, she scrubbed down the bathroom, cleaned the toilet and sink. She hung up fresh towels. When the floor dried, she carried one of the kitchen chairs into the bathroom and climbed on it.

Emily stared at her reflection. "Hello, Emily," she said quietly. She stared at the Emily Thorn in the mirror until her eyes watered. "It's me. I have something to tell you, Emily Thorn, something I was too stupid to figure out until I talked with Father Michael. You can't go back, you can't ever regain the past. I tried, I even succeeded in dressing up my shell so that I look like the Emily I remembered, wanted to be again. I was so busy trying to recapture that exterior I never gave any thought to . . . what I did was *I shut down inside.* I ceased to feel. I wasted more of my life. I want that part of me back. I want to be able to laugh and smile. I want to *feel* again. And if I get hurt again, I'll know I'm alive. How else will I know I'm alive?"

Emily reached up and gently tugged at the piece of mirror on the wall. "Good-by, Emily Thorn. You're a fraud, a phony, a make-believe." She carried the chair back to the kitchen, but left the light on and the door open.

Back at the table, Emily picked up the note where she'd scribbled the name and phone number of the mountain retreat Father Michael had given her. She dialed direct, asked for information, scribbled some more. "I'd like to make a reservation for tomorrow. I'm not sure when I'll arrive. Yes, I'd like a cabin to myself. Bedroom, sitting room, bath. Yes, that's fine. How long will I be staying? Indefinitely!" She scribbled additional directions.

It took thirty minutes to pack four suitcases. Indefinitely meant she needed a lot of clothes. She carried the suitcases down the stairs to the front door, then called the women and Ben to ask them if they'd drop everything and come by the house. "It's important," she said. The last thing she did before making fresh coffee was to call the airport and book a flight to Asheville, North Carolina, then phone a car rental agency and reserve a four-by-four. Her plan was to stay in Asheville for the night and start out for the retreat early in the morning.

Emily set out the cups, cream, and sugar along with the spoons and napkins. She sat down to wait.

They knew there was something different when they walked in the door. Emily could see it on their faces. As one, they looked toward the open powder room door.

"It was the last thing I had to do. Listen, all of you, there's something else I have to do. I know you can all get along without me for a while. I say a while because I don't know how long I'm going to be gone. I need to find my-self." She smiled, a genuine smile of warmth. "Corny, huh? Unfortunately, it's exactly what I have to do. I guess you can say I'm one of those late starters, late bloomer . . . what-ever. I'm one of those people who need to be pounded over the head to get a message through. But I got it. Finally. You guys can handle things. Heck, right now the business pretty much runs itself, thanks to all of you. Nothing is going to change. You can stay here as long as you like, carry on as before."

"Where are you going?" they asked in unison.

"Black Mountain in North Carolina. It's not far from Tennessee. It's in the Great Smoky Mountains. It's a re-treat of sorts. I left the phone number by the telephone. You call, leave a message, and then I have to call you back. There aren't any phones in the cabins. Stop looking so skeptical." Emily laughed. "I can handle it."

"I'm going to miss you," Ben said simply.

"And I'm going to miss you. I'm going to miss all of you. I already miss you and I haven't even left yet. I know you want to know why and the best answer I can give you is, I reached the goal I set for myself and for all of you. Today is the anniversary of Ian's death. Don't read more into that than there is. We shouldn't waste our lives and I don't intend to waste even one more day. You know what I'm talking about. I was so damn busy fixing up myself on the outside I forgot about the inside. I shut down inside and I never opened up. Ben knows that better than any-one. I swear to all of you, I didn't realize I'd done that until a very wise man pointed it out to me this morning. You know me, I jumped on it right away. This isn't going to be any quick fix and I know it. That's why I can't tell you how long I'll be gone."

"Good for you, Emily," Ben said in a husky voice. "We'll all be here when you get back."

"Take as long as you need."

"I feel so blessed," Emily said, blowing her nose. "I don't want to cry and I don't want any of you blubbering either. So . . . who's driving me to the airport?"

"Are you kidding? We're all taking you," the Demster twins shouted.

Emily cried then. "I love you all so much. Thanks for understanding."

"I'm outa here," Ben said, turning away so they wouldn't see the tears in his eyes. "I'll load the van. I assume the bags by the door are what you're taking." Emily nodded.

Emily followed Ben out to the van. She stepped into his arms and cried on his shoulder. "I have to do this," she whispered.

"I know you do, Emily. If it feels right, do it."

Emily smiled tearfully. "Yes, that's what you always say. You're such a good friend, Ben. You're always there for me. I know we got off to a rocky start, but we got on with it. My life is richer because of you. I never really enjoyed a picnic until you took me on one. I never thought I would ever go hot-air ballooning, but I did. You taught me not to be afraid of myself. I learned so much from you. There's one thing I don't understand, though. You never once mentioned my face-lift. Why is that?"

"What face-lift? You look the same to me." Ben grinned. "Sure, I noticed it, but to me it wasn't important. I love the Emily Thorn I first met and that isn't going to change. C'mon now, no tears. You're going off on an adventure and it's going to be whatever you make it. Think about me, the women, the business, but only if you have time. I love you, Emily. I'll be here when you get back. You are coming back, aren't you?" he asked anxiously.

"Of course I'm coming back. I don't know when, though."

"As long as you come back, that's all that's important."

He kissed her long and lingeringly. "You're a hell of a person, Emily, and remember that I'm the one who said it first. Well, maybe I'm not the first, but I'm the one who counts."

"You are the first one, Ben. I'll remember and you're the nicest guy walking this earth. You remember that I'm the one who said it. I don't care if I'm the first one or not."

"You're the first," Ben said wryly. "C'mon, climb in and let's get this show on the road. The sooner you leave, the sooner you'll get back."

Ten minutes later the door to the white van slammed shut. Two hours later there was a round of hugs and kisses and more tears as Emily prepared to walk down the jetway. To Ben she whispered, "Keep your eyes on things and take care of them. You're probably the only man I'll ever trust for the rest of my life. I'm going to work on that, but right now thanks for being my friend, Ben."

"Go on, get the hell out of here," Ben said gruffly. Emily kissed each one of them again and then ran, her tote bag flip-flopping against her side. "Bye, Emily! Call us! We love you!"

"No more crying. That's an order," Ben said firmly. "Come on, ladies, I'm taking you all to dinner! She'll be back before we know it."

Emily massaged her neck muscles before she climbed out of the jeep. The four-hour drive over rocky terrain wasn't something she was going to want to repeat for a long time. This was definitely the woods, Emily thought as she looked around. She was parked in a gravel lot that faced the main building of the Black Mountain Retreat. It was beautiful and it was so quiet she thought she was deaf for an instant. She sucked in her breath, remembering another time when the heady scent of pine weakened every bone and muscle in her body. But that wasn't completely true either. Ian had a lot to do with her rubbery knees and mushy muscles. Tall evergreens, so tall she had to step back to crane her neck upward. Smaller evergreens, low bushy evergreens, each smelling better than the other.

The main structure looked like a post card log cabin. A swing hung from rafters on the front porch and barrels of bright red geraniums were everywhere.

Serene.

Emily felt the tension leave her shoulders the moment a nun in a dark habit came out onto the front porch.

Sister Phyllis, or Phillie, as she preferred to be called, was gorgeous, with huge dark eyes, perfect teeth, rosy cheeks and a disposition Emily would have killed for.

"You must be Mrs. Thorn. Father Michael called us. He said we were to roll out our red carpet. Sad to say," Phillie said, laughing, "we don't have a red carpet. We have a prayer rug, worn in spots and it's hard to see what color it really is. It works, though, that's the main thing." Her chuckle was rich and warm. Emily felt drawn to her immediately.

"It's beautiful here. Quiet."

"Oh, yes, it is quiet. We liven up at meal time and we've been known to have sing-alongs."

"No!" Emily said in mock surprise.

"Let's get you signed in and I'll show you to your cabin. I just hate paperwork. I'd rather say five rosaries."

Emily laughed when she noticed the paperwork consisted of her signing her name and writing a check.

"This particular path is called Archangel Trail," Phillie said. "Since you aren't of the Catholic faith, archangel means an angel of high rank. Father Michael said you belong on this trail. He said you'd know why."

"Bless his heart. Yes, I know why. It's lovely. Who tends the flowers?"

"You do as long as you live here. I personally check for

weeds each day at sundown. Well, what do you think of it?"

"It's charming. I don't see any other cabins. Am I the only one here?"

"Good heavens no. There is only one cabin on Archangel Trail, though. They more or less all meander along and come together at the main cabin where you drove in. You absolutely cannot get lost. There's a map of the area inside. It will show you where the ranger station is. They check on us twice a day. We're filled up right now. That means there are forty-six guests. Meals are taken in the hall behind the main cabin and it is clearly marked. We have a chapel that is on Ascension Trail. You only attend services if you want to. The religious classes are marked on your calendar. Nothing is mandatory here. We have a recreation hall on Holy Cross Trail. We have a television, library, soda fountain, and a stereo system. The phone is in the hall. If someone calls you, we send someone to your cabin and a clothespin is attached to your mailbox. We get mail every day. Is there anything you want to ask me?"

"Mealtimes. What happens if you miss one?"

"Then you miss it," Phillie said cheerfully. "We only have one seating. Breakfast is at seven, lunch at noon, and dinner is at six. Our food is plain but robust. One of the sisters makes fresh bread every day and bakes pies. All our food is grown and cooked here. As I said, it's plain, but in all the years we've been operating, we haven't had one complaint."

"Remarkable."

"Let's go inside. I always like to see the guest's first impression."

"It's . . . it's . . ."

"Spartan?"

"Not really. It's lovely, Sister. I think I expected something a little more rustic."

"Ah, rustic. I see. Will you be comfortable here?"

Emily looked around at the plain, comfortable furniture. The fireplace was fieldstone with two tubs of pink flowers on the hearth. Mountain scenes hung on the walls. The lighting looked good. She moved into the bedroom. Double bed, huge closet, dresser, an easy chair with a floor lamp. The bathroom was small with a sink, toilet, and stall shower, all tiled in blue. A hooked rug was on the floor.

"I'll be very comfortable here, Sister," Emily said.

"Don't be alarmed when you hear the bells ring. We ring the Angelus three times a day. We call it a devotion. It's loud. Now, is there anything else I can do for you?"

"No, Sister."

"I'll have one of the boys bring your bags down in the next half hour. Your vehicle has to stay in the parking lot. You can keep your bicycle here, though. Do you ride?"

"I never have. I bought the bike in town. Back home I rode for miles on my stationary bike."

"That must have been boring," Phillie quipped.

"Well, I used to watch Sue Simmons and Al Roker when I pedaled. Sometimes I watched Sally Jessy Raphael in the mornings. It helped the time pass, but you're right, it's boring."

"There's so much for you to see. Don't be surprised to see the squirrels and rabbits at your door begging for food. They come as far as the steps and wait ever so patiently. You'll see several containers on the porch. It's rabbit pellets and nuts for the squirrels. I'll see you at dinner, Emily. Is it all right to call you Emily?"

"Of course."

"Then you must call me Phillie."

"Okay, Phillie."

Emily flopped down on a wooden chair to stare at her view. She wondered when the peace and quiet would get to her? Probably by tomorrow. She was dozing off when she heard the sound of a horn and tires crunching the gravel of the trail. She shook her head to clear it.

"Miss Thorn, I have your things here. Where do you want them?"

"The porch will be fine. I guess the bike should be up here too."

"You could park it between those two hemlocks. Good shelter from the rain." He waited for her response. She nodded.

This was no boy. She wondered if he was a priest. He was tall with sandy hair and a boyish smile. Well-built, he filled out his khakis. He wore mountain boots that were worn but neat.

"I see you got the best cabin in this retreat." Deep voice. She liked that. Maybe it was going to be interesting here after all. "Most times it's empty. Story goes that you have to be somebody pretty important to get Archangel Trail. Of course the nuns won't admit that. So, you're all set. Matt Haliday," he said, holding out his hand.

"Emily Thorn." She pulled two wrinkled one-dollar bills from her pants pocket and held them out. "Isn't it enough?" she asked as she rummaged in her pocket only to feel change.

"I'm sure it's enough, but what's it for?" A devilish light shone in his eyes.

"For bringing down my gear. Phillie said a boy would bring it all down. Nuns might . . . mix up men with boys since they lead such a sheltered life . . ." Damn, she was babbling like a schoolgirl and she was still holding the two dollars.

Long slender fingers raked at his hair. "I don't know if I should be flattered or insulted. I think I'm flattered. I'm a ranger. I stopped by to check on things. We do it twice a day and Bobby was off doing something else so Phillie asked me to bring down your things. It was a favor. Save that two bucks and I'll let you buy me an ice cream cone on Sunday. The sisters make ice cream on Sunday afternoon. All you can eat for fifty cents."

Emily stuffed the money back into her pocket. She felt embarrassed. "Okay, you got a deal. What flavors?"

"She wants flavors yet," the ranger chuckled. "They alternate, one Sunday it's vanilla, one Sunday it's chocolate, one Sunday it's butter pecan, the fourth Sunday it's banana, and if there's a fifth week in the month, the sisters really get screwed up and end up making butterscotch. Best damn ice cream in the whole state. I make sure I show up every Sunday with my kids."

Emily thought about Ben and Ted. She'd have to write and tell them about the ice cream. "How old are they?"

"Nine and fourteen." She was about to ask where Mrs. Ranger was and why didn't she come for the ice cream when he said curtly, "I'm a widower. The sisters are real good to my kids. They love coming here. They help out when things get going. Phillie can get frazzled real easy. Gilly goes off the deep end every Friday night during the fish fry, but then I'm giving away all the secrets of this here retreat," he joked. Emily laughed and was still laughing when he hopped in his jeep and backed up the trail.

"Guess he's the only one allowed to drive the trails," she mused. A widower. He showed up for ice cream every Sunday. Three more days till Sunday.

Emily unpacked. It took her ten minutes until everything was in its proper place. Another minute to shove her suitcases under the bed. She grabbed for the folder on the dresser and headed back to the front porch. Just how far was the ranger station?

Emily finished the slim brochure, set it aside, peered at the weeds in the pots of flowers. Should she weed now or wait till tomorrow? Should she shower? Nap and go to dinner or should she get up and explore her surroundings?

"I am just going to sit here and soak up this pine-scented air. I am also going to smoke a cigarette. I might think about things, but then I might not. What I will do is think about making out a schedule for myself so I don't go nuts. Breakfast, a hike, a swim and then a bicycle ride, some weeding, lunch, a nap, another walk, some more gardening, shower, dinner, and then . . . zip. Nothing. Watch the stars come out, count my blessings. Read up on the Appalachian Trail and the Smoky Mountains." She positively itched to break in her new hiking boots and mountain bike.

If she got bored, she could drive to Gatlinburg. She wondered how far she was from Memphis and if it would be worth her while to drive to Graceland to see Elvis's memorial. It was something to think about if the time came when she got bored with living in the woods.

Emily dozed and then slipped into a deep sleep. She woke at the first peel of the Angelus. She bolted down the steps, disturbing two squirrels at the base of a deformed pine tree next to her steps. As she ran, she called over her shoulder, "I'm sorry." She didn't feel silly at all.

Dinner was lively with Sister Celestine, Tiny for short, offering the blessing. The food was served family-style, which meant dig in and help yourself and there's more in the kitchen. Emily ate heartily of the pork roast, baby carrots, and potatoes from the garden. The garden salad was so fresh, also from the garden, that the vegetables actually crackled and crunched. The bread was homemade as was the butter and jam sitting at each end of the table. The cherries jubilee were so delicious Emily had to force herself to move away from the table.

"No, no, no, Mrs. Thorn. Everyone carries their plate and silverware to the sideboard at the end of the room."

Emily blushed. "I'm sorry we forgot to tell you that," Sister Tiny said with a smile.

As Emily walked away from the dining hall, other guests came up to her and introduced themselves. Outside, under the canopy of pines where coffee was being served, Emily had a chance to listen to various tales of misfortune and tales with happy endings, thanks to the Black Mountain Retreat. As one happy guest put it, "You commune with God, nature, and yourself. Here in this tranquil place you can't fool anyone, least of all yourself." Emily wasn't sure she understood what the woman was talking about. Obviously it had something to do with the spiritual side of things.

"I'm Rosie Finneran," a plump woman of an age with Emily said, holding out her hand. "It's nice to see some new blood here. Every year it's the same old people and I see you're on Archangel Trail. Now that has everyone buzzing, I can tell you. Only special people get that cabin. To my way of thinking, it's usually a person who doesn't mix in and has a delicate problem of some kind. There are others who say it's a VIP kind of thing and of course the *habits* don't divulge secrets. Personally I don't really care, but I would think you'd be lonely all the way down there by yourself. I talk a lot," she said breathlessly. "A lot of the people here don't talk at all. They pray. Prayer's fine, but there are other things in life. Do you like it so far? Wait till you meet the Rangers. *Verrrrryyyy* nice. I'm looking for a partner. Most of the people on Easter Trail where I am are a bunch of old farts. How come you're here?"

"You're right, you do talk a lot." Emily grinned to take the sting out of her words.

"That's because I come from a family of eleven kids and you really had to get in there and say what you had to say. I myself have eight children and it was the same kind of thing. They're all gone now and leading their own lives. I come here every summer. Ten years now."

Rosie was short, basketball round with plump cheeks, tight, gray curls held in place with colored barrettes with metallic streamers hanging down past her ears. Piercing blue eyes hid behind ornate shell-rimmed glasses. Emily was reminded of a busy, precocious squirrel.

"This is my first year," Emily said.

"This place hooks you. When you leave at the end of the summer, you can't wait to get back home among your own things, and then after a week or so, you wish you were back here. Everyone says the same thing. I think you and I will get along swell and we can buddy up if you lighten up. You look much too serious. Later we can talk about whatever you think is your problem. You also look like you're full of questions, so fire away."

"How many nuns are here? Do laypeople work here? It must take a lot of people to keep everything as nice as it is. How often do the rangers come here? I met the one called Matt. He brought my gear down to the cabin."

"Whoa. One at a time. We have six nuns. They aren't your regulation nuns. They let us call them by their nicknames. They join in and have fun with us. We have a softball game in August and they play right along with us. Phillie is a real slugger and Tiny can catch a pop fly like you wouldn't believe. They pray a lot and they swim by themselves. The others don't intrude. They're friendly and trust me when I tell you they keep their lips zipped. Every time I talk to one of them I feel so . . . peaceful. It's hard to explain. They have no worries, they live for God and to do good deeds. I guess the word I'm looking for is *pure.* So when you talk to them about a problem, they always seem to have the right answer. I'm not a Catholic, but I go to their mass on Sunday. A lot of the rangers come too. A priest from Gatlinburg comes every Sunday. It's real nice and sets the mood for the rest of the day.

"Nine laypeople work here. There are five groundskeepers;

two of them are retarded boys whose parents work here. They're lovely boys. The rangers come by twice a day. Usually it's Matt, but sometimes Ivan comes. Depends on who's off during the week and who's off during the weekends. Both of them are real nice and friendly. Matt's a widower and Ivan is a bachelor. I've been trying to snag him for ten years, but he won't bite. Neither will Matt. I think every single woman who's ever come here has tried to hit on both of them. They're sociable and even friendly, but it doesn't go beyond that."

Emily laughed. "Maybe you need to change your bait. Where are you from, Rosie?"

"Barnesboro, Pennsylvania. I'm a hick from the sticks. I've been thinking about moving south to get away from the cold winters, but the thought of packing up all my belongings is enough to make me change my mind every time I think about it. So I go to Florida in the winter and go home in the spring. Let's go for a walk. We need to walk off that dinner. Unless you have other plans."

"Right," Emily giggled. "Let's go. I ate too much."

"It's easy to do that here. The fresh air really gives you an appetite but then you work it off during the day. Everything you do here is one form of exercise or another. It's your turn to talk. You can't let me keep going on like I do or you'll never get to say anything. Tell me about yourself, Emily. Only what you want to tell me," she added hastily.

"There really isn't much to tell. I was divorced and my ex-husband died last year. I'm rather boring. Do you work, Rosie?"

"I never worked a day in my life, for money that is. I worked my tail off in the house, though. I went straight from my parents' house into marriage and I had a baby right away. My husband was a very good provider. He was in insurance and he believed in his product so we had plenty of it. I'm not rich, but well enough off that I don't have to worry about working or my old age. I can even offer my kids some modest help if they need it. My Harry died on the golf course. I was so angry. That's a story in itself. So, tell me, how do you like it here?"

"It's lovely. Do people come here in the winter?"

"Yes. In fact, they have to turn people away. I came here one year for Christmas after Harry died. I felt it was something I had to do. All I did was cry the whole time so I cut the visit short and went home. It's different here in the winter. There's skiing, snowmobiling, horseback riding. The horses love the snow. Bet you didn't know that. Cozy fires, warm friendships, cups of cheer. Sister Cookie makes a mulled wine that will sizzle your socks right off your feet."

"I'm going to go bike riding tomorrow. Would you like to join me, Rosie?"

"I'd love to. I think we should be going back. I have this bunion that is a killer. I want to put my slippers on, but first I'm going to walk you home."

"You don't have to do that," Emily demurred.

"Sure I do. You aren't familiar with the trails yet and it's dark now. The torches along the paths are something you have to get used to. The first time I was here I was lost for a couple of hours. They sent people out to look for me. I felt incredibly stupid. We need to stop by the camp store and get you some soft drinks and juice. You run a tab and pay up at the end of the month. You just more or less help yourself and write down what you take. I thought we could sit on your porch and have a cola, sort of unwind and talk."

"I'd like that." Emily realized she meant the words. She liked Rosie Finneran. The woods and the loneliness didn't seem quite so grim now.

Later, as they approached Emily's cabin on Archangel Trail, Rosie scurried up to the front porch and returned to the trail with a torch she ignited from the one on the trail.

"See, you would have walked up there in the dark. When you left, it was light and you didn't light it. Think of this," she said, returning the torch to its cement bucket on the porch, "as your porch light. You're supposed to put it out yourself when you retire. The ones on the trail burn all night."

"What shall we toast?" Emily asked, remembering the many toasts she and the women had made back home.

"How about to friendship and becoming good friends."

"Sounds good to me," Emily said, clinking her bottle of Snapple against Rosie's.

They sat in companionable silence, listening to the sounds of the bullfrogs and crickets, content to sip their drinks and stare out at the star-filled night. At ten o'clock, Rosie said it was time to call it a night.

Inside, undressing for bed, Emily realized how alone she was. Without warning she started to cry. Her shoulders shook with the force of her sobs. God, what was wrong with her? *What do you want, Emily? What will make you happy? What the hell is happiness? Blow your nose, light a cigarette, and go sit on the front porch. Count your blessings and get on with it.*

Huddled in her robe, Emily leaned back into the pillows she'd carried out with her. It was warm; she didn't need a blanket. She felt safe with the torch at the far end of the porch. Eventually she dozed and was awakened with a bright light shining in her face a little after three in the morning. "Wha—Who are you? Oh, Mr. Haliday. Is something wrong?" Emily asked.

"I was about to ask you the same question. I'm sorry I woke you, but we take our safety seriously around here. I'm covering for Ivan this evening. He threw his back out today trying to move a tree trunk that came down in a storm a few days ago."

"I . . . didn't want to sleep inside. Actually, I didn't . . . I couldn't sleep. I came out here to count my blessings, that kind of thing and . . . well, that's what I did. I guess the fresh air hasn't gotten to me yet."

"Takes a few days," Haliday said.

"Do you always come around in the middle of the night?"

"Midnight and then again at three. It's extra money. With two kids going to college in a few years, it will come in handy."

"I never had any children," Emily said quietly.

"There are days when I don't number them among my blessings," Haliday said. "When they were little, they were little problems, and now that they're bigger, they're bigger problems. I don't know if it gets worse or better."

"Who watches them when you're on patrol?"

"I have a lady who sleeps in when I'm on duty. During the day they manage by themselves. The neighbors keep an eye on them and they're up here a lot in the summer. Winters they're in school. They aren't being neglected."

"I didn't mean to infer that they were," Emily said stiffly.

"Do you like it here?"

"Yes, but it's awfully quiet. I'm not used to it, I guess. Rosie Finneran and I hit if off pretty well. I think I made a friend. That part of it is nice. I like people, but I miss my friends and I've only been here a day."

"Five dollars says inside of a month you won't want to go home. And I'm not a betting man."

"I'll take that bet. I'm not sure if I'm a gambling woman or not. I guess I am," she said thoughtfully. "I gambled some pretty high stakes back home. With my life and my financial security."

"Did you win?"

Emily laughed. My God, I'm laughing at three o'clock in the morning. "I guess you could say I won. I looked at it then as reaching a goal I had set up for myself. Then when I attained that goal, I wasn't sure if it was what I wanted . . . I wanted it, but it didn't seem to be enough, if you know what I mean."

"Are you married, Mrs. Thorn?"

"I was once. I got divorced and then my ex-husband died last year. Perhaps you heard about it on the news; it was quite sensational. Ian was gunned down outside an abortion clinic in Los Angeles. I had a hard time with that, but I went on because I had to go on. Then I spoke with a priest who told me about Black Mountain. That's why I'm here. What about you, Mr. Haliday?"

"Call me Matt. Everyone does."

"Then you can call me Emily."

"Okay. I've lived here all my life. I've never been away except to go to school. I came back here as soon as I graduated and got a job with the Park Service. Then I got married and had kids."

Emily didn't think it strange at all that here she was, in a strange place in the woods, having a conversation with a park ranger at three o'clock in the morning.

"And almost lived happily ever after," Emily said quietly.

"Almost. Sometimes things aren't meant to be. I don't know why that is," he said sadly.

"Are you happy, Matt?"

"Contented. I'm not sure I know what happiness is. I thought I was happy when I was married, but maybe it was just contented. They talk a lot around here about peace, contentment, and spiritual well-being. They don't use the word *happy* much. How about you, Emily?"

She wasn't about to confide in this perfect stranger even

though he made her feel like she'd known him for a while. "I'm up for whatever gets me through the days. Maybe we all need to search for the meaning of that word and then see if we're capable of experiencing it. Instinctively we may shy away from it because we're afraid the feeling won't last and maybe it's better not to go through the feeling and then have a letdown."

Matt chuckled. "I suppose you could be right and then again you could be wrong."

"Spoken like a true politician." Emily smiled in the darkness.

"Are you one of those career females?"

"Now, why does that question sound obscene?" Emily asked coolly.

"A lot of them come here searching for something. They enter a man's world, fight, kick, and scratch, and when they get what they want, they can't handle it so they come here to do their soul searching. Then they go home, get married, and give up their jobs."

"Well, if that doesn't sound chauvinistic, I don't know what does," Emily bristled. "Does that mean you think women belong in the kitchen, barefoot and pregnant?"

"If that's what they want. If it isn't what they want, then they should be prepared to pay the price. The only problem is they don't want to pay that price. I'm only speaking about what I've heard. The sisters talk about it a lot. As far as counseling goes, they leave much to be desired. Their habits help a bit. The men, the CEOs who come here to get off the fast track, aren't any better than the women. The men pack it in and go off and sail around the world, and the women go back and get married. I don't understand. Why can't these people do things in moderation?

"So," Matt said, "I guess I've taken up enough of your

time. I should be getting back to the main building and write up my report. I'm sorry I woke you."

"That's okay, Matt. I'm wide awake now. I'll probably just sit here and watch the sun come up."

"My favorite time of day. Wait till you see how the dew sparkles in the early hours. It looks like this whole place is speckled with tiny diamonds. You can get drunk on the smell of the pines."

"I had a Christmas tree once that made me dizzy with the scent."

Matt scoffed. "You people in the city don't know the first thing about trees. You need to cut one from the woods and drag it home. We don't put chemicals and junk in our soil up here. Makes a world of difference. You take one of these trees home and you can smell it all over the house. You'll learn," he said, getting up from the step where he'd been sitting. "Were you serious about me being a male chauvinist?"

"Uh-huh." Emily tried to hide her smile at the serious look on his face.

"My daughter said the same thing. Guess I have to work on that."

"I would if I were you. Thanks for stopping by."

"My job," he said curtly. "You wait till tomorrow. Phillie and Tiny will know we were sitting here talking. I don't know how they do it, but they know everything that goes on here. They're renegades."

"I'll remember that. Night, Matt."

"Night, Emily."

Emily curled up in the chair, and before she knew it, she was sound asleep. A sound at the bottom of the steps woke her just as the sun was coming up. Her breakfast guests. A smile worked its way around her mouth. "Okay, guys, give me a minute to get it ready."

"Amazing," she said over and over as she walked

among the squirrels and rabbits that were eating the food she put out.

Emily's smile stretched from ear to ear as she stared at the necklaces of diamonds that circled the shrubbery and trees. She was walking on a carpet of sparkling brilliants that so delighted her she clapped her hands in pure pleasure. "Good morning, world."

Chapter 17

Emily settled into her new, temporary life in the mountains. She established a routine that included Rosie Finneran and to some extent Matt Haliday. She was sleeping like the proverbial log, eating like the proverbial pig, and exercising like the proverbial guru. She loved every minute of it. She laughed, giggled, joked with the other guests. Some she knew by name; others, who she thought of as religious, were nodding acquaintances. "It seems I live in anticipation of the next meal," she said to Rosie when she pushed her chair back from the table at breakfast time.

"Well, let's see, you've been here ten days and you seem to me like a new person. You have rosy cheeks, Emily Thorn." Rosie grimaced.

"What's wrong?"

"Gas," Rosie said, massaging her stomach. "Everyone has noticed that Matt Haliday sort of seeks you out or comes around wherever you are. People are talking."

"Stop it, Rosie. He'd be here anyway. How do you know I'm not where he is? Chew on that one, my friend." Emily smiled.

"You sly little devil. He's nice. I could see you with him. He's not sexy-looking, though." She grimaced again. "Let's walk a little."

"I think he is. Sexy I mean. What you see isn't necessarily what you get. He could be a dynamo in bed."

"He could also be a dud," Rosie shot back. "I thought you said he was a male chauvinist."

"That too. Look, he's not interested in me, he's just being nice. He treats you the same way he treats me. I have to admit, I'm a little interested in him. He intrigues me."

"Why is that?" Rosie asked, bending over to tie her sneaker. She gasped when she straightened up. Emily, who was walking ahead of her, didn't hear the frightening sound.

"I never met anyone content to live his life in . . . these types of surroundings. I know he lives in town, but by his own admission he's rarely there except to sleep. He pretty much lives up here with the trees and moss."

"I don't know, Emily. He gets to meet new people every year and gets to renew old friendships. He looks out for people. That's very rewarding in itself. He tends to nature and that's rewarding too. It's his life. He strikes me as a man who has it all together and loves what he does. How does he compare to that guy Ben back home?"

"Apples and oranges," Emily said loftily. "Hey, it's quarter to nine. We said we were leaving at eight-thirty for our hike. I'll meet you here at the crossroads. I have our lunch." Emily held up a cardboard box Sister Gilly had handed over after breakfast.

"It's not my fault you wanted a second helping of those butternut pancakes. Bring the map in case we get lost," Rosie called over her shoulder.

Emily sprinted back to her cabin, stuffed her gear in her purple backpack, and slid her arms through the hoops. At the last minute she shoved the map of the retreat in the hip pocket of her shorts. She was walking through the door when she turned around, entered the cabin, and removed her boots and shorts to pull on a pair of twill khaki slacks. She laced her boots. Now she was ready. Or was she? She stood perfectly still on the last step and mentally ticked off the items in her backpack. Knife, first aid kit, flashlight, small but powerful, lunch, a heavy sweatshirt, and a can of insect repellent. She went back into the cabin for the third time and picked up the three Hershey bars on the end table in the sitting room. "Enough already, move," she muttered.

"Appalachian Trail, here we come," Rosie said.

"How are you feeling? Look, if you aren't up to this, we can go another time. A ten-mile hike is something to think about. Are you sure, Rosie, that you're up to it?"

"I do it every year, but only four miles. What's six more? I have to make pit stops, but I can do it. Are you getting nervous?"

"Not at all. I'm looking forward to this. I can't wait to write to my friends and tell them I went hiking on the Appalachian Trail. They are going to be so jealous. Well, maybe they'll be relieved they aren't here. Hiking isn't something they're fond of."

"Bet we see Matt at some point."

"Today is his day off," Emily said.

"Ah, so you are keeping track of him." Rosie burst out laughing at the look of chagrin on Emily's face. "Hey, it's okay, don't be embarrassed. Wild anticipation is better than the actual happening, whatever that happening is. An affair, a trip, whatever. Usually the event is pretty much of a letdown. It's that wild, wicked, anticipation that makes it all worthwhile. Take me, I've been lusting after Ivan for so long I lost track of time. If anything ever happened, I don't think I'd know what to do. First, though, I have to lose some weight and give myself a new do, a new, what's that called, a makeover? When he sees me, he sees this roly-poly, gray-haired woman who is a grandmother."

"Don't do that to yourself, Rosie. I used to do that."

Emily confided about her bathroom escapade and the broken mirror. "That was then; this is now. If you're serious, I can put you on a health and exercise program, and if you extend your time here, when it's time to leave I can personally guarantee a significant weight loss. I can even do your makeover. I know all about makeup. I worked in a lounge for a long time and makeup was important. I can color your hair and even cut it for you. If there's a way to save money, I know it. Do you know there are over two hundred ways to serve tuna fish, three hundred and sixty ways to make chicken? I know them all!" Emily giggled.

"I don't have any willpower," Rosie groaned.

"Okay, I can deal with that. Think about it like this. There you are, a svelte one hundred and fifteen pounds with a sleek new hairdo, fashionable makeup, a gorgeous outfit, and out of the woods comes Ivan the . . . hunk. He sweeps you up over his shoulder and takes you to his . . . his cave, where you make wild, passionate love. He ravages and plunders and you love it. You cry for more, more, and still more until he's nothing but a quivering mass of jelly. You get up, rearrange your clothes, and look down, disdainfully, at this heap of quivering manhood and say . . . what will you say, Rosie?" Emily doubled over laughing.

"See you around," Rosie gurgled. "I'm in your hands, Emily. Do it."

"Okay, tomorrow we start. Let's stop for lunch. I think we've come about four miles, maybe a little more. We deserve to rest."

Emily handed over a plastic-wrapped ham and cheese sandwich and a peach to Rosie, who said she wasn't hungry. Emily ate hers hungrily and could have eaten Rosie's too, but she didn't. The juice from the peach dribbled down her chin, dropping to her T-shirt. "Oh, shit, now it's going to stain my shirt. I'm such a slob." She wiped her mouth with the back of her hand. "Want some water?"

"Yes, but what I'd really like is a couple of aspirin. Do you have any in the first aid kit?"

"I don't think it's going to help, if it's your stomach that hurts. Is it bad?"

"It isn't *as* bad, but it's still there. It must be a pocket of gas and that's the worst. I get it sometimes when I eat the wrong things. I think it's from the three weenies I ate last night. Maybe it's from those char-blackened, roasted potatoes with all that dripping butter."

"Best potatoes and weenies I've ever eaten," Emily said happily.

"Then how come *you* don't have gas?" Rosie grumbled.

"This is some conversation. I ate sauerkraut with my weenies. It makes you *go*. Did you *go?*"

"No, I didn't go. The aspirin is for a headache. Give me three." Emily obediently shook out three aspirin from the bottle and handed them over to Rosie, who gulped them down with a swig of water from the bottle in Emily's backpack.

"We have to get moving. Our goal is to make it back to the retreat by dusk. Gilly promised to hold dinner for us if we were late. She made me swear not to tell the others. I put ten bucks in her personal poor box."

"Bribing a nun is shameful. And she let you do it?" Rosie asked.

"Yep, and she smiled. Here, let me give you a hand," Emily said, reaching down to grab Rosie's arm. She staggered backward, regained her footing, but in doing so turned completely around. Huffing and puffing, Rosie took the lead, but veered to the right, leaving the trail. Emily followed, whacking at the brush with her arms.

Emily looked at her watch two hours later when Rosie said, "I have to stop, Emily. My side is killing me. Let's see if we can figure out where we are exactly. Where's the map? I haven't seen any markings for a long time now.

The trail is clear, not like this path we're on. Do you suppose we made a mistake and somehow got off?"

"Don't tell me that, Rosie," Emily grimaced. "I don't want to be lost. My God, there's nothing around for miles and miles. If you even *think* we're lost, let's head back the way we came and go back to the retreat. We can do this another time. It's almost two o'clock." She handed over the water bottle. Rosie drank greedily and asked for more aspirin, while Emily rummaged in her pockets for the map. "I left it in my shorts," she wailed.

"Feel my head, Emily."

"Rosie, you're *hot!* We're going back! Now!"

"Not till this pain in my side lets up. How hot do you think I am?"

"Maybe 102. Did you have a fever when we started out?"

"No. I just felt sluggish. I hate to tell you this, but I don't think the pain in my side is gas either."

"Are you telling me . . . ? Did you ever have your appendix out? Are you telling me you think you have appendicitis?"

"There's nothing wrong with my ovaries because I had my GYN checkup before I came up here. What else is there but your appendix? My kidneys are okay. God, Emily, what if it bursts? I'll try, but I don't think I can make it back."

"Let's take a few more minutes. I can help support you, but if it really is your appendix, maybe you shouldn't even be walking. The fever is going to slow you down. I don't want to leave you here and go on to try and find help. If we are lost, I could get even more lost on my own without the map. The sisters will know something's wrong if we don't make it back by dusk, but that's six or seven hours from now. A lot can happen in that time. There's no guarantee Gilly will even be aware that we aren't back. Our suppers will be in the oven and she'll be at Devotions. Maybe we won't be missed till nine o'clock or even later. Tell me what to do, Rosie," Emily said tightly.

"Go back and . . . get help. I can't make it, Emily, and even if I could, I'd just slow you down. Take the bandages from the first aid kit and tie strings on the bushes so the rangers can find their way here. Once you find the trail, you can jog the rest of the way. You're in good shape."

"Oh, God, look at you, you're drenched. I'll leave you the water bottle and the backpack. What if it gets dark and you're here alone?" Emily wailed.

"I have your flashlight and my own. Go, Emily, please. I'll be okay till you get back. It's my fault. I went off the trail."

Emily's heart fluttered in her chest. "Rosie, I can't leave you here alone. What if some wild animal attacks you? I don't know the first thing about tracking, finding my way back. I could get lost again. Maybe we could burn something and try and contain the fire so just the smoke rises. Surely someone will see it."

"Fires are out. They can spread. I'm not experienced in this camping business. Don't even think about it. The pain is getting worse, Emily. Please go. I'll be okay as long as I know you're trying. You can do this, Emily. Just think about all the things you accomplished after your husband left you."

"God, Rosie, that was different. No one's life was at stake then."

"You're wrong, your life was at stake. Stop talking, Emily, and go. Please."

"All right, all right, but first let me make you comfortable. Rest your head on my backpack. The flashlights are beside you. If it rains, you have some pretty good foliage overhead. I'll leave the water with you. Drink it, Rosie. Keep chewing these aspirin." She slipped the bottle into the breast pocket of Rosie's shirt. She leaned over to kiss her friend on the cheek. "Count the leaves on the trees, and when you've counted them all, start to count the pine needles. I'm going to be giving you a quiz when we get you out of here."

"Just go, Emily. I'm counting," Rosie grimaced.

Emily looked over her shoulder as she started off. Rosie's eyes were closed, her face full of pain. *I can do this. I know I can do this. I have to do this or something will happen to Rosie. I goddamn well will do this.*

Emily thought about bears and wolves and other creatures of the forest. Snakes. She looked around wildly for a big stick. Should she try to be quiet or should she make noise? She had no idea. Walk. Stay alert. Don't lose the stick. She waved it threateningly for her own benefit.

She walked for hours, following the beaten back bushes they'd attacked earlier. She hoped and prayed she would recognize the place where they'd stopped for lunch. She looked at her watch. She'd been alone for two hours, which meant she should be coming to their luncheon spot any minute now.

Sweat dripped down her face, down her neck, soaking the T-shirt. The heavy twill of her pants was chafing her thighs. She looked around, her eyes wild, when she felt a gust of wind as it whistled through the dense trees. What the hell did that mean? A temperature drop? The dimness of the forest pressed around her. Alarming her. She still hadn't found their picnic spot. Had they struggled uphill or had they gone downhill? She couldn't remember. All she could think about was Rosie and the place where she'd left her. She ripped off another piece of the sterile gauze and tied it to a thorny bush. She felt her heart ripple in her chest when she unrolled the rest of the roll. There wasn't much left.

Emily stopped, hoping to see something that looked familiar, something to indicate they'd come this way before.

The trail was steep, slick with the resin from the pine needles. Twice she slipped, going down on her knees, but righting herself immediately. She tried to run, but her lungs wouldn't permit it. *She should be going downhill, not uphill.* She stopped, her ears buzzing. She was aware now that there was no sun. Earlier she'd noticed the lacy pattern ahead of her. It was darker now too. "Oh shit!" she muttered for the hundredth time.

For the first time Emily smelled her own fear. Her eyes started to burn with the salty sweat dripping into them. She was lost and she knew it. "You shouldn't have trusted me, Rosie," Emily wailed.

Suddenly Ian's voice rang in her ears. "Bitch, Emily, you do that best. And when you're done bitching, cry and whine. No one does it better."

"Shut up, Ian. You're dead. Ashes in the desert. You can't talk to me anymore and you can't tell me what to do either. I'd like to see you find your way in these woods. I can do this, you wait and see, you son of a bitch! I'm not really hearing you. You're just a figment of my imagination," Emily snarled.

Which direction should she be going—west, east, north, or south? She had no idea. Where was the sun going to set? It was impossible to tell with the way the clouds were streaking across the sky. The canopy overhead was so dense, so chilling, she felt bile rise in her throat. She lashed out with the stick, closed her eyes, and moved to the left only because it felt right to do so. She slipped then, the sturdy mountain boots going out from under her. She was on her back, sliding over rocks, brush and the sticky, oozing pine needles. She felt something graze her cheek and then she felt the pain and wetness.

The wind knocked out of her, Emily didn't move. A trembling hand reached up to touch her face. Blood. She pulled up her shirt to wipe at it. Head and face wounds bled profusely and didn't necessarily mean a serious injury. She stared overhead at the patch of grayness directly in her line of vision. Any fool would know it was going to rain and rain soon. The cooling breeze she'd felt before was stronger now. Definitely wind.

Emily got to her knees, shook her head to clear it, and started off again. She thought she was going the same way, but at a lower level, one that wasn't so dense with under-growth. She was still on high ground, but her breathing was easier. She tied a piece of bandage onto a bush, winced at the sight of her own blood.

She struggled on, glancing at her watch every few min-utes. It was a quarter to five. She still had hours of daylight if a storm didn't come up. Winded, she leaned against a tree and bellowed at the top of her lungs. She called for help over and over until she was hoarse and then she started off again. "I can do this. I have to do this. You can do whatever you set out to do if you have the will." Well, by God, she had the will. It was nature and the forest that were not cooperating. She plowed on, wiping at the ooz-ing blood on her cheek with the back of her hand.

She thought about the inspiration hour that she and Rosie had attended the week before. It had started out se-riously and ended on a silly note, but she'd walked away with a wonderful feeling. Part of it was Sister Cookie and her dry sense of humor. Basically it was a list of things to do, suggestions that were an inspiration guide.

Now, if she could just remember some of those things, it might help. She plunged ahead, her head reeling dizzily. It was darker, the trees and shrubbery more dense. Soon it was going to be totally black within the forest. Open a book, to any page, choose a paragraph, and let it be your inspi-ration. Sure, sure, what if it's one of those romance novels full of sex and mayhem? Emily muttered as she whacked at the dense growth along the trail. Don't for one minute think or even tolerate negative thinking. Don't listen to people with negative tongues. Easier said than done. You take me now, Sister Cookie, just what the hell is positive about the situation I'm in right now? Don't lose your sense of humor. If you temporarily misplace it, find it. It takes more muscles to frown than it does to laugh. Laugh often. Ha, ha, Emily snorted.

Emily stopped, took a deep breath. She was exhausted, winded. She leaned back against a tree, her legs spread, her hands on her knees. She took deep breaths. She swore then that she heard Ian's voice soughing through the treetops. It was unmistakable. She should know, she'd listened to it for years and years.

"You screwed up, Emily. Now you're copping out. You never think, you just plunge ahead. For once in your life take charge."

"Shut up, Ian, you're dead. You aren't even buried so you can't rise from the dead. You're spread all over the Mojave Desert with those stupid tulips. I'm here and I'm doing the best I can. It's black as pitch. I can't see. I think I might have a concussion and Rosie is depending on me to get help. Don't talk to me, Ian. I refuse to listen to a dead person. Get the hell away from me."

Let your mind and spirit be open to receiving a miracle. Here I am, Lord, you can send one this way any minute now. No, no, don't direct it at me, send it to Rosie. You're full of it, Sister Cookie. I liked the one where you said it was a wise man or woman who knows when to retreat. That one was made for me. A close second was when you said we should all be on the lookout for His Messengers. God, I can't even see. What if He's here and misses me? bullshit!

Suddenly she was on the ground, rolling, rolling, rolling, until she slammed against an outcropping of boulders at the base of a tree. She wanted to scream her agony,

but the pain in her shoulder was so bad all she could do
was bite down on her lip, rock her body in misery. She felt
a rush of warmth on her arm. Was it ripped open?

It was lighter here with a break in the overhead canopy
of pines. By squinting she could just barely make out the
hands on her watch. And stuck into the outcropping of rocks
was a wooden arrow with the words APPALACHIAN TRAIL.
Five o'clock. Was she going toward the Black Mountain
Retreat or toward Maine? Providing she could even get up.
She rolled on to her left side, waited a moment until the
pain eased, and then struggled to one knee. Pain rocked
her body, spears of pain shooting up and down her arm.
Broken shoulder, collarbone, arm? Probably all three. She
was on her feet now, her face contorted with the effort.

"Goddamnit, Emily, move!" Was it Ian's voice that shouted
encouragement? Impossible. Ian was dead, gone forever.
"Stop feeling sorry for yourself. You're going the wrong
way. I always said you were stupid. Turn around and go
the other way. Do it, Emily."

"Shut up, Ian. You can't tell me what to do anymore."

"I don't want your death on my conscience."

Was it really her ex-husband talking? Was she delirious,
hallucinating? From long years of habit she turned around,
each step agony.

"If I'm really talking to you, Ian, what are my chances
of getting help for Rosie? How far am I from the retreat?"

She was on the ground again, her body one massive raw
nerve ending. She knew she was going to black out. "You
pushed me, you son of a bitch!"

"That's it, Emily, get mad. Real mad. Get on your feet
and *move!*"

"Help me, Ian. Please. If you hate me so much, then
help me to get help for Rosie. Rosie never did anything to
you. Please. I can't do this. I cannot take another step. I
have to lie down. Sooner or later someone will find us.

Leave me alone, Ian. My arm and shoulder are broken. You're a doctor, you know how painful that is. You went to bed when you got a pimple."

"Quitter! You're going to let your friend die because you're too damn lazy to pick up your feet. I gave you an order, Emily, and you damn well better obey me. You just sprained your arm and shoulder. Nothing's broken. You only have a gash on your arm. Trust me."

"I'm not a quitter and I'm not lazy. Another thing, you bastard, when I get back, I'm turning you in for practicing medicine when you're dead. So there!"

She was moving. She must be crazy for talking to a dead person. On the other hand, maybe talking to a dead person was what Sister Cookie meant when she said she should be ready to receive one of His Messengers.

Ian a Messenger of God? It was too ludicrous for words. Wasn't it?

What time was it? How much time had gone by since she fell? Talking to a Messenger of God, even if it was Ian, took time. Five-thirty, six? Probably five forty-five.

"Keep moving, Emily." His voice was gentle this time, prodding her on. Maybe he really cared if she made it. For Rosie's sake, of course. I can do this. I have to do this. I *will* do this.

At the Black Mountain Retreat, Sister Cookie looked at the clock. Goodness, time had gotten away from her. She looked around, checked the ovens, slid the trays of scrubbed potatoes into the one that was free. The rump roasts were baking to perfection. The salad was all ready, the tables set, the vegetables ready to be steamed. The home-baked rolls were in the warming oven, the peach cobbler cooling on a long table on the back porch.

A tray with pitchers of ice tea and glasses waited for her to carry out to the back porch, the one place, besides their bedrooms, that was off limits to their guests. Here in this private, secluded place that was all theirs, they congregated to smoke a forbidden cigarette and drink their ice tea. Once a month they confessed their vice and then forgot about it until the following month.

None of the nuns really knew where the cigarettes came from—the fresh packs anyway. The ones left on the tables after meals were placed in a shoe box in the kitchen waiting to be claimed. Usually they waited three days before they smoked them. "Finders, keepers," Phillie chortled as she fired up. The fresh packs appeared as if by magic, usually every other day. Most times they were left on the steps of the back porch, where they sat during their morning and afternoon break. The sisters were divided on their opinions as to who left the awful things. Gilly, Cookie, and Tiny thought it was Matt. Phillie, Gussie, and Millie thought it was Ivan.

Tiny poured the ice tea. Gussie handed out the cigarettes. Millie held the lighter.

"Terrible, filthy habit," Phillie said, leaning back as she drew deeply on the cigarette.

"Disgusting," the others said cheerfully.

They took turns blowing perfect smoke rings.

"I know for a fact that God isn't going to punish us," Gilly said happily. "Because He lets us find these terrible things. If He didn't want us to have them, He'd keep them out of our sight."

"Baloney. That's a crock," Eric Clapton's biggest fan, Sister Gussie, said happily. "I'm not giving them up."

"We aren't either," the other nuns chorused.

"We might roast in hell," Sister Tiny said.

"Then we'll roast together," Sister Millie said.

"Time to stub out," Sister Gilly said, holding up the stub of her Marlboro Light. "See, nothing but the filter. Absolutely sinful."

"Do you think Mother Teresa smokes?" Sister Phillie asked fretfully.

"Probably, with all the stress she's under, how could she not?" Sister Cookie said. "I think the sky is pretty black. Oh, I hope we don't have a storm this evening. I wanted to finish that blood and guts book I'm reading. If the power goes out, I won't know who killed Darlene."

"Her sister Marlene did it, so stop fretting," Sister Gussie said. "Plus, it was the gardener who gored the guard at the gate. That other stuff was just a red herring. Now you don't have to worry if the power goes off. I have a new book you can start tomorrow called *Missing Beauty*. Matt dropped it off yesterday."

"I do hope Rosie and Emily are all right. It gets pretty dark up there around this time of day even when the sun is out. With a storm coming, it will be dark as Hades," Sister Tiny said.

"Rosie's been on the trail before," Gilly said.

"The most she's ever hiked is four miles. Today they planned on ten miles. Emily isn't familiar with the trail at all."

"I'd feel better if we asked Ivan to go take a look when he gets here with the mail. He's late. Usually he's ringing the bell by the time we finish our . . . sinful vice," Millie said.

"I promised to save them a dinner plate."

"Breaking the rules again, Gilly," Gussie said.

"Rules are meant to be broken. They aren't hikers like some of the others," Gilly dithered.

"I hear the bell. Ivan's here with the mail."

The sisters gathered up the tray and the dirty ashtray. It was left to Gilly to walk around to the front of the building to accept the mail.

Ivan was a bear of a man, six foot four and weighing in

at two hundred and sixty pounds, a monolith with tree trunk arms and hands like slabs of beef. The khaki uniform and the Stetson did nothing to dispel his giant size.

"Big storm coming Sister, but not till later. Maybe ten o'clock. Make sure everyone is inside." His voice was soft and gentle, comforting.

"Oh, well, if it isn't going to hit until ten, then I guess I don't have to worry about Rosie and Emily. They went for a ten-mile hike up on the trail this morning."

"What time did they leave?" the giant asked quietly.

"After breakfast. I promised to hold dinner for them. Actually, I said I would fix their plates and put them in the oven. I know it's breaking the rules, but I don't care. They'll both be starving when they get back."

"That was nice of you, Sister. Rules can be broken from time to time. Did Rosie feel confident to hike ten miles? Perhaps I should take a look. The woods will be pretty dark about now. Rosie is afraid of field mice so she might get spooked."

"How do you know Rosie is afraid of field mice?" Gilly asked.

"Matt told me. I'll take the jeep up and look around. If they left at eight-thirty, nine at the latest, they should have been back by now, even allowing for a lunch break and other pit stops. I'm going to take a look. If I miss them, send up one of the flares we left with you. Will you do that, Sister?"

"Of course I will. I'll tell the others. I cautioned Rosie to stick close to the trail and not to get off. I even told her to mark it. Each hiker is told the same thing. They should be back by now. I must go or dinner will be late this evening."

Ivan handed over a light sack of mail, turned on his heel, and marched around the side of the building to the front where he'd left his jeep. He waited until he was a quarter of the mile away from the retreat before he pulled his mountain vehicle to the side of the road. Using the mobile phone, he called Matt Haliday.

"Trust me when I tell you those two women did not hike ten miles, and if they aren't back by now, something is wrong. Rosie has a bunion. Everyone in Black Mountain knows about her bunions."

"Let me get someone in to look after the kids and I'll come up. Light some flares as you go along. It's going to storm before long, Ivan. At the most it will take me forty minutes."

"I'll see you later," Ivan said, breaking the connection.

Ivan thought about the few emergencies he'd had over the years at the retreat. For the most part, the guests never ventured far and there had been no serious problems. He liked this job, related to all the people who came to the retreat seeking comfort and solace. He himself had done the same thing years and years ago when his fiancée was killed in a car accident. Fifty now, unmarried, a lover of children and all animals, he worked virtually around the clock.

He liked Rosie Finneran, but then everyone liked Rosie. Once or twice he'd thought about asking her to take in a picture show, but he'd never acted on his thought. Now he was sorry. Rosie made him laugh. Rosie winked at him when she thought no one was looking. He never winked back and didn't know why. Now he wished he had. Sometimes, though, Rosie didn't have enough sense to come in out of the rain, but that was okay too. Sometimes he did stupid things too.

He thought about Emily Thorn and Matt Haliday. He knew Matt was interested in the lady from New Jersey. He tried to hide it, but wasn't successful. He always asked what went on at the retreat when he was off duty. He'd start by mentioning the nuns and a few of the guests and then he'd hit on Rosie and Emily last. Ivan liked to see the sparkle in

Matt's eyes when he talked about Emily Thorn. Just last week Matt had carried an ice cream cone over to her and then sat with her and Rosie. He'd wanted to join them, but they all looked like they were having such a good time he didn't want to intrude so he'd eaten his ice cream cone and left, taking a second one with him.

Ivan parked the jeep. He slung his backpack, which was as big as a bushel basket, over his shoulder and set off, his high beam flashlight lighting the way. His long-legged strides were awesome and thunder loud.

She was on the ground again, facedown, her foot caught in something. She tried to wiggle, to move, but the knifelike pain in her neck, shoulder, and arm took her breath away. She lay still, her face buried in pine needles and coarse earth. She sneezed again and again from the resin in the needles.

If she could just sleep, even if it was for just ten minutes. In her life she'd never been this tired, this ridden with pain.

"Get up, Emily. This is no time to go to sleep. If you're too lazy to do it for yourself, think about your friend. She's counting on you. Listen to me, Emily."

"Why should I? I thought I told you to leave me alone. I don't want to talk to a dead person. God's going to punish you for tormenting me like this. Leave me alone."

Emily struggled to get up on her knees as she balanced herself with her hand. She toppled forward, her face again mashing into the pine needles on the ground. "I hurt my knee and my ankle hurts," she whimpered.

"Your friend hurts a whole lot more, Emily. Get your ass in gear and get up and do what you set out to do. That's an order, Emily."

"Damn you and your orders, Ian. What about me?"

"You aren't important now, Emily. Your friend is important. If her appendix bursts, she's gone and you know it. I'm a doctor. For once in your life, listen to me."

"You *were* a doctor. Shut the hell up. I know . . . I don't need you to tell me . . . I can't see . . . I know I'm hopelessly lost. Help me to get up."

"Do it yourself, Emily. I'm watching you."

"Stop telling me what to do." She was on her feet, listing to the right and then to the left, but she was upright. She reached out with her left foot, trying to find the stick she'd been carrying. She knew if she bent over she'd fall again. She stomped on the end and it bounced upright. She caught it. The prize at the end of the rainbow.

Thunder rolled across the sky, once, twice, three times, followed by dancing lightning that lit up the forest for a few brief seconds. "They let you do that?" Emily asked in awe. "How'd you do that, Ian?"

"Magic. Are you satisfied that you're on the trail?"

"Yeah, yeah, I am. How much further is it?"

"If I told you how far it is, you'd give up. If I told you were within sight of the retreat, you'd do something stupid like run into a tree. I don't know how far it is. Just keep moving."

"I know your game, you louse—you're trying to make me mad. Ian, I am too tired to get mad. What you did to me was terrible. I did what I had to do. You didn't even know me when I walked into your office. I'm the old Emily now."

Lightning ripped across the sky, streak after streak until Emily thought she was watching a fire works display. By jamming the stick between two massive boulders, she was able to move forward, her injured arm hanging at her side as she dragged her bad leg. She was moving and that was all that mattered. "That was some show. What'd you do, wrinkle your nose or something?"

"Stop wasting your energy talking. You should have kept one of the flashlights and a flare. You're doing good, Emily."

Emily was so pleased with the compliment she tried to move faster, tried not to think about Rosie and Ian and his . . . spirit world. It was probably all a bad dream anyway. She vowed never to tell anyone about the conversations she was having with her dead husband.

More lightning danced across the sky. She saw it then and thought her heart was going to pound its way right out of her chest. *Sasquatch.* God, no. Al Roker with his Doppler radar gear on his back. A living nightmare. She gripped the stick in her hands and cried, out of fear, not for herself, but for Rosie. She was losing touch with reality and she knew it. What would the NBC weatherman be doing here in the Smoky Mountains? And if it was Al Roker, where the hell was that giddy Sue Simmons, the five o'clock news anchor? "Ian, help me, don't leave me here with this . . . this *thing.* Ian, I swear I'll . . . I'll do something . . . good and kind . . . you can do it, use your powers, Ian. Don't let me die."

But there was no answer.

Then a light was in her face, blinding her. She shrank back as she tried to shield her eyes. "Mrs. Thorn."

She recognized his deep, comforting voice. "Ivan," she croaked. Her relief was so overwhelming she slid to the ground. It didn't matter now if she could get up again or not.

"Jesus, God, what happened to you, Mrs. Thorn?"

"It's Rosie. I left her . . . way back there, up there, somewhere. I tied bandages for a while to mark the trail. Then I ripped my socks and underwear until I ran out. Something's wrong with Rosie's appendix. I left her with the flashlights and the backpacks. It got dark and I got lost and . . . none of that's important. I can't tell you where she is. She's up there. She was running a fever and she was in a lot of pain. You can get her, can't you?"

"Of course. What about you? Is anything broken?"

"No, I'm just banged up. You can leave me here. Just get Rosie."

"I thought I heard you talking to someone."

"I was . . . I was . . . talking to myself. I think you should hurry, Ivan."

Ivan was already on the mobile phone he carried in his oversize backpack. "Think, Mrs. Thorn, how far, how long did it take you to get here?"

"Hours, but I got lost, it got dark, I fell down a ravine, it was very slow-going for me. I think I've been walking for five, maybe six hours. I left the flares with Rosie and the flashlights. Maybe if you set one off, she'll set hers off and you'll get a sense of direction. You're going to need a litter to carry her. I know you're big, but I don't know if you can bring her down by yourself."

Ivan slapped the phone back into his pack. "Matt's on his way. I'm going on ahead."

Within minutes, Emily was surrounded by light from low-burning torches Ivan stuck in the ground. "Take good care of her, she's sweet on you," Emily said. Now, where did that come from, Emily wondered as she curled up on the mossy ground.

"Is she now?" Ivan said with a chuckle in his voice.

When Ivan was gone, Emily whispered, "Is it okay to go to sleep, Ian?" She knew there would be no response. She smiled as she cradled her head against her hands. An instant later she was sound asleep. Thunder and lightning ricocheted over and around her, the pelting rain doing its best to douse the torches Ivan had left for her. She woke hours later when she felt herself being picked up and carried a distance. She felt every bounce and jar as she was settled into Matt Haliday's jeep.

"My God, Emily, you look . . . are you sure nothing's broken?"

"Don't even think about taking me to a hospital. All I

need is a hot bath, some bandages and ointment, and maybe some TLC from the sisters. I think I probably look worse than I am. How's Rosie?"

"Being operated on as we speak. It's appendicitis. Ivan stayed at the hospital with her."

"She kind of likes Ivan," Emily said, trying to brace her injured shoulder against the door.

Matt laughed. "Ivan kind of likes her too. You did really well, Emily. For a tenderfoot."

"I thought that was a cowboy term."

"We use it a lot for people who aren't experienced on the trail. You made it. I've seen, over the years, experienced men get hopelessly lost. We've had to send out search parties more than once. Rosie will be just fine, thanks to you."

Emily clenched her teeth. "I had a little help. Actually, I had a lot of help."

"I don't think I want to know," Matt said quietly.

"That's good, because I wasn't about to share."

"You really should have a doctor look you over, Emily. I'll be more than happy to drive you to an all-night clinic if you don't want to go to the hospital. I'd feel a lot better if you'd agree to go."

"I've already had a doctor . . . I'm fine. The sisters will take good care of me. Gussie told me she would have been a vet if she hadn't had a calling, as she put it. She loves patching up people. Talk to me, Matt, tell me about those nuns. They don't seem . . . they are real, right?"

"There's all kinds of stories. The one I think is closest to the truth is that they once belonged to an order of Benedictines. One of them, Cookie, I think, had a very rich relative who left all his money to her. He used to come here twice a year. The place fell on hard times and she bought it up, after she left the order. She's quite modern, as are the others. They believe in divorce, birth control, think priests should be allowed to marry, and think there is a place for female priests. The Vatican didn't see it their way so they left. The Black Mountain Retreat is their home and they're the happiest bunch of women I've ever seen. Their habits are a design of their own. They still consider themselves nuns and they do lead a good life, ministering to one and all. I guess you could say they're progressive renegades. I don't personally know if this is true or not, but it's been said that more than one person has mentioned them in their will. This place is very solvent, and as fast as they take in money, they put it back into the business. And it is a business. There's a two-year waiting period for reservations for new guests."

"That can't be," Emily said groggily. "I just called up and they took me right away."

"Then you must be someone very special," Matt said briskly. "It's one rule they *don't* break. I told you that first night only special people go to Archangel."

In spite of herself, Emily felt pleased. She'd never, to her knowledge, been considered special. It must be because of Father Michael.

"What time is it, Matt?"

"Almost midnight. The sisters are waiting up for you. I radioed ahead. There might be news of Rosie when we get there."

"I hope so." A moment later Emily was asleep.

The sisters dithered and fretted when Matt carried Emily into the kitchen by way of the back door. He was shooed out almost immediately. "Any news of Rosie?" he called through the screendoor.

"Not yet. Let us know if you hear something."

As one, they clucked their tongues like mother hens as they shepherded Emily into a huge bathroom.

"There's no way we're going to try and take your clothes off. They're stuck to you with your own dried blood so we're going to stand you under the warm water and let you remove them. Then we'll take you into the Jacuzzi. A good belt of this plum brandy and a couple of aspirin will have you feeling better quickly. We'll tape up your shoulder and ribs, patch up your knees and arms. You'll be good as new in about a week," Cookie said.

"Should we pour the peroxide over her while she has her clothes on or off?" Gussie asked as she removed the cap from a gallon jug.

"After," Cookie said briskly. "I think we can all use a slug of that brandy. It's going to be a long night."

"I'll get the glasses," Phillie said happily. "This is so nice, being able to do something good for Father Michael's friend. He's going to be so pleased when we tell him."

At four o'clock, when the nuns led Emily out to the porch where she was to sleep on the chaise lounge for the remainder of the night, she felt almost as good as new. She said so, quite happily.

"That's because you're drunk. One drink in the Jacuzzi is equal to four. Maybe it's three. It has to do with the hot water. You had three glasses of brandy so that's either nine or twelve drinks. Sleep well, dear Emily," Gilly said, covering her with a light summer blanket.

Chapter 18

"It's hard to believe it's been five whole days since Rosie's operation," Sister Cookie said as she held out a glass of lemonade to Emily. "It's going to be so wonderful for you when you see her. What time is Matt picking you up?"

"In about twenty minutes. Sister, I came up here because I wanted to talk to you about something. Now look, I'm not of your faith so I don't . . . what I mean is I believe in God and . . . you and the others always talk about miracles and . . . what makes a miracle?"

"God."

"That night, something very strange happened to me. I swore to myself I wasn't going to ever talk about it, but I can't get it out of my mind. If you have a minute, I want to tell you a little about what happened up there on the trail."

"I have as many minutes as you need, Emily. Now, take a deep breath and tell me."

"I see," Sister Cookie said when Emily had finished.

"Was it my subconscious or was it really Ian? I need to know, Sister. It was so real. I swear, Sister, on all that is holy, that he physically picked me up at one point. I felt . . . I felt him. Now, am I crazy or did that happen?"

"I don't know, Emily. If I were you, I think I would want to believe the Almighty's hand was on your shoulder. In this case, Ian's hand if he was one of God's Messengers. God takes care of us, Emily. All you have to do is ask and He's there for you. You needed Him. For you, it was Ian. Believe that and hold on to it. It could have happened, and I for one would classify that as a miracle, but then I'm one of those renegade nuns everyone talks about. It could have been your subconscious at work too. If it's important for you to believe it was Ian, then there are two of us who believe it. You and me. Ian came through for you when you really needed him. It doesn't matter how or why. He did. And that alone, Emily, should erase a lot of the bad that has shackled you for so long."

"I tried calling him back, but he didn't respond. He's gone forever now, isn't he, Sister?"

"Maybe he's going to be your Guardian Angel," Cookie said with a twinkle in her eye.

"Now that's a hoot," Emily replied. "Thanks for talking to me, Sister. Thanks for believing with me. I do, you know."

"Isn't it a wonderful feeling?"

"I woke up with a smile these past days. I feel lighter, buoyant somehow. Is that crazy or what?"

"Not at all. Was there a song in your heart?"

"Not really."

"There will be. I hear Matt's jeep. Don't forget the basket for Rosie and give her our love."

"I will."

"Matt Haliday is a fine man," Cookie said slyly.

Matt looked fit, clean-shaven, slicked-down hair, clean khakis, polished loafers, and he smells good too, Emily thought as she settled herself.

"How are you feeling?"

He sounds like he cares. "Still a little stiff if I sit too

long. I have lots and lots of scabs; that's why I'm wearing long sleeves. Makeup can't cover my facial abrasions, but I can live with them. I have to thank Ivan. What if he hadn't decided to go up on the trail? I could still be wandering around. You too, Matt. I wanted to call you, but . . . I didn't."

"You can call me anytime, Emily. My home phone number is on the bulletin board. That's why we're here. It's our job to look after the guests and to do our best to keep the forests safe. I hear Rosie is ready to come home, but she's running a slight fever. Maybe tomorrow. Do you know why she didn't want her children called?"

"I guess she didn't want to worry them. Mothers are like that."

"But . . ."

"I'm sure one of the sisters would have called if things . . . went from bad to serious. What do you do on your days off besides drive guests around?"

"Usually just hang out. Cook a roast. I like to cook. I do some gardening, take the kids places. They went with friends on an overnight camping trip so I'm at loose ends. Listen, would you like to have dinner with me? I made a pot of spaghetti earlier. I even used some sun-dried tomatoes. I know how to make garlic bread and I've got some real good beer to wash it all down with."

"I'd like that, Matt."

Matt stared at her and then back at the road. For some strange reason she felt comfortable with this man. There was no fear, no anxiety. It seemed as if she'd known him for a long time.

"You look pretty spiffy."

"Me?"

"Yep, you." God, why had she said that?

"Am I supposed to say you look spiffy too?"

Emily laughed. "It would be nice. Clotheswise, that is. Forget the flesh with all the scratches and scabs. I just hope

I don't scare Rosie." He had seven freckles marching across the bridge of his nose that were still easy to see with his deep tan. She felt a smile work its way around her mouth.

"Emily, would you like to talk about your hours on the trail? I'm a good listener if you do."

Emily thought about the question. Anything less than an honest answer to this new friend—and he was a friend— would have been cheating. "No. Maybe sometime, but not now."

"Okay. Yeah, you look spiffy, too," he said with a wry grin.

"Now that wasn't so hard, was it?" She was flirting and he was flirting back. At their ages. A silly grin attached itself to her face.

"Do you like horror flicks?"

Emily shrugged. "Why?"

"I thought if you didn't have to go right back after dinner we could watch one. The sisters have them by the bushel. My son likes to watch them so Gussie loans them to me. I cannot get used to the idea that those gentle souls like that stuff. Chain-saw murders, decapitations, the gorier the better. They read that stuff too. You know that and then you see them kneeling, saying their rosaries. It doesn't compute."

"They're human like the rest of us. I don't understand all that much about priests and nuns, but it seems unnatural for them to give up everything from the outside world. Not only unnatural, but unfair. They can still do all their good works and keep that part of themselves that belongs to the outside world. That's only my opinion," she added hastily.

"Are we talking about sex here or the blood and guts movies and books?" Matt asked, his eyes on the road straight ahead.

"Everything. I wouldn't want to give up sex, would

you? I kind of like it. What I mean is . . . oh, Lord, I don't believe I said that." Emily blushed.

Matt guffawed. "I'll pretend you didn't say it."

"Why don't we talk about something else? What do you put in your sauce?"

Still laughing, Matt explained. "Tomatoes, paste, a little oil, oregano, some pork neck bones. I cook it for seven hours."

"Why?" Emily asked, perplexed.

"It gets thicker. I hate watery sauce. Am I doing it wrong?"

"I don't know. I only cook mine for three hours. It tastes pretty good to me. Doesn't it get bitter?"

"Maybe that's why the kids like to eat at their friends' houses. Well, you can tell me tonight. It'll be cooking seven hours by the time we get home."

"It must be hard for you to be both mother and father to your children. How do you do it with all the hours you put in?"

"In the beginning it was hard. The neighbors helped. The sisters did their share and Ivan plays at being an uncle. They adore him as well as the sisters. The kids cooperated all the way. Gradually things got easier. We have a routine and we all try to stick to it. Everyone has chores. In the beginning I . . . didn't handle it very well. You know, Why me, why did this have to happen to me, that kind of thing? The sisters worked me through that. It seems like a very long time ago."

He sounds, Emily thought, like he's still in love with his wife. The smile left her face.

"We're here. There's Ivan's four by four." He winked at Emily, who stared at him blankly.

"Is something wrong, Emily?"

"No. I started to think about Rosie. Remembering." She reached behind her for the picnic basket.

"Here, let me carry that."

"I can carry it," Emily said tightly.

"I know you can. I was trying to be a gentleman about it. If you're one of those uptight females, that's okay with me." There was laughter in his voice that Emily ignored.

She was miffed and it was silly and stupid of her. Why shouldn't he still be in love with his wife? He'd obviously had a good marriage, and when it ended, he grieved. Like I did, only I didn't have a good marriage. He has children, constant reminders of his wife. Open your heart, Emily, and be generous of spirit, she scolded herself.

She liked him. A lot. It was going to be a problem for her if she didn't . . . do what? She was jumping ahead of herself here. So far he'd expressed no serious interest in her. So what if he invited her for dinner and then asked her to stay and watch a movie? So what? Lots of people did things like that and it didn't mean a thing. Friendships were made up of little encounters like this. She was hardly in a position to expect more. She'd only known the man for a few short weeks.

"Here," she said, handing over the picnic basket. Matt reached out and took it from her, his hand touching hers. She felt a tingle race up her arm. "I'm used to doing everything for myself. It's nice when someone offers to help. I find it . . . very difficult to . . . to ask. I'm not referring to the picnic basket . . . well, yes, in a way I am."

Matt wiped imaginary sweat from his brow and said, "Whew, I'm glad we settled *that*. For a minute there I thought maybe we'd come to blows."

Emily giggled at his lopsided grin. A sense of humor, a prime requisite for a prime friendship that might, just might, turn into something more.

In the elevator, Emily tried not to stare at her companion. She was aware of the closeness of him, the very cleanness of him. She loved khakis, loved uniforms of any kind.

She thought about Ian's white lab coats, his white shirts, and then she thought about Ben and the sweat suits he wore all the time. Damn, she didn't want to think about Ben, not when she was in the company of someone like Matt.

"I'll buy you an ice cream cone if you tell me what you're thinking right this minute," Matt said.

"I was thinking about how creased and pressed you look," Emily lied. "What were you thinking about at the same moment?"

"I was thinking maybe I should kiss you right here in this elevator."

"Sometimes it doesn't pay to think. Sometimes it pays to act on what one thinks," Emily said boldly.

"Uh-huh," Matt said, setting the picnic basket down on the floor.

He drew his arms around her, holding her close to him. She realized how tall he was, towering over her, lifting her chin with the tips of his fingers to look down into her eyes. His lips, when they touched hers, were soft, giving as well as taking, gently persuading her to respond. His arm cradling her against him was firm and strong, but his fingers still touching her face were tender, trailing whispery shadows over her bruised cheekbones. Having him kiss her seemed to be the most natural beginning to their new friendship. It was just that. A kiss. A tender gesture, tempting an answer but demanding none.

Matt stepped back, his gaze locked with hers. "I'm too old to play emotional games," he said. "Seventeen-year-olds do that and I'm a far cry from seventeen. Besides, more often than not they hurt rather than give pleasure. I like you, Emily. I'd like to get to know you better."

Emily's heart thumped. She nodded. "I'd like to get to know you better too. Maybe when you see me eating spaghetti, you'll change your mind. I tend to drip it down my shirt. Usually I wear something red when I'm going Italian."

"So I'll give you a bib. I'm fifty-five, Emily." He looked away for a moment as he waited for her response.

Emily laughed. "If that's a hint for me to declare my age, think again. Everyone knows the second half of one's life is supposed to be the best."

"I heard that too. Guess we'll just have to see if we can prove it. I already know how old you are. I tricked Sister Phillie into letting me see your reservation. Date of birth, etc, etc, etc."

Emily flushed. He'd looked up her reservation. That meant serious interest on his part. She herself had asked questions about Matt Haliday, which meant she, too, was interested. Chemistry.

"The elevator door's been open for a while," she said. "We should probably get off."

"I noticed that." Matt laughed. "We could ride down again and then ride up and do the same thing all over again. Want to?"

"Yeah. Yeah, I do," Emily said, backing farther into the elevator.

His arms were around her the moment the door closed. This time the kiss lasted longer, but was just as sweet and tender as the first time. He was still kissing her when the elevator rose. When the elevator stopped on the fourth floor, Matt relaxed his hold on her. "Damn good thing it stopped. I was seriously thinking about sex in an elevator."

Emily gurgled with laughter. "I was too."

"*Ahhhh,*" was all he could say.

Emily followed Matt down the corridor to Rosie's room. She winked at Rosie and gave her head a slight nod. Rosie smiled from ear to ear.

"You just missed Ivan."

"Good thing," Matt said. "Otherwise there would be nothing left in this basket for you. The sisters, according to Emily here, packed everything you love. How's the food here?"

"Terrible. Emily, how are you?" Rosie asked with such concern that Emily felt tears prick her eyelids.

"I guess I do look like five miles of used road. Actually, I feel pretty good. My joints don't feel as stiff as they did. The bruising is fading and so is the swelling. A lot of the scabs are starting to itch so I guess that means I'm healing. You look great; how do you feel?"

"Fine. I'm walking better. I thought an appendectomy was a piece of cake, but it isn't. I'm running a slight fever. If it goes down, I can go home tomorrow. Ivan said he'd pick me up and drive me back. He's been coming by every day. He said he feels responsible for me since he carried me down the mountain. You saved my life, Emily. I don't know how I'll ever repay you."

"I'm just sorry it took me so long. God, Rosie, when it got dark, I thought for sure we were both done for. We both made it thanks to Ivan and . . . and a friend. Let's not think negative thoughts. Everything happens for a reason. You can just forget that repayment business too. Not another word, Rosie."

"Okay. So, what are you two up to?" Rosie grinned.

"Up to? As compared to what?" Matt asked, matching her grin.

"You know, are you off today? What's going on at the Retreat? How are those renegade sisters doing? Ivan has told me some pretty wild stories."

"Don't believe half of them. Those sisters are the finest people I've ever met. They contribute to this hospital every year. Did you know that?"

Rosie and Emily shook their heads.

"They give to the old age home and the orphanage too. Money as well as their time. They practice what they preach. Not too many people do that," Matt said.

"I wasn't criticizing them," Rosie said. "I think it's wonderful and funny at the same time. I wish I had their philosophy and disposition. Guess what, I lost twelve pounds."

"No!" Emily laughed.

"Yes, I did. It's going to be that much easier to start that regimen you're going to map out for me."

"Only when the doctor gives the okay," Emily said firmly.

A nurse bustled into the room. "Doctor is making rounds now. Visitors can wait in the waiting room or they can leave," she said briskly.

"This takes forever, guys, so you might as well leave. Thanks for coming by. I'm sure I'll see you tomorrow. Did you bring me anything to read?"

Emily nodded. *"The Woodchopper Murder* and *Venom in the Blood.* I passed on *Nights in the Bayou.* It's about alligators chewing up the residents at a religious retreat." Matt burst out laughing. Emily joined him. Rosie threw a box of tissues at their retreating backs.

In Matt's car on the way to his house, Emily realized something strange was happening to her. She was feeling. The process, as she thought about it, was like pinpricks of awareness making her alive again. Really and truly alive. She risked a side glance at Matt. Great profile. Maturity. Muscular in all the right places. Her neck felt warm.

She was feeling. I'm Emily Thorn. Divorced. Widowed. CEO of a thriving company. Successful. It hit her like a bolt of lightning. Those are things I did . . . do, not who I am. I'm Emily Thorn. Me, Emily the person.

Something was happening to her, had been slowly happening since her arrival here in the Smoky Mountains. She was viewing things differently, feeling *everything.*

"Well, here we are, my humble abode. It looks small from the outside," he said, hopping from the jeep. He walked around to the side and opened the door for Emily.

"It used to be a summer cottage and I added on and winterized it. I was born about a mile from here. Do you like it?"

"It's very nice," Emily said. "I love front porches. Do you ever sit out here?" she asked as Matt guided her up to the wide plank porch.

"When I have the time. Usually late at night when I have things to think about. I tend to fall asleep in the chair and wake up with a crick in my neck. Come on, I'll give you the two-minute tour."

"It smells wonderful," Emily said, wrinkling her nose in approval.

"Garlic. And onions. This is the living room," he said airily, his arm waving about.

Emily looked around. The room was square with deep furniture covered with flowered chintz that matched the drapes. A braided rug was in the middle of the floor. It looked homemade. Everywhere she looked there were pictures of a smiling young woman. Emily felt her tongue grow thick in her mouth. Too many pictures. Too many memories. She wondered how she compared to the smiling woman with the pony tail and laughing eyes.

"This is the dining room, which is really an extension of the living room. We eat in the kitchen. The truth is I think we live in the kitchen. As you can see, it's big. I extended it when I added the family room on to the back of the house. A bathroom too. Those kids of mine stay in there for hours. I'd never make it to work if we only had one."

It was a wonderful kitchen, sunny and warm with green plants tucked into corners and on the windowsill. Copper that needed to be shined hung from long chains hooked into the rafters as did net bags of garlic and herbs. The cushions on the burled oak table and chairs were bright red and matched the placemats, which were old and worn.

A braided rug rested by the sink, another by the stove. Notes and memos were plastered all over the front of the refrigerator. And on all the walls were framed petit point pictures. The kitchen held two, one a bowl of striking red apples, another of lemons and limes next to a pitcher of lemonade. The ones in the living room were different, more personal. A sailboat with figures of four people. A family. Matt's family. Another of a little boy and girl playing ball in the yard. Emily felt something catch in her throat. This family lived with their memories the way she had.

"The bedrooms are just bedrooms. Kind of messy. How do you like my deck? Ivan helped me build it."

"Oh, it's wonderful. What a magnificent view. It takes your breath away. You must love it here very much."

"I do. I don't think I could ever live anywhere else."

He's making a statement, Emily thought. Warning me ahead of time that this is where he belongs.

"Who's Al Roker?" Matt asked quietly.

"Why do you want to know?" Emily asked, flustered with the question.

"Ivan said that when he found you, you thought he was Al Roker. I'm asking you who he is."

Emily laughed, a nervous sound even to her own ears. "I thought there, right before Ivan found me, that I was becoming delirious. At first I thought he was a Sasquatch. Then I thought he was Al Roker. Back home I always watched the five o'clock news and weather when I could. He's the weatherman and he's always talking about his Doppler radar. I don't even know what Doppler radar means. When I saw Ivan I thought it was Roker with the Doppler radar strapped to his back. I didn't know if I was dreaming . . . I don't know what I thought. I was scared out of my wits."

"Uh-huh."

"What does uh-huh mean, Matt? Are you trying to ask me something without actually coming out and asking me. Like, is there a man in my life or something like that?"

Matt's head bobbed up and down. "Something like that. Is there?"

"Yes and no. I have a very good friend back home. We have an understanding of sorts. He's free to do as he pleases and so am I. We get along well. He has no real baggage and I don't either. He's seen me through some rough times. He's a very good friend. What about you?"

"No, no one. I don't know why that is," he said.

"I think I might be able to give you a clue," Emily said quietly.

"Oh yeah."

"Yeah. Your living room is like a shrine to your wife. I just walked through it and I counted twenty-four pictures, nine on the mantel, two or three on every table, several on the wall, not to mention the needlework pictures. It's the same thing here in the kitchen. I would imagine it intimidates women if you bring them here."

"Does it intimidate you, Emily?"

"Very much so. I could never kiss you here, or if we ever decided to go to bed, it can't be in this house."

"The kids . . ."

"The kids should have the pictures in their rooms. You should have one too. There comes a time, Matt, when you have to put it all away if you want to get on with your life. If you're happy looking at the pictures, happy with your memories, then you don't have to do anything. This is just my opinion. Am I still invited for supper?"

"Yes. Of course. I don't really bring women here, Emily. Perhaps one or two, but they were really just friends. They were a little jittery now that I think about it."

"Can I set the table?"

"End of discussion, right?"

"Right." Emily smiled.

He was clumsy, but at home in the kitchen. Emily sat in her chair and fought the urge to offer to help, knowing instinctively he wanted to perform for her.

"I'll never be a renowned chef," Matt said, dropping spaghetti into the boiling water.

"Guess what, I'm never going to be a trail blazer either. We each have to accept little things like that in life."

"You're funny. I like that. Not too many people have a sense of humor."

"I used to be as dry as year-old mud. I've been involved in a steady learning process for the past few years. Life's just too damn short to dwell on the past, even yesterday for that matter. It's gone. What's that saying, the past is prologue, something like that? What do you want to be when you grow up, Matt?" she teased.

"A caring human being. Bet you thought I was going to say a fireman. How about you?"

"I met my goals. I guess I want to do something . . . meaningful. Hopefully, all the bad times are behind me. This portion of my life is important to me. Whatever I do has to do with who I am now. One of the sisters put the idea into my head, but I happen to think she's right when she said God had a design for me. He got me this far and now I have to figure out what He wants me to do. One of these days I'm going to figure it out."

"How long are you staying at the retreat?"

"I'm not sure. It's kind of open for me. Certainly as long as Rosie stays. The sisters said I could stay as long as I want. Hey, I may never leave."

"Gets pretty cold here in the winter."

"It's cold in New Jersey too," Emily said, her voice neutral-sounding. "The reason your sauce is so watery is because you aren't letting the spaghetti drain and I never rinse mine."

"Oh, yeah?"

"Yeah. And the vinegar in the salad contributes to the wateriness of the sauce. I thought chefs, even good cooks, liked criticism."

"Not this cook. Eat."

"Tell me about your kids, Matt."

"Benjy's twelve. He's a good kid. Into sports. He does well in school if I keep after him. He loves the outdoors as much as I do. He looks just like his mother. He has her temper too, I'm sorry to say. Molly is like me. She's easygoing, pretty. She doesn't think she's pretty, though. She's fourteen and she has definitely discovered boys. I think the phone is growing out of her ear. She accepted her mother's death very well. Benjy had a lot of problems we had to work through.

"They both worry about me. Back then . . . they were afraid every time I left the house that I wouldn't come back. They're very close. I've never had to really deal with the problem of another woman. I don't really know what their reaction will be. I guess that sounds like I'm giving you a warning."

Emily nodded. "Forewarned is forearmed, that kind of thing? This is . . . not exactly hypothetical, but what if we do . . . start to see each other and the children don't like or approve of me? What happens then?"

"I don't know, Emily."

"I don't know then if I can let myself be open to something like that. I like you, I feel attracted to you. I liked it when you kissed me. But I don't need any more heartache in my life, Matt. It's taken me a long time to get where I am." Her pulse was beating so fast she was sure he could see it bouncing up and down. "Why don't we go back to being friends. Let's not plan anything and that way . . ."

Matt leaned across the table. "Listen to me, Emily. I take my relationships seriously. My body is telling me I want to go to bed with you and I think your body is telling you the same thing. Now, that's the physical side of things. We can deal with that when the time comes. I like you. I find myself trying to find ways to be in your company. I was worried sick when Ivan brought you down from the mountain. I wanted to take care of you, to make you better, to dress your wounds. I never felt like that about anyone except my wife. I wanted to tell you, but it seemed kind of . . . wimpish. My kids are a separate issue. I'll deal with them as a father. What we're talking about here is you and me. I really tuned into you that first night when I came by your cabin and woke you up. You sneaked into my heart, Emily."

Emily's eyes misted. "I think you sneaked into mine too. There's every possibility your kids *might* like me."

"Molly will. Benjy won't. I'll deal with it, Emily."

"I don't know the first thing about kids. I'll probably make things worse. I'll say something when I shouldn't. I'll bend over backwards when I should be stern."

"I cooked so you can clean up," Matt said airily.

Emily got up from the chair, her thoughts in a turmoil. She could feel prickles of electricity run up and down her arms as she carried her plate to the sink.

His embrace, when it came, was neither expected nor unexpected. It was natural, just the way it was in the elevator. She felt herself melting into his arms as though she'd been doing it for years and years. He felt good. He felt so right, she was dizzy with the thought. She felt his lips, his fingertips, his hard body. She couldn't help it, she wanted this man. But not here, not now. She said so.

Matt backed away, swatted her rump, and handed her the dishtowel at the same time. "Just put them in to soak. I'll do them later."

"That's good because I had no intention of doing them. I'm a guest." The charge of electricity ricocheting between them was so strong, Emily moved to the other side of the kitchen.

"I think you should take me home," she said quietly.

Matt nodded. "I think so too."

"Supper wasn't bad, thanks for inviting me."

"My pleasure," Matt said formally.

"Why don't we have dessert at my cabin?"

"Let's go, lady."

They ran like two kids to the jeep. They were driving away, the wind blowing in their faces, when Emily said, "You didn't lock your door."

"I never lock my door."

"We know why we're going to my place, right?"

"Right. No game playing. We're going to have sex. Good, old-fashioned sex. Jesus, I feel like a kid. It's been a while, Emily. I might be a little rusty." She laughed and laughed until he joined her, throwing back his head in delight.

They tripped over each other as they ran up the four steps to Emily's porch. Both of them tried to squeeze through the door opening at the same time. Thinner than Matt, Emily bounded through, turning on the lights as she went along. "Forget the damn lights and come here," Matt ordered.

Their eyes met in the dimness of the bedroom, and without a trace of modesty or embarrassment, she was aware she could drown in Matt's incredibly dark gaze and emerge again as the woman she needed to become.

Seeing her moist lips part and offer themselves to him, he lowered his mouth to hers, touching her lips, tasting their sweetness, drawing a kiss, gentle, yet passionate. Searing flames licked her body; the pulsating beat of her heart thundered in her ears.

When he stepped away, his arms dropping to his sides, his eyes searched hers. What he saw reassured him.

Emily closed the distance between them with one forward step. She kissed him then as she had never kissed another man, a kiss so deep with longing and yearning she felt her knees grow weak. Her head buzzed with emotions she'd thought were gone forever. She knew then, in that one dizzying moment, that this man belonged to her, for however long their time would be together. She had finally found a man who could make her feel like the woman she wanted to be.

"Tell me you want me to make love to you," Matt whispered.

"Yes, yes, make love to me, here, now." Her voice was deep, singing with desire, a voice that was new to Matt and new to her too.

He tore away his clothes, eager to be naked against her, wanting the warmth of her touch on his body. Rolling over on his back, he took her with him, trailing his fingers down the length of her spine and returning over and over again to the roundness of her bottom. He invited her touch, inspired her caresses, always watching her in the dim moonlight filtering into the room, reveling in the heavy-lidded smoldering in her eyes. He wanted her to take pleasure in him, wanted her to find him worthy of her finely tuned passions. Did he please her, he wondered as she smoothed the flat of her palms over his chest, her fingertips gripping and pulling at the thicket of hair. Her mouth found his nipples, licking, tasting, lowering her explorations to the tautness of his belly and the hardness of his thighs. He reveled in her touch, in the expression of her eyes as he took her face in his hands and held it for his kiss.

Putting her beneath him once again, he kissed the sweetness of her mouth, her eyes, the soft curve of her jaw. Her breasts awakened beneath his kisses, and she arched beneath his touch.

She sought him with her lips, possessed him with her hands, her own passions growing as she realized the pleasure she was giving him. The hardness of his sex was somehow tender and vulnerable beneath her hand as she felt it quiver with excitement and desire . . . for her. His hands never left her body, seeking, exploring, touching . . . she wanted to lie back and render herself to him, touch him, commit him to memory and know him as she had never known another man. Instead of being alien to her, his body was as familiar to her as her own. She felt her body sing with pleasure and she knew her display of passion was food for his.

Emily was ravaged by the hunger he created in her. She wanted to feel him inside her, joining with her, bringing her to her own release. "Matt," she breathed, imploring him with her eyes, feeling as though she would die if he did not enter her, yet hating to put an end to the excruciating pleasure.

He put himself between her opened thighs, his eyes devouring her as she lay waiting for him. Her soft hair reflected the silver of the moon, her skin was bathed in a sleek sheen that emphasized her womanly curves and enhanced the contact between their flesh. He sat back on his heels, his gaze locking with hers as his hands moved over her body. Emily met his eyes, unashamedly, letting him see the hungers that dwelled there and the flutter of her lashes that mirrored the trembling in her loins. His hands slipped to her sex and she cried out softly, arching her back to press herself closer against his gently circling fingers. "You're so beautiful here," he told her, watching her eyes close and her lips part with a little gasp.

He gentled her passions, fed her desires, brought her to

the point of no return, and smiled tenderly when she sobbed with the sweetness of her passions. She climaxed beneath his touch, uttering her surprise, whispering his name. His hands eased the tautness of her thighs, kneading the firmness of her haunches and smoothing over her belly.

When she thought the sensation too exquisite to be surpassed, he leaned forward, driving himself into her, filling her with his pulsating masculinity. Her body strained beneath his, willing itself to partake of his pleasure, to be his pleasure. The fine hairs of his chest rubbed against her breasts. His mouth took hers, deeply, lovingly. His movements were smooth as he stroked within her, demanding she match his rhythm, driving her once again to the sweetness she knew could be hers.

Her fingers raked his back, feeling the play of his muscles beneath his skin. She found the firmness of his buttocks, holding fast, driving him forward, feeling him buried deep within her. He doubled her delight and she climaxed again, and only then did he rise up, grasping her bottom in his hands and lifting it, thrusting himself into her with shorter, quicker strokes.

Her body was exquisite, her responses delicious, but it was the expression on her lovely face and the delight and pleasure he saw there that pushed him over the edge and destroyed his restraint. The total joy, the hint of disbelief in her clear eyes, the purity of a single tear on her smooth cheek were his undoing. He found relief in her, her name exploding on his lips.

They lay together, legs entwined, her head upon his shoulder as he stroked the softness of her arm and fullness of her breasts. His lips were in her hair, soft, teasing, against her brow. "You're a beautiful lover," he breathed, tightening his embrace, delighting in the intimacy between them.

"So are you," Emily murmured.

"Would it surprise you, Emily, if I told you I think I'm falling in love with you?"

"Would it surprise you, Matt, if I told you the same thing?"

"I guess that means we're halfway in love."

"Sounds good to me," Emily said, snuggling as close to him as she could. They slept, each dreaming of the other.

Chapter 19

It was late when Emily woke. She remembered instantly all the details of the previous evening. Her arm snaked out to touch the pillow Matt had slept on. He was gone, but she knew that. She rolled over, burying her face in the pillow. His body scent was faint, but noticeable. She took a deep breath before she stretched like a cat.

It was going to be another beautiful day with a cloudless sky and warm breezes. A glance at the little traveling clock on the nightstand told her she'd slept through breakfast and it was almost time for lunch. It didn't matter in the least; she wasn't hungry. She was hungry only to feast her eyes on Matt Haliday.

Was it possible she was in love with the ranger? In so short a time? All the slick magazines, all the love stories on television told about eyes meeting across a room and then boom, everyone rode off into the sunset and lived happily ever after. Yeah, well, things like that didn't happen to the Emily Thorns of this life.

Emily bounded from the bed like a teenager. She showered, dressed, and was on her front porch ready to feed the squirrels and rabbits. The moment she finished and pulled the last weed from the flowers on the porch, she was running down the trail to the recreation building to call the hospital. Perhaps she could pick Rosie up.

"Mrs. Finneran was discharged an hour ago," the charge nurse said happily.

Emily clapped her hands. How wonderful. Now she could sit for hours and talk to Rosie about Matt. Providing she wanted to listen. What to do now? Call home, talk to her friends; Ben. Ben. She owed them all a phone call. The basket of mail on her dresser from all of them was still unopened. It was sinful that she'd been so lax.

Her calling card in hand, Emily placed a call first to Ben. Her happiness sizzled over the wire as she announced herself. "How's it all going, Ben?"

"It's going. Obviously things are going well for you too. I don't think I ever heard you sound so happy. Or are you drunk on the scent of the pine trees? Nah, that can't be it. You must have made friends with the four-legged creatures roaming about. What *do* you do there all day?"

"This and that. The hours seem to fly by. I've made some friends. In fact one of them is on her way home from the hospital as we speak." She told him about Rosie's operation and getting lost on the trail. "You should see my face, Ben. It looks like a peanut butter and jelly open-faced sandwich. I was so stiff for a few days, I could barely walk. I'm fine now, though."

"For God's sake, Emily. What ever possessed you to go hiking like that? You aren't exactly the outdoor type. Something serious could have happened to you."

There was such worry and concern in Ben's voice, Emily felt a wave of guilt wash over her. "Nothing happened to me. I'm the outdoor type now. I love it, Ben. You can't believe how busy I am, how I fill up my days."

"When are you coming back, Emily? It's almost the end of August. I miss you. Your friends miss you too. Martha called off her . . . whatever it was she had with that old geezer. Seems he was looking for a nurse to take care of him; not that Martha is a nurse. He's due for some kind of serious surgery. But then I guess you know all about that; she said she wrote you a long letter."

"*Hmmmnn,*" was all Emily could think of to say.

"Are you so busy, Emily, that you couldn't call or write?"

Damn, his voice sounds so sad, so weary, Emily thought guiltily. "No, Ben, I just needed to . . . I guess I didn't want to have any kind of responsibility for a while. No pressures, if you know what I mean. I don't have a phone here, Ben. I have to go to the recreation hall. Besides, phone calls are frowned on. There's no one to run messages back and forth." How lame her voice sounded.

"Do you miss us at least a little bit? Me in particular."

"I do and I don't," Emily said truthfully. "I do think of all of you. You're all well, things are going well too, right?"

"Of course."

"See, I'm expendable. I really think I'm going to stay on awhile longer. It's still nice here through October. They tell me September is beautiful."

"Did you tell your friends you weren't coming back on Labor Day? They're planning a big barbecue. Lots of clients, friends, etc. As of last night they were still under the assumption you were coming back on schedule."

"Are you trying to make me feel guilty, Ben?"

"Yes."

"Well, stop it because it isn't going to work. I could see it if I was needed, but I'm not. And don't tell me I'm slacking off either."

"You sound defensive," Ben said coolly.

"You're making me sound this way, Ben. You and I had an agreement. I never made any promises. I'm sorry if this call has upset you. I will call the women and talk to them and explain why I'm staying on for a while. Good-by, Ben, it was nice talking to you. Take care of yourself. I'll drop you a line this week." As she finished speaking, she broke the connection with her index finger hovering over the bracket.

The happiness was gone now, replaced with guilt.

She was scuffing her way back down the trail to her cabin, her eyes on the ground, when she heard a sharp whistle. She turned. "Matt!"

He looks embarrassed, she thought. "Whatcha got in the sack?"

"Lunch. I brought some meatball sandwiches from home. Want to sit on your porch and eat them?"

"I'd love to. I have some soft drinks inside. I love picnics."

"I do too. Listen, tonight is the fish fry. Sister Tiny asked me if Molly will help. I said she probably would. I have to pick them up in town at three o'clock. I thought maybe we could all eat together. Ivan and Rosie, my kids, you and me. I'd like you to get to know my kids. Are you up to it?"

"Absolutely. I can't wait to get Rosie settled in. I would have picked her up, but when I called, they said she'd been discharged and Ivan was bringing her here. I'll look forward to it. These are, ah . . . tasty," Emily said, biting into the meatball sandwich.

"Tell the truth. They taste like hard rubber spiced with parsley."

"That too. I missed you when I woke up."

"I hated to leave. You're nice to sleep with."

"So are you. I decided to stay on awhile longer, at least till the end of September. I think Rosie is going to stay on too."

"You'll pretty much have the place to yourself for September. Mostly everyone leaves either the day before or the day after Labor Day. For some reason October is busy. Harvest moons, pumpkins brought up from town, the changing of the leaves. Cooler weather. The sisters get a reprieve. They work very hard, but then I guess you noticed that. By the way, Sister Tiny really did a number on her ankle yesterday. She stepped into a gopher hole. They took her to the doctor and he said she had to stay off it for a week or so. That's why they need Molly tonight. You smell good," he blurted out.

"I could smell your body scent in the bed when I woke up," Emily said, meeting Matt's gaze. "Are you off this weekend?"

Matt nodded. "I promised to go to Benjy's soccer practice and Molly wants to go roller skating. Weekends are pretty busy. I don't usually have them off, and when I do, I have to cram everything I can into the hours."

"I see," Emily said.

"What are you going to do?" He crumpled up the wax paper and napkin. He reached for hers and stuffed it into the paper bag he was holding.

"Read, spend time with Rosie. Call home. Help out if the sisters need me. I never have a problem filling up my hours. Maybe I'll go into town with Rosie and take in a movie."

"Will you miss me?"

Of course she would. Right now she wished she had magical powers so she could stuff herself into Matt's pocket and be with him all day. "Probably not," she lied. "How about you?"

"Probably not."

"Liar!" Emily laughed.

Matt looked chagrined. "Did you lie too?"

"No," she lied again. "Come on, I'll walk you over to your vehicle. Then I'm going over to see Rosie."

When they reached the jeep, Emily waved airily and sprinted down the trail, a smile on her face. He was going to kiss her, but on the off chance she read his intentions wrong, she took off.

"Rosie! When did you get home?"

"About half an hour ago. It's great to be back. I'm going to sit here all day and let people wait on me."

"What people?" Emily asked, looking around. "Where's Ivan?"

"He went fishing. He dumped me off. Actually, he carried me up to the porch. Don't go reading anything into any of this. He's not the least bit interested in me. He visited me every day. I think he felt responsible for me for some reason. He is *borrrrrriinnnng*. All he wanted to talk about was trees, animals, and fish. And Matt and his kids. I pretended to fall asleep so he'd leave."

"And I thought—"

"Sister Phillie brought down a pitcher of lemonade and some cookies. It's inside. They said they'd bring lunch and dinner too."

"I can do that. Matt told me Sister Tiny hurt her ankle and his daughter is going to help out with the fish fry tonight. If they have a wheelchair, I can wheel you up. It's too far for you to walk. They're going to be shorthanded. How do you feel, Rosie?"

"Good. I get twinges, but the doctor said it's gas. I must be the stupidest person in the world. How can you not know gas from appendicitis?"

"I don't know if I would. It's over and done with—you're okay, I'm okay. Let's not look back. I did enough of that these past years. Listen, have I got something to tell you. You aren't going to believe this. I hardly believe it. I keep pinching myself. Listen . . ."

"Oh, my God!" Rosie said when Emily told her about the night before. "That's wonderful. It is wonderful, isn't it?"

"I think so. He wants me to meet the kids tonight. I met them before, but I think this is different. I wonder what they're going to think."

"The little girl is sweet. The sisters adore her. The boy, he's rather sullen, fretful if you follow me. Four or five years ago Matt . . . well, he made friends with a woman who was here named Angela. She really liked him and he seemed to like her too. Whatever there was ended as quickly as it began. Supposedly she told someone who told someone else who told me, that the boy didn't like her and refused to even be polite. That was the end of that. It's a rumor and I probably shouldn't even repeat it. I'd hate to see you get hurt, Emily. Matt takes his parenting very seriously, as well he should."

Emily frowned. "Are you trying to tell me I have to suck up to some nine-year-old kid?"

"Yep, I guess that's what I'm telling you. From everything I've heard, Matt's kids, the boy especially, rule his personal life."

"That's terrible." A worm of fear skittered around inside her stomach. "I think you just scared me, Rosie. I like Matt. In fact, I think it goes beyond *like*. What should I do?"

"Nothing," Rosie said emphatically. "Be yourself. If Matt feels the way you do and if he's willing to allow his son to botch up your relationship, and I'm not saying the boy will do it, but if he does, then Matt isn't worth much, is he? If Benjy . . . that's his name, right?" Emily nodded. "Well, if Benjy has a problem, it probably stems from his mother's death, but that was a long time ago. Matt should have taken him for counseling or something. The schools back home are big on picking up on stuff like that. Maybe it was easier for Matt *not* to deal with it. There might not be a problem at all and we're worrying over nothing." Her voice belied her words.

"Baggage."

"I beg your pardon."

"Baggage, Rosie. That's a slang expression people use

when a relationship is under way and there's a wife or children in the background. They refer to them as baggage. It sounds terrible, I admit, but true nonetheless. What . . . what if he hates me? Kids of nine are pretty smart, aren't they?"

"I'd say so. Manipulative too. I would have thought it would be the girl. Girls are so protective of a parent. But she may relate better and she might be looking for a step-mother."

"Who said anything about marriage?" Emily yelped.

"Relationships, if they're serious, usually lead toward marriage. Don't go coy on me, Emily. I'm sure you've thought about it. Fantasized maybe." She smiled at Emily's flushed face.

"Want to play Scrabble?"

"Sure."

"Okay, I'll walk up and get the game and bring you back something for lunch."

The two women played Scrabble until three-thirty, when Emily called a halt. "I think you need to take a nap and I'm going to go for a bike ride. I'll be back by five-thirty. I asked about a wheelchair and the sisters said someone would have it down here by five forty-five. Once you get there, you can walk around. Okay?"

Rosie nodded. "Emily?"

"Yes."

"Don't spend too much time thinking about all of this. If it's meant to be, it will be. Sister Gussie's philosophy. Do what you did that night on the trail; think about that inspiration class we went to."

"Good idea. See you later."

Back at her cabin, Emily rummaged in the dresser drawer for the list of inspirational sayings and stuffed it into the pocket of her shorts. Thirty, or was it forty, suggestions on how to find inspiration in everyday life. Like she was really going to put food coloring in her bath water. With no bathtub on the premises, that one wasn't going to be hard to discount. There was no problem with admiring herself or dreaming a little. She knew them all—why she'd brought the list was a mystery, she thought as she pedaled along, her mind half on Matt, half on the sayings in her pocket. Do something new and different every day. Yeah, sure. Change your moods like clothes. Well, hell, that wasn't hard to do; she did that automatically. The one that was going to give her the most trouble was refusing to sit still for negative thoughts. She was going to have to ask one of the sisters how she should exercise her soul. Was that even possible? If she had a favorite of all the suggestions, she supposed it was the one that said, Let the world heal you. She'd tried that now for years and it seemed to be working.

Emily stopped her bike an hour later, looked at the uphill bike trail, and climbed off. She sat down, cross-legged, and lit a cigarette. She still hadn't given up the filthy things. Maybe she never would.

What would she do if Matt asked her to marry him? Did she really and truly love him? What about Ben? So many questions with no ready answers. "I don't think I'm mother material. In fact, I know I'm not." She was muttering to herself, a habit she'd thought she'd broken. Affairs were nice, relationships even nicer. Baggage. Package deal. "So, I'll have a little fling, and when it's over, I'll go home." The kids would always come first with Matt. And that's the way it should be. She lit a second cigarette from the stub of the first one. That was another thing—she wouldn't be able to smoke in Matt's house. "I do care about him." She was muttering again. What she needed right now was to shift into neutral.

Emily tried not to think. Instead she did her best to look around, savor, lock away the memory of this beautiful place. It was almost perfect with the sun filtering through the lacy overhang of trees. Everything was green and lush, the pines so aromatic she wanted to stay there forever. Banks and banks of wild fern were everywhere, their fronds long and graceful.

Because she couldn't quiet her mind, she thought about Ben and her friends back home. She hadn't read the mail either. "Damn."

Emily lit a third cigarette from the crumpled pack in her pocket. She ripped at the foil paper. Three left. She was going to smoke them all, bury the butts, and then pretend she hadn't smoked any of them. To what end, she questioned herself.

"Rosie's right. If any of this is meant to be, it will be," Emily muttered as she climbed back on her bike and pedaled back to her cabin.

She was nervous, twitchy, when she walked into the recreation room for the wheelchair. Thank God it was the electric kind. Just for the hell of it, she sat down and wheeled herself to Rosie's cabin. "It's a fun ride," she called cheerfully. "And it's electric so it isn't going to get stuck in the pine needles. Everything smells delicious as usual."

The fish fry was always held outside in the picnic area with gaily colored cloths on the redwood tables. Candles in wine bottles and cans of bug spray were at the ends of every table.

"What's on the menu?" Rosie asked.

"Catfish, expertly boned and fried to perfection, those slab potatoes topped with cheese, corn on the cob, fresh peas, homemade bread and butter, salad, and I think dessert is a secret. I saw a sign in the recreation room that said they were having an old-fashioned taffy pull tonight."

"I'll pass," Rosie said.

"Me too. I don't see Matt, do you? Okay, you can get out of the chair here. We can sit under this tree and we'll have a real good view when the sun goes down."

"This is fine. The breeze is nice, and no, I do not see Matt. Go look for him. I'll be fine here."

"No. I'll sit here with you. Want a cigarette?"

"Sure. A beer too."

"Gotcha. There's a keg tonight. Guess we have Ivan to thank for that. Those guys from Alabama can really sock away the beer. Last week they said a keg was needed. They paid for it too. Have you noticed how generous everyone is here?"

"You're simply talking to hear yourself, Emily. Go get the beer, leave the cigarettes, and if you meet Matt, don't hurry back."

"Am I that obvious?" Emily asked.

"Only to me. Don't bring me all suds either."

"I hear you," Emily said, trotting off for the beer. She returned carrying a tray with three glasses, two for Rosie and one for herself.

"Emily, Rosie, mind if Benjy and I join you? You've both met Benjy."

Emily and Rosie nodded.

Emily was about to light a cigarette and then changed her mind. Young people didn't care for cigarettes these days, which was good. She watched as Rosie blew a perfect smoke ring. Damn, she really wanted a cigarette. She hated drinking beer without a cigarette in her hand. "Everything smells good, doesn't it? Dessert is a secret tonight."

Benjy nodded, his face sullen. Clearly he would much rather be someplace else.

"Are you ready to go back to school, Benjy?" Emily asked quietly.

"No."

Emily tried again. "Your dad said you play soccer. Do you belong to a school team or is it a summer program?"

"School team. I don't like it, but my father said I have to play."

The belligerent expression on Benjy's face warned Emily that the boy was about to erupt and very soon. She noticed Matt's fingers drumming on the table top, a sure sign of nervousness.

I don't need this, Emily thought.

"Why don't you see if you can help the sisters in the kitchen, Benjy?" Matt suggested.

"Why? Do you want to get rid of me? It's not my turn to help."

"Because it would be the nice thing to do. No, I don't want to get rid of you, and turns don't count."

"Yeah, they do. Molly gets paid to wait on tables. I clean up and take the trash out to the dumpster and I get a free meal. Where's the fairness? I could have had pizza at home." He was out of his chair, heading for the kitchen, shouting his last words over his shoulder.

Matt closed his eyes wearily. "He has a terrible attitude. I don't know what to do with him anymore."

They were like night and day, Emily thought when Molly, carrying a tray with their dinners on it, set it down to give her father a loud smacking kiss. "Gee, it's nice to see you up and around, Mrs. Finneran. Mrs. Thorn, you look real good. Your bruises are almost gone. Bet you're happy. Guess what, Dad, when the sisters pay me tonight, I'll have enough money for the installation of my very own phone. By next week I'll have enough for the first month's bill. You aren't going to change your mind, are you?" she said, her words tumbling out with machine-gun speed.

Matt smiled. "A deal's a deal."

"If you want beer, you have to get it, Dad. I'm not allowed to do that."

"The ice tea is fine, honey."

She kissed the top of her father's head before she ran back to the kitchen.

"She's going to be a real beauty as she gets older. She's pretty now, but in a few more years she's going to be gorgeous."

"I know," Matt said modestly, "and then my problems will really begin."

"Think positive," Rosie said cheerfully. "This fish is perfect. I love fish. I love these potatoes too. I just plain love food."

She's nervous, just the way I am. Matt's antsy too, Emily thought. She wished he'd look at her, say something that was only understood by the two of them. A wink, a touch to her hand. It wasn't going to happen; that much she knew. He was caught up in his son's behavior to the exclusion of all else. She felt as if someone were poking at her heart with a stick. Children always come first. Get used to it, Emily. Second fiddle. Can you handle that?

Matt wolfed his food then excused himself, saying he wanted to check on Benjy. He gave Emily a brief, apologetic glance before he sprinted off.

Emily stirred the food on her plate, separating the fish into flakes and then mashing them into the potatoes. She felt miserable.

"The boy doesn't like me," Emily said. "I don't like him either. It's not a good place for either one of us to be."

"That boy doesn't like anyone," Rosie said. "Let's go for a little walk. By the time we get back, that mysterious dessert should be ready. I bet it's fruit. When the sisters can't think up something new, they spread the rumor that dessert is going to be something special, and it's usually watermelon filled with ice cream with rum poured over it and then set it on fire."

Emily burst out laughing. "That's funny, Rosie."

"Why don't we walk up and around the kitchen and come out in the parking lot and then back down the path to here. I can handle that. I'm supposed to walk, but then the incision starts to pull and I cramp up. I guess the more I walk the easier it will get."

"I don't need or want any more problems in my life," Emily said as they walked. "Sometimes I'm sorry I came here and met Matt. One minute I like him, well, I more than like him. Then a few minutes later I think about Ben and wish I was back home. I think this is just a fling and I'm not . . . I care a great deal about Ben. I feel so damn guilty. Guilt, Rosie, is a terrible thing."

When they were back at their table, Emily whispered, "Do you know what I'm afraid of, Rosie? I think it will break my heart if Matt . . . if Matt finds a way to come to my cabin tonight. So, would you mind if I stayed with you. I don't want to know . . . if he does . . . I'd just rather not be . . . available."

"Sure. I don't think that's going to happen. Matt will take the kids home and he won't drive all the way back here, not if Benjy is in the mood he's in. We can go now, Emily, if you like."

"I like."

Chapter 20

The dog days of August gave way to the bright, colorful days of September. The temperature dropped, the leaves began to turn, and the majority of the guests packed up and waved good-by, promising to return the following year. Two elderly couples along with their companions, Rosie, and Emily were the only guests that stayed on.

With two weeks to go on her extended stay, Emily found herself living for the hours she could spend with Matt. Her fling was becoming obsessive, but she didn't know how to turn her emotions off. The rest of the time she spent with Rosie, playing board games, biking, and hiking.

It's going to be so hard to leave here, Emily thought for the thousandth time.

She was dressing now for an evening in town. "Wear your best bib and tucker," Matt had said. "I have something important to talk to you about." Of course she'd agreed, and between herself and Rosie, not to mention the nuns, she was already married and living happily ever after. If such a thing was possible.

Her stomach was quivering and her throat felt as if a walnut were stuck in it. Twice she'd had to remove her eye shadow and start over because of the shakiness of her hand.

Emily stared at her reflection in the mirror. The person staring back at her was an Emily she didn't really know. There was a sparkle in this person's eyes, a certain looseness around her mouth that meant that mouth smiled a lot. All the time, as a matter of fact. This wasn't the same person who was married to Ian Thorn or the person who was deeply involved with Ben Jackson back in New Jersey.

Two weeks more and then she had to return to New Jersey and the house on Sleepy Hollow Road. If she wanted to.

If her instincts were right and Matt was ready to commit, was she ready to take on an instant family? She liked Molly and tolerated Benjy, but the boy was going to require a lot of time and effort on her part if she *wanted* to become a member of the family. For now he accepted her as someone who stopped by occasionally, someone who went out with their father once in a while, someone who sat with them at the fish fries on Friday and licked ice cream cones on Sunday afternoon.

One thing she knew for certain was she could never live in Matt's house, but how was she to tell him that? Was she even marriage material?

Emily lowered the seat on the toilet and sat down. Marriage meant different things to different people. Matt . . . what would Matt expect? Susy Homemaker? Someone to cook, clean, and scrub? Someone to be there for him twenty-four hours a day?

The happy Emily in the mirror was frowning; she could see her reflection from where she sat. And Emily, are you ready to do all that at this point in your life? You've come so far, done so much, suffered untold agonies. Can you go back and do all the things Matt would expect, those very same things you expected of yourself when you married Ian and weren't able to experience? She had to admit she didn't know.

She was also going to have to fess up that she did more than conduct exercise classes. Matt had no idea how well off she was or how successful she was back home. Several times she'd been tempted to tell him, but for one reason or another, she hadn't because she was afraid she would intimidate him.

Two more weeks.

Summer fling?

What happened when the fling was over?

You pack up, go home, nurse your bruised heart, and go on from there.

Who *was* this person in the mirror?

Emily gave herself a shake, pulled her orange dress over her head, straightened it, buckled the belt, slipped her feet into her sandals. She fluffed out her hair, added a spritz of perfume, and clipped on her earrings.

"You might be happy, but you're just too damn negative for me," Emily said to the person staring back at her.

Her car keys in hand, Emily snapped off the light in her bathroom.

Rosie was on the front porch, to Emily's surprise. "I thought I'd walk down and walk you up to the parking lot and then go on to dinner. You look jittery," she said, taking Emily's arm. "Don't be. You don't have to commit to anything, assuming we're right about this little dinner. You are your own person, Emily. Believe in yourself. Whatever you do will be right for you."

"Oh sure, look how I screwed up things with Ian."

"Who screwed things up?"

"Okay, we both screwed up. I made some terrible decisions that were very hard to live with."

"But you did live with them. Look at you now. Emily, you literally have it all. Think about that. You have a successful business you and your friends created. You have a man back home who loves you and you have a man here who loves you. You are a lovely woman, sensitive, caring. You, my dear, have come full circle, as the saying goes."

"I'm going to miss you, Rosie. Have you given any more thought to my offer of joining me in New Jersey?"

"That sounds like you're going back. I want to go home and see my children and grandchildren. I want to be home for Christmas; it's a special time for my family. The first of the year will be time enough to make a decision. Well, here we are, Emily. Drive carefully and be home by nine-thirty." Rosie laughed. "You look great, Emily. You'll blow his socks off."

Emily hugged her new friend. "Don't eat too much of that pot roast and go easy on Cookie's gravy; it's a killer."

"Tell me about it," Rosie said, falling into a jog to make her way to the dining room.

The plan for the evening was that Emily was to drive to Matt's house to save him the trip back up the mountain. He would fix dinner for his kids, and make sure homework was being attended to before he left. Obviously tonight was going to be a sexless evening unless Matt followed her back to her cabin, which was unlikely since it was a school night. She felt disgruntled with the knowledge.

Emily switched on the radio. Tears blurred her eyes as she listened to the words of a popular song... *a few stolen moments is all we share... I just break down and cry... I'm saving all my love for you...* Emily dabbed at her eyes, switching the station.

It was still light when Emily pulled her jeep into the driveway. Benjy was sitting on the steps, a ball of fur in his lap.

"Is he yours?" Emily crooned, stooping down to pet the furry little head. "He's gorgeous. Does he have a name?"

"Not yet. Some camper dumped him and I found him on the way home from school. If Dad lets me keep him, I'll give him a name. Do you think he will, Emily?"

"Does your dad like animals?"

"Sure. We weren't allowed to have a dog because ... because my mother said it made her allergies worse."

"If he was yours, what would you call him?"

"Bizzy. Not b-u-s-y, but B-i-z-z-y."

"Guess that means he gets around a lot. Very clever," Emily said, tousling his hair. "Want me to speak to your dad?" she whispered.

"Yeah," the boy said, raising hopeful eyes.

"Okay. You'll take care of him, right? That means feeding him, walking him, and giving him a bath when he needs it."

"I'll do everything," the boy promised.

Emily entered the house. "Matt, I'm here," she called. She squeezed her eyes shut, hoping that when she opened them, the pictures in the living room would be gone. This time she crossed her fingers, but when she opened her eyes, they were still there. She felt her shoulders go slack.

God, he's handsome, Emily thought as she held up her face for his light kiss. She felt annoyed for some reason. Why was it men grew distinguished as they grew older and women just got older? She thought about her weight loss, the loose skin, and her face-lift. If she hadn't done all that, she knew she wouldn't be standing here in Matt Haliday's living room with his first wife's spirit looking on. She thought she felt a piece of her heart chip away.

"Did you meet our new guest?"

"Bizzy? Yes, he's adorable. Are you going to keep him?"

"Yeah. Benjy needs him and the pup needs an owner. I hate it when someone dumps an animal. It makes my blood boil."

"When are you going to tell him?"

Matt looked at her curiously, as much as to say, Interfering already? Damn, that's not what the look meant at all. As usual, she was overreacting.

"Right now. He can give him a bath while we're gone and have someone to keep him company. Molly, of course, is in her room with the phone stuck to her ear."

"It's all part of growing up, Matt."

They were on the porch. Benjy had the pup curled up against his cheek. He looked up at his father. Matt nodded. "He's your responsibility. Remember now, if you don't take care of him, you'll be no better than the person who dumped him. I want your word, Benjy."

"I promise, Dad. Should I give him a bath now?"

"Good idea. Try not to get water in his ears and soap in his eyes. Dry him real good, and yes, he can sleep with you. Put some papers down on the floor in the kitchen, by the doors, and in your room."

"Okay, Dad." When he passed Emily, he gave her skirt a twitch by way of a thank-you.

"Where are we going, Matt?"

"I thought we'd go to Solly's. The ribs are great, the steak soft as butter, and the fish is fresh every day. They serve a great peach pie for dessert. It isn't really a classy restaurant, just a good one."

"Any way is fine, Matt. I'm not fussy."

"That's one of the things I like about you," he said, taking his hand off the wheel to reach for hers. "You aren't a phony, you aren't pretentious, and you don't expect . . . things. You're simple like myself."

Simple. He meant it as a compliment. "What you see is what you get."

"Exactly. Women always know exactly how to put things. You look pretty tonight, Emily. You always look pretty, though. Even when you were all banged up."

"Are you buttering me up for something, Matt?" she teased lightly.

"Lord, no. Molly is forever telling me I have to express myself. She says people aren't mind readers and she's right.

It's helped me a lot with Benjy. I miss you already, Emily and you still have two weeks to go before you leave."

"I'll just be a phone call away," Emily said lightly.

"It won't be the same."

"No, it won't," Emily said. "I'll miss you too."

"Whoever would have thought I would, at the age of fifty-five, fall in love and feel like a kid again? Do you feel that way?"

"Pretty much."

Matt was silent for several minutes. "Do you ever find it curious that neither one of us has really talked about our past?"

"I think about it sometimes," Emily said.

"Why do you suppose that is?" Matt asked.

"I guess we didn't want to clutter up our moments with the past. Is there something you feel you want to say? You don't have to, you know."

They were in the parking lot of Solly's. Matt turned off the ignition and pocketed the key. He reached for Emily's hand. "I got married late. I was forty-one. I thought I was going to be a bachelor all my life, charm women and walk away. Then I met my wife, who was twenty-one years younger than me. I fell hopelessly in love in the time it took my heart to beat once. Caroline was . . . there was something ethereal about her. She was small, fragile, with eyes the color of dark opals. She had the loveliest smile. My heart would swell every time she smiled at me. She was too young for me, but I didn't care. I swore I would take care of her forever and ever. What I did was put her on a cushion and then I never let her get off."

"Matt, you don't have to tell me any of this."

"No, I want you to know. Caroline didn't know the first thing about keeping house or cooking. I don't know how that was possible, but she made such a disaster out of everything it was simpler to do it myself. I cooked, I cleaned, and when Molly was born, I started working two jobs so I could pay someone to come in and take care of her.

"Caroline's life consisted of needlepoint, television, and books. She said she loved me, loved Molly, but I don't think she knew the meaning of the word *love*. We made love, but it wasn't satisfying. I didn't know it was supposed to be like it is with us. I had affairs, but they were all physical, there was no emotional involvement.

"Caroline . . . after Benjy's birth, to me was never the same. She was deteriorating right before my eyes and I didn't recognize it. When it was too late, I asked her why she didn't complain or say she wasn't feeling well and she said . . . she said . . . she thought it was her punishment for not loving the children and me. I went berserk. I started to drink, almost lost my job. Ivan covered for me, often working both shifts. Hell, I was so drunk the day Caroline died I couldn't get up off the floor. Ivan said I went to the funeral, but I don't remember it. That time, while I was married, is all a blur to me. How could I . . . ?"

"It's over, Matt. Please, let's talk about something else."

"I need for you to know, Emily. The other reason is I don't want to make another mistake. Are we a mistake, Emily?"

He's giving me an out if I want to take it. She needed to give him an out too. "Only if we rush into something neither of us is prepared to handle."

"Let's go inside."

"Would you rather go back to the cabin? We can get down on our knees and beg Sister Cookie to give us some leftovers. I wouldn't mind in the least, Matt."

"You really wouldn't?"

"Not at all."

"I wanted to show you one nice evening, Emily. And you look so pretty."

"I think I'd rather go back."

They were roaring out of the parking lot a moment later.

With the wind in her hair and singing in her ears, Emily smiled in the darkness.

"I love you, Emily."

"Would you love me if I was fat, had a double chin, and lots and lots of wrinkles?"

There was a five-second wait until he responded. "Of course. Those are outside things. I didn't fall in love with you because of your looks."

Emily's heart skipped a beat. Ben had said the same thing, but there hadn't been that little pause. Ben had seen her at her worst and at her best. Matt was seeing the new refurbished Emily. He hadn't even realized she'd gotten a face-lift. How was this possible? It must be that inner beauty thing people always talked about. She was definitely going to have to talk to the sisters again, maybe even Father Michael.

When they arrived back at the retreat, Emily slid from the jeep in time to step into Matt's arms. He swung her around and then lifted her high in the air.

"I love you, Emily Thorn," he growled. "I want to marry you!"

"Wow!" Emily growled back before she kissed him soundly. "Listen, I'm not really hungry. Let's go for a walk. I love this time of day, when the day is done and you can sit back and review what went on and think about how you can make tomorrow even better. How about you, Matt?"

"I'm partial to sunrises." He reached for her hand. "You know, new days and all that. Do you think there's anything wrong with falling in love when you're fifty-five?"

"It's probably the best time. You're older, wiser, and

your emotions are at an all-time high," Emily said quietly. When was he going to realize she hadn't said she loved him too?

"Emily, how hard will it be for you to give up New Jersey and your . . . that fitness class you teach? Can you be happy here?"

Fitness class? Could she give all that up? She should have told him who she was a long time ago. For some reason it hadn't seemed important then. Men have such egos. How would her success affect their relationship? "I don't know, Matt. Marriage is a tremendous step. We haven't known each other that long. We aren't kids anymore. I'm not sure I'm stepmother material. Can we talk about this tomorrow or the next day? Tonight is . . . I don't know, kind of special. I feel something I can't explain. It's a perfect night, it's lovely here, and we're together. We're sharing and that's so important." But she wasn't sharing; she was cheating by not telling him about her life back home. She could rectify that later. If it became a serious issue, she'd deal with it then.

Two proposals of marriage. And she'd thought no one would ever want her again.

"Speaking of sharing . . . Emily, have you ever done something so out of character people looked at you like you'd sprouted a second head?"

She laughed. "I don't think so. Why?"

"Right before I turned fifty, I did something . . . something I always wanted to do. I went out and bought this . . . what I did was buy a motorcycle, a Harley Davidson. A low rider. I got it for fifty bucks because it was a total wreck. I rebuilt it from the bottom up. The engine purrs like a kitten, but I've never taken it out. I didn't want people to say I was trying to be a kid again so I go out in the garage, polish it, and sit on it. I even bought a black leather jacket. Would you like to go for a ride?" he asked breathlessly.

"You mean sit on the back and whiz down the road?" Emily asked, excitement bubbling in her voice. "In the dark?"

"Yeah!"

"On the road or . . . back here?"

"Well, part of it is whizzing down the road like you said. The wind is in your face, your arms are spread, and you experience that awesome feeling of power. They call the Harley I have a Hog. You game, Emily?"

His excitement was so contagious, Emily nodded. Together they sprinted back to the jeep. Forty minutes later they were opening the door of Matt's garage.

"Is this a beauty or what?"

It must be a man-boy thing, Emily thought. To her, it was nothing more than a bicycle with an engine. She eyed the seat where she was to sit. "I'm not getting on that thing unless you wear the black leather jacket. Does it have silver studs and emblems?"

"It's got *everything*, even a zipper," Matt said, his eyes wild with anticipation. "I wish you had one."

Emily looked down at her sheer dress, thought about her panty hose and high heels. She burst out laughing. They'd be in the woods so no one would ever know she wasn't an experienced biker or hanger-on or whatever the term was for the person who rode on the back.

"I saw this picture once of a girl on the back of a motorcycle who was wearing a black vest, probably leather, with all this silver stuff on it, and her boobs were hanging out. Almost hanging out. She even had a tattoo on her arm and one in the cleavage."

"You can work on that for the next time," Matt said, slipping his arms into the jacket. "Jesus, I can't believe we're doing this. Are you excited, Emily?"

Was she? "Petrified would be more like it."

"Don't you trust me?"

"Of course. It's just that at my age a stationary bike is more my style. Shouldn't you be wearing leather boots with steel toes or something?"

"That's my next purchase. Okay, get on. We're going to go slow when we're on the open road. The light is good, but I've never driven this in the dark or on the road. Put your hands around my waist and crinkle your dress up around you."

Emily did as instructed. With his feet on the ground, Matt maneuvered the Harley out to the driveway, where they coasted down to the road. He turned on the engine and it roared to life. In spite of herself, Emily was so thrilled she yelled, "Whoopee!" Her heart roared in her chest.

"Isn't this great?" Matt yelled as they rode up the mountain.

"I wish we were going to New Mexico with just a backpack," Matt shouted. Emily knew he was saying something, but she couldn't hear the words. She squeezed his sides to show her support.

In her life she'd never felt this free, this wild, this happy. She wondered what it would be like to ride this thing all the way back to New Jersey, pull into the driveway at the Sleepy Hollow house, and have everyone rush out to see her in the black leather vest that she was going to buy as soon as possible. Surely there was a catalog just for biker attire. She threw her head back and laughed as she'd never laughed in her life.

The bike was slowing, ready to turn into the entrance of the Black Mountain Retreat. "So what do you think?" Matt said, stopping the bike.

"I think, Matt Haliday, that we're both nuts, but I love it. Are you sure it will be okay to take this thing on the bike trail? Won't the sisters have a fit?"

"No one is here except the elderly couples and they

don't bike. The sisters don't bicycle either. It's night; everyone is indoors. Ivan and I patrol the trails. I say it's okay. The jack rabbits and squirrels are safe for the night. We aren't going to go up the mountains; we're just going to ride around the trails. I don't even know if this is the kind of bike for this terrain. I think a dirt bike is more in order, but since this is all we have at our disposal, I say we go for it."

"I'm ready," Emily said, squaring her rear end on the seat. "Matt, be careful, some of the trails really dip. There's one real bad one a mile or so down the second trail, the one with the black and white sign that says TRAIL DIPS."

"I know the one you mean. We pack that down five or six times a year and it still dips. Ivan did it a week or so ago so it should be okay. We can't figure out why that happens. We even filled it with rock and thirty or forty inches of hard-backed dirt. I'll be careful. Are you ready?"

"Make my blood sing, Matt," Emily said happily. "Are you sure you have enough gas?"

"This baby can go forever on a tank of gas."

They started out slow with Matt talking about everything and anything. When they picked up speed, Emily hardly noticed. The headlight, brighter than the spot lights at the retreat, picked up every rock, pebble, and bush along the way. She had no idea where they were after a while because she was so exhilarated, losing all her sense of direction. She found herself glued to Matt's muscular back, her hair whipping behind her in wild disarray.

Twenty minutes into the ride, Emily's stomach muscles started to knot up with anxiety. They were going too fast, Matt wasn't experienced enough with the cycle, and they were riding on slick pine needles, thick with resin. The trees rushed by in a blur, the wind making her eyes tear. Matt was shouting something, but the wind carried his words off in a rush. She herself was screaming for him to slow down, but her words trailed behind, no more than a whisper. The Harley roared ahead. She felt frightened for her life. The thrills and excitement she'd felt earlier were now two miles back on the trail. Her life as she'd known it flashed before her. Oh, God, she was never going to see her friends or Ben again. Ben. Dear sweet, gentle, kind Ben. Any minute now she was going to be killed because she'd come along on this stupid ride. Without a helmet. She screamed again, her voice hoarse and crackly. When Matt didn't slow the cycle, she butted her head against his back as hard as she could. The result was a sharp pain in the center of her forehead.

"Get off, Emily, NOW! Tell him to slow down, Emily, and get the hell off that machine."

"He can't hear me," Emily screamed.

"Use your hands, squeeze his sides, butt his head with yours. Do it now, Emily. This is right up there with every stupid thing you've ever done."

Emily brought her head closer to Matt's helmet and banged it. She gouged his sides, but she knew he didn't feel it through the leather jacket.

"Slow down, Matt! You're scaring me!" Emily screamed.

Her left arm glued to Matt's left side, Emily worked her right hand up under Matt's jacket to dig at his side. She knew he would take the gesture as excitement. *"Stop!"* she screamed at the top of her lungs.

She saw the branch ahead, its width as round as her wrist with fingers jutting out, thick with leaves. She saw the dip in the road at the same time she thought she heard Ian's words, *Jump off, NOW!*

She saw the piles of rocks, the thickness of the tree trunks, the prickly brush; she even thought she saw a raccoon perched in a tree to her left. Then, as if in slow motion she saw and felt Matt swerve the bike to the right, saw the broken end of the tree limb swing upward, felt it strike her, and then she felt nothing, heard nothing, but her own moans as she stared at the top of the trees outlined in the bright light from the headlight on the Harley.

Emily struggled to move. Wave after wave of dizziness assailed her. "Matt, where are you? Matt!" She thought she was screaming, but her words were no more than whispers. She tried again and again, calling Matt's name, begging him to answer her. The headlight continued to shine upward like a beacon. Surely Ivan would see it and come to their aid the way he had the last time.

She saw Matt then, spread-eagled on the pile of boulders. She had to get to him, try and help him.

The minutes crawled by until she heard the crackle of the underbrush and saw the moving spear of light.

"Jesus Christ!" The words exploded from Ivan's mouth like gunshots.

"Is he alive, Ivan? Take care of him. I'm okay for now. I think my shoulder might be fractured. I can't move my arm."

"What the hell were you two doing up here on a motorcycle?" Ivan said, his words blistering in the quiet night. She watched as his fingers probed Matt's body. He really didn't expect an answer and she was in too much pain to offer one. If she wanted to close her eyes now, she could. Ivan was here; Ivan would see that she and Matt were taken care of. She could hear him on the portable phone issuing orders for a litter, a team of medics, and an ambulance.

He was beside her, squatting down so he was almost eye level with her. "I can strap up your shoulder and move you away from these rocks. You were lucky, Emily, that you landed in the brush. The limb gave you a hell of a whack, though. Guess that's what did the damage."

"Is Matt okay?"

"Yes," Ivan growled. "He's never taken the bike out before. It was something to tinker with, to polish and admire. You shouldn't have let him take it out."

He was blaming her. Just the way Ian always blamed her. "Like I could have stopped him," she retaliated. "I told him to slow down, but he was going so fast and the engine is so loud he couldn't hear me. I tried." As a defense it was lame, even to her own ears.

"You never should have gotten on the damn bike. If you hadn't gotten on, he would have left it in the fucking garage where it belongs."

"That's not fair," Emily cried. "You can't blame me for this."

"I am blaming you. Matt would never have taken that Harley out of the garage if it wasn't for you. He's fifty-five years old and trying to act like he's twenty-five. For you. You should have had more sense."

Suddenly there were blinding lights, commotion, and voices. Far away in the distance Emily could hear the sounds of sirens. Ambulances. "I will not allow you to blame me for this, Ivan, not now, not ever, and don't ever say that to me again." Emily closed her eyes. She felt herself being raised to go on the litter, heard herself repeat Ian's words, heard the reassuring reply.

The next hours were nothing more than a blur for Emily. She knew her shoulder was being set, knew she was fighting the anesthetic.

It was midmorning when Emily awoke fully. The first thing she saw were the nuns, in full habit, their sweet faces filled with worry. They advanced as one, spoke as one. "Thank God you're all right."

They patted her hands, smoothed her hair back from her forehead, wiped her tears, straightened the covers.

"Tell me about Matt."

"Ivan said it was my fault. Maybe it was. If it's true, Sisters, how will I live with that?"

"You can't blame yourself, child. Matt . . . Matt knew what he was doing and he broke the rules. You can't blame yourself," Sister Gussie said quietly.

"I had . . . a guiding hand. I was going to . . . to jump off and take my chances when the tree limb came up out of nowhere. I tried to warn him, but the motorcycle made so much noise Matt couldn't hear me. I did try, Sisters. I need you to believe me. If you don't, I'm going to . . . I can't go through that again. Can't we call, ask someone? Where's Ivan?"

"He's with Matt. We can try the ranger service. We can call the hospital ourselves or we can get in the van and drive there. What would you like us to do, Emily?"

"Go there. Please."

It was decided that Sisters Tiny and Cookie would go back to the retreat to take care of the two elderly couples and Sister Phillie would stay with her, the others going to Asheville.

The hours dragged by, one after the other, the wait interminable.

Emily woke a little after eight in the evening to see Sister Phillie saying her rosary on the chair in the corner of the room.

"I thought I heard the others."

"I thought the same thing. Perhaps they're out by the desk. I'll check and see. She was no sooner off the chair than the door opened. Emily wiggled and squirmed in the bed as she tried to slide upward for a better look at the weary nuns. She drew a deep breath, her eyes fearful.

"Matt will live. He's got a concussion, a broken arm, and a few of his ribs are fractured. He'll need some surgery on one of his knees. A full recovery is expected."

"The children?"

"Matt's sister is with them. She'll take care of things. The children adore her. She and Matt were very close."

"Go home, Sisters. I think I need to be alone for a while. I truly appreciate everything you've done. You all look so weary. The doctor told me I can leave in the morning if I promise to stay in bed and rest. Is it possible for me to camp out with you? If not, I can call one of my friends from home to come and stay with me."

"It will be our pleasure, Emily. We have a spare room in the main cabin. We wouldn't think about leaving you on your own. Good night, child."

"Sisters?"

"Yes, Emily," they said in unison.

"Pray for Matt."

"We've been doing that all day, child. We'll continue to pray until he's well. Try and get some sleep," Sister Gilly said.

She would probably never sleep again.

Emily pressed the button-on gadget hooked to the rail of her bed. The light went out. She pressed another button and the picture on the television disappeared. She lay in the dark, tears rolling down her cheeks.

"Ian, can you hear me? I need to talk to you. Come out, come out, wherever you are." She called him again and again until she was hoarse with the effort. "You were never there at all, were you? It was all in my mind. I wanted . . . I *needed* to believe you would help me. It's all mixed up in my mind. The sisters believe; at least I think they do. Do you only come out . . . down . . . appear, whatever, when I'm in physical danger? I need you now so where the hell are you? See, that's what I meant the first time. I needed you emotionally and you were never there for me. You're a son of a bitch, Ian. Here I am talking to someone who's dead. They're going to lock me up and throw away the key. I need to know, Ian—did I or didn't I hear you? *Answer me, damn you.*

"I don't want to go crazy, Ian. I have some good years left and I want to enjoy them. Don't take those from me too. Damn you, answer me."

When there was no response, Emily beat at the bed with her good arm. "I knew it!" she shrieked. "It was all in my mind. I should have known better than to expect you to ever do anything for me. I did it myself. I used my own guts, my own will, my own mind. You were like a straw in the wind that I tried to clutch at. Good-by, Ian."

Emily was so exhausted with her tirade she started to drift into sleep.

Maybe it was the swishing sound of the door opening, or maybe it was the sound of the nurse's rubber-soled shoes, or maybe it was even her own breathing, but she thought, as she slipped into sleep, that she heard the words "Good-by, dear Emily."

Emily slept, with a smile on her face and tears on her cheeks.

In the morning, when Sister Phillie came to pick her up, she told her about her dream of Ian. The two women looked at one another and smiled knowingly.

There were dreams and then there were dreams.

Chapter 21

It was the day before Halloween when the cast came off Emily's shoulder. And it was the same day she was driving to Asheville with Sister Phillie to see Matt.

Three weeks since the accident on the bike trail. Three, long, endless weeks since she'd seen Matt. She didn't even know if he'd see her when she did get there. When she told him she was going to stop by to see him, he said fine, but there was no change in his flat voice. It was as if he didn't care if she visited him or not.

It wasn't that they didn't call; they did, every day, sometimes twice a day. But she was the one who did the calling. She shivered when she thought about how impersonal Matt's voice was. Oh, he was polite, asking about her shoulder, asking how things were at the retreat, and he always asked about the sisters. In those same three weeks he never once said he loved her, never said anything about their relationship. He did talk about his kids, and that should have been her first clue that something was seriously wrong.

Ivan was absolutely no help. He worked long hours, sometimes double shifts, and he avoided her as though she'd come down with a plague of some kind. He even avoided the sisters, saying only that Matt was coming along and would fully recover.

On every one of her calls she asked the charge nurse if Matt had asked for her. She was always told the same thing: no. On those days when he was in therapy or out of the room, she left her name and a brief message—Get well soon.

She'd made three trips with the sisters to Matt's house, but it was closed up, which meant Matt's sister must have taken the kids to her home, wherever that was.

"My arm feels stiff and my shoulder aches," Emily complained when she followed Sister Phillie out of the clinic. "Lord, I cannot wait to take a shower. Can I stand in there until the water runs cold, Sister?"

"Absolutely. Look around, Emily. It's typical October weather, cold, dreary, and rainy. That's part of the reason your shoulder aches. I imagine you'll feel it from now on as the weather changes."

"I don't have a good feeling about this, Phillie. I thought Matt loved me. He said he did. I wish I knew if I really and truly loved him. It's all mixed up for me. On that wild, crazy ride, I remember thinking this wasn't what I'd signed up for. You know, thrills and excitement. I am what I am, a stick in the mud, a career person. The children . . . Matt loves and adores them and that's the way it should be. I guess I'm just too selfish. I don't know how to be a mother. I don't even know if I want to be a stepmother. I'm all mixed up, Phillie."

"Then I guess you'll have to get unmixed up. I do believe it's time for you to make decisions. You must be the one to make them. Now, before we go to the hospital. You've had three very long weeks to do nothing but think about your relationship with Matt. In your sleep we heard you talk about Ben. I imagine . . . he's part of all of this. Now, buckle up, you know I drive too fast."

"Then slow down, Sister," Emily grumbled. "I've had enough speed to last me a lifetime."

An hour later, Emily, her hair damp dry, dressed in slacks and a hooded sweatshirt, climbed into the passenger side of the retreat's van. The ride was made in virtual silence.

In the parking lot, Phillie pulled up next to a florist's van. Matt loved flowers. Maybe she should have sent him some. Maybe she should have done a lot of things. Maybe-maybemaybe . . .

"We're going to stop and see Mrs. Blanchard. It's my duty. When she was in better shape, she used to bring her home-made lentil soup to the retreat. We threw it out because we couldn't define the ingredients. She meant well." Phillie rolled her eyes to show what she thought of Mrs. Blanchard's culinary efforts.

"Good idea," Emily agreed.

Mrs. Blanchard was a cantankerous curmudgeon who shrieked at them as they stood in the doorway. "Go away, I don't need your prayers and your sticky, sweet words. Where were you when they were cutting off my big toe? Nowhere to be seen, that's where. Go on, scat, get out of here and let me die in peace."

"People don't die from amputated toes," Phillie said knowledgeably.

"You don't know that for a fact. You're no doctor. Let me die in peace."

"Will you be disappointed if you don't die?" Phillie asked curiously.

The woman stared at them, her mouth hanging open. Emily yanked at Phillie's arm.

"What was the point to all that?" Emily asked.

"She's afraid. She's old. She uses nastiness as a defense. I'm going back. You go on down to the third floor and see Matt. I'll meet you in the lobby. This lady needs me."

"All right, Sister," Emily said, hugging her. Emily knew in her gut that Mrs. Blanchard would be at the Black Mountain Retreat for Thanksgiving and probably Christmas. God does work in mysterious ways, she thought as she made her way to the elevator.

Emily peeked into Matt's room. There was such an array of machinery, pulleys, contraptions, and wheelchairs she didn't know where to look first. Where was the bed? She stepped into the room on tiptoe. Behind the curtain she could make out the dim outlines of a bed. Matt was being balanced on some kind of board attached to pulleys above the bed. Emily walked around the curtain.

"Matt, it's Emily."

"It's nice you stopped by. I guess I should say thank you. They're taking all this junk off me tomorrow. Then it will be physical therapy for a while. Life goes on," he said flatly.

"Yes, life goes on. We learn as we go along. I'm the living proof. My shoulder will heal and your body will heal. We're alive—that's what we have to remember. It was a stupid thing we did, Matt."

"We? It was my idea. I knew better. You . . . it was like I was trying to . . . to be young for you. To do something wild and reckless. I didn't think about my kids. I didn't think about anything but showing off for you. You were just as excited as I was. I thought women were supposed to have more sense, have that sixth sense everyone always talks about. Where was it that night?"

"I think I'm missing something here, Matt. Are you blaming *me* for the accident? If you are, you need to change your thinking. I'm willing to take *half* the blame. It took me a long time to learn that each of us has to take responsibility for our actions. Obviously, we don't know each other. And I was less than honest with you. I don't just conduct exercise classes. I'm a corporation. I, along with a group of friends, own Emily's Fitness Centers. We're on the Stock Exchange. I wanted to tell you. But something held me back. I wanted to see, I guess, if you'd be interested in me—plain, old Emily. There's something else too. I had a makeover. I didn't always look like this. Face-lift, boob job, the works. I suppose I should have told you that too. I've come to the conclusion that I knew all along this was a summer fling, for want of a better word. Summer romances rarely work. In novels they do. However, this is my life and your life we're talking about. It's entirely possible both of us were in love with the word *love*. Some people would say we're over the hill. Your children have to come first. You're a father. I was never a parent. Starting with a ready-made family is not something I'm comfortable with. The bottom line is, Matt, I came here to say good-by."

"I see."

"That's it? 'You see'? Do you at least think I'm right?"

"If it's right for you, Emily, then it's right. I believe I said I love you three or four times. You never said you loved me. I guess I knew you didn't. That wild ride . . . that was to make you think I was exciting. Living in the mountains can be pretty boring. I knew you were a city girl. I kept asking myself what you would want with a guy like me. I live in a shitty little house, I can't cook worth a damn, and my kids have some problems. I was born here and I'll die here. You're pretty much a free spirit. I can respect that. Why don't we just say we had a nice summer and let it go at that? You'll send me a Christmas card and I'll have the kids send you one."

"I'm sorry, Matt."

"I am too, Emily. The sisters, when they talk about it, and they will talk about it, will say it was meant to be. They'll console me with cakes and cookies and cheerful conversation. You should go now, Emily, before you have me blubbering in my beard. Christ, it itches. I can't wait to shave it off."

"If there's ever anything . . ."

"I'll call you. Get the hell out of here, Emily."

Tears streaming down her face, Emily blew him a kiss. She ran from the room. In the long corridor, she bumped into Phillie. Together they raced outside, where Emily collapsed in the nun's warm arms. "I'm not sure why I'm crying, Phillie. For myself, I think. I think I wanted it to be otherwise, but I guess it wasn't meant to be. Ben's . . . Ben's face kept getting in the way."

"Emily, honey, I wasn't going to tell you this, but I think now might be a good time to speak up. I discussed this with the other sisters after your arrival. It's not our way to interfere; I want you to understand that right off. Every summer Matt has . . . a romance with one of our guests. I believe Rosie tried to tell you without actually saying every summer. We believe he was . . . is . . . looking for a mother for his children. Matt is a fine man. I personally believe he's still in love with Caroline. He blames himself in so many ways for the way things turned out."

"If things had gotten serious between us, you know, marriage plans and the like, would you have spoken up, Phillie?"

"I don't know, Emily. Would you have accepted his proposal?"

"I don't know. I realize now I didn't love him the way I loved Ian. That was a sick, obsessive love that never should have been. I was expecting those same feelings. Ben . . . my feelings for Ben were . . . are totally different. There weren't any bells and whistles. I wanted . . . felt I deserved the bells and whistles." A moment later she said, "Nah, I wouldn't have said yes. It doesn't say much for me, does it, Phillie?"

"My dear, it says more than you know. Ben?"

Emily's heart skipped a beat at the mention of Ben's name. "I'm going to tell him about Matt. You know what, Phillie? He'll understand. He's given me so much, helped me in so many ways, and he never asked, expected, anything in return. I'm afraid. I don't know if I can ever commit to anyone, ever again. My choices, Phillie, no one making them for me. Is this where you say, if it's meant to be, it will be?"

"I wouldn't touch that for anything. You've come a long way, Emily. You still have some distance to travel, though. In my opinion. Think about your life, what you've accomplished, how you've turned your life around. Think about all the good you've done for others. Think about all the people who love you and whom you love. Take it one day at a time. You give, you get, a hundredfold. Trust me."

"That business with Ian up on the trail. Both times. It was me, wasn't it? It was my own intelligence, my own spirit. It was never Ian. I wanted it to be Ian so bad. I wanted him to do just one grand, wonderful thing for me. Saving my life was the grandest thing I could think of. In the end I did it myself. Me. God, Phillie, it was me all the time. He fooled me, though. He left his entire estate to me. Did I ever tell you that?" There was such excitement in her voice, Phillie leaned back against the wall and smiled.

"He did. It's worth millions. Do you have any idea of the good I can do with that?"

"I would hope you'd remember us and maybe build something here that we can tend to. There are a lot of women who could use our help and so many troubled children. Am I being too forward?"

"God, no. I'll take care of it, Phillie."

"Let's go sit in the car and puff on some cigarettes," Phillie said. "You have some, don't you?"

"You bet—two whole packs under the seat. Thanks, Phillie, for everything. Listen, I can send you cigarettes once a month and some *really* good whiskey and brandy."

"We'd like that a lot, Emily," Phillie said, drawing deeply on the cigarette in her hand.

Emily blew a perfect smoke ring, which Phillie matched. "I think I'll head out this afternoon. I don't have much to pack. Hell, I could just hop in the jeep and go. You can give my stuff away. Yeah, that's exactly what I'm going to do. I'm going *home*, Phillie. I think the word *home* is the most beautiful, the sweetest word in the English language. Did you hear me, Phillie, I'm going home!"

"I heard you and I think it's wonderful. Give me another cigarette."

An hour later with her overnight case and shoulder bag slung over her shoulder, Emily said her good-byes to all the nuns. There were tears and promises to write and to return for visits from time to time. When she handed over the remaining packages of cigarettes, the sisters lit up immediately. Her send-off was completed in a cloud of smoke. Emily drove with her left hand on the steering wheel, her right hand flapping back and forth in a wild waving motion until the black-garbed figures faded from her rearview mirror.

She was going home.

Emily walked into the house on Sleepy Hollow Road a little before midnight. Clad in her flannel shirt, cords, and hiking boots, shearling jacket over her arm, she shouted, "Hey, I'm home!"

They came on the run, from all directions, their slippers flip-flopping on the hardwood floors, their robes swishing about their ankles. "Emily! God, you're home. This calls for a toast. Jeez, you look like a million dollars! We missed you! We really missed you! Does Ben know you're back?"

"I just decided to come back this morning. I would have been here sooner, but I had a layover in Atlanta for a few hours. I'm so glad to be back home," Emily said, hugging each of her friends in turn. "Just this morning I told Sister Phillie that the sweetest word in the English language is *home.* I could use a drink. I have stories to tell and secrets to share."

"Ben?"

Emily smiled. "Tomorrow, when the day is new and fresh, I'll call Ben. Tonight is for us. I need to thank all of you again for . . . for being you, for being my friends when I needed friends the most . . . the whole nine yards. Come on, let's get into our campfire circle and yack till the sun comes up. I missed that. Wow, look at those herbs on the windowsill! They were just buds when I left."

"You were gone a long time," Martina said.

"Yes, but I'm back. Isn't it funny how the one place in the world that will always welcome you is home. That one place we consider to be safe, that place that warms your heart. Shit, I wish I was a writer so I could express it better."

"I think you did a pretty good job of it just now. You're right. It's that wonderful, warm house that welcomes you at the end of the day and greets you the first thing in the morning."

In the basement they formed their usual circle and sat cross-legged. Fuzzy Navels in long-stemmed glasses were passed around by the Demster twins. "I think we should make our first toast to HOME. Our home," Emily said.

"Hear, hear!" they chorused.

"To home!"

Emily woke slowly, and knew instantly that she was home in her own bed. She stretched luxuriously as she stared at the young rays of sun creeping into her room. A new day. Maybe this was the first day of her new life. No, that can't be, she told herself. This wasn't her new life and it wasn't her old life either. It was simply life. Her life that she'd made better by caring and sharing.

The bedside clock, a gift from Matt on her birthday,

said it was five forty-five. That meant she'd slept a total of one hour. She stretched again. Damn, she felt good. Rested, raring to go. Where? To Ben's house, of course.

That's it, Emily, finish up one affair and go on to good old Ben. Tacky. You don't deserve Ben. She kicked off her slippers and slid back into bed. With the pillows propped up behind her, and a cigarette that was making her cough, she tried to bring her thoughts to some kind of order. Yes, she was back. Yes, she and her friends were together and they weren't blaming her for her long vacation. They understood about Matt. None of them had chastised her for her fling. "As long as it helped you get your shit together," Nancy said. She crushed out the cigarette. She hated smoking in her bedroom; and only did it when she was confronting a stressful situation.

What is it I'm looking for? How am I supposed to know "it" when and if I do find it? This was probably one of those times when she should be making a list. And then she thought about the list Ian had made of the things she wanted. Be careful, Emily, you just might get what you wish for. Better to think and not commit to paper. Go to Ben, talk to him, explain your feelings. *Settle your goddamn life already! It's time.*

At seven-thirty, Emily was barreling down Watchung Avenue on her way to Ben's house. She stopped for Dunkin Donuts and two cups of their own special coffee at the shop on Park Avenue. Fifteen minutes later she was ringing Ben's doorbell. When there was no response after three long peals, she used her key, opened the door, and called Ben's name. A quick trip to the kitchen and upstairs convinced her Ben wasn't in the house. Where could he be so early on a Sunday morning? He liked to sleep in on the weekends. She looked around the tidy rooms and felt as though she was trespassing. She let herself out, locked the door, and sat down on the stoop, where she drank both cups of coffee and ate three donuts. She was finishing her third cigarette when Ben swerved into his parking space, tooted the horn, and waved. She didn't move. He looked great in his sweats. For one, wild moment she felt as though her heart had turned over in her chest.

"Been waiting long?" he asked coolly.

"Not that long." Why wasn't he swooping her into his arms? Why wasn't he saying something like, God, Emily, I thought you were never coming back? Maybe she was supposed to do the talking and moving. She felt like it. Wanted to do it. *Then goddamn it, do it!*

"Looks like you drank my coffee. Did you at least save me one of those donuts? Come on, I'll make some fresh. I was up at the crack of dawn to get Ted ready. I waited with him till his flight was called."

"Did you have a nice visit? Of course you did; I don't even know why I said that. I want to say so many things, Ben, I don't know where to start. I want . . . expected you to . . . swoop me up and kiss me till I cried for mercy. Right now I feel kind of lost. I don't know why that is. I couldn't wait to see you. Look at me, Ben, that damn coffee can wait. We need to . . . to . . . talk."

Ben settled the basket of coffee grounds firmly in the pot, turned it on, and then faced Emily. "I'm listening."

"We, Ben. Not just me. Us."

"Wrong. I did all my talking. You know how I feel, what I want. You talk."

"You aren't going to make this easy, are you?" Emily said miserably.

"No, I'm not."

"I wanted . . . expected . . . bells and whistles. I wanted my blood to sing. I thought if I imagined those things, I would know I was in love. Maybe that only happens in novels and movies. Damn it, I wanted that. My life, my marriage, it was so screwed up . . . what did I know? Out in the woods I had a lot of time to think. The funny thing is, I didn't realize I was thinking until . . . well, until I made charts, lists, memorized inspirational sayings that I thought I could apply to my life. And . . . I came to the conclusion that . . . well, what I . . . I did was . . . I put you . . . our relationship right up there with home. Safe, happy, warm. You know, when things aren't going well, and you go home and sort of snuggle in . . . I know I'm not explaining this right. Don't say anything, Ben. I have to get this out in my own way. That house on Sleepy Hollow Road was, and still is, my sanctuary. That's how I feel about you. It must be love, Ben, because if you . . . if you moved or left me, I'd be . . . devastated. Just the way I'd feel if I lost the house on Sleepy Hollow Road. Now, if you put that together, it tells me I'm in love with you. I never said that to you before because I wasn't sure . . . I'm about as sure now as I can be. I don't want to get married right away. That piece of paper scares me. I don't really want to live in sin either. Those nuns got to me. They drink and smoke—did I tell you that? And they play five-card stud on Sunday afternoons. Sunday yet! Now, you can say something."

"Wait here," Ben said, a strange look on his face.

Emily waited. She thought about her little speech, wondered if her heart would ever beat normally again, before Ben returned fifteen minutes later.

"Close your eyes," he called from the hallway. Emily obediently closed her eyes.

"Okay, now you can open them."

His voice sounds funny, Emily thought as she opened her eyes. Clamped between his teeth was a silver whistle. In both hands he held Christmas bells. "Do you hear them now?" he said around the whistle in his mouth. The bells rang and the whistle shrilled.

Emily whooped with laughter. "Only you, Ben. I swear, this makes it all right. Thank you, thank you so much.

C'mere," she said, crooking her index finger. "I want you to make love to me right here on the kitchen floor."

"Lady, I thought you'd never ask. Can I stop with the bells and whistles now?"

"The way I look at it, you can't kiss me with that whistle in your mouth, and I have other plans for those hands of yours."

The whistle landed in the sink and the two bells sailed across the room. "Emily, I'm all yours. For now and forever."

"*Shhhh,* you talk too much. You made it possible for me to love again, Ben, so let's do what we do best."

It was midafternoon before Emily and Ben were willing to untangle themselves from the bedclothes. "You are a man of endurance, Mr. Jackson," Emily said contentedly.

"And you, Miz Thorn, fueled and stoked that endurance. I love you, Emily, so much it hurts me sometimes."

"So that's what all those twinges are. I thought it was the aging process." How wonderful it felt to be here with this man who understood and loved her the way she needed to be loved. "I love you, Ben. I guess I always loved you. I was afraid to say the words. Afraid if I said them aloud it would . . . be like before. I didn't want that. This is what I want. I'm sorry it's taken me so long to realize . . . to come to you and be honest."

"All good things come to those who wait. I told you I'd wait forever. I meant it. Look at us now, you crazy kid."

"Ben, let's go home. I want to tell my friends. I want to . . . I have so many ideas and I want you all there to hear them because each of you has a voice in our future."

"Okay. But I have an even better idea. Let's take a shower together first."

"You devil," Emily squealed as she beelined for the bathroom.

* * *

"What *is* this?" Emily demanded as she pushed her chair away from the table. "It tastes like one of Sister Tiny's secret surprises."

"It's a bunch of cookie crumbs with pudding and brandy for zip. Tell us! Don't play dumb either. All of us watched you two walk up the driveway and we all decided that, in the whole of our lives, we've never seen such sappy expressions. We're calling it love. Are we right?"

Emily flushed and nodded. Ben displayed a silly grin.

"Toast! Toast! All we have left is, Bud Ice."

"Sounds good to me." Ben's silly smile grew wider.

Emily stood, her beer bottle held high. "This is a special toast. Listen up. To bells and whistles. Who needs them? Okay, now down to business."

They talked intensely for two hours. "Then we're in agreement. We're going to sell our shares in Emily's Fitness Centers and move on. The lawyers will handle everything. Our pensions are intact; we all have excellent health insurance. We have enough money in the bank to last all of us the rest of our lives, and the money we set aside for Ben's son's college will grow so that, when he's ready to go off to college, he'll be able to go on for his MBA or Ph.D. if he wants to. The choice will be his. So, I say we start to do some good deeds. With Ian's money. He had this house . . . a monster house, lots of grounds, quite a few acres. I suggest, and you all have a voice in this, but I suggest we turn that house and grounds into some kind of women's shelter so that women who are in the same situation we were in won't have to live with the fear we lived with. It will mean we'll be pretty much going back to the basics, but I think we can do it. Yes, there's a lot of money, but it won't last forever, so we'll have to make our endeavor a working endeavor. There won't be a time limit as to how long they can stay either. Maybe we could buy an extra piece of property, raise chickens, sell eggs, plant gardens, and peddle the fruits of our labors. We could even board dogs and do grooming. Whatever we have to do, we can do. We proved that some time ago. That's it," Emily said.

"Vote!" the Demster twins shouted.

"The ayes have it!" Ben said. "Listen, this wouldn't have anything to do with Ted living in California with his mother, would it?"

"It has everything to do with it. I suggest we make another toast. I'll get the beer," Emily said. Her head was half in the refrigerator, the cold air swirling about her. *Atta girl, Emily. I couldn't have done it better myself. He's the one for you. Good-by, dear Emily.*

"Hey, what's holding up the works?" Ben shouted.

Emily turned, a smile on her face. She set the beer on the table before she wrapped her arms around Ben's shoulders from behind. "I just want you all to know I love this guy. And . . . and I have it on good authority that he's the one for me." The silly smile was back on Ben's face, but Emily couldn't see it.

The girls whistled and hooted. Emily sat on Ben's lap and nuzzled close. She was happier than she'd ever been in her life and all because Ben had taught her how to love again. She felt herself being pulled closer, heard the whispered words, "I love you, Emily Thorn."

"Not as much as I love you, Ben Jackson."

"Wanna bet?"